A Farmhouse in the Rain

A Farmhouse in the Rain

Joe Kilgore

TOP HAT BOOKS

Winchester, UK
Washington, USA

First published by Top Hat Books, 2016
Top Hat Books is an imprint of John Hunt Publishing Ltd., Laurel House, Station Approach,
Alresford, Hants, SO24 9JH, UK
office1@jhpbooks.net
www.johnhuntpublishing.com
www.tophat-books.com

For distributor details and how to order please visit the 'Ordering' section on our website.

ISBN: 978 1 78535 434 2
Library of Congress Control Number: 2016931755

A CIP catalogue record for this book is available from the British Library.

Design: Stuart Davies

Printed and bound by CPI Group (UK) Ltd, Croydon, CR0 4YY, UK

For Claudia, Dorothy, and Willie.

"The real test of a man is not how well he plays the role he has invented for himself,

but how well he plays the role that destiny assigned to him."— Jan Patocka

Prologue

Near Flamanville, France, 1944

His right arm hung useless at his side. Rivulets of blood had dried on the back of his hand and along his fingers, but he had lost no strength in his other limb. With his good hand, he pulled the gag from the boy's mouth, then slipped the blindfold from his eyes.

"Vos mains," he said. And the boy turned so the man could untie his hands.

"Venez avec moi," the man commanded, and the boy followed him up the short flight of stairs and into the room. Then the man gripped his shoulder tightly and guided him toward the closed door. The boy's heart was pounding like a boxer's jab, threatening at any moment to punch its way through his sunken chest.

"Ouvrez-le," the man said. So the boy reached up slowly, grasped the knob, turned it, and pushed the door open.

The squeak of the hinge momentarily diverted his attention but did not hold it. The boy's eyes cut immediately to the bed where the blankets had been pulled all the way up, covering some sort of lump beneath it. Still with his hand on the boy's shoulder, the man walked him to the edge of the bed. There, he removed his hand and pulled the blankets away.

The boy gasped. And the man grabbed him again, holding him firm and making him stare at the nude woman on the bed. The blue scarf that had choked the life from her was still wrapped tightly around her throat.

The boy had never seen his mother naked. He tried to gaze on the parts that had always been hidden to him, rather than focusing on her white lips, bloodstained nose, and still-open eyes. But the man was intent upon the boy seeing her face frozen in its death mask. He walked the boy closer, pointed to her throat, drew his finger across his own, and said, "Américains … Américains."

The boy nodded his head as if he understood.

When the man had gone, the boy went back in the bedroom. He opened the top drawer of the dresser, reached in as far as he could, and pulled out a framed photograph. It was a picture of his mother and father in Paris. She often showed it to him and told him it was taken the afternoon before the evening he was conceived. He wasn't sure what conceived meant precisely. But he knew it always made his mother smile, each time she shared the picture and the story with him.

Then he went and sat beside his mother on the bed. He sat there for hours. Sat there staring as her head and neck turned turquoise. Sat there as blisters began to form and fluids began to leak. Sat there as her body began to bloat and swell. Sat there as the pungent odor of rotting meat began to fill the tiny room. And all the while he sat, he would look back and forth from the decaying corpse to the photograph in his hands and marvel at how one could become the other.

He was still sitting there when the men found him. Men in uniforms who let him keep his photograph but took him from his house. Men who spoke words he could not understand. Men whom the man with one good arm had branded as his mother's murderers. *Les Américains*.

Part 1

Providence

Chapter 1

Pilot Hill, Texas, January 1943

Thump. Thump. Thump. Each time the round ball hit the red dirt, a wisp of dust would dart from beneath it, then dissipate while wafting to earth. The constant pounding had worn away the green grass, leaving a pockmarked and dimpled surface serviceable only when the weather was dry. But it was often dry enough to repeatedly conjure visions of packed arenas, riotous fans, and that last second shot to beat the buzzer and claim the championship. Glory is ever present when young men dream.

From her kitchen window, Riley's mother watched him spinning, jumping, and shooting over and over again. *Maybe luck was on his side,* she thought. Maybe he'd grow tall enough and work hard enough and be good enough to escape what he was born into. Perhaps that round, leather basketball was the ticket that would take him away from the life around him. An oil field life of hard labor, forgotten hopes, compromised aspirations, and eventually acceptance. Acceptance of the shallow canals, wooden derricks, and gravel roads that surrounded them like prison walls. *Regret is inevitable,* she thought to herself. The lint in the pocket of every life. But maybe it wouldn't have to be in his.

He had just sailed a silent twenty-footer through the netless rim on the battered backboard his father had set up for him behind the clothesline in the tiny backyard. A shot that set off the high school senior's imagined victory celebration, until his mother's voice cut short the jubilation.

"Riley…time for supper. Come on in." She never had to yell twice.

They sat at the booth his father had built in one corner of the kitchen. It negated the need for a table and chairs; there was little room for them anyway. The kitchen was small like the rest of the clapboard house. There were two bedrooms, a shared bath, a small area that could be called a living room, though very little living went on in it. Most nights were passed with Riley reading in his room. His mother and father sitting on the front porch until it was time to retire. People in Pilot Hill went to bed early and got up even earlier.

There was no meat this evening. But a meal of eggs and potatoes, with diced onions seasoned to please, did more than assuage the trio's hunger; it delighted their taste buds as well. So much so that when Glenn Miller's band on the ever-present radio cranked up "Chattanooga Choo Choo," Riley's father rose, extended his hand, swept his slightly hesitant wife to her feet, and began to twirl her around the kitchen. The big oil field roughneck who was used to lifting massive pipe and dragging heavy chain was surprisingly light on his feet and gentle with his touch. It warmed Riley's heart to see his parents forgetting for the moment that bills hadn't been paid and repairs hadn't been made, and simply enjoying the music and the movement and each other. It was one of those snapshots the mind involuntarily takes and stores to be recalled sometime in the future. Most often when there's a pressing need for happiness.

Later that evening, Riley drove the family Ford past a long line of vehicles to the far side of a big, tented roller rink. Winter had little meaning in Southeast Texas. Temperatures never fell very far. So young people enjoyed the outdoors as much in winter as they did in spring. Especially when something out of the ordinary set up shop for a while. The rink was usually a fixture for a few weeks only in summer. But with the exceedingly mild weather, the owner had decided to have another go at the oil field community.

Beneath a giant canvas the portable wooden floor had been assembled. Racks of rental skates stood row upon row just inside the entrance. A red picket fence rimmed the floor to keep clumsy skaters from going over the side. The loud speakers continuously blared "A String of Pearls," "Moonlight Cocktail," "Tangerine," and other big band hits. Men, women, boys, and girls stepped, stumbled, and skated round and round as music filled their ears and a myriad of thoughts filled their minds. The older set nostalgically wondered where their youth had gone. Children and adolescents imagined their futures in fast cars they'd never own or at fancy balls they'd never attend. Teenagers fantasized about the topic of most young people's reveries, the opposite sex. It was a night for reflection, contemplation, dreaming. Such nights were now few and far between. Thirteen months earlier the Japanese had bombed Pearl Harbor.

Riley could have parked closer, behind automobiles that had arrived earlier, but he wanted a front row seat to watch the skaters from the privacy of his car. He never really liked being in the middle of crowds. Sure, he put up with it when he was on the gym floor in the middle of a game and everyone else was in the grandstands. But he wasn't one for mixing, mingling, being part of the throng. He liked being somewhat apart. There but not there. Participating his way. On his own terms.

The night was clear, cool, and much more comfortable than winter had any right to be. Riley watched the skaters as they circled. The tentative ones, who walked more than they rolled. The speedsters who annoyingly zipped in and out of the crowd, grabbing the middle tent pole to whip themselves around the corners even faster. The cruisers, content to take it slow and steady. Among the latter, one in particular caught his eye. And the eyes of virtually every other young man in attendance. She was wearing a sleeveless black tunic and short white shorts that hugged her in all the right places. Hers was a figure men ogled and women envied. Slim, smooth legs, thin waist, tight tummy, and curves that were pinup promises of heaven to every male beyond puberty. Her golden hair was short by the standards of the day. It bobbed about the tops of her shoulders dancing this way and that in time with the music. Her nose was small, her lips full, and under dark brows her coffee colored eyes glowed like gemstones. Literally sparkled like Tiger's eye, particularly when she smiled.

Riley knew who she was. Her name was Gwen. She was the daughter of Sam Taylor, the tool pusher who worked for the same company as his father. The same company virtually everyone in Pilot Hill worked for. She was a year behind him in school. He had seen her there, but he had never quite seen her as he did this night. There was something magical about the way she glided round the rink. He couldn't take his eyes off her. And the more he gazed, the more he wondered why he had never thought about her this way before. Getting out of the car, he walked slowly beside the fence toward the entrance. Still watching. Still wondering.

Stepping inside the entrance, Riley casually leaned against the counter. As he debated with himself on what he might say, fate made him hurry his decision. The two girls Gwen had been skating with became tangled, tilted precariously, and were about to fall right in front of him. He caught one by the arm. Gwen reached out and grabbed the other's elbow to keep them upright. She giggled as she said, "Hey, you two, leave the fancy stuff to the experts."

It was out of his mouth before he had time to take it back, which upon reflection he would have. "Now, we don't need any more of your lip, Miss Taylor. At least not that way."

The two girls giggled this time. But Gwen didn't. She caught his clumsy flirtation exactly the way it was intended. It made her smile and she responded, "Well, if it isn't Riley Cross, the basketball star. Why don't you put on a pair of skates and show us how it's done?"

"Don't think my coach would want me to take a chance on turning my ankle just now. Still got a few games to play, you know."

"I know. I watch you at all the home games," Gwen answered.

"Come on, Gwen," one of her friends chided.

"Yeah," the other said, "let's keep skating."

"Think I'll rest for a minute. You two go ahead."

The girls looked at Gwen, then Riley, then giggled as they took off on their own.

"Say," Riley stammered, "I...I didn't mean what I said before. I mean, I didn't quite mean it the way it came out. I was just kidding, you know."

"I know a kidder when I see one. I thought it was a pretty cute thing to say."

"Guys don't like to be called cute."

"Well, I don't know why not. You certainly are. Though I guess you'd prefer to be called handsome, wouldn't you?"

"Think I'd prefer to be called Riley."

Hers was an appropriate description. Riley Cross was an above average example of the male species. Six feet, one inch tall. A hundred and seventy pounds of trim physique, the result of running up and down gymnasium floors thousands of times. His full head of brown hair was trimmed neatly and parted on one side in the style of the times. His long, straight nose, green eyes, and thin lips set off an appealing face that didn't have that lived-in look it would eventually take on.

"You skate well," Riley said. "You look good out there."

Gwen replied, "Now, are you talking about my skating, or are you talking about me?"

"I was talking about your skating. But I have a sneaky suspicion you know exactly how good you look."

"My, my, Mr. Cross. Are you flirting with me?"

"Actually, I thought it was the other way around."

By the time her friends came around a third time, Gwen already had her skates off. She stopped them and said, "Don't wait for me, okay; I'm going to catch a ride with Riley."

"Are you sure?" one asked. The other said, "Go ahead. Go out and come back, if you like. We can meet you here when the rink closes."

"No, it's okay. He's already said he'd give me a ride home. I'll be fine," Gwen added.

The girls looked at each other and shook their heads but skated off dutifully.

Driving away from the rink, Riley surveyed the night sky as Gwen sipped on the bottle of Coke he had bought her. He looked at the stars and full moon mainly as an excuse to keep from staring at her.

"What do you think you're going to find up there? Enemy planes?"

"I doubt that they'd be in the skies over Texas. Just looking at the moon. It's so bright, I bet we could drive without the lights."

"Turn them off and let's see," Gwen dared him.

There were no cars behind or in front of him at the moment, so he took her challenge and turned them off. The change was abrupt, but the moonlight was so encompassing that they were able to easily navigate without headlamps.

"Oh, wow," Gwen laughed, "this is so weird." Then sliding across the front seat and wrapping her arm around his, she said, "Let's see how far we can go without turning them back on."

Riley was immediately aware of her touch and the scent of her. He didn't know what kind of perfume she had on, but he knew he liked it. Almost as much as the feel of her body next to his.

"Wouldn't it be great to just go on like this forever," she said. More a statement than a question. "Just riding through the moonlight to wherever the road might take us."

"This road will take us to the processing plant," Riley responded drily.

"Oh, that's not what I meant, silly. I meant, wouldn't you like to just start driving and never stop until you were someplace totally different, totally wonderful."

"Is there some place that's totally wonderful?"

"There must be," she said. "I know there has to be."

"Where do you think we might find it?" Riley asked.

"Anyplace away from here," Gwen responded. "Anyplace with mountains and oceans and maybe even palm trees."

"You're a funny one," Riley said.

"Funny how? Funny ha-ha? Or funny in the head?"

"I can't tell yet."

"Oh, come on, Riley Cross. You can't tell me you haven't thought about getting away from here to some place with city lights and music and excitement."

"I guess I have," Riley agreed. "I know my mom talks about it from time to time. She says if I'm able to get a college scholarship playing basketball, then I'll be able to learn a lot more and see a lot more of the world."

"Is that what you want to do, Riley? See the world? Me too. I guess most people from small towns want to see what they're missing, huh?"

"I don't know," he responded. "Some people like small towns. Like my dad. I don't think he'd have any problem living here the rest of his life."

"Not me," Gwen countered. "I want to go places and see things and do things I've never done before."

"Maybe we ought to turn the headlights back on," Riley said. "My folks would kill me if we had an accident."

"Not just yet, okay," she asked, squeezing his arm. "Let's get off this main road so we won't have to worry about it."

There was a side road thirty yards ahead of them on their right. A dirt trail that wound its way through derricks and rocking horse wells and eventually made its way to a shed where cement, pipe, and other drilling equipment was kept. Riley maneuvered his way down the trail and pulled the car to a stop behind the shed.

"This is nice," Gwen said. Then sliding over to the passenger side of the car, she added, "Come on, let's roll the windows down and get some fresh air."

Riley complied.

"I bet you take girls out here to park all the time, don't you?"

"No. I just pulled onto this trail because you said you wanted to get off the main road."

"Well, you seemed to have chosen a pretty secluded spot. I bet you've been out here before. With older girls, right?"

"Or maybe," Riley began, "you knew exactly where we were when you asked me to pull over. Maybe you're the one who's been out here."

"Absolutely not. What kind of girl do you think I am?"

"A very pretty one."

"Well, that's very nice of you to say. Why haven't you ever told me that before?"

"Gee, I don't know. I guess I've been so involved with my studies and the team, I haven't paid a lot of attention to other things."

"Like girls, you mean?"

"Like you, I mean. You are pretty, Gwen. Really pretty."

"Am I the prettiest girl in school?"

"You're the prettiest girl in this car."

"Well, that's no compliment. Am I the prettiest girl you've ever had in this car?"

He could have lied or joked some more but he didn't. "Yes. Yes, you are."

She noted the sincerity in his voice. And, for a moment, changed the subject. "Gosh, it's so quiet out here," she said. "All you can hear is the pumping of the wells and the croak of the cicadas."

"Yeah," Riley ventured. "Unfortunately, they're pumping for somebody else."

"It's a shame, isn't it? A shame we don't have our very own oil well, pumping out money for us day and night."

"Yeah, it is. Guess we can't all be rich though."

"It would be fun to be rich. Wouldn't it? Fun to have all the money we wanted…to do whatever we pleased."

"I kinda think you do what you please now."

"Well, I'm not sure that's a nice thing to say."

"I didn't mean anything bad by it. I like girls who are independent. Girls who don't need to have guys waiting on them hand and foot. You know, like rich girls seem to do in the movies and all."

"Well, I'm glad you think I'm independent, Riley, because I am. And I'm really glad you think I'm pretty. Because I think you're about the most handsome boy in town. But…I still bet you that rich people have a lot more fun than we do."

"I might take that bet. Watching you skate tonight…you seemed to be having a lot of fun."

"It was fun," Gwen said, slowly sliding back to Riley's side of the car. "It was fun skating, and even more fun having you watch me. You're fun to talk to, Riley. You really are. I don't know why we haven't done it before. And you know, maybe you're right. Maybe there are some things people can do to have fun whether they have a lot of money or not."

"And just what might that be?" Riley questioned, hoping he knew the answer already.

"Oh, I don't know," Gwen purred. "Maybe something like this." She bent over, titled her head, and pressed her lips against his.

It was a kiss both held, then paused to look in each other's eyes, and kissed again. Even harder this time. More passionately. They kept kissing for what seemed like a long time. Kissing lips, ears, necks, and lips again.

"You can touch me if you want to," Gwen whispered. "I've never let anyone touch me before. But I'll let you. If you want to." At that moment, there was nothing in the world Riley wanted more. He explored her body with his hands, caressing her gently, then firmly, as his passion rose. She answered in kind, bending her body to his touch, then she unfastened her bra and pulled the tunic over her head and let it drop to the floor of the car. He kissed her again and again. Then she reached for him, smiling as she said, "Is that you, or the Coke bottle?"

"It's me," Riley said. "God, you're so beautiful." Then he watched her smile turn to hunger as he bent to kiss her again.

For the next two weeks, they were inseparable. At school they had lunch together. She would wait for him after his games. On weekends they would return to their off-road hideaway. Between them, there was no talk of the future. They were too immersed in the moment. But moments, like everything else in life, have a beginning and an end.

Riley came home from school on a Wednesday afternoon and entered the house through the back door as he always did. When he stepped into the kitchen he immediately knew something was wrong. His mother was sitting at the booth. He could see she had been crying. There was an envelope on the table in front of her. It was unopened.

"Mom, what's the matter? Are you okay?"

She had to clear her throat before she spoke. "I kept telling myself this wouldn't happen. I didn't want to face it, I guess. It was silly of me to think it would somehow just pass us by."

"What would pass us by, mom? What are you talking about?"

"Your dad read about it in the newspaper some time ago. He saw that they had lowered the age requirement from twenty-one to eighteen. He said it was something we should prepare for. I just couldn't bring myself to talk about it."

"It's for me, isn't it, mom?"

"Yes, Riley. It's for you. It's from the Selective Service…the draft board."

Chapter 2

Chicago, Illinois, February 1943

The cold air mass started in Canada, moved across Lake Michigan, and blanketed Chicago in lake-effect snow. In the bars, old-timers warmed themselves with single malt scotch and told visiting businessmen this was nothing. "Should have been here twelve years ago in 1930. The white ice was twenty inches thick. Hell, this is barely a dusting."

At Finnegan's, muted conversations, bleated expletives over missed shots, and disgruntled exchanges of five-spots were interwoven with the recurring clack of cue balls. Brendon Killian O'Byrne was having a particularly bad day. His game was off. Not much, but enough. He had rushed his entry. Now he was paying for it.

Normally, Brendon would spend half an hour or so at the bar before suggesting a friendly game with one of the patrons. This afforded him plenty of time to study the skills of the various players. He would then choose one who wouldn't necessarily be a pushover. Beating your opponent too badly too quickly caps the competitive spirit. Thereby stopping the goose from continuing to lay golden eggs. So he would choose someone he believed he could master, but someone who would actually keep the contests competitive. Today however, he had been in a hurry. And haste had put him on a green felt table with someone doing a rather handy job of taking Brendon's green.

"Up for another?" the winner asked.

"Got a lot going on today," Brendon said. "Let me make a quick phone call and then I'll let you know."

He walked over to the bar, put a dollar down, and said to the bartender, "Mike, can I get some change for the phone?"

When the barkeep brought his coins, Brendon whispered his question.

"Do you know this guy I'm playing?"

"Never laid eyes on him before today."

"He's better than I thought he was."

"Life is full of surprises. Then you die."

"Thanks for the comforting words."

"I dispense good beer, not good cheer."

Brendon entered the phone booth, closed the folding door behind him, and called the number he had memorized long ago.

"We still on for tonight?"

"Sure. Why wouldn't we be?"

"I was just checking to make sure nothing has changed."

"Nothing's changed. Why would it?"

"Oh, I don't know. The weather, I guess. I was just wondering, you know."

"You're not getting cold feet, are you kid? This thing's been set up for some time. Too late to back out now. Plus the snow will probably help. Cops don't like to get out much when it's wet and nasty."

"I said I was in, and I am," Brendon answered. "See you guys at nine."

That's the way Brendon was. He didn't make commitments easily. But when he made them, he kept them. Even if he thought less of them later. And he was definitely thinking less of this particular commitment. It wasn't fear that was gnawing at him. He wasn't afraid to steal things. Of course, the only stealing he had done so far was shoplifting, and that wasn't real stealing. Well, at least it wasn't in Brendon's mind. He had a selective sense of right and wrong. He felt like storekeepers never even missed boosted items. At least, not the ones Brendon had hit. Or if they did, they didn't whine about it and call the police. It was the price of doing business. And he figured what they lost from shoplifters was infinitesimal compared to what it cost them to pay off cops on the take or greedy ward politicians in control of who did and who didn't get the licenses they needed to operate in the first place. Everybody takes from everybody, in one way or another. That's what had been drummed into Brendon from cradle to his ripe old age of twenty. And what you learn on the tough streets of Chicago's south side, you don't forget.

Brendon was a stocky kid. Not muscles for muscle's sake. Just firm. And hard where it was good to be hard. He had black hair and black eyes and was often referred to as a black Irishman. An endearment meant to describe his demeanor as much as his appearance. Those who knew him knew he was always up for a pint, or a party, or a pretty girl if the chance presented itself. And like most of the Irish from his part of the city, he could handle himself in a tussle if the ale turned to anger, which it sometimes did when there was too much of the former.

Like virtually all of the youth in his neighborhood, Brendon came from a working class family that always seemed to get by but never seemed to get ahead. His dad was a union man through and through. He believed the most important things in life were your union card, going to work every day, dinner with your wife and family, sharing a pint with your pals at the local pub, getting a good night's sleep, and doing all of it over again the next day.

Brendon though, being young, sharp, and eager for opportunity, however it presented itself, was convinced there must be more to life than endless routine. So he always kept one eye open for locals who seemed to be doing a little bit better than everyone else. He'd gravitate toward the guys who were buying the most drinks, or wearing suits instead of dungarees and jackets, or the swells with polished shoes. If it wasn't summer, and your shoes were polished in Chicago, you definitely had more money in your pocket than you knew what to do with. And the way Brendon saw it, if a shortcut was required here and there to be in that league, he was willing to take it.

The decision to knock over Feldman's Pawn Shop hadn't been

that difficult for Ian and Snapper. They were used to supplementing their income with occasional breaking and entering. But this would definitely be a step up for Brendon. Even though he was only to be the lookout. The rationale had been simple enough. Feldman was a Jew who lived off the hard times of his neighbors. Why shouldn't three good Irish boys advance their stature in life by pocketing a week's proceeds of the kike's ill-gotten gains? It sounded eminently reasonable, even righteous after the third pint. But now that the day had come, Brendon was less than anxious for the hour to arrive. Which might have been why he picked the wrong opponent to challenge for a game. So he made the decision to stop throwing good money after bad.

Leaving the phone booth and walking toward the door, Brendon said, "Sorry friend. Have to take a rain check on that rematch. Too much to do now."

"Better luck next time," his nemesis replied.

With you, sport, I'd need more than luck, Brendon thought to himself, but didn't say as he stepped out of Finnegan's and headed up the snowy street toward Hightower's Drugstore.

In addition to dispensing pills, patent medicines and a vast array of medicinal remedies, Hightower's had one of the busiest soda fountains in the neighborhood. Brendon wasn't particularly addicted to sweets but he was powerfully attracted to the young lady who worked behind the counter. Her dark hair, blue eyes, and trim figure had caused him to watch many a milkshake melt in his glass.

"So, Jilly McIntyre, what are you serving today?"

"As I've told you before, Mr. Brendon O'Byrne, it's Jillian. And our menu hasn't changed since you were in here yesterday."

"Well then, you better give me whatever you gave me yesterday."

"And I'm supposed to remember every customer's order from day to day, am I?"

"Not every customer. Just me. Surely you can't forget the

conversation we had and how it started."

"Well, I suppose it started with what it always starts with, right? A chocolate milkshake that you'll wind up not finishing. Or even starting for that matter."

"You're the one says I have to order something. I'd much rather just sit here and talk to you."

"It's not me, you know. It's Mr. Hightower. He doesn't like us fraternizing with customers who are too cheap to buy something."

"You wouldn't be calling me cheap, would you Jilly, darlin'?"

"No. I wouldn't. But Mr. Hightower would probably have worse names than that for you."

"Well, just to show you that I'm no cheapskate, suppose I take you out to dinner tomorrow night?"

"Dinner, is it? And just where were you thinking of taking me to dinner? Down the street for the free finger sandwiches at Finnegan's?"

"No, I was thinking that you might want to accompany me to dinner at The Drake Hotel."

Jillian spilled the milk she was fixing the shake with. "The Drake Hotel? Well, I had no idea I was being asked out by such a high roller. Since when do you have the price of dinner at The Drake? Not to mention the cab fare to get there."

"Oh, I have a little work to do tonight. And once it's done, I'll be a man of means and I thought you just might like to have a night on the town."

"Now what kind of work would you be doing at night that's going to get you enough money to—" she stopped in mid question, put her hands on her hips and stared accusingly.

"Don't be jumping to any conclusions now. You always tend to think the worst of me. I just happen to have a job cleaning out this big warehouse, with a couple of friends of mine, and it's going to pay enough for us to mix with the swells if you're up to it."

"And just why is this job being done at night?"

Without hesitation, the falsehoods continued to roll out of Brendon's mouth. "The warehouse owner waited too long to get started. He's got new merchandise coming in tomorrow morning. So the place has to be cleaned out tonight. That's why he's paying so much."

"The Drake, you say. Brendon, I've never been to such a ritzy place. I'm not sure I have the right thing to wear."

"Jilly, you dress up anything you put on. Every man in the place will have his eyes on you. And every woman will wonder who that good-looking young man in the pinstriped suit is. A swell couple arm-in-arm."

"I didn't even know you had a suit. I've never seen you in one."

"I'll have one by tomorrow night. And we'll be something to see, Jilly. Something to see. Say you'll come with me."

The smile on her face grew wide as a banana split. "I wouldn't miss it for the world," she beamed. "Now here, drink this milkshake. Mr. Hightower is coming over."

By nine o'clock that night the snow had begun to fall even harder. Brendon stood on the corner of 87th Street and Stony Island Avenue beneath a green canvas awning now cupcaked with a layer of white. He had gone home for dinner, told his parents he was going out to shoot pool with his friends, and now he stood rocking from one foot to the other with a cigarette dangling from his lips while his hands remained stuffed in his pockets to ward off the cold.

Keeping his eyes peeled for Ian's 1939 DeSoto Coupe, Brendon didn't immediately notice the street waif who rounded the corner and walked up beside him. A tug on his pant leg got his attention.

"Flowers, mister? Want to buy some flowers?"

"Hey, it's kind of late for a kid like you to be out, ain't it? Shouldn't you be home by now?"

"My mom says I have to sell all my flowers before I come

home."

She can't be more than eleven or twelve, Brendon thought, as he looked down at the skinny little girl in the well-worn coat. *Must be tough on the kid in weather like this.* "Why don't you just dump them somewhere? Tell your mother a bum stole them from you."

"No, that would be lying," she innocently answered. "Anyway, mom says we need the money."

"Well, I can't buy any tonight, sweetheart, but I tell you what. If you're here tomorrow night…earlier, say around seven, I'll buy all the flowers you have with you."

"Honest, mister? You will?"

"I said it and I'll do it. And you know what, there's a hospital just a few blocks from here, down 87th. Why don't you head over? I bet lots of people will want to buy flowers there."

"For the people who are sick?"

"That's right. I bet you'll sell out there."

She took off down the sidewalk, through the drifting snow, shouting without turning around, "See you here tomorrow night, mister. At seven."

"Seven it is, sweetheart," Brendon yelled back. But she had already turned the corner.

Ten minutes later the black DeSoto pulled up; Ian was behind the wheel and Snapper was in the back seat. Snapper Dooley was a mental deficient who made up for his lack of intelligence with an abundance of meanness. Growing up, he spent most of his time in and out of reform schools. He would have gotten into even more trouble than he did were it not for Ian Donovan. Ian's misspent youth was no less checkered than Snapper's. But Ian was smarter and infinitely more cunning. He used people like rungs on a ladder, and he always found ways for someone other than himself to take the fall for whatever nefarious endeavor he was engaged in. But he had a knack for endearing himself to others before his true colors unfurled. That's how he had pulled Brendon into his orbit. On the surface he seemed like a sharp operator who really knew the score. Plus what corners to cut without getting into trouble he couldn't get out of. But Brendon was about to find the surface a lot slicker than he realized.

"I'll slide over, you drive from here," Ian told Brendon.

Five minutes after that, all three were sitting in the car across the street from Feldman's. *So far*, Brendon thought, *everything was going according to plan*. But so far only goes so far.

"Okay, it's almost nine thirty," Ian said. "Now, when Feldman comes out, if he's not carrying any sort of satchel, or package, that means the week's take is still inside. But if he's got something under his arm, just drive up ahead of him. Snapper and I will jump out, shove him in the alley and take it from him there."

Brendon's response was instantaneous. "What? What are you talking about? You didn't say anything about jumping anybody on the street. You said he always leaves the take inside."

"Well if he doesn't my lad, we've got to be prepared to adjust," Ian answered.

"Look, this isn't what we talked about. You said all I had to do was sit in the car and wait. You said I should hit the horn if a patrolman got too nosy, and pick you guys up at the back entrance five minutes after you went in. You said that's all I had to do."

"Well, laddy boy," Ian retorted, "as the legendary Robert once said, the best laid schemes o' mice and men gang aft agley."

Snapper piped up from the back seat. "Not goin' all weak-knees on us, are you, boy?"

"It just not what we talked about. It's not what I agreed to."

"Agreements be damned," Ian countered. "You heard what to do if he comes out with something under his arm."

"But Feldman's an old guy," Brendon said. "If he struggles, or resists, he could wind up getting hurt. I never agreed to be part of hurting anybody."

"Oh, I doubt very seriously that he'll be resisting," Snapper said coyly, pulling a revolver from his inside coat pocket.

"A gun! You brought a gun?" Brendon couldn't believe it. "Look, breaking and entering is one thing. Armed robbery is something else. This is crazy. I'm not going to be part of—"

"Look," Ian said, pointing across the street and cutting off Brendon's protests.

The lights inside Feldman's were going out. Any moment now the old man would be stepping outside and locking the door. Snow continued to fall. The temperature continued to drop. But Brendon had broken into a sweat. A sweat that rimmed his collar, beaded on his forehead, and wet the top of his upper lip. *Don't have anything with you,* he said silently to himself. *Leave it inside. Don't be carrying anything. Please.*

The door swung open. Feldman stepped outside. He was wearing a fedora and a big brown overcoat. It took him a second to find his keys and lock the door because he had to take the big manila package he was carrying and put it under his arm.

"Start the car," Ian said.

"But look," Brendon began. Then he felt the cold muzzle of the revolver pressed against his neck.

"Start the car," Snapper added.

The engine turned over as Ian said, "Start off slowly. Let him get almost to the corner. Then cut in front of him quickly so he can't cross."

Brendon pulled away from the curb and started down the street. How had he gotten himself into this? He knew the answer. It was another short cut. Another way to get money without really working for it. But it was all going to go wrong. He could just feel it.

Feldman was getting closer to the corner. "Alright, get ready to hit it," Ian said. "Get ready. Get ready. Now!"

Brendon stomped the gas pedal hard and cut the steering wheel sharply to the left, sliding Ian and Snapper to the right side of the car. But just as he was coming to an abrupt halt in front of

Feldman, he knew he didn't want to be part of what might happen. With no thought of the consequences, he whipped the wheel back to the right and hit the pedal again. The speed of the thrust and the icy streets caused the DeSoto to fishtail. In a panic to straighten the car but get away from Feldman, Brendon jerked the wheel again. But the overcorrection on the slick pavement sent the car into a spin. Centrifugal force took over as the Coupe spun like a top down the middle of the street barely missing the parked cars on both sides. Then the tires hit the curb jolting the front of the vehicle upward and bouncing it onto the sidewalk. When the wheels came down with a thump, Brendon could swear they barely preceded a muffled cry.

By the time Ian and Snapper had climbed up from the floorboards and made sure they were in one piece, Brendon had opened the driver's door and stepped out into the street. The first things he saw were crimson rose petals scattered over white snow.

"Get back in the car," Ian yelled, "we can catch up with Feldman in the next block."

But Brendon didn't respond. His gaze was now fixed on the little girl lying in a heap against the side of a building. "We hit her," Brendon said, almost too softly to be heard.

"We didn't hit her. You hit her," Snapper barked.

Ian yelled, "Get back in the car!"

By now, Brendon was on the sidewalk, leaning over her. "We have to help. She's still breathing."

"You help her, altar boy. She's your doing," Snapper growled.

"But not a word about us, you hear?" Ian threatened. "Not a word about us if you know what's good for you. This is all your fault anyway."

With that, Ian slid behind the wheel, Snapper joined him in the front seat, and the DeSoto backed off the curb and drove away into the black Chicago night.

An hour later, on the third floor of Mercy Hospital, a

policeman who had recently stepped out of the elevator was wrapping up a conversation with the duty nurse. The last thing he asked was "Who brought her in?"

"That young man sitting over there on the bench," she replied.

The policeman walked over and put his hand on Brendon's shoulder. It startled him out of an exhausted sleep. The first thing out of his mouth was, "Is she going to be okay…officer?"

"No, son. I'm afraid she's not going to be okay," the policeman answered. "Now, suppose you tell me exactly what happened."

Brendon couldn't believe it. He felt sick inside. He knew it was an accident—knew that the car was out of control—knew he had never even seen her there. But when he spoke, words just started pouring out. Words that were far from the truth. "I don't really know. I was on the next street over. I heard some tires squealing. And when I turned the corner, there she was. I picked her up and carried her here, to the hospital."

"The night nurse confirms you brought her in, son. But now that you've told me what you've told me, it might interest you to know that Shamus McElwane has a newsstand near that very corner, and he witnessed the whole thing. You better come with me."

At the pre-trial hearing, Brendon relented and admitted he was driving the car. But he said he didn't know the other two men the newsstand operator had seen. *What good would it have done,* he told himself. He was driving. They weren't. He had agreed to go with them. He had acquiesced and made the decision to do as he was told and start toward Feldman. And he was the one who then lost control of the car. So he told the court there were two fellows who had come out of a nightclub too drunk to drive. He offered to drive them back to their hotel for five dollars and they accepted. But when the accident happened, they panicked and took off in the car.

It seemed plausible, the judge thought. The witness had indicated it appeared the car was sliding on the slick street. The event itself seemed to be simply a tragic accident. And the young man had tried to render aid by taking the victim to the hospital. But the district attorney was an ambitious man, hungry for notches on his belt that could help him move up the political ladder. He reminded the court that a young, innocent life had been snuffed out. He felt that it was his duty to at least pursue a charge of vehicular manslaughter.

Unsure that one tragic event should lead to another, and times being what they were, the judge proffered a Solomonesque proposal to the prosecution and defense. Alternative one; the boy would stand trial for manslaughter, where the next years of his life would be dependent upon a jury of twelve good citizens, well and true. Alternative two, the manslaughter charge would be dropped and the death ruled accidental if the young man would enlist in the army, where able-bodied men were needed and his ultimate fate would be left to the almighty.

The prosecution, not wanting to be seen in any way as unpatriotic, agreed.

The defense, after consulting with their still guilt-ridden client, rejected the unknowable outcome of a jury trial, and Brendon Killian O'Byrne accepted the offer of service to his country.

Chapter 3

Los Angeles, California, March 1943

The corners of the white linen tablecloth rose and fell with the vicissitudes of the cavalier breeze coming off the astoundingly blue Pacific. White china, cut crystal, and filigreed silverware kept it firmly anchored even when Paul Cassidy raised the glass of California Chardonnay to his lips. Which he did often. He wasn't exactly sure when having lunch with his parents had become such a trial. He only knew that it was now something to be endured rather than enjoyed.

A violent hacking cough broke the stillness of one of the many silent pauses that filled their familial gatherings. The elder Cassidy had held it in as long as he could. But what must come out will. Be it phlegm or philosophical differences.

"Oh, Charles, do you have to do that at the table? Drink more water. I'm continually telling him to drink more water. But he won't do it, Paul. You know how stubborn he is."

Clearing his throat, Paul's father responded, "Don't like water. Never have. You know what Bill Fields said about it. He said I never drink water. Fish fuck in it."

Wincing, Paul's mother replied, "How absolutely vulgar. What a vulgar thing to say over lunch, Charles."

"Nonsense. It's funny," the older man replied. "Dirty is dirty if it's dirty for dirty's sake. But if it's dirty for fun's sake, that's a different matter."

"I know vulgar when I hear it, and that was vulgar. Wasn't it, Paul?"

"Shockingly so, father. Can't you see how offended I am? In fact, you may well have put me off my wine. Let's see." He raised his glass and took another swallow. "Ah, luckily I've survived.

Still tastes pleasant as it did prior to your atrocious vulgarity."

"Paul, you're making fun of me," his mother said. "How rude. What a rude thing to do."

"Afraid your mother's lost her sense of humor, son. A terrible thing to lose one's sense of humor. Or one's sense of proportion. That's important too, I guess. But not as important as a sense of humor."

"I would never make fun of you, mother. I was just having fun with you. Just injecting a bit of levity."

"Well, at least your humor wasn't vulgar, like your father's. He's becoming less and less refined, I'm afraid. Probably because of those objectionable people he has to deal with now."

"I am here at the table, you know, Margaret. You can address me directly rather than referring to me."

"I just don't see why you had to take that position, Charles."

"It was my duty, dear. We all have a duty to do something for the war effort."

"That's silly," Paul's mother responded. "We have no duty to involve ourselves in Mr. Roosevelt's war."

"It's hardly Mr. Roosevelt's war, mother. I mean Pearl Harbor was bombed, you know." Then he couldn't help himself from adding, "It was in all the papers."

"Heading up our district's War Relocation Authority is not only an honor, dear," Charles's father said, "it is vitally important."

"Absolutely, mother," Paul piped up. "Can't have those subversive Japanese gardeners running amuck in Pacific Palisades."

"No need to make light of it, Paul," his father replied. "Sabotage is no laughing matter. There's too much at stake to take chances."

"I think the chances of a seven year old Japanese schoolgirl blowing up one of our west coast refineries is a bit far-fetched. Don't you, father?"

"Well, the kids might not be a threat, but we can't just relocate the parents. Who would take care of the children?"

"Oh yes, I see, dad. It's the humane thing to do. Just round up the parents, grandparents, kids, babies and all, and ship the lot of them to the Arizona desert so they can all be together."

"We're at war, son. Our whole way of life is at stake. Don't you understand that?"

The wine was helpful but it had not been consumed in sufficient quantities to chill Paul's rising temper. "I understand that we are rounding up Americans like cattle, and sending them off to God knows where to be kept for God knows how long."

"They're not Americans son, they're Japanese!"

"Charles, be mindful of your blood pressure," Paul's mother inserted.

"The majority were born and raised here, dad. I thought being born in America made you an American."

"There's nothing deeper than blood, son. Where you're born is never as important as who you come from."

"What a depressing thought," Paul snapped, pulling the linen napkin from his lap and tossing it on the table.

His mother quickly said, "Well, who would like some kiwi and sherbet?"

On the way back to his apartment, Paul took the coast road. He liked the way the wind felt coming off the ocean, tossing his blond hair back and forth on his forehead. He liked the sound of the waves lapping the shore. He even liked the salty smell of the sea and the way the light glinted off his windshield, moving from one side to the other and flaring a bright gold when the snaking path he was on turned toward the sun. All were sensations that helped him put things in perspective, and these days he seemed to need all the help he could get where that was concerned.

Paul Cassidy had always known he was a son of privilege. But for most of his youth, like most of his peers, he simply took it for granted that the houses in his neighborhood had swimming pools and tennis courts and servants of one particular ethnic persuasion or another. That's just the way life was. When he thought about it at all, which was seldom, he rationalized that he had no choice as to his parentage, or how grand his home was, or how well off his family, friends, and neighbors happened to be. But when he started taking classes at the University of California at Los Angeles, he met all kinds of young people whose lot in life was decidedly different than his. And he began to ruminate more often on the rather good hand fate had dealt him.

Paul's mother had wanted to send him to college in the east. She had grown up in Massachusetts and felt that one of the older, more traditional schools would provide a more impressive pedigree. But his father was a self-made westerner who had borrowed a thousand dollars for a real estate investment and subsequently turned it into a fortune. He saw no need to round rough edges off Paul, and he liked having his only son close by. Even if the boy had shown no interest whatsoever in land, high finance, or the inevitable convergence of the two.

When he entered college four years ago, he had taken an apartment near the school. His mother wasn't keen on the idea. She thought he should continue to live at home. But his father simply said, "Do the boy good to get out and see how the other half lives. Maybe make him appreciate what he's got a little more. And how hard you need to work to keep it."

The effect, however, had been closer to the reverse. He became self-conscious that while he always had spending money in his pockets, his fellow students seldom did. He noticed that they seemed to study harder and cram more for exams, but he generally wound up with higher marks. He couldn't help but observe that many of them had to take jobs at school, or off campus, simply to continue their education, while he never had to give tuition a second thought. And over his last year, he noticed that more and more of his male friends were having to leave school because they were being drafted. When he mentioned to his parents what was happening to so many of them, his mother would simply make a derogatory remark about the President and his father would mumble something about needs, quotas, and whatnot. But he'd always end his side of the conversation with "They don't need everyone, you know, son. Don't worry about it."

There was a diner near campus that Paul and a number of his friends frequented in the evenings. The food was relatively good and remarkably inexpensive. Due to the location, the owner of the diner knew he was going to need a lot of students if he was to have a steady stream of customers. So he priced accordingly, which enabled the place to turn a reasonable profit and serve as convenient hangout for students and neighborhood residents as well.

When Paul came in after his last class, on the evening following his Sunday lunch with his parents, he noticed three acquaintances in a corner booth. Coffee cups rimmed their table. On his way over, he said to the girl behind the counter, "I'll have a cup of coffee. And they'd probably like some more."

He had barely slid in beside them when Tina Morton, from his journalism class, said, "Did you hear about Professor Hiroshi?"

"No," Paul replied. "I don't have any of his classes this semester."

"Well," Jaime Martinez said, "neither will anyone else for a while."

"What do you mean?"

Tina answered before Jaime could. "He's gone. The substitute Prof said he was on an extended leave of absence. You know what that means?"

Paul answered dejectedly. "It means he's been relocated."

"Yeah, relocated. You'd know all about that wouldn't you, Cassidy?"

The undisguised sarcasm came from the third member of the

group, Lev Goldman, a short, bespectacled, rather rumpled young man with dark hair and an attitude to match. His disdain for wealthy goyim was seldom masked. It wasn't financial envy that flamed it. It was their exclusionary tendencies he found distasteful. And if some of them were like that, which they most certainly were, then all of them must be. At least that's the way Lev saw it. In his mind, Paul's friendship with those of a decidedly lower social strata was simply good-natured slumming. Nothing more. And as such, no quarter need be given.

"What do you mean, I'd know all about that?"

"Well, it's no secret your father is head of one of the War Relocation Authority districts. It's public knowledge, you know. The names of Authority members were printed in The LA Times the other day in an article suggesting readers write them and tell them what they think about this racist, anti-American practice. Seems that not enough people gave dear old dad the message."

"There's no way for you to know my father was involved," Paul replied. "Different districts are responsible for different sections of the county."

"See," Lev quickly pounced. "You do know all about it. Or, at least more than you want to share."

"Oh, give it a rest, Lev," Tina interrupted. "Paul's not responsible for what his father may or may not do."

"Yeah, Lev," Jaime chimed in. "Don't be such a jerk."

"Oh, I'm the jerk, am I? Well I don't think Professor Hiroshi would think I'm such a jerk. He's probably in the back of a truck now. Or on a railroad car being shipped off to an internment camp while we sit around talking about what a swell guy Paul is."

"Look," Tina said, "nobody likes what happen to Professor Hiroshi. And nobody likes what's happening to all the other Japanese on the west coast. But when there's a war on, all sorts of bad things happen to people. Sometimes with the best of intentions."

"Oh, good intentions, is that it? Good intentions gone astray," Lev began. "Well, you know I'm pretty sure people like Paul's dad have the best of intentions. He's intent on keeping California safe. So he carts off all the Japanese. Mussolini's intent on keeping Italy safe. So Fascists bust heads and root out all the undesirables. Hitler's intent on keeping Germany pure. So he rounds up all the Jews. You know who knows the most about good intentions gone astray? It's the people who are affected by those good intentions. The people whose lives are turned into a living nightmare. But of course it's not all of those people. Some actually get away. Some are tricky enough, or smart enough, or rich enough to get out while the getting is good. Right, Paul?"

"What are you asking me for? How the hell should I know?"

"Well, you should know," Lev said, raising a folded newspaper above his head, "because it's all here. Right here in the city news." Quoting a headline, he read, "Famous European artists relocating to America." Then he did his own editorializing. "To Los Angeles. To Pacific Palisades, that particularly upscale neighborhood one of us at this table is from. Of course you realize, European artist is simply a euphemism for Jewish artist. That's right. Famous author, Thomas Mann, and renowned actor, Oskar Homolka. That's right. Jewish author. Jewish actor. But then, I guess you don't keep up with everyone in your neighborhood, do you, Paul? Just some people. The right people."

"Lev, you know I don't even live there anymore. My parents do. Give me a break, will you?"

Jaime added, "Yeah, Lev. Cool off, okay? What's bugging you today, man?"

"It's this war," Tina said, before Lev could reply. "This damn war. It's got everyone crazy jumpy. Especially everyone our age. You never know who's going to get called next."

"I just wish we could get it over with," Paul added. "I think the sooner it's over, the sooner everyone can get back to some sort of real life, you know."

Lev, who had been ranting just a few seconds ago, now seem deflated, like an unknotted balloon that zigs and zags uncontrollably, then sinks to earth limp and lifeless. "Listen. Paul, forget what I said, okay. I got a bit carried away. I shouldn't have lumped you in with the rest of the swell set. I didn't mean to imply you were a rich shkutz."

"No, you didn't mean to imply it," Paul said. "You meant to come right out and say it."

The group giggled. But only for a moment.

Then Lev said, "Maybe Paul's right. Maybe all we need is to get the war over sooner. You know who thinks that? The government, that's who. I mean they must think that. Or why else would I have gotten this today?" Reaching in his pocket, he pulled out an envelope and dropped it in the middle of the table.

Everyone looked at it, but no one wanted to open it. So Lev continued. "It's rather short and to the point, actually. It simply says I am hereby notified that I am being ordered to report for a physical examination pursuant to military service. So. Do you think that will help get the war over sooner, Paul?"

Paul looked at Lev but didn't answer. Instead, he turned toward the girl he had spoken to when he came in, raised his voice and said, "Forget the coffee. Bring us four beers."

* * *

Paul woke up early the next morning, fortunately no worse for wear after the multiple rounds of beers he and his mates had the night before. He showered, dressed, made himself a cup of coffee, then decided he'd walk to class because the sun-splashed California morning was simply too beautiful to spend inside. Leaving early, he ambled along a cement path that wound its way through manicured Bermuda grass, sculpted boxwood hedges, and trimmed sycamores. Coming upon an empty bench he decided to do something he almost never did—pause for a moment and take stock of his life.

Only a few weeks remained before graduation. He wouldn't be at the top of his class but he was a lot closer to the top than the bottom. He had interned at a public relations firm the past two summers and they told him upon completion of his studies to see them first. There was no doubt in his mind they'd offer him a job. And there was no doubt why. The firm represented a number of his father's real estate interests. They did what they thought was good for them. *Who doesn't,* Paul thought. But that wasn't all he thought.

How long could he keep it up, he wondered. How long could he keep acting like he was independent while accepting his father's money, influence, and connections to pave the way for him. And how far did that influence go? Lev wasn't the only friend he knew who got that letter in the mail. All around him, young men his age were being plucked off college campuses, pulled from grocery store stocking aisles, lifted from mechanic shops, factories, farms, even high schools to fill the swelling ranks needed to fight a world war. But somehow, he remained untouched, apart from it all, with his father's words ringing in his ears. "They don't need everyone, you know, son. Don't worry about it."

Paul wasn't naive. He understood his father's meaning. He was not to worry about what virtually every healthy young man in America had to worry about. His father would pull enough strings to make sure Paul wasn't forced into anything. But how could his father pull enough strings to keep Paul from looking in the mirror every morning and being disappointed in the man he saw there. A man who took advantage of the advantages he had. A man content to let others carry the burden while he reaped the rewards. A man who would never know how much of a man he really was.

Three weeks from the day Paul sat on that bench, he

graduated from college. Afterwards, he celebrated late into the evening with friends and family.

The following morning, unbeknownst to his mother and father, Paul decided not to go see the public relations firm about a job. Instead, he met with an army recruiter at the Hollywood station. The soldier told him there was an urgent need for men who could lead other men. In most demand he said, were college graduates who, after completing basic combat training, would move on to officer candidate school, followed by a commission in the United States Army. It wasn't the recruiter's well-rehearsed pitch that convinced Paul Cassidy to sign on the dotted line. It was something more. It was the thought of staring at that face in the mirror every morning for the rest of his life, and not truly knowing who was staring back.

Chapter 4

Sabine River, May 1943

Pine trees are immune to borders. The ones in east Texas are indistinguishable from the ones in west Louisiana. But Riley stared out the window anyway, thinking he might be able to spot some minor difference between the two. After all, he had been told all his life that everything was bigger in Texas. He knew such talk was ninety percent exaggeration, but still he scanned the treetops for any noticeable differences.

The Greyhound bus taking him to the mobilization training center at Camp Polk rolled through the Piney woods more like the tortoise than the hare, continually picking up and dropping off passengers at drug stores, post offices, and bus stops in hamlets too tiny to even be referred to as towns. More often than not, the passengers were young men in the same situation as Riley. Now and then, there were older women and men on their way to visit ailing family members. Leisure had yet to become a reason for travel in this part of the South.

The draft board let Riley finish his semester and graduate before having to report. Board members were tasked with meeting quotas but allowed to exercise some degree of restraint where timing was concerned. In their tiny corner of the world, they knew most of the boys and the parents of the boys they were sending off to war. So they did what they could to be flexible. Within limits of course. A country building an army of citizen soldiers couldn't rely on patriotism alone. Only about a third of the fighting force needed was made up of voluntary enlistment. The other two-thirds had to come from conscription. It was the proverbial dirty job someone had to do.

In the days and weeks prior to Riley's departure, he and Gwen saw each other as often as they could. It was easy during breaks at school. Nights were harder. Gwen's parents didn't allow her to date during the week. So most of their time spent alone was on weekends. Weekends that seemed to fly by once they knew their time together would soon be ending. Both tried to keep from repeating what had happened their first night together. But noble objectives were no match for young love and raging hormones. And while the talk after their lovemaking centered on how much they cared for each other, each had a foreboding sense of finality that kept them from discussing the future. She thought hard about asking him to marry her before he had to leave. He thought hard about asking her to wait for him. But their thoughts never quite made it into words. Eventually, she promised she'd write him every day. He promised he'd get word to her as often as he could. Their last time together was the day before he left. They didn't try to find a secluded place to make love. It somehow didn't seem appropriate on so solemn an occasion. Not knowing quite what to say, their goodbye was awkward and more abbreviated than it needed to be. Each wanted to be strong for the other. So neither cried. Both saved their tears and shed them once they were alone.

Chapter 5

Illinois Central, May 1943

The Main Line of Mid-America clicked and clacked its way along the iron rails that connected Chicago to New Orleans and Birmingham. The Illinois Central railroad had recently upgraded to diesel-electric power, cutting two hours off the twenty it had previously taken to make the run. Switching from steam to a more powerful mode of locomotion was just one of the changes a wartime footing was bringing to the country. The sooner passengers could get from one place to another, the faster they could get on with what they had to do. For most it was conducting business. For some it was familial obligations. For others, like Brendon, it was simply transport to training. The government, in its infinite wisdom and frequently inexplicable logic, had bundled its monthly quota of conscripts and enlistees from the Midwest and shipped them off to be taught soldiering in Louisiana. Apparently more facilities existed there for combat training. At least that's what Brendon heard the other recruits saying as they boarded the train.

He had never been south. In fact, he had never been out of Illinois. When you live in Chicago you don't think much about going other places. *Why would you,* Brendon mused. Inhabitants of the windy city had virtually everything anyone might need. If not in your own neighborhood, in someone else's. A self-contained universe, that's what it was. But now he had been expelled from that universe and he was on his way to Dixie.

Eighteen hours is a long time to spend on a train. Reflection becomes inevitable. Brendon had no second thoughts about his decision. Spending time in prison was not something he wanted to risk. No matter how slight the chance might have been of his actually being convicted of vehicular manslaughter. *What an awful word,* Brendon thought, *manslaughter.* In his case it was even worse. *Child slaughter. How do you ever get over that?* The tragedy had lingered in his mind, never completely out of his thoughts, since the night it happened. He knew it was an accident. He knew he never saw her when the car was spinning. But he knew just as certainly he had been involved in something awful. He couldn't forget the way her body hung limp in his arms. The way she never opened her eyes as he carried her through the snowy streets. The way she just seemed to crumple onto the stretcher like a rag doll when he reached the hospital. Was she already dead? Had he carried a little dead girl from a street corner to the hospital? Did they simply not want to tell him right away? Did they even really try to save her? Or was he simply looking for some way, any way, to have someone else share responsibility for what had happened?

From Illinois through Kentucky, Tennessee, Mississippi, and into Louisiana, the thoughts and the guilt kept bouncing back and forth in his mind. Thoughts of what he had done, and what he hadn't done. He hadn't gone back to see Jillian. He was too ashamed. Unless she read something about it in the paper, or heard something from a friend, she never knew what happened. He hadn't called. Hadn't gone back to Hightower's Drug Store. Hadn't taken her to dinner at The Drake Hotel. Brendon told himself she must think he was the worst kind of heel to just vanish that way, without a word. But he rationalized that was somehow better than trying to tell her he had caused a little girl's death.

Though he may not have been conscious of it initially, and while he may have assumed the primary reason he chose not to go to trial was to avoid any chance of prison, he began to wonder if perhaps there was another reason for his choice as well. A reason that might have been just as strong. Maybe going to war was a way for him to make up for what he did. Maybe helping some unknown civilians, or saving some of his fellow soldiers' lives, was a way for him to balance the books. Maybe that was it. Or maybe he just wanted to do whatever he could to stop thinking about the night and the snow and the child.

After saying goodbye to his parents, before going to Union Station, Brendon stopped at the church in his neighborhood to make confession to his parish priest. He told Father Donovan what he had done and that he was on his way to join the army. The priest reminded him that while we can't always understand God's ways, we can do our best to atone for our own transgressions. And taking up arms against evil was indeed one way to do that. Brendon acknowledged what Father Donovan said. He sincerely hoped it was true. But he also understood that if this was his penance, it was only just beginning.

Chapter 6

Highway 101, California, May 1943

When Paul informed his parents of his decision to enlist, his mother cried and his father blustered about undoing all that he had done to keep Paul out of harm's way. But once they fully understood their son had no intention of reversing his decision, his mother put on the bravest face she could muster and his father insisted on driving Paul to the induction center at Fort Ord. It would be a long drive from Los Angeles to Monterrey, but the elder saw it as an opportunity to recapture some semblance of the kind of relationship he had with Paul as a boy. And the younger saw it as perhaps a small way to make his father happy. A meager down payment on a major debt he knew he owed.

The sea-green Packard 120 Club Sedan cruised northward at a leisurely pace. Paul had suggested he drive up the coast, as his father would have to drive back alone. No point in one man having to do all the driving, he said. And Paul reminded his dad that he probably wouldn't be behind the wheel of anything for some time to come. The elder agreed, accepting the inevitability that all father-son hierarchies eventually realign and become more man-to-man.

Ahead of them and to their left, the view was about as spectacular as America has to offer. The curving coastline of California mountains reached toward the rocky shores of Big Sur like knuckles on the hand of God. Salt air and sea spray wafted through their open windows reinforcing the eternity of the Pacific, and silently reminding them of man's limited time to enjoy it.

"You'll write your mother often, son. It's important, you know. It'll calm her worries a good deal just hearing from you."

"I will, dad. Often as I can. You know I'm not shy when it comes to talking about myself."

Now and again, along the way, Paul's father would nod off, slipping into reverie induced by the afternoon sun. He daydreamed of taking this same route in earlier times when Paul was young and precocious, and his wife's windblown hair and gleaming smile made it seem like his entire existence was a chamber of commerce billboard. An advert for the good life when one never had to wonder if beyond the sea's horizon a Japanese fleet was steaming landward.

The conversation that passed between Paul and his father as they made their way up the coast was more about the past than the future. It was far easier to talk about the pleasant times behind them than the uncertain times ahead. They recounted vacations they had taken, schools Paul had attended, neighbors and friends they had known, family picnics they had enjoyed in picturesque locales. It was, in effect, a long goodbye that neither felt comfortable addressing directly.

By the time they were nearing Monterrey and Carmel by the Sea, they could no longer avoid the real reason for their trip.

"Paul, you're going to make a first-rate officer. Of that, I have no doubt."

"I appreciate your confidence in me, dad. Frankly, right now, it's a lot more than I have in myself."

"I know I gave you a hard time about it before, son. But the truth is, having thought it over, I want you to know I'm very proud of you. If I were still your age, I think it's something I would have done myself."

"I think you probably would have, too. You always did seem to take the bull by the horns, didn't you, dad?"

"Maybe so, I don't really know. I seem to be a lot better at shooting the bull, these days."

"I want you to know something too," Paul began. "I know I've never said it. And I know for sure I've probably never shown it.

And though there are definitely a lot of things I know we don't agree on, I've always looked up to you, dad. I know you worked very hard for all you've been able to give mother and me."

"That's what a man does, son. He works hard and shares what he accomplishes with his family. You're going to have a new family for a while now, Paul, the army, and all the men in it. You'll need to work hard for them."

"I'll try my best. I hope it's good enough."

"If it's your best, son, it will be more than good enough."

"Any other sage wisdom you might be able to impart to me, dad?"

"Yes, son, there is. Keep your head down. And give those Japs or Nazi bastards hell!"

Outside Fort Ord's main gate, Paul watched his father drive away. As the Packard got smaller and smaller, it felt as if everything that had happened to him until now was fading away as well. He knew he was entering a world where it made no difference whatsoever who his father was, or what neighborhood he lived in, or how much money his family had. He was entering a world where the only thing that mattered was performance. He had never felt quite so alone. Or quite so exhilarated.

Chapter 7

Camp Polk, Leesville, Louisiana, May 1943

The assembly area for incoming recruits was outdoors. It consisted of portable aluminum grandstands beneath an overhanging tarpaulin to ward off the sun or rain or both. Beneath it, men became acquainted with the first rule of military life—hurry up and wait.

Riley had been there almost an hour when the latest group of inductees made their way to the grandstands. It was the third group to arrive since he had taken a seat. This bunch looked much like the ones that had preceded it. Mostly young men in their late teens or early twenties. Some a little older. One or two a lot older. But virtually all were rumpled, tired, apprehensive.

Every fifteen minutes or so, a non-commissioned officer would emerge from a wood-framed building and call a list of names. Those called would follow the NCO into the building. Those not called would wait. Even though it was only May, it was already hot and muggy with the temperature just over ninety degrees. Riley had moved higher up in the grandstands to take advantage of what little breeze occasionally made its way under the tarp. The majority of new arrivals took a seat on the lower level. One or two climbed a few rungs not wanting to be at the front of the pack. One fellow, a darker young man with black hair and eyes to match, moved all the way up to the level Riley was on and took a seat beside him. He took a pack of cigarettes from his shirt pocket, pulled one out and said without looking at Riley, "Okay to smoke here?"

"I don't think so," Riley answered.

"Why not?"

"Don't really know. But the soldier who keeps coming out of

that building, tells guys who are smoking to stop."

"Oh, yeah. How often does he come out?"

"Every now and then. Seems like, I don't know, every ten or fifteen minutes."

"Well, he's not here now, so I think I'll light up. Want one?"

"Don't smoke," Riley answered.

"Don't smoke because you don't smoke? Or because of that soldier you mentioned?"

"Don't smoke because I don't smoke. Just never took it up."

"Wish I hadn't," he said, just before lighting up and taking a big drag. Then he sighed and said, "No I don't. Can't think why I said that. A little nervous, I guess."

"Yeah, I was nervous too when I first got here."

"You been here a while?"

"Seems like a long time. Don't have a watch. Wouldn't matter if I did, I guess. I mean whatever's going to happen is going to happen. In whatever time it takes. Guess all our time is the army's now."

"You're right there, friend. Good way to look at it. We're here for the duration, as they say. Might as well sit back and take it as it comes, huh?"

"That's what I'm doing. Until I'm told to do something different."

"Makes sense, friend. Makes sense. Hey, what's your name? Mine's Brendon. Brendon O'Byrne from Chicago," he said, extending his hand.

Riley reached over and gave him a firm handshake as his father had taught him. "I'm Riley Cross, from Texas."

"Texas," Brendon echoed. "I never met anyone from Texas before."

"That makes us even I guess. I never met anyone from Chicago."

The NCO had returned, and the first thing he saw was the cigarette in Brendon's mouth. "No smoking here," the sergeant said. "Put it out and put the butt in your pocket. Or you'll be policing the entire area."

"Policing?" Brendon muttered, almost to himself.

"He means cleaning up," Riley added. "I heard him use that word earlier."

Brendon ground the cigarette into the aluminum bench he was sitting on, blew the ashes off the end, then dropped the butt into his shirt pocket. "Sorry, didn't know," Brendon explained, without really knowing why.

The sergeant asked gruffly, "What's your name, recruit?"

"Me?"

"Yes, you, meathead. What's your name?"

"Brendon. Brendon O'Byrne."

"O'Byrne, Brendon," the sergeant began, running his finger down the long list of names on his clipboard. "Yeah, you're on here. Come on down and start a line over there."

Brendon started to stand up when Riley tugged at his sleeve. "Ask him about me," Riley said, almost under his breath.

"Hey Sir, what about my friend, here?"

"Riley Cross," the Texan reminded him.

"Riley Cross. He's been here longer than I have, Sir."

"I'm no Sir," the NCO barked. "It's sergeant. Sir is for officers. What'd you say his name was?"

"Cross," Riley answered. "Riley Cross."

The sergeant had to flip four pages back before he spotted his name. "Yeah. Cross, Riley. You should have moved through earlier. Why the hell are you still here, Cross?"

"You never called my name, Sergeant. I've just been sitting here waiting for you to call my name."

"Well, I just called it, dumbass. Now get off your lazy butt and get in line there behind O'Byrne."

Inside the building recruits were instructed to repeat an oath of allegiance. They all did so compliantly. Each had already passed a physical examination prior to receiving orders to report so there was no need for another. The men were then marched to the base Barber Shop where their heads were checked for lice and their hair was trimmed short. After that it was on to supply where they were given two sets of fatigue uniforms, boots, belts, packs, entrenching tools, helmet liners, sheets, a blanket and a pillow. Then they moved on to the barracks that would be their home for the next eight to twelve weeks. The barracks were long wood-framed buildings painted white and stacked one next to the other with approximately forty feet between them. Inside each, a long walkway ran down the center of the structure. On each side of the walkway, double bunk beds rimmed the walls. Individual footlockers were provided to hold each man's gear and civilian clothes. There was a privy on one end with ten sinks and mirrors, ten non-partitioned toilets, and a long row of showerheads for bathing. On the other end, right beside the door, there was one small private room for the NCO in charge.

Riley and Brendon's incidental alignment held as they went through the various processing stations. By the time they got to their barracks there was an unspoken agreement that they might as well stick together. Fate is as good a guide as any when you're young, alone, and completely unsure of what the future will bring.

"You want to be up or down?" Brendon asked.

"Either one," Riley answered, "it's all the same to me."

"Okay," Brendon came back. "I'll take the lower. You have longer legs, anyway. Easier for you to climb up and down."

Riley stepped on the metal railing and hoisted himself up on the top bunk. He stretched out, put his hands behind his head and said, "Well, I guess as they say, we're in the army now."

Brendon was about to respond but he never got the chance. Another NCO banged the door open and strode down the middle walkway booming, "Alright ladies, out of your civvies, in your fatigues and outside in ten minutes. And I don't mean eleven. Now, let's see you ladies move."

Ten minutes later the inhabitants of each building were outside, assembled into ranks and columns, and marched to the center of the compound. There, they stood at attention while a soldier mounted the small platform that fronted them. The soldier was trim, with ramrod straight posture and a starched, wrinkle-free uniform that made Riley aware of how rumpled he must look in his hastily assembled fatigues. The man was probably in his mid-thirties, Brendon thought. His well-trimmed mustache made him look a bit older than his years. The NCO in charge ordered the company to stand at parade rest. A position they had only learned moments before. Then it was time for the soldier on the platform to speak. When he spoke, his voice was clear and strong and gave those assembled their first insights into what was ahead of them.

"Men, my name is Captain Williams. I am your Company Commander. That means I am responsible for you. This is a charge and a duty I do not take lightly. It is up to me to see that each and every one of you is transformed from a raw recruit into a fighting soldier. You are not soldiers yet, and will not be addressed as such until you complete your basic training. And complete it you will. Because the training you receive here is what will enable you to survive in combat, and it is what will enable America to be victorious in this war. That, gentlemen, is why you are here. To help win a war that must be won. The unprovoked, unannounced, and cowardly attack on our forces at Pearl Harbor by the Japanese, and the indiscriminate bombing, blitzkrieg and occupation of European countries and cities by the heinous Nazis, cannot and will not stand. If German and Japanese atrocities are allowed to go unpunished, the world that you and your loved ones have known all your lives, will cease to exist. Freedom, as we know it, will vanish from this earth. We are here gentlemen…you and I…to make sure that does not happen."

"Becoming a soldier is not an easy task. More will be required of you over the next few days, weeks, and months, than has ever been required. You will be stretched to the limit of physical and mental endurance. Why? Because this is the only way we, and you, will know that you are prepared to participate in the battles ahead. You won't always know why we are having you do something. You will initially feel that we are simply being harsh because we like it, because we're vindictive, or because we're simply enamored with the power we wield over you. Nothing could be further from the truth. Everything we order you to do is for a purpose. If you are going to stay alive to appreciate the ultimate victory that is to come, you must learn to react without thinking, to comply without debate, to follow orders as if they come from God almighty. Because in combat, your leader is your God. Defy him and you put at risk not only your body, but also your immortal soul."

As the captain paused for effect, some were impressed. Some were unmoved. Some thought the speaker a pompous ass. And some wondered what they had gotten themselves into. Such is always the case with individuals. Individuals who have yet to become a unit.

"You should know," the captain continued, "that it makes no difference whatsoever whether you enlisted or whether you were drafted. You are here now, and you will learn, and train, and fight shoulder to shoulder with the man beside you. How you got here is of no consequence. What you do here is all that matters."

"In the days ahead, you will not see me often. The officers and non-commissioned officers in charge of the different platoons and squads will be directing your individual training while I oversee the progress of the entire company. But rest assured gentlemen, I will be completely familiar with the individual performance of each and every one of you. And I expect that performance to be outstanding. Anything less than that is unacceptable. It is unacceptable because the truth of the matter is this: not all of us here will come out of this conflict alive. When this company musters after the war, many who are standing beside you now will be lying beneath the ground on some far-flung, distant shore. The harder you train, the more you accomplish, the more likely you will be a victor and not a casualty."

"One last thing. Once you are all quartered properly, you will each be given pencils and papers with which to write letters. Write them. Write to your fathers and mothers, your brothers and sisters, your aunts and uncles, your wives and your girlfriends. Why? Because those are the people you are fighting for. They are the people who care the most about you and how you are doing. They are the people who will write you back and keep you informed about the life you once knew and the life you want to go back to. And believe me, gentlemen, Mail Call will become your most cherished time while you are here. You will ache for knowledge of the outside world. But you will only get it, if your relatives know that you are alive and well and want to hear from them. So write. And write often."

"In closing, let me simply state what I know you all believe. Our cause is just. Our objectives are honorable. We will oppose and defeat the enemies of freedom because it must be done. You and I are going to do it. Good luck, recruits. I look forward to next addressing you as soldiers."

The first sergeant called the company to attention. The captain then executed an about face, stepped off the platform, returned the top's salute, and strode away. Riley, Brendon, and every man standing on the gravel parade ground beneath the hot Louisiana sun, knew that for better or worse, their lives were beginning anew.

Chapter 8

The Settlement, near Pilot Hill

The rocker creaked as its occupant moved back and forth, rhythmically keeping time with the fall of raindrops from the leaves of an ancient ash. The old black woman was crumpled within the chair as if she were part of it. Her bone-thin arms and gnarled fingers wrapped around the rocker arms while the toes of her worn leather shoes pushed against the wooden porch, slowly moving her back and forth. It was late afternoon, before twilight, but the sun was already making its intentions clear. Soon it would drop below the horizon silhouetting the scattered oilrigs against the dying orange light.

She heard the rattle, thump, and rumble of the truck's engine before she actually saw it coming up the muddy road in front of her shack. It came to a full stop, but the driver kept the engine running. For a number of seconds nothing happened. Then the passenger door on the bruised and battered 1937 Chevrolet opened, and a young woman in a raincoat stepped out and started up the footpath. The old woman took her to be something more than sixteen but less than twenty. Older than many who had come to her. Younger than some. A pretty girl, the old woman could see. Even though a scarf covered her head as she walked.

"Are you the one they call Granny Moses?" Gwen asked.

"I suspect you knew that before you stopped," the old woman replied.

"I was told this was where you lived."

"That wasn't all you was told, was it, child?"

"No. It wasn't."

"You the one come for the potion, right?"

Gwen paused before she answered, then said, "Yes. I'm the one."

"How long you been late, girl?"

"A few weeks."

"Always on time before?"

"Yes."

"You know it gonna make you real sick, now."

"That's what I heard," Gwen answered. "But it will work, right?"

"Oh, it work alright. It work for plenty before you."

"Well, I want it then, okay?"

"You bring the money?"

Gwen took her hand out of the raincoat's pocket. The bills were wadded in her fist.

"I have it," she said.

"Just step up here and put the money in my hand. Then take this jar beside me."

Slowly, cautiously, Gwen mounted the three steps leading up to the porch, picked up the jar and extended her hand with the cash in it.

The old woman slowly peeled her hands off the arms of the rocker, reached out and wrapped both of them around Gwen's hand as she took the money. Still holding on, and pointing her head toward the truck, she asked, "Is he the one that done it?"

"No. That's my brother."

"One that done it not man enough to come hisself?"

"He doesn't know," Gwen said. "He's in the army."

"You sure you want to do this, child?"

"Yes. I'm sure."

The old woman released her hand and said, "You feel bad for a day or two, but then you be okay. Don't worry. You be okay. I helped lots of girls like you."

"Thank you," Gwen barely managed to get out before hurrying down the steps and running back to the pickup truck.

The old woman watched the truck leave ruts when it tore out of the wet earth. She slipped the bills into the pocket of her tattered sweater as the sun sank closer to the far horizon. Then she began to rock, as she had done so many times before, and as she knew, life being the way it was, she would continue to do again and again.

Chapter 9

Hightower's Drug Store, Chicago

Jillian's routine didn't change much. Take the order, scoop the ice cream and wedge it in the glass, pull the lever on the soda machine and fill it to the brim, then put in the straw and the long spoon and set it in front of the customer at the counter. No, her routine didn't change, but her customers did. There was no denying that fewer and fewer young men were coming to the soda fountain. The war seemed to be sucking them out of communities like she drained the last remains of Coca-Cola, root beer, and strawberry soda from the containers in front of her. Of course, whether she'd admit it to herself or not, the volume of young men who were vanishing didn't seem to concern her so much as the quality of those no longer there. Such as the black Irishman who had made a big show of inviting her to dinner at The Drake Hotel, only to stand her up and virtually vanish from Hightower's, the neighborhood, maybe even Chicago itself. She thought she had read him better. That's why every time someone who appeared to be in their approximate age range saddled up to the counter, Jillian would find a way to ask them about that fast-talking Brendon O'Byrne.

No one seemed to know him. Or, none seemed willing to admit it if they did. But she'd continue to ask, even if she was in no particular hurry to talk to strangers at the counter who seemed more creepy than cordial. As was the case with the skinny, pockmarked loner who sat on a stool slumped over his root beer float like a vulture enjoying newly found carrion.

"Hey, there," Jillian began. "You from the neighborhood?"

Snapper took the straw out of his mouth long enough to mumble, "Why do you ask?"

"Oh, just curious, you know. We don't get many young guys in here anymore. What with the war and all."

Snapper proceeded, as he usually did, to give himself too much credit. "And you're feeling a little lonely. Is that it, cutie?"

Jillian back-peddled as fast as she could. "Oh no. Nothing like that. Just wondered if you might know something about a friend of mine, that's all."

"Well, if he's a friend of yours…why are you having to ask strangers about him?"

"Yeah, that's true. Don't worry about it. Forget I asked."

Slurping the last remains of his float up the straw with a noise that sounded like a bird choking to death, Snapper went on with the implement still between his teeth. "Come on, sister, give. What's this friend's name? Maybe I know him."

"It's O'Byrne. He's Irish."

Finally taking his eyes off the empty remains of his glass, he looked over at Jillian and said, "You're kidding."

Buoyed, Jillian responded, "Why? Do you know him? His first name's Brendon. Brendon O'Byrne."

"Yeah, I know the Mick," Snapper responded warily. "What's it to you? Did he say something to you about me?"

"No. No. I didn't even know you knew him. I was just taking a shot in the dark."

"You didn't hear what happened to him? Didn't hear nothin' about it?"

"I haven't heard from him in a number of weeks." Jillian said. "That's why I was curious."

"Well, cutie," Snapper began, obviously pleased to be imparting bad news, "your friend got himself in all kinds of trouble. Almost got sent to Joliet."

"The penitentiary? You can't be serious. Not Brendon."

"I'm serious as the grave, sweetie-pie. Because that's where he put a little kid. A little girl."

Jillian's shock was apparent. She had a hard time processing what he said. "But that just can't be. You must be thinking of someone else. Brendon wouldn't do something like that. Not the Brendon I know."

"Brendon O'Byrne," Snapper said. "Not too tall. Black hair, black eyes, smart mouth. I doubt there would be two of him in this vicinity."

"But you said almost. You said he almost got sent to Joliet. What happened to him?"

"Lucked out, he did. Luck of the Irish, I guess. Skated by a vehicular homicide wrap by saying it was an accident, and that he'd agree to join the army rather than risk going to trial. Army's pretty hard up for soldier boys these days, I guess."

"The army! You mean he's already gone. Already left Chicago?"

"Far as I know," Snapper crowed, feeling self-satisfied at being such a font of knowledge. "Got sent down to Louisiana, I hear. For boot camp. Next stop…a little eye-to-eye with some very nasty Krauts or a bunch of monkey-faced Japanese, I guess. What's it to you?"

Jillian didn't answer. She really didn't know what to say. They hadn't exactly been an item. But they might have been. He seemed so energetic, so much fun, so full of life. *It must have been an accident,* she thought. It must have been. He never would have intentionally hurt a child. Not the Brendon, she knew. The one who was going to take her to dinner at The Drake Hotel.

"Hey, listen," Snapper boomed. "Forget that Irishman for a minute and bring me another root beer float. And this time, put a cherry on top. It reminds me of your lips."

Jesus, Jillian thought to herself, *what a jerk.*

Chapter 10

Basic Training

Two thousand miles separated Camp Polk in Louisiana from Fort Ord in California. But in 1943, basic combat training in one place was very similar to basic combat training in the other. At the lowest level, individuals became part of a squad that consisted of four to ten men. There were three to four squads in a platoon and three to four platoons in a company. Three to five companies made up a battalion with three or more battalions in a brigade. A division consisted of three brigades and encompassed ten to eighteen thousand men. But no recruit ever thought of himself as part of a group nearly twenty thousand strong. All recruits ever thought about was making it through eight weeks of impending hell. Which came with a certified devil for every three to four squads—the platoon drill sergeant.

"Good morning, girls!" the starched and pressed noncom bellowed.

In unison, the platoon answered as one. "Good morning, Drill Sergeant!"

"I can't hearrr you!"

"Good morning Drill Sergeant!" The collected scream was louder this time.

"My name is Drill Sergeant Herman Ferris. But we need not be that formal, girls. You may address me by my Christian name. Which is what, recruit?"

Riley had sensed it was not good to wind up at the front of a column. But the C at the head of his last name had alphabetized him into the precarious position in which he now found himself.

"Herman?" Riley answered by asking.

"You weren't listening, were you, Alice? Now drop and give

me twenty!"

Riley fell to the ground in one motion and starting immediately doing push-ups. As he went up and down like a piston, the sergeant continued addressing the platoon.

"I said my name is Drill Sergeant Herman Ferris. That would make my Christian name…Drill Sergeant. Would it not?"

The answer boomed back by all present. "Yes, Drill Sergeant."

Lean, trim, his face, neck, and the back of his hands browned by the Louisiana sun, he began to pace back and forth in front of the men as he talked. "Yes, I am Drill Sergeant Ferris. And I am sure some of you, in your infinite lack of wisdom, will get it into your heads to refer to me, behind my back, as Drill Sergeant Fair Ass. You will probably giggle with your little girlfriends and think this is particularly clever and cute. Well, let me assure you women of something. There is absolutely nothing clever, cute, or fair about me. As you will soon come to know. Fairness, by the way, has nothing to do with the army. The army is not about being fair. The army is about being effective. It is my job to see to it that you become effective soldiers. I am very good at my job. Do you know why I am very good at my job, recruit?"

The young man he was staring at didn't answer immediately.

"Yes, you, fat boy. Do you know why I'm very good at my job?"

This time the reply came fast and loud. "No, Drill Sergeant."

"Of course you don't," Ferris began anew. "You don't know one thing about me, the army, or you, for that matter. You don't know anything because your head is full of muck and mush, and I'm going to clean it out and hose it down and make sure you learn how to act like a soldier."

In time, the platoon would become accustomed to Ferris's soliloquies and take them with infinitely more irreverence. But first exposure always has the most impact.

"You will learn everything you need to know to become an effective soldier because you will be taught everything you are taught the army way. What is the army way? Don't bother trying to answer because I've already told you that you don't know anything. The army way is to tell you what we're going to tell you. Then, we tell you. Then, we tell you what we've told you. In this way you will not forget what you have been taught."

Brendon thought to himself that it almost sounded reasonable. He wondered if he was already beginning to lose his personal perspective on things. He didn't have to wait long to realize that was part of the process.

"The first, and most important thing you ladies will learn, is how to follow orders. There is only one way to follow orders. That way is quickly. You follow orders quickly. You do not think about how to follow orders. You do not think about why you follow orders. You damn sure don't think about if you should follow orders. In fact, you do not think at all. You simply respond. And you respond quickly. Do I make myself clear?"

Again in unison. This time, loudest of all. "Yes, Drill Sergeant!"

"If you do not respond quickly it must be because you do not know what to do. If you do not know what to do, it must be because you were not paying attention when you received army instruction. If you do not pay attention when you receive army instruction, then you must be an idiot. Why? Because lack of knowledge…that leads to inability to follow orders…will get you killed. Not only will it get you killed, it will likely get the men on either side of you killed as well. It really is quite simple, ladies. In combat, you follow orders or you die. That is why you will learn to follow orders one way and one way only. And what is that way?"

The response was deafening. "Quickly, Drill Sergeant."

With various stylistic differences, Paul was hearing a similar diatribe on the other side of the country. He absorbed it all, less with the passion of an acolyte, and more with the practicality of a protégé. If he was going to eventually join the management ranks of this man's army, he knew he better become skilled at performing labor's role as long as his situation called for it. Buried unconsciously somewhere in the far reaches of his brain, lay his father's oft repeated admonition to "do the first thing well before you move on to the second."

In California, Louisiana, and camps and forts across the country, each day began long before the sun came up. Recruits' individual and collective slumber was violently interrupted with piercing brightness from bare light bulbs plus the banging and clanging of trash can lids amid shouts of "Drop your cocks and grab your socks! Formation in ten minutes!"

Most of the men assumed these rude awakenings were typical army harassment and noncom bluster. In point of fact, they were being trained to awake instantly and become mobile immediately. In the field, the enemy wouldn't wait for them to yawn and stretch and leisurely prepare for battle. Individual reaction time could mean the difference between life and death.

Conditioning was the first order of business. Very few draftees were in good physical shape. Even enlistees who thought they were fit, found that the army had different ideas about what constituted fighting readiness. Morning formations began with calisthenics. Jumping jacks, pushups, squat thrusts, knee bends, sit-ups, leg lifts, and more. Repetition after repetition. Then the runs would begin.

"At the command…double-time!"

A quarter mile followed by a hundred yards of walking. Then back to double-time for another quarter mile. Eventually the running would increase to a half mile at a time. Then a mile at the double. Initially it was difficult for the majority of troops. Particularly those overweight. Riley's basketball training came in handy. He seldom got as winded as others in his platoon. Brendon's pool table prowess was of no benefit. He'd tire quickly, but then summon the wherewithal to keep going. He wasn't about to break formation and run to the side of the trail to vomit like some. Those recruits who quit, gasping and wheezing and fighting for breath, weren't given a pat on the back and encouraging motivation. They were simply given more double time once the platoon had moved on. There were enough of those underperformers, however, to cause Drill Sergeant Ferris to institute a somewhat more rigorous program.

"Ladies," Sergeant Ferris barked, "from now until further notice, our entire quadrant of the base...meaning the barracks, the chow hall, the motor pool, the latrines...in fact any area I can see with my naked eye...is a double-time area. That means when you are moving about...for whatever reason...you will double-time. You will double-time to and from breakfast, lunch, and dinner. You will double-time to and from formations. You will double time any time you are not within the confines of a building...executing an assigned detail...or performing any close-order drill that is not being performed double-time. If I see any of you girls walking anywhere out here, you will immediately regret it. Do I make myself clear?"

"Yes Drill Sergeant!"

Marching and close-order drill were part of the daily routine as well. Over and over and over again the platoon would march in formation executing turns, stops and starts at the drill sergeant's command. Though few of the recruits realized it, the objective of all the marching had less to do with looking good on the parade ground, and more to do with the instantaneous execution of direct orders. There was no time to think or prepare. There was only time to react, or the man behind you would walk up your back. And individual stumbling, bumping, or any movement not in sync, would only result in more marching for the entire platoon. Peer pressure was as motivating as the drill sergeant's lambasts.

A break from the confines of marching in columns and ranks was provided by more physical training via the obstacle course, which had to be executed at double-double- time. One after the other, with only seconds in between, recruits would run as fast as they could from one impediment to the next. The obstacles consisted of a latticework of rope squares that would have to be stepped in and out of at top speed, followed by a balance beam to be mounted and walked across. There was a knee-high tunnel that could only be traversed by crawling under it flat on the belly using elbows and ankles to push forward. Then, a ladder led to monkey bars that required hand-over-hand swinging from one rung to the next. There were a series of poles that had to be zigzagged through. Beyond them, a rope dangled from a mounted beam. It was to be gripped, then climbed twenty feet to the top and back down again. After that, a massive round pole sat astride two stumps some fifty feet apart. It was to be mounted like a saddle and crossed by using one's hands to guide and one's butt to bump forward. Next came a crossbar for leaping, grabbing, and executing ten chin-ups before dropping back to the ground. It was followed by a rope strung from one platform to the next. Recruits would have to hang beneath it then swing their feet up to grab hold and cross by inching their way underneath, from one side to the next. Finally, a wooden wall stood square in the path. Recruits had to scale it by jumping up, grasping the ledge, pulling themselves up, then throwing their legs and their bodies across the top and dropping to the earth below. From there, running the remaining twenty yards full tilt constituted completion.

The rigorous path of physically challenging hindrances served not only to toughen those who took them on, it also provided officers and noncoms with a way to evaluate the men. Strength, stamina, and endurance made for potential squad leaders. Perseverance, while commendable, seldom was rewarded. Failure to complete the course in requisite time resulted in immediate retrial from start to finish.

Meals were to be consumed within fifteen minutes of entering the mess hall. Various classroom instruction would follow the meals allowing one half hour for digestion before some form of physical activity would begin again.

Morning and post-chow formations were always highlighted with some type of practical demonstration. Early in their training, Riley and Brendon participated in one.

"Right," Sergeant Ferris began. "Now I need two volunteers for a special detail. Come on ladies, two volunteers."

Riley looked over at Brendon who raised his eyebrows as if to say why not. "I'll volunteer," said Riley.

"Me too," echoed Brendon.

"Right. Good. You two men step forward and stand here, in front of the platoon."

They did as ordered and listened as Ferris continued. "These two girls have just volunteered to clean the grease traps on the kitchen stoves immediately following the evening meal."

It was one of the dirtier and more loathsome tasks recruits had to perform. Brendon's eyes closed shut. Riley sighed. The rest of the platoon started to chuckle until Ferris called them to attention and went on.

"This is an object lesson for all of you pretties. Never volunteer for anything! The army doesn't need volunteers. The army knows exactly what needs to be done and who needs to do it. We tell you what to do. We don't ask who wants to do something. If some nincompoop officer or some noncom high on bootleg hooch asks for volunteers...it's because he doesn't know what the hell he's doing. So keep your mouths shut and your hands down until he figures it out. Is that clear?"

"Yes, Drill Sergeant."

"You two," Ferris said, motioning to Riley and Brendon, "report to the cook immediately after chow. Now get back in formation."

Chapter 11

Mail Call

Days ended with filthy and exhausted men straggling back to their barracks. Most would crash on top of their bunks and take their sweet time about getting undressed. Some, like Paul, would put aside the crushing weariness and hurriedly peel away the dirty fatigues so they could be first to the sinks and showers and have at least a little time to themselves before lights out.

Paul had been a tennis player and swimmer in school so he was able to cope with the physical training better than many. It didn't get to him nearly as much as the psychological fatigue of constantly being told when to eat, when to sleep, and what to do virtually every waking hour. He had been used to living on his own and coming and going as he pleased. The inability to do so and the constant dictatorial browbeating made him vow to himself that when he became an officer he would lead his men like men, not like cattle.

Clean and shaved and lying atop his bunk with the cool California breeze coming through the open barracks window, he worshiped this relatively quiet time. More than once he questioned why he enlisted in the first place. Why put himself through all this when chances were he could have bypassed service entirely based on his father's connections. But those questions were always answered before he nodded off to sleep. There was a king-size job to be done and he never would have been able to think much of himself if he had just left it to everyone else. He didn't see it as bravery. In fact he didn't know if he was brave or not. He'd have to find that out later. It was more a sense of responsibility. A feeling that he simply had to do his part. *One either has integrity or one doesn't,* he reasoned. And for some reason, he felt he had to convince himself that he had it.

As the weeks moved on, mornings found Riley and Brendon, sweaty and hot, crammed between fellow recruits in the back of two-and-a-half-ton trucks rolling toward a daily destination. The deuce and a halves, as they were called, always seemed to have the tarps in place and any semblance of fresh air cut off entirely. Across the country, Paul was usually stacked shoulder to shoulder with his mates, shivering from the pre-dawn cold in the back of open-topped flat bed trailers headed for a similar destination. Was it more training masquerading as enforced acclimatization, or was it merely operational incompetence? Little matter, really. From the army's point of view it wasn't about getting to and from the rifle range. It was about what you did once you go there.

Proficiency with the M1 Garand rifle was mandatory. It was the army's primary weapon for combat infantry. Relatively heavy at just under ten pounds, it fired a .30-06 cartridge, had an eight round en bloc clip, and an effective firing range of five hundred yards. Recruits would spend more time with it than with any other piece of equipment. And rightly so. Of all the things they carried, it was the one most likely to influence whether they would come out of the war alive or dead.

Marksmanship, maintenance, assembly and disassembly in light and dark, were gone over again and again. Riley proved to be one of the better marksmen in the platoon. His father had often taken him hunting, and shooting came more naturally to him than others.

Brendon was an average shot at best. But he understood how important his rifle was so he soaked up every piece of information about how to keep it clean and functioning. The last thing he wanted was a weapon that jammed or misfired when he needed it most.

The more training progressed, the more each and every recruit began to internalize that the primary thing they were being trained for was killing. On the rifle range, distance had a way of making it all seem more like the development of a skill. But the first day they fixed bayonets, everything seemed to take on a more somber mood. The whole concept of taking another life took on an entirely new dimension when it was up close and personal. In addition to individual instruction in the thrusts and parries of bayonet fighting, recruits were also made to engage in one-on-one pugil stick bouts. Using heavily padded, pole-like training weapons, aggression was the order of the day. Before the first bout of each session, the instructor would make things perfectly clear.

"Here's the situation. You're out of ammo. The enemy's out of ammo. There's nothing between you and him but the length of your rifle and the bayonet on the end of it. It's stick or be stuck. Cut or be cut. You have to be aggressive. But you also have to be smart. The last thing you want to do is run headlong into his steel. Remember, when it comes down to this level, you won't survive playing defense. You have to be both meaner and smarter. Attack! Pummel the bastard if you have to. But do it under control. Be hard. Be quick. Be relentless. And you just might come out alive."

In both pugil stick and hand-to-hand combat drills, Brendon and Riley often took on one another. More often than not, Brendon's stockier build, quickness, and overall strength, would get the best of Riley. They could both smile and shrug it off after they had banged, bumped, twisted and thrown one another to the ground with a padded stick at the throat of whoever was on his back. But they also knew days were coming in fields far away where such contests would never end without blood.

There was little, if any, time off. Training went on six days a week. No overnight or weekend passes were granted until basic training was over. On Sundays when recruits didn't train, most were still assigned details on base. Cutting the grass, cleaning the barracks, kitchen police—it seemed there was no end to menial jobs someone had to do. When he had any free time, Paul would generally spend it on his own. He didn't dislike the men he trained with, he simply valued the miniscule private time he could carve out for himself. Even on those occasions when his turn came around for barracks fire watch at night, he complained about it far less than his comrades because it offered him the opportunity for quiet reflection the days never did.

Of the many things Captain Williams covered when he addressed his company upon their arrival, virtually all agreed he had been right about one thing. Mail Call was the recruits' favorite part of the day. Letters and packages from home brightened faces, buoyed spirits, and helped men remember there was actually another world outside the confines of their camp. Having each and every day filled to the brim with drills, training, instruction, and physical exertion from pre-dawn to dusk, it was easy to forget that real people existed outside that environment—people who didn't wear olive drab and bark orders—people who treated other people like individuals, not just numbers in never-ending ranks and columns of even more numbers.

Names were called at random by the noncom distributing the mail. When Riley heard his, he elbowed his way through the crowd to grab the letter before it got flipped to the back of the stack. His mother was good about writing. Which was to say, consistent. He had gotten a letter from her virtually every week he had been in basic. Once he had written initially and given her the correct mailing address, her letters starting appearing like clockwork. That first week he had mailed his address to Gwen as well. Mailed it with just a short note saying he'd like to hear from her. And that he'd write her often if she wanted to hear from him. He never received a reply.

As Riley tore open the envelope and began to read, he realized that this letter was much like the others from his mom. She always started by saying his father sent his love and hoped everything was going okay. Reminding Riley that his dad was not really a letter writer but that he liked her to read out loud all the letters that Riley sent to them. There was the usual dissertation of local events. How his dad seemed to be coming home from work looking more tired and drawn than usual. What the Pilot Hill athletic teams had been up to recently. Any boys he might have known from school that enlisted or received their draft notices. It was a small town, she reminded him, with everyone eventually knowing everyone else's business.

There was one item at the end of his mother's letter this time, which held his attention and wouldn't let it go. An item he read and reread at least three times. She casually mentioned that one of the families in town had moved away. The Taylors, she said. Sam Taylor who worked for the same company as Riley's dad. No real reason had been given for why they moved. She said she didn't know whether Mr. Taylor had gotten a better job somewhere else or not. But there had been some idle gossip about it, she mentioned. Loose talk from old busybodies with nothing better to do, she suggested. The talk had centered on the Taylor's daughter, Gwen. His mom said she thought the girl was a year or two behind Riley in school. She wasn't one to repeat such talk, she reminded Riley, but she went on to say that there were suggestions the girl had gotten herself in a family way and that the Taylors had left town to avoid the shame and embarrassment of the whole situation. Of course, there was no way to know if it was true, she went on. Small towns breed gossip at the speed of rabbits, she said. Then she went on to say good-bye and encouraged him to write whenever he could.

Riley sat on the steps of the barracks with the letter in his hands. At first he wondered if his mother was simply repeating what she had heard or whether she was trying to send him a message of her own. *No,* he thought. His mom generally came right out and said whatever she was thinking. He had not told her about Gwen. He had kept their relationship to himself. The entire time he'd been at Camp Polk he had continued to wonder why he never received a response from Gwen. He thought perhaps it was just too difficult. Too painful for her to write someone she was in love with whom she might never see again. But maybe there had been more to it than that, Riley pondered. Maybe there had been a lot more.

* * *

Two nights later, at 0100 hours, Brendon was standing barracks fire watch. In another hour his shift would be up and he could climb back into the sack and grab at least a couple of hours' shuteye before the day began. The day that would hold the recruits' toughest test to date. As he walked slowly and quietly down the center aisle he grinned at how each man seemed to have a different way of sleeping. Some completely beneath the covers. Some sprawled atop them. Some on their backs snoring away. Some on their sides quiet as a mouse. One big lump after another filling each bunk until he came to his own. The sheets looked inviting, but he knew he still had sixty minutes to go. *Funny*, he thought. Sleeping below Riley, he never really knew whether the Texan was an over, under, on-his-back or on-his-side sleeper. *Now's the time to find out,* he thought. Stepping over to their side of the barracks, he raised up on his toes to see the top bunk.

What he saw didn't compute. It was empty, and flat as a board, hospital corners pulled taught.

I didn't see him get up, Brendon told himself. *I didn't hear him going to the latrine. And if he did, why would he make his bed? He'd just be coming right back to it. Of course, if he's getting up to stay up, he'd make it. But why get up in the middle of the night and blow off all that sleep when you don't have to? Something was definitely out of plumb,* Brendon thought. He walked quickly back to the latrine to check it out. Everything looked normal. Nobody on the toilets.

Nobody at the sinks. Nobody in the showers.

This is crazy, Brendon thought. He stepped over to the side door of the barracks and shined his flashlight on the steps outside. Seeing no one, he then walked the length of the building to the back door. Shining his flashlight outside and scanning from side to side, he saw something he found hard to believe. There was Riley in civilian clothes, kit bag in hand, pressed up against the corner of the barracks with his back to the wall. When Brendon's light hit his eyes, Riley turned his head quickly and used his free hand to motion up and down for Brendon to douse the light.

"What the hell are you doing out here? And dressed like that?"

"I have to go back to Texas," Riley mumbled. "I have to."

"Hey, this ain't summer camp, you know," Brendon replied. "You can't just swing in and out of here when the mood strikes. Going AWOL is bad news, my friend. You don't want any part of that."

"You don't understand. Something has happened. Something that I'm responsible for."

"Well," Brendon answered, as he pulled his fellow recruit back to the steps, "enlighten me. Tell me what's important enough to risk stockade time for."

"You don't walk away from your responsibilities," Riley began, almost as if he were talking to himself. "Not if you're a man, you don't."

"Just spit it out, okay. Tell me. You know you can trust me."

It wasn't easy for Riley. He never liked talking about his personal feelings to anyone. He disliked intensely the idea of sharing what had gone on between Gwen and him. Their relationship was private. It was just between the two of them. But somehow their intimacy had become grist for the local gossip mill. And he felt ashamed that he wasn't there to help her deal with it, and perhaps a lot more.

"Riley, tell me what it is, damn it. Before we both get in trouble for being where we're not supposed to be."

Confused, unsure of what he should or shouldn't do, he was torn between breaking Brendon's grip and stealing off the base to the bus station, or going back inside, climbing onto his bunk, and trying to put it all out of his mind. But the latter hadn't worked before, and Riley had little hope it would now. So he started to talk. About himself, Gwen, and the letter from his mom. When it looked like he had said all he was going to say, Brendon spoke.

"You know what I think, man?"

"What?"

"I think she sounds like a great girl. The kind of girl who knows how to take care of herself. And I think you're taking too much of this on yourself."

"But I—"

"I know what you did. And I know what you didn't do. From what you've said, you didn't make her any promises. And she didn't make you any."

"Some promises are unspoken," Riley said.

"Yes. And some promises are spoken out loud. Like the promise…the oath…that you and I and all the other guys took when we signed up."

"I know, but…"

"You don't think the other guys here have things in the outside world they'd like to deal with? Think about the married guys. The guys with kids already. You don't think they'd rather be home taking care of their business? Sure they would. But you don't see them going over the hill, do you?"

"I just feel like I did something I shouldn't have done," Riley countered. "And I ought to try and make it right."

"You don't even know where the girl is. Or where her family has gone. And by the way, it takes two to do what you think you did wrong. You didn't do anything by yourself. And hell, who says it was wrong, anyway? If it was what you both wanted, well, that's just life, you know. Things sometimes turn out differently than we think they will. I can vouch for that, man. And I can vouch for doing something wrong too. A lot more wrong than what you did."

Then Brendon began to talk about what he had kept inside until now. The story of a snowy night in Chicago, a botched stick-up, slick streets and a dead little girl he tried to save but couldn't.

"But that was an accident," Riley said. "Accidents just happen. You can't blame yourself for something you never meant to do."

"Seems like we blame ourselves for all kinds of things, don't we? Things we never wanted to happen, and things we can do nothing about once they have. Maybe we just have to find a way to—"

Brendon didn't get a chance to finish his sentence. It was cut off by the booming voice they both knew so well. Though this time it seemed a lot less clear and emphatic than usual.

"What in holy hell is going on here?" Sergeant Ferris asked, and wobbling a bit as he did so.

Startled, Brendon reacted first. "Drill Sergeant! We, uh, we were just…" he tried to begin.

"O'Byrne? Aren't you supposed to be on fire watch? Fire watch inside the barracks?" Though barracks came out a lot more like *barrachhks*.

"Yes, Drill Sergeant, but—"

"And who the hell is this civilian? What the Sam Hill is he doing here?"

Riley wasn't going to let Brendon take what was coming alone. He said, "It's me, Drill Sergeant. Private Cross."

"Cross? Cross? Why are you out here? And what are you doing in those civvies?"

By now Ferris was weaving erratically. Both Brendon and Riley spotted the unfinished but severely depleted bottle of Jack Daniel's clutched in the sergeant's right hand.

Brendon piped up quickly with the first thing that came to

mind. "He walks in his sleep, Drill Sergeant."

"He what?"

"Walks in his sleep. Gets up sometimes. Puts on his civvies and just walks around. I'm his bunkmate, Sergeant, I've seen him do it lots of times before. Then he always gets undressed and goes right back to bed."

"That's the stupidest thing…the stupid…the st…aughhhh!" Ferris bent at the waist and vomited profusely over the tops of his own spit-shined combat boots.

"Oh! You must be sick, Sergeant," Brendon said, motioning to Riley to take his left arm while he took his right. "Come over here to the steps and sit down for a second, okay?"

Ferris put up no fight and let himself be guided to the steps where he plopped down and mumbled, "Yes…sick…I must be sick. Better take some of this medicine." Whereupon he pulled the bottle to his lips and took a swig that would choke even the Irishmen that Brendon knew. "Medicine helps when you're sick. So does rest. Rest helps too," he said. Then Ferris leaned back on the steps until his head was touching the top one like a pillow. In less than ten seconds he was out cold, still clutching the bottle in his hand.

"Come on," Brendon said, "this is our chance."

"What do you mean?" Riley asked.

"We'll take him to his room, put him to bed, clean his boots. There's a good chance he won't remember any of this tomorrow. If he starts to recall something, or if he asks, we'll just deny everything. He'll be in no shape to disagree. And he won't want it known he was so stewed that he threw up and passed out."

"Maybe, I don't know. Maybe you're right," Riley said. "Maybe there's nothing I really could do about Gwen and all."

"I am right. The best thing you can do now is just let it go. She'll write you if she wants to. Or if something happens. If you don't hear from her…it's because she doesn't want you to hear from her."

"I guess you're right. I guess I just wasn't thinking about all the consequences."

"That's for sure. Consequences like both of us landing in a world of trouble. Maybe even stockade time. Listen, we lucked out and caught a break with Ferris being plastered. Let's just get him inside and put to bed, okay? Man, would I hate to have his head in the morning."

Riley had no more to say in reply. He helped carry Sergeant Ferris back inside. Then he undressed quietly, stepped up on the top bunk, and lay there another hour, staring at the ceiling, before finally falling asleep.

Chapter 12

Live Fire

The truck pulled off the paved parkway and onto the gravel road leading to the field where the final exercise was being held. Paul, like all the other recruits huddled in the bed of the truck, was thinking about what their platoon sergeant had said to them.

"It's called a live fire drill because that's what it is. You need to know what it's like to be under fire in combat and we need to know exactly how you'll react. Each of you will enter a seven-foot trench where you will proceed to a pre-marked position. On the command you will exit the trench and begin to advance forward on your bellies. And I mean like a snake. The only thing that should be off the ground is your rifle, which you will keep dry and out of the muck at all times. I cannot over-stress the need for you to stay low and keep advancing. You must keep going because when you exit that trench and start forward, another recruit will be coming up right behind you. And you must stay low because live ammunition will be fired over your head as you move."

"Now…some of you may think we're not serious. You may think the army would not intentionally fire live ammunition over the heads of our own troops. Well, think again. We are dead serious. If you get up on your knees, you will be hit. If you stop moving forward and block the movement of those behind you, you will be hit. If you stand up at any time you will assuredly be hit and you will just as assuredly be killed. The rather unpleasant fact is this. We need to know now if you've got what it takes. It is regrettable if you suffer injury or death during this exercise. But it is preferable to having you get yourself and your fellow soldiers killed when you freeze, panic, or bolt in the face of enemy fire. Do I make myself clear?"

"Yes, Drill Sergeant."

It was dark when the trucks reached their destination. No moon shone overhead to light the way. The men quickly assembled into platoon formation and were marched single file to a path that wound through the woods.

"Keep no more than an arm's length of space between you and the man in front of you," the platoon sergeant barked. Paul quickly realized the order was necessary to keep men from wandering off the path and into briars, limbs, rocks, or uninvited animals along the way.

Halfway to their destination the men began to hear sporadic gunfire. Bursts of rat-tat-tat from machine guns. Occasional explosions that sounded like grenades going off. Even though there was a chill in the air, Paul had begun to sweat under the weight of his fully loaded backpack, heavy weapon and building apprehension. The moonless night had left things so dark it was virtually impossible for the recruits to know exactly where they were going. They simply had to trust that the man in front of them was headed in the right direction.

Ahead of him, Paul could hear the voice of a soldier repeating, "Watch your step. Ground slants down here. Careful, watch your step." When he got even with the soldier, he realized the need for guidance. The earth had been dug away leading to the trench the men were now entering, one behind the other. If you weren't ready for the quick drop-off you could easily tumble ass over elbow.

Paul said nothing and spoke to no one as he entered the trench and took up his position. Mentally he kept repeating to himself "Stay low, stay low...keep moving forward...keep moving forward." He couldn't help but notice what was underfoot, though. The dirt in the trench was no longer dirt. It had been watered down so that wet clay and mud clung to his boots as he stood and waited for the command. He wondered if the ground he'd have to cross would be as awful.

"One minute!" he heard the sergeant shout. *Focus,* he kept saying to himself. *Stay focused.* But for some unknown reason the view of the Pacific Ocean from the back of his parents' house kept darting into and out of his mind. *Forget it,* he told himself. *Just stay low and keep going. Stay low and keep going.*

It didn't feel like a minute when he heard the sergeant shout, "Alright, let's go! Over the top! Now!" He stepped in the footholds that had been dug in the trench wall and began to move up. As his head cleared the top he could see what was ahead of him. Arc lamps had been strategically placed along the sides of the field to throw crisscross light over the open ground. Staying low might not be the problem he thought it was. Barbed wire stretched across the length and width of the course he had to travel. It appeared to be approximately knee high. Staying under it without snagging his pack, his weapon, or himself would be the trick. That and keeping going.

On his belly, using his elbows, the insides of his knees, and his feet to move forward, he quickly became aware that the ground was even wetter and muddier than in the trench. Liquid gook quickly soaked the entire front of his uniform. The thick clay and mud made moving forward an inch-by-inch process. It took all his strength to keep his rifle off the ground but under the barbed wire. More than once he had to stop and hold his position because the man in front of him would stop. It was like cars bunching up at a traffic light. He couldn't go until the man in front of him moved. The man behind him was in the same predicament. On and on the starting and stopping and starting again kept him lying in the mud and muck as much as moving through it. Then the firing began.

There was no mistaking the rapid fire of the machine guns. What he hadn't been prepared for were the orange tracers zipping overhead. Red bolts of fire seemed to scream all around him. The continuing rattle of the distant guns gave way to the fire bolts racing by. *My God,* he thought. *What must it feel like to have one of those rip into you? To tear off part of your flesh or slice through a vital organ?* But as frightening as the thought was, he couldn't focus on that, he just couldn't. He had to keep inching forward. At one point, he saw the men in front of him turning over and moving ahead on their backs. They were using their hands and their rifles to keep the barbed wire from snagging as they went under. Paul immediately did the same thing. As he rolled over he felt the wet water and mud spill down his back and chill his spine. How far had he come? How far did he have to go? Just then, grenades started to go off on the perimeter of the field. The concussions carved muck and mud even deeper into the recesses of the wet ground. Surely he must be nearing the end. *Surely,* he hoped.

Sweat was pouring down his face and into his eyes. Shots and shouts and explosions were pounding the earth on either side of him. He dared not look to his left or right to try and get his bearings. All he could think of was that he must be getting close to the end of the field. He must be. Then, so close it startled him, he heard the barbed wire scrape across the top of his helmet. He took one hand off his rifle to lift the wire above his face as he went under it. Then the noises around him began to sound strange. They sounded like shuffling, grunting, running. *But they can't be,* he thought. *They can't be standing up and running. They'll be hit. They'll be killed.* Just then a voice cut through the clutter of his addled consciousness. "Alright soldier, off your ass and on your feet. And get the hell out of here."

Looking toward the sound of the voice, he saw a noncom standing above him, hands on hips, feet spread wide apart. He was standing up. He was standing up and he was yelling at Paul, "What are you waiting for? Double time!"

It was only then that Paul finally comprehended what had happened. He had made it. He had made it across just as he was supposed to. Scrambling to his feet, he staggered forward at the run, almost falling, but he managed to maintain his balance as he saw the men ahead of him heading toward another path that lead away from the field, away from the mud and the guns and the noise.

He caught his breath as he caught up with the other men. On the path, each slowed to a walk and tramped along until they came to a clearing where trucks were now assembled to pick them up and take them back to the base. Every man there was caked with grime and muck and overcome with fatigue. Each had crawled nearly a hundred yards on their elbows, bellies, and backs. They were soaking wet and chilled to the bone as the night wind swept through the trees around them. But each one knew he had done what he had come to do. He had passed the test. He had taken what the army had dished out and come through it. Come through it like men were supposed to. As wet and cold and uncomfortable as he was, Paul was happy. Happy to know he'd soon be back at his barracks where he could take a shower and hit the sack. And happy because for the first time since he had entered the gates of Fort Ord to begin basic training, someone had actually referred to him as soldier.

Chapter 13

Santa Fe Super Chief, en route to Union Station, Los Angeles

No matter how hard you try to put things behind you, they just keep coming back. That's what Gwen was thinking as she gazed out the window of the train rumbling westward. Behind rock formations in New Mexico and Arizona, alongside arroyos and towering saguaros, visions of Riley kept floating into her consciousness. The way he'd look at her and smile when she hadn't said anything at all. The slope of his shoulders as he ran down the basketball court. The downward tilt of his head when he wasn't sure what to say. Why couldn't she forget these things? That's what she wanted. To lock them away somewhere so the ache would go away. The heartache of parting with him and with the child that might have been.

Why was life so unfair, she wondered. Why was there this awful war that came between people who loved one another? Why did things have to end just as they were beginning? She hoped with all her heart that he would be okay. She prayed that he would. And that he would somehow understand. Understand that what she had done was for both of them. So each could have a brand new start at life when this terrible conflict was over.

Miles and hours later, as the Super Chief neared the outskirts of Los Angeles, Gwen almost said aloud, "Keep him safe, Lord. And give me the strength to deal with whatever my future holds. I know I probably don't deserve your help, but I ask for it anyway. And I swear I'll try with all my heart to do whatever I can to deserve it."

In Union Station, a lone figure sat in one of the tufted leather armchairs alongside the building's central strip of inlaid marble.

If the original architects of the combined Dutch Colonial and Mission Revival train station had placed tiny dolls in their original scale model, surely one of them would have looked like him. He wore a dark fedora, cocked rakishly to the side. An appropriately restrained suit of brown plaid was not uncomplimentary to the station's terracotta tile floors. His yellow tie accented a crisp white shirt, the collar tips held together by a gold bar and tiny chain that matched his cufflinks. The shine on his handcrafted Italian leather shoes caught the light of the chandeliers when he crossed his legs and flicked the ash off the black cigarette protruding from its polished bamboo holder.

Felix Pressman was a midday fixture every Thursday at Union Station. And despite his dapper appearance, he came to see rather than to be seen. Now in his mid-fifties, his hair was gray and well trimmed, including his thin mustache, and his skin was more bronze than most of the movie stars he represented. He was one of Hollywood's top agents and he got that way by trusting his instincts and his first impressions. Every day hundreds of bright-eyed young people came through the turnstiles after stepping off the Atchison, Topeka and Santa Fe, the Southern Pacific, and the Union Pacific Railways. And every Thursday, Felix was there to see for himself what the great melting pot of America was delivering to his door.

This wasn't something he had to do. The Pressman Talent Agency kept his bank account burgeoning and his appointment book was full to overflowing. This was something Felix did for the sake of nostalgia and to keep his powers of observation and discernment sharp as the tip of his Waterman pen. He himself had been picked out of a group of new arrivals to the City of Angels by a long-dead agent named Harry Arbane. Harry had a keen eye for faces in the waning years of silent films and Felix had the kind of face studios were looking for. Chiseled features. Piercing eyes. Devilish smile. His was a face that belonged in Arrow shirt advertisements, and it went with a body that looked good in tuxedos or tennis wear. So it was not surprising that Felix made a reasonable living as a model and oft-employed extra in both drawing room dramas and sword and sandal epics. But he never made the transition to leading man or even featured player due to his high-pitched, almost feminine voice, and the fact that as an actor he was absolutely awful. Nevertheless, he always seemed to be on the guest list at all the right parties and wound up marrying a rather dour widow who had the good grace to die shortly thereafter, leaving Felix with a considerable amount of money that he used to open a theatrical agency.

His personal charm and exquisite manners made him perfect for hobnobbing with studio bigwigs and aspiring starlets. So much so that it wasn't long before Felix had turned his initial seed money into a profitable business. And while the ensuing years added gray to his temples and green to his bottom line in equal measure, he never forgot how he had been fortuitously plucked out of a crowd of nobodies. And he never failed to make his weekly sojourn to the start of it all in search of the next Clark Gable or Jean Harlow.

Felix spotted Gwen amid a gaggle of uniformed soldiers and sailors. They were circling her like hungry sharks moving in for the kill. On leave and on the make, they had no doubt gravitated to the pick of the litter. Felix noted that the young knockout was doing her best to smile and parry the whistles and catcalls, but it was obvious she wasn't encouraging them, and even more obvious that it was becoming difficult for her to keep walking due to the GIs' increasing intensity. As they drew near, Felix rose from his chair, stepped through the school of servicemen, and immediately stopped their flow.

Bringing his fingertips to the brim of his hat, he nodded slightly and said to Gwen, "Hello. So good to have you home, dear."

"Hey," one sailor blurted, "is this your old man?"

A soldier quickly followed, "Well, he's way too old to be her husband."

Gwen stood in silence, not quite sure what to say. Then she asked, "Uncle Henry?"

"Jeeze, it's her uncle. Just our luck," one of the group said, disappointedly.

"Thank you so much for watching over my niece, gentlemen. It's good to know our lads are not only taking the fight to the enemy, but protecting our loved ones at home as well."

The buzz seemed to quickly fizzle out of the military mob. Amid various goodbyes like "So long, cutie," "Maybe next time, doll face" and "See you around, beautiful," they all moved on to what they hoped would be greener and less adult-supervised pastures.

Gwen said, "Gosh, Uncle Henry, I had no idea you'd look…well…the way you look. I mean I was expecting something totally different. I —"

Felix interrupted, "I'm terribly sorry, my dear. I have to apologize. You see, I'm not your Uncle Henry. My name is Felix Pressman."

"What? But why did you tell them you were my uncle?"

"Well, it seemed to me as if you were having a bit of a problem with the fervor of the lads, and I thought I might be of some assistance."

"Oh, they were just boys being boys, I guess. I could have handled them." Gwen said unconvincingly.

"I'm sure you could. I imagine you're constantly besieged by eager young men, aren't you?"

"Well, I don't know about constantly, but yes, a lot I guess."

"Yes, I don't doubt it. You are quite attractive, dear, of course. But you also seem to have an almost instantaneous magnetism. A sort of glow and allure that is a very rare thing."

"Ah, that's very nice of you to say, Sir, but I'm really supposed to be meeting my uncle here and I should be trying to find him."

"Yes, your Uncle Henry I believe you said. But am I given to believe you don't actually know what he looks like? Your own uncle?"

"Well, he's supposed to look a little like my father. I haven't actually seen him since I was a little girl. I came out from Texas to stay with him and my aunt for a while. If I can find a job, maybe even live here for good, you know?"

"Was he supposed to meet you here at the station? Do you have a picture of him?"

"I have a picture of me and my dad. Here, let me show you," she said, putting her suitcase down and reaching into her purse to retrieve the photograph.

"Well, if you like…ah, I don't believe I know your name yet."

"It's Gwen. Gwen Taylor."

"Lovely. Well, if you like, Gwen, I can try and help you find your uncle."

"Oh that's very kind of you, Mr.…Mr.…"

"Pressman. Felix Pressman."

"I'm so sorry, I'm terrible at names," Gwen said.

"Don't give it a second thought, my dear. I'm sure you're tired, coming all the way from Texas. These surroundings are foreign to you, as am I. Anyone would have a hard time remembering minor details under such circumstances."

"Mr. Pressman, you seem like a really kind man, but I don't want to put you to any trouble. I'm sure I can find my uncle on my own."

"I wouldn't hear of it, my dear. A beautiful young woman like you…alone in a crowded station such as this…I'd never forgive myself if I didn't make sure that no one took advantage of you. Los Angeles is a rather large city, you know. No doubt larger than where you came from in Texas."

"Oh, Mr. Pressman, you don't know how right you are. The small town I came from in Texas is so small you can't even call it a town. It's more like, well, just sort of a bump in the road."

"All the more reason I should help you find your uncle. Let's get to it."

Felix insisted on carrying her bag as they walked over to the concession area where they had a better view of people coming through the main doors as well as people sitting, standing, and waiting for other people to arrive. As they waited, they talked. Felix found Gwen charmingly unaffected. Naive, unsophisticated, unsure of herself. But with a smile photogenic as any cameraman could ask for. Eyes capable of melting any man's heart. And a body that kept turning the heads of just about every male passing by.

Gwen was overwhelmed with the elegance and grace that was Felix Pressman. The clothes, the manners, the vocabulary. All bespoke her ideal of what a rich, successful, businessman should be. Especially a rich, successful, Hollywood businessman. One who was now igniting her senses with stories of his agency, the movie studios, and the actors and actresses he represented. Her head was virtually spinning so that the man who walked up to their table had to say "Excuse me" twice before she turned to look at him.

"I'm Henry Taylor. Are you Gwen? Sam's daughter? I saw the Texas sticker on your suitcase and thought I'd ask."

Taylor did look a bit like Gwen's dad. A little thinner, if that was possible. A little older too. But the resemblance was definitely there.

Before Gwen could answer, Felix was on his feet introducing himself and bringing the man up to speed on what had recently transpired. He also went to great lengths to assure Mr. Taylor that his desire to help his niece was purely platonic and done with no ill intentions whatsoever. Gwen quickly added her commentary on how kind Felix had been.

"Well, I want to thank you then, Mr. Pressman, for looking out for my brother's child. We'll be on our way now."

Reaching into his inside suit pocket, Felix pulled out two embossed business cards and gave one to each of them. He told

Taylor that Gwen had mentioned she would be looking for work when in Los Angeles and that there was the possibility there might soon be a clerical vacancy at his agency. He asked that Gwen or Mr. Taylor call him at the number on the card in the next day or two. Gwen's eyes grew round as half-dollars. Taylor thanked him again and motioned for Gwen to join him. "Best be on our way," he said.

"There is just one more thing," Felix injected.

Taylor stopped and asked, "What is it?"

"I sincerely hope you won't take offense, Mr. Taylor. You certainly do bear a striking resemblance to Gwen's father. But I would very much appreciate it if you wouldn't mind letting me see some sort of identification with your name on it. You have my card, and while I have absolutely no doubt that you are indeed Gwen's uncle, well, I'd just feel infinitely better if I knew for sure Gwen was under the protection of her father's brother."

Taylor stared at Felix for a moment. The corners of his mouth turned down. Then he reached in his back pocket, pulled out his billfold and removed his driver's license from it. "This should be sufficient," Taylor said, letting Felix look at it but not hold it.

"Yes. Yes, I see, Henry Taylor. Thank you so much. Please drive carefully on your way home and Gwen, do call me in a couple of days. By then I should know more about that potential clerical position."

Gwen thanked him, Taylor nodded, and the man and his niece walked away. As they did so, Taylor was thinking that fellow was just a touch too fancy for his liking. Gwen was thinking that Los Angeles must indeed be the City of Angels and perhaps she had just met hers. Felix was thinking he hadn't lost his ability to spot a diamond in a sea of costume jewelry. He was thinking that as he was also memorizing the address he'd seen on Taylor's driver's license.

Chapter 14

Chicago

The black DeSoto was parked by the curb. Ian was behind the wheel and Snapper in the passenger seat. They both smoked and flicked their ashes out the open windows as they sat and watched the flow of pedestrians walking past, into, and out of Hightower's.

"A drug store, huh? That would be a novelty."

"The place is a gold mine, I tell you," Snapper said, as he attempted to blow smoke rings that never quite came full circle. Or even half circle. "A virtual goldmine."

Ian was dubious. It had been Snapper's idea. The wellspring from which all bad concepts flowed. But he had to admit, "They definitely get a lot of business. What about the hours?"

"I'm pretty sure they're open until midnight."

"What makes you say that?"

"I saw it written on the door."

Ian closed and opened his eyes before he spoke. "And does reading the front door constitute the sum total of how you cased this particular joint?"

"Nah. I been in there a lot. Mostly at the soda fountain. They make these great root beer floats."

"What about cash registers? How many are there? Where are they located? Is there a back room? Maybe a safe behind the counter?"

Specifics were obviously not in Snapper's wheelhouse. "Look, they got plenty of those things. Maybe all of them, I don't know."

Heaven help me, Ian thought. *He's like the Scarecrow in that Wizard of Oz movie. If he only had a brain.* "Tell me again about the girl you mentioned. The one who was asking you about

O'Byrne."

"She's a looker, like I said. Brunette. Good figure. Perky. Yeah, that's the word for her, perky."

"Yes, but what about her work habits. Is she always behind the soda fountain? Does she rotate and work in other positions in the store? Ever seen her behind the counter, up front?"

Snapper's intellectual resources had been depleted with the earlier queries. These new ones taxed his patience as well as his mind. "Look…when I'm here, I see her at the soda fountain. That's all I know. That and the fact she knows O'Byrne. Why don't we just go in and you can see the rest for yourself."

"When you want something done right," Ian began, but didn't finish the cliché. "Okay, let's go see this place."

A few moments later when they stepped inside, Snapper made straight for the soda fountain. Ian noticed there was a cute girl manning it. But that wasn't all he noticed. He saw a glass counter next to the front door with a large cash register atop it. There was a second cash register on the end of the counter in the soda fountain as well. Plus a third one in the corner that housed the pharmacy. Walking slowly, he eventually made his way to the back and took the stool beside Snapper who was already enjoying his coveted root beer float.

Ian said, "I see my friend's already ordered."

"He's getting to be a regular in here. Got a sweet tooth, I guess," Jillian answered. "You going to have what he's having?"

"No. I think I'll just have a Coke."

"One Coke coming up."

When she turned to get a glass, then filled it at the fountain, Ian gave her figure the once over and had to agree with Snapper that perky was the right word for her. But unlike Snapper, he wouldn't think of mentioning it. He simply kept the conversation on a small talk level. And made mental notes as he went.

"Lot of folks here. This your busiest time of day?"

"Not really," Jillian replied. "Lunch hour, and early evening, when people get off from work. That's when the place really fills up."

"Yes, I guess those would be busy times. Probably again at dinner I guess, huh?"

"We get a few teenagers and younger people coming in at night. But not enough to call it crowded, you know?"

"Well, people go other places for dinner I guess. Lucky for you, right. Less work to do?"

"Oh, I'm generally gone before then, I work the eleven to seven shift."

"Must be boring spending all those hours behind this counter. Of course, I guess your boss shifts you to other spots in the store now and then to break up the monotony."

"I wish," Jillian cheerily replied. 'He's says I'm the fastest soda jerk he has. So he keeps me here where I can keep things moving. Doesn't want his customers to wait long for anything."

"A smart businessman," Ian commented.

"And a good judge of human nature," Jillian added. "He knows I'm kind of talkative. Likes to keep the atmosphere friendly in here. Guess he thinks this is the best place for me to do that."

"Sounds like an excellent employer. How long you worked for him?"

"Oh gosh, let me see. I guess it's a couple of years now. A couple of years this August."

"I'll have another," Snapper intruded, pushing his empty glass toward Jillian.

"One more root beer float, on its way."

"And take your time making it. I like to watch you when you turn around."

Ian winced. "You'll have to pardon my friend, here. He sometimes says things he shouldn't."

Jillian replied, "Actually, he frequently says things that he shouldn't. At least that's been my experience."

"Yes, that's right," Ian said. Then, doing a marvelous job of acting like it just popped into his head, he said, "Oh yes, I believe he mentioned to me that you and he had a mutual acquaintance, Brendon O'Byrne. Turns out I know Brendon as well."

Jillian turned in mid-fill. "You know Brendon?"

"Yes, yes I do," said Ian.

She quickly wiped off the excess foam that was running over the side of Snapper's float and slid it down the counter to him. "Is it true he's in the army now? And that other stuff too?"

"Afraid so," Ian answered. "A bit of nasty business it was. Particularly for a good guy like Brendon."

"You were a friend of his?"

"I was, yes. A good friend. And regardless of the rumors that swirl around an event like the one that happened to Brendon, I'm convinced it really was an accident. That little girl being killed, I mean."

"That's what I think," Jillian said. "It had to be. Brendon wasn't the kind to do something like that. In fact, I bet he felt so badly about it…so guilty…whether it was really his fault or not…that he went and joined the army just to try and make up for it."

"You know, I think you may be right, miss."

"Say…you don't happen to know where his folks live, do you? I mean, if it's somewhere in the neighborhood, here…I'd like to go and see them. Maybe see if they have an address for wherever Brendon is in the army. So I could write to him."

"As it turns out, I do know where his parents live. He was still living with them before he left. I bet they do have an address where you can reach him."

"Oh, can you give it to me now. I'll jot it down."

"Well, the thing is, I don't really remember the exact number. But I know the street. It's not far from here. Didn't you say that you get off at seven? I could drop by and pick you up. It will only take a few minutes to get there and I know I'll recognize the house when I see it again. I used to pick him up there now and then."

"Well, gee, I don't know, Mister, I mean I don't really know you or anything."

"Oh, you're right. I haven't even introduced myself. My name's Ian Donovan. Ask anyone in the neighborhood, I'm sure they know the Donovans. You also know I'm a friend of Brendon's, so how bad could I be? Anyway, I'll just take you right there, wait while you get your address, and run you straight home. It's the least I can do for the fastest soda jerk in Chicago."

Jillian hesitated for a moment, then she said, "Well, I guess it will be okay. I really would like to write him. But just there and then straight to my place, okay? I live with my parents too."

"It's a deal," Ian said, putting enough money on the counter to pay for his Coke, Snapper's floats, and a sizable tip as well. "See you at seven."

Seeing it, Jillian said, "Oh, that's too much, really. You don't have to do that. I mean you're already doing me a favor."

"My pleasure," Ian responded. "Anyway, maybe one day…you can return the favor."

Chapter 15

Graduation

Cigarette smoke swirled in the air, rose, but never completely dissipated. It hung just below the ceiling and cast a faint haze over the room like early morning fog. The clanking of beer bottles and incessant chatter almost drowned out Harry James' version of Two O'clock Jump coming over the jukebox. The Buck Horn was a town girl's dream. Fifteen guys to every gal with fourteen of those guys in uniform. Pretty girls had their pick of any GI in the room. Even fat and ugly became fair and urgent to most of the dogfaces who hadn't so much as seen a real live woman for the past eight weeks.

Basic training had ended, resulting in Riley and Brendon's first weekend pass. They would start Advanced Infantry Training at Camp Polk Monday morning, but this was Saturday night and they were determined to enjoy their time off.

Luck and a gut-twisting hangover had been on their side. Sergeant Ferris was so sick the morning after he had run into Brendon and Riley outside the barracks, that he performed a minor miracle simply calling the platoon to formation. There was certainly no room in his head for anything that happened the night before. And no room in his stomach for anything at all. As witnessed by his several trips to the side of the parade ground to expunge whatever had the temerity to cling to the insides of his rampaging belly.

After the graduation ceremony, Riley and Brendon's company had received the standard lecture, accompanied by moan-inducing slides of disfigured genitals, regarding the evils of participating in unseemly activities off base. They, like so many companies before them, had been advised to avoid the bars just outside the camp in the nearby town of Leesville, which had been given by officers and enlisted alike the appropriate nickname, Disease Ville. And like virtually all of those who had come before them, they ignored the warnings in favor of the close proximity to alcohol and women.

For their first two beers, Brendon and Riley stood at the bar wedged shoulder to shoulder with other mates from their company. But when a table with two chairs crammed against the side of the wall became vacant, they sprung to the open seats like flies to carrion.

"You think what they said about this place is true?" Riley asked. "That it's one of those dens of iniquity?"

"God, I hope so," Brendon answered. "So far it just looks like the YMCA. Young men in khaki uniforms."

"That would make it the YMKU."

"Oh yeah, must be the beer. Tastes pretty good though, huh?"

"I guess so," Riley said. "I was never a big drinker. Too involved in sports and all."

"Yeah," Brendon replied. "The sports I was involved with always involved a little drinking. Take shooting pool for instance. Used to do quite a bit of that at Finnegan's in my old neighborhood."

"Were you any good?"

"Good enough to make a buck or two now and then."

"Oh yeah? Good enough to best those guys shooting over there?"

"Not sure. Have to check them out a bit first. A fellow can make a big mistake rushing into something before he knows what the outcome's going to be."

There was a slight pause. Then Riley said, "You talking about me now?"

Brendon, genuinely concerned that what he said might have been taken incorrectly, quickly answered, "No, man. No way. I was just talking about my own situation, you know?"

When Riley didn't respond immediately, and just took another pull on his longneck, Brendon went on. "I mean…I'm glad you decided not to try to make a quick turnaround to Texas on your weekend pass. You really wouldn't have had any time to spend there at all before you'd have to head straight back. And as you said, you have no idea where she or her family went. But, I wasn't talking about that. I was talking about pool, and how you need to take a look at who you might be going up against and how well the fellow plays."

Riley, unused to drinking, was already beginning to feel the effects. "Yeah, what's done is done, I guess. People move on, don't they? I'm just sorry I never got the chance to tell her goodbye. Or to tell her that we didn't need to say goodbye. I mean…she might have waited…if I had asked her. You think?"

"No, I don't think she would have, Riley. From what you've told me, I think she wanted to kind of start her life over. Make a clean break, you know. Not your fault. Nothing you could have done about it. Just the war, man. This damn war."

"Maybe you're right. Though it would have been nice to really say goodbye."

"I know what you mean, pal. That girl who worked in the drug store…the one I told you about…the one I was going to take to dinner at The Drake Hotel. Well, I never told her goodbye. I know I should have. But after what happened and all, I just couldn't bring myself to face her again. We all do things…or don't do things…we wish we had done a lot differently. Don't we?"

"I'll drink to that," Riley said, raising the bottle to his lips and taking a swig.

Brendon started to join him, then realized his bottle was empty. "Hey, mine's bottomed out. Think I'll have another. You up for another round?"

"Might as well," replied Riley, "we got all day tomorrow to get over what happens tonight. Then it's AIT. Advanced Infantry Training. We're going to be some badass soldiers, are we not,

Private O'Byrne?"

"That we are, Private Cross. That we are. Waitress! Two more over here!"

* * *

Across the country in Monterey, California, Paul was celebrating his completion of basic training with his mother and father. They had insisted on driving up the coast to see his company's graduation ceremony and to have dinner with him over the weekend before he left for Fort Benning, Georgia and Officers' Candidate School. He had tried to talk them out of it, feeling he had merely taken the first step in what was to be a long journey. But they had indicated how badly they wanted to see him and he had acquiesced.

Paul's father booked rooms at The Monterey Hotel on Alvarado Street. One for him and his wife, and one for Paul. The Monterey was one of the oldest hotels in the city. Since 1904, its classic European architecture and elegant furnishings put travelers in mind of what they might have experienced at the turn-of-the-century. Fireplaces in bedrooms and uniquely handcrafted details provided an ambience of luxury for those fortunate enough to be able to afford it.

In the pink-walled and plush-carpeted dining room, Champagne was followed by a steak dinner for Paul and his father while his mother nibbled at swordfish and showered her son with one compliment after the other.

"Oh, Paul, you looked so dashing in your uniform yesterday. Why didn't you wear it to dinner this evening?"

"Well, I haven't had the chance to wear civilian clothes for a while. They're a lot more comfortable. And frankly I felt a bit odd wearing it out in public since I haven't actually done anything to really earn it yet."

"Nonsense," his mother went on. "I heard those officer

people saying what an exemplary job your group…your…oh, what's it called?"

"Company, mother."

"Yes, what an exemplary job your company had done."

"They say that about all the basic training companies, mother. To say less would imply they hadn't done as good a job at instruction as they're supposed to."

"Well, you should have worn it anyway, it makes you look even more handsome that you already are."

"Give the lad a rest, dear," his father interjected. "Nothing wrong with that pinstripe he's wearing."

"Anyway, you'll see me in it again, mother, when we say goodbye. I'll be wearing it on the train I'm taking to Georgia."

"Well, I just don't understand why you have to go all the way to Georgia to become an officer. Couldn't they just as easily make you an officer here?"

"Mother, the only infantry officer candidate schools the army has are in Georgia, Oklahoma, and Virginia. I've been assigned to the one in Georgia. So that's where I have to go."

"But why do you have to leave so soon? You just completed this basic training thing. You'd think they'd give you some vacation time at least."

"Yes," his father jumped in jokingly, "why don't you tell them to put the war on hold for a week or two while you work on your tan at the beach."

"Oh, you're dreadful, Charles, you really are. You knew what I meant, didn't you, Paul?"

"Yes, mother, I knew exactly what you meant. But alas it's not to be. I leave for Fort Benning tomorrow. And frankly, I'm glad it turned out to be Georgia."

"Why on earth would you be glad about going to Georgia?"

"In addition to OCS, Fort Benning also happens to have a jump school there. Once I finish my officer training, I'm thinking about volunteering for parachute training."

"A paratrooper!" his father exclaimed. "I'll give you this, son, when you go, you go all the way, don't you?"

For one of the few times in her life, Paul's mother actually found herself speechless. She simply sat there staring at her son with a rather stricken look on her face.

* * *

After three more beers each, plus two pool games where Brendon had taken a couple of townies for twenty bucks, he and Riley had checked back in at the camp gate and were walking toward their barracks.

"Say," Riley began, "do you remember that officer that came and talked to the unit the other day?"

"Which officer? We hear from quite a few, you know."

"The one who wore the beret and had his dress greens tucked into his boots."

"Oh, you mean the guy making the pitch for paratroopers. Yeah, I remember him."

"Well," Riley announced, "once we get AIT behind us, I'm thinking about volunteering for jump school."

"Whoa," Brendon said, grabbing Riley by the arm. "That's the beer talking."

"No it's not. I'm really thinking about doing it."

"Why in the world would you be thinking about that? Have you forgotten the last time we volunteered for something?"

"No. But I'm thinking about the extra dough each month. That would be worth having, wouldn't it?"

"Yeah, if you're around to spend it. Stop and think for a minute. Why would we want to do something that's even more dangerous than what we're going to have to do in the infantry anyway?"

"Well," Riley said, "because it pays more, like I said. It's additional training. So that's three more weeks we get to spend stateside before we get shipped off to God knows where. And because the guys who do it are kind of thought of as the best of the best in the entire infantry, you know?"

"You're telling me that you're seriously considering jumping out of a perfectly good airplane?"

"I'm not only considering it," Riley began, feeling the effects of the brews more than ever now. "I'm considering that we both ought to be considering it. Wouldn't want to break up a good team, now would we?"

"No, I don't guess we would. But jumping out of an airplane? What's the deal? Did you have a bad experience in one, or what?"

"Hell," Riley answered, "I've never even been in an airplane. I figure it won't be any scarier to jump out than to land in one of them. You are familiar with the term crash landing, right?"

"Look, I kept you from going AWOL. Is there any way I can keep you from going airborne?"

"Nope."

This time Brendon knew it wasn't the beer talking. That nope had a feeling of finality to it.

"Then, hell. Guess I might as well go with you. It's not like we've got much of a chance of getting out of this war alive anyway."

"Private O'Byrne," Riley said. "We are definitely going to be some badass soldiers."

"That we are, Private Cross. That we are."

Chapter 16

Jump School, Fort Benning, Georgia

Riley and Brendon completed their Advanced Infantry Training, which included additional weapons instruction in side arms, grenade launchers, bazookas, machine guns and more, as well as extended bivouacs plus escape and evasion drills. Brendon proved far more skilled with a forty-five than he had with his rifle. He even matched Riley shot for shot on range scores. Of course, it was a moot point. Riflemen didn't carry pistols. But it buoyed Brendon's confidence nevertheless. And they both left Camp Polk with a sense of pride, accomplishment, and readiness to take on the rigors of parachute training.

Paul's OCS training steeped him in basic leadership skills, advanced physical fitness tests, additional weapons qualifications, infantry tactics, and operational orders. The latter outlined a specific situation, mission of the unit encountering it, tasks involved in the execution of the mission, support required for the sustainment of the execution, plus command and control throughout. At the conclusion of his training, Paul's scores topped his class. And he officially became Second Lieutenant Paul Cassidy. He had attained a level of respect that would automatically be afforded him via the army's class system of rank. However, it was one that would be postponed for three weeks as he entered the jump school at Fort Benning. There, officers and enlisted men trained side by side.

The first formation of the first week of training occurred at 0500 hours and found Private Riley Cross standing next to Second Lieutenant Paul Cassidy. Brendon was two rows behind them. The enlisted men had been a bit dubious when they were told that everyone would go through exactly the same training regimen regardless of rank. They assumed that officers would be afforded some level of privilege. They weren't. While they were billeted separately in officers' quarters, as it related to training, they had to stand the same formations, do the same calisthenics, make the same runs, and suffer the same consequences if they failed to do any of it as ordered. More than once, an instructor would drop an officer for some infraction or other and that lieutenant, captain, major, even colonel, would have to knock out twenty pushups just like any sergeant, corporal or private. After the first day or two, the GIs had no doubt that generals would be forced to do the same had they been part of the class.

Training was broken up into three basic sections; run week, tower week, and jump week.

While classroom and practical instruction went on each week relating to safety, performance, and technique, the emphasis of each week was focused on one thing. That one thing the first week was conditioning. And the focus of conditioning was running. Paratroopers were required to double-time in formation for three miles without stopping. Initially this was done in fatigues only. As the week went on, more and more equipment was added. Full gear runs were the toughest. And so were the standards. If you fell out of formation, dropped too far back, or couldn't complete the run, you washed out. And if you washed out at any time, you had to start the three-week course all over again.

Often, after a long run, or a break in the exercise that was being conducted, Riley and Paul would find themselves in close proximity due to both their last names starting with C. And more often than not, Brendon would amble over to take his break with them. Paul had introduced himself to Riley and Brendon early on. He didn't want to appear to be aloof or distant simply because of his officer status. And they rather enjoyed the opportunity to treat an officer like just another soldier, at least during training hours.

"So, Lieutenant, why did you want to be a gung ho paratrooper, anyway?" Brendon asked.

After a long drag on his cigarette, Paul responded. "Well, I thought if I was going to have to lead men in battle, it made a lot more sense to lead the best. The better the men, the better my chance of staying in one piece."

"Pretty smart," Riley interjected. "You think the other officers here think like that?"

Brendon spoke before Paul had a chance to answer. "I think some of them might be here just so they can wear jump wings on their chest."

Paul replied, "Hard to say. Motivation's a very personal thing. But this is a lot to put yourself through just to look good to others."

"Maybe when it really comes down to it," Riley offered, "they're just doing this to prove something to themselves, you know? To see if they've really got what it takes to measure up."

"You may have something there, Private," Paul added. "But I wouldn't attach that motivation to officers only. I think every man feels the need to test himself now and then."

"Not us, Lieutenant," Brendon piped up. "Cross is doing it for the extra money, and I'm doing it to impress the ladies later on."

"Well, you'll have to let me know how that works out for you. If it does, I just might sport a pair of jump wings at the next officers' club dance myself."

"Course, we all have to earn 'em first," Riley reminded them.

"On your feet!" the instructor barked.

"You're right there, Private. And it looks like we're going to continue doing that right now."

The intense physical regimen didn't let up when they moved to tower week. Morning runs continued to be part of the program. Conditioning received such emphasis for practical reasons. It was paramount that parachutists be able to evacuate their drop zones with all possible speed. Lingering gave the enemy more time to reach them. And frequently, paratroopers would have to hike long distances after they landed. The quicker they could cover the ground between them and their objective, the better chance they stood of completing their mission, and staying alive.

The first tower was thirty-four feet high. Hearing the height bore no relation whatsoever to the troopers' initial climb to the top. Once there, they had little time to deal with the lumps in their throats and the butterflies in their stomachs. They were strapped in and hooked to harness lines that would catch the soldier at the bottom of the drop and slide him along a cable where he would de-rig, then get back in line to do it all over again.

Riley's heart was beating in his chest like a Comanche war drum when he toed the edge of the tower and heard the instructor shout "Go!" He had every intention of doing exactly as he had been taught—to jump up and away with all the spring his legs could muster. Instead, he did like most first-timers and simply stepped off feebly and dropped like a stone. He knew he was falling because he could feel his stomach racing up through his throat. He couldn't see how fast he was plummeting because his eyes were clinched shut. When he felt the harness catch, his eyelids opened and he saw other troopers waiting in line laughing and giggling. *God,* he thought, *I must have looked as scared as I actually was.* After two full days of training on the thirty-four foot tower, however, Riley and the rest of his company were bounding off the edge like their legs were coiled springs.

The two hundred and fifty foot tower was next. On the ground, soldiers were strapped in parachutes that were fastened to cables. Then they were slowly hoisted skyward. When each reached the top, the fasteners would be released and with the parachute already deployed, the soldier would float to the ground enabling troopers to more closely experience actual landings.

Brendon thought the thirty-four foot tower seemed high. As his feet left the ground on the way to two hundred and fifty feet in the sky, he marveled at the fact that full-grown men could actually resemble ants walking about on their respective mounds. He didn't have long to contemplate this phenomenon, however; upon reaching the top his chute was released and he began his descent to the ground. *Jesus,* he said to himself, *I'm dropping so much faster than I thought I would, better get into my landing position and prepare to—Umph!* He hit the ground before he could finish and consequently didn't tuck and roll as he had been taught. His instructor likened his landing to a sack of potatoes falling from the back of a truck. Repetition is a marvelous teaching aid, though. By the end of the week Brendon and the others in his class were tucking, hitting, rolling, jumping up and moving smartly away just as they had been taught.

Marches away from the towers and back to their respective barracks were accompanied with cadence that seemed to grow in intensity with each obstacle overcome and each task accomplished. Knowing that showers and sack time lay ahead, the men would sing out as they marched.

"Stand up, hook up, shuffle to the door.
Jump right out and count to four.
If that chute don't open wide.
Spill my guts on the countryside."

A verse that would take on added meaning as they entered the final week of their training, jump week.

As they marched onto the aircraft, each man in the outfit was mentally going over what he had learned in the two weeks leading up to this—running the five points of performance over and over again so none would be omitted. One: proper exit, check body position, count. The count was particularly important. If the opening shock wasn't reached by the count of four, the reserve shoot must be activated. Two: check canopy and gain control by seizing the toggles and risers so maneuvering is possible. Three: keep a sharp lookout for jumpers during descent. Mid-air collisions can lead to entanglements which can lead to collapsed canopies. Four: slip, turn into the wind and prepare to land. Feet and knees together, knees slightly bent, elbows tight to the sides, chin on chest, eyes open. Five: land and hit all five points of contact—balls of feet, calf, thigh, buttocks, and the pull-up muscle. Be sure to hit the canopy release while still on the ground to avoid being dragged.

The rumble of engines was only slightly louder than the beating hearts of the men inside the planes. This was what it had all been for. The running, the towers, the instruction, the repetition. All was in preparation for this moment. As the aircraft lifted off the ground, an audible gasp was heard from more than one soldier. Paul checked his gear to make sure all was in readiness. Brendon felt the sweat running down the sides of his face and thought about the chilly lightness of the snow in Chicago winters past. Riley couldn't believe he was actually flying. He couldn't believe that in minutes from now he'd be leaping from a big metal bird into the sky and through clouds he had only known from the earth below.

As the drop zone drew near, the men were given the order to stand up. Each did so on legs somewhat shakier than they had been when boarding the plane. Then came the order to hook up. And each man took his static line and hooked it over the cable running overhead. Check equipment came next. Each man was to check his own equipment in front, and the equipment on the back of the man in front of him. Most ended this preparation by making sure the straps between their legs were duly pulled apart and rested against their thighs as they were supposed to. Were they not, the opening shock of the parachute could turn a baritone into a soprano.

The opening of the door in flight brought a roar of wind and engines that sent a chill up the spine of each man. This was real.

It was really happening. They were all about to jump from the relative safety of the plane to the potential danger of the sky. Then came the command.

"Stand in the door!"

The trooper at the front of the line took up a position in the door. Feet slightly spread, lead toe over the edge, hands gripping the skin of the aircraft. Each man shuffled up so he was tight on the man in front of him. No one wanted to slow down the exit causing the last men in line to miss the drop zone.

Then the red light turned green and the order was shouted, "Go!" From each side of the aircraft, men began leaving the plane. A sergeant at each door staggered the exits so the men wouldn't be jumping at exactly the same time, increasing the possibility of banging into one another when driven toward the center by the prop wash. Like a traffic jam at rush hour, the line would start and stop as each man was told to go or hold momentarily. Paul kept telling himself, "Don't freeze. Don't freeze. When you get to the door, go!" And before he knew it, the man in front of him left the plane. He quickly stepped up and then the sergeant waved him out. Mustering all the courage he could engage, he jumped.

Paul immediately felt as if he were in a tornado. The prop wash hurled him back so violently he was convinced he was rushing through the sky laterally rather than dropping. He was in mid count when he was suddenly pulled upward as if being lifted by the hand of God. *That's good,* he thought. *My chute is opening. My canopy is deploying*. Then he continued to go through his performance points. Check canopy. But just as he was doing so, a strange sensation overtook him. His feet were literally being pushed upward. It felt as he was standing on a bed of some sort. Glancing down, his heart sprang into his throat. He was actually standing atop another jumper's parachute. *My God,* he thought, *how is this possible?* Then another thought broke into his consciousness: "Wait a second…if I'm on top of his chute…then he'll get all the air beneath him…and my canopy will collapse." Paul immediately looked up and swore he could see his canopy beginning to billow and turn in. "I've got to get off," he told himself. "I've got to get off this other chute." He quickly began to run. Second Lieutenant Paul Cassidy was literally running in mid-air atop another soldier's parachute. He bounded along the top like a crazed clown on a trampoline, and in moments that seemed like hours, he hopped off.

Again he felt the rush of air and the rise upward as his canopy fully deployed once more. *I've done it,* he told himself. *I've gotten free.* Then he heard a sound like no other he had ever experienced. A deafening silence all around him. The roar of the engines was gone. The barking of orders was stilled. The shouts and yelling of other soldiers became distant as one planet to another. The breeze cooled his face and he floated like a winged bird on an updraft. This was the closest thing to flight that man would ever know. This was peace and serenity supreme. This was remarkable. He had jumped from an airplane in flight. He was not injured. He still had all his limbs and apparently his faculties. He had not died. He was floating slowly to earth.

Oh yeah, the earth, he quickly reminded himself. *The ground. It's coming closer and closer.* Around him he could see other soldiers hitting the ground, rolling and getting up. He knew he must prepare to land and execute as he was taught. Once again a rush of wind made him feel he was moving faster horizontally than he was downward. But then his feet hit the turf and he banged down on his side and his back. Hitting the quick release, one side of the chute turned inward and the canopy lost its wind, crumpling behind him. He quickly rose. Nothing hurt. Nothing was broken. He could move. He could walk. He had made it. He had actually made it.

All of a sudden, someone was behind him, patting him on the back. Patting him on the back and sharing the thrill of a lifetime.

"Wow! Was that something? I mean, was that really

something?" Riley was apparently as happy to be in one piece as Paul.

"Incredible, Private Cross. Just incredible."

The word Private immediately brought Riley back to the reality of the moment. He quickly jerked his hand off Paul's back. "Oh, sorry, Lieutenant. I was just fired up, you know?"

"I do know. I know exactly how you feel."

"I don't mind telling you, Lieutenant, I was scared plenty."

"Rest assured, you weren't the only one."

"Wow. You think it's always like that?"

"Well, Private, we'll soon know. We've got another jump scheduled for this afternoon."

The unit completed four more jumps that week, two of which were at night. Night jumps were particularly frightening to Brendon. *At least during the day,* he thought, *you could see that there was ground below you. Albeit fifteen hundred feet below you.* At night, particularly if you weren't standing in the door, you had no time for your eyes to adjust and you were virtually leaping into darkness. On the kind of moonless nights they encountered, it really wasn't until you were low enough to see the outline of the tops of the trees that you knew you were about to land. The ground arrived fast with little time to adjust and make a five-point landing. More often than not, and as was the case with Brendon, you hit flat-footed, jarred the hell out of your knees and wound up falling directly on your face or your ass. At least darkness kept the indignity from being so obvious to your mates.

At the end of the week, all of the men who completed the three-week training course were awarded their jump wings. Privates Riley Cross, Brendon O'Byrne, and Second Lieutenant Paul Cassidy were now Army Paratroopers. Soon they would be receiving their orders and shipping out. Then the real soldiering would begin.

Chapter 17

Los Angeles

A week and a half after he had rescued Gwen from the gaggle of GIs in Union Station, it occurred to Felix Pressman that he had not heard from her. Then it occurred to him that he probably knew the reason why. And the reason's name was Gladys. Gladys Mallory had answered a Want Ad the first week Felix opened his agency and she had been with him ever since. With a near photographic memory and formidable demeanor she became indispensable at filing information, filtering random phone callers, and fortressing the owner from anyone and everyone he had not specifically said he wanted to see. And Felix recalled that he had not told Gladys he wanted to see Gwen.

"Gladys, has a young lady called recently? A young lady named Gwen Taylor."

"Yes, Mr. Pressman, I believe a woman by that name did call. Of course I have no way of knowing whether she's a lady or not. She did sound young, however."

"Well, why didn't you put her through to me? I asked her to call me."

"She did say that you asked her to call, Mr. Pressman."

"Well?"

"Well, what? Do you know how many people call and say that you asked them to call you?"

"A lot?"

"Something exceeding the population of Boise, Idaho, I would say."

"And you never let them through?"

"I most certainly do not. You were very explicit, Mr. Pressman. You said if you wanted to speak to any individual, then you would give me the name of that individual. And if you had not done so, then you didn't want to take up your valuable time talking to every would-be model, every aspiring actor or actress, and every washed-up writer or director. You were quite emphatic about it."

"And I didn't mention to you that I wanted to talk to Gwen Taylor?"

"You did not."

"But I do."

"You do what?"

"I do want to talk to Gwen Taylor."

"Well, all you had to do was tell me, Sir. I'll telephone her and I'll let you know when she's on the line."

"Thank you, Gladys."

"By the way, Mr. Pressman, I believe this is the young woman who mentioned something about an upcoming clerical position."

"Yes, that's right."

"But we have no clerical positions…upcoming or otherwise."

"We'll make one."

"And why will we do that, Sir? If you don't mind me asking?"

"I don't mind you asking at all, Gladys. I simply thought it might be good for you to have an assistant. That's all."

"Are you saying, Mr. Pressman, that I'm in need of assistance? That my work has been insufficient in some way?"

"Not at all, Gladys. You continue to perform at the top of your game."

"Well, then, I don't see the need…"

"It's not a real need, Gladys, it's more like a want. I want this young woman here because I think she might really become something. She has a certain quality about her that you just don't find in every pretty face and figure that comes along. But she's very young and her naivety is as immense as the state she comes from. Which is Texas, by the way. She needs molding and shaping. She needs to learn discipline and punctuality and discretion and all the excellent traits you can teach her, Gladys. That way she'll get exposure to our business and our clientele but she'll be under our wing. Then, when the time is right…when I think she's ready…I'll start her out slowly. Modeling assignments. Work as an extra. Believe me, Gladys, she has a face made for the camera. And yes, a figure too. I tell you, Gladys, if we do this right, if we bring her along slowly and correctly, exposing her to just the right people at just the right time…well, we just might be able to make her eternally loyal to us and perhaps…perhaps…a star."

"And having done so, we will then be in a position to make a considerable amount of money from her for quite a long time. Is that the idea, Mr. Pressman?"

"Gladys, your acuity is keen as ever."

"But, Mr. Pressman, what if it turns out that she's all potential and no payoff? It happens quite often, does it not?"

"That it does, Gladys. But I have a feeling about this one. And as the saying goes, nothing ventured…nothing gained."

"I'll get her on the phone."

Chapter 18

Chicago

They sat in the car outside Brendon's parents' house. Ian in the front and Snapper in back. Jillian had gone to the front door and introduced herself. Then Mrs. O'Byrne asked her in and she had been inside for close to twenty minutes. If Snapper possessed any particular virtues, which of course, he didn't, patience would never have been one of them.

"This is taking forever."

"Good things come to he who waits," Ian replied.

"My ass. I never got anything good from waiting."

"Snapper, my friend, you're in too much of a hurry. If you don't watch out, you just might run yourself into the grave."

"Yeah, well, a fella could die of old age waiting for this dame."

"Well, just don't rush things when she comes back. Follow my lead, okay?"

"Sure, sure."

The rote reply didn't do much to increase Ian's confidence that Snapper would indeed take things slowly, but he had no time to address it further as he saw the door open and Jillian emerged from the house. She walked to the curb, opened the door, and got in the front seat.

"Say, thanks again for bringing me over. His parents are so nice. And now I have the mailing address where I can write to him."

"Swell," Ian said. "Seems like you were in there quite a while just to get an address."

"Well, older people like to talk, you know. Especially about their children. And it was just like I thought. His mom and dad both said that the thing with the little girl had been a terrible accident. Brendon never even saw her. They said after the car stopped sliding on the icy road, he got out to see if there was any damage. That's when he found her. Then he rushed her to the hospital. But it was too late."

"What'd you expect them to say?" Snapper grunted.

"What do you mean?"

Ian answered for him. "He just means that parents never think their kids are guilty of anything. They always give them the benefit of the doubt, so to speak."

"Oh, I'm sure that's not the case here. I'm positive it was just an accident. Anyway, you said you thought so too?"

"Yes, I know I said that," Ian replied, starting the engine, "but sometimes you say things to people you don't know very well…just to move the conversation along."

"What does that mean?" Jillian snapped.

"It means, maybe we know more about Mr. Brendon O'Byrne than we're saying."

"Oh, you two don't know what you're talking about. Just take me home, like you said you would. Go up to the end of the block and turn right."

"Sure," Ian soothed. "Nothing to get upset about. We're on our way."

The next few blocks were driven in relative silence, except for Jillian telling Ian which streets to take. The mood inside the car had taken a decidedly chillier turn. Jillian wasn't completely sure why. But she was sure she wanted to get home. When Ian turned onto Kinzie Street, Jillian said, "That's it. On the corner. The house on the left."

Ian slowly pulled the car to the curb, nearly fifty yards from the house Jillian had indicated. She asked, "Why are you stopping here? I told you it's the one up ahead."

"Well," Ian began, "I wouldn't want your folks, or the neighbors, getting the wrong impression."

"Wrong impression? What are you talking about?"

"You know. A pretty girl like you, riding in a car with two men. People jump to conclusions, you know." Before Jillian had a chance to reply, Ian went on. "Just like you've jumped to conclusions about O'Byrne…and maybe about us."

"What are you saying?"

"I'm saying that maybe O'Byrne isn't the great guy you think he is. Maybe he told his parents what he wanted to tell them, and left out some of the less flattering parts."

"Like what?"

"Like what he was really doing on 87th street that night."

"And just what do you think that was?" Jillian questioned.

"Oh, I don't have to think," Ian said, "I know."

"Yeah," Snapper jumped in, "we know what he was doing there. We know."

Jillian looked from one to the other, then said, "How do you know? How?"

Ian responded. "Because we were with him, doll. We were right there with him."

"Well," Jillian said, beginning to get a bit flustered, "then you know. You know it was an accident if you were there."

"It sort of was and wasn't an accident," Ian said. "Hitting the kid was accidental, but gunning the engine and jerking the steering wheel around like crazy, and trying to screw us out of a score…well, that part wasn't accidental."

"A score? What do you mean, a score?"

"A heist," Snapper answered. "A robbery, if you don't know what heist means."

Now Jillian was really confused. She couldn't believe Brendon would do anything like that. But she certainly wouldn't put it past these two.

Ian began to spell it out for her. "Now, you see what I mean, kid? You see what I mean about jumping to conclusions about people? You assumed O'Byrne was clean as the driven snow. Not exactly true. You assumed my friend and I were relatively harmless. Or you wouldn't have gotten into the car with us. Not exactly true."

Jillian hurriedly reached for door handle but Snapper reached over the backseat, grabbed her by the shoulders, and held her firm as Ian continued.

"You see, we helped you get something you wanted. Now, you're going to help us get something we want."

"If you touch me," Jillian said with what little bravado she could muster, "I'll scream to high heaven. I'll kick up such a fuss everyone around here will hear."

"Don't flatter yourself," Ian said. "We have no intention of hurting you. All we want is what we helped you get. Some information."

"What kind of information?"

"Nothing special. Just stuff like how much cash is in each one of those cash registers where you work...whether there's a safe somewhere in the back of the store...what Hightower does with the daily take...or what day or days he usually takes it to the bank."

"But...I don't know any of that."

"You may not know now. But you've got lots of opportunities to find out. When the old guy's not looking....from your coworkers...you know. We're not in a big hurry. We'll even give you a week."

Now that Jillian assumed she wasn't about to be assaulted, or worse, she summoned the courage to be a bit combative. "And just what makes you think I would do that? For that matter...what's to keep me from going to the police and telling them what you two are planning?"

Snapper pulled her back harder against the seat, as Ian said, "Well, for one thing, the police won't necessarily believe you. We haven't committed any crime. We'd just tell them we were having some fun with you. Kidding you along, you know. And as for why you might do it, well…we figure you'd rather have us knock over where you work than where you live. You did just tell us where that was, didn't you? I also don't think you'd want Snapper wandering through the O'Byrne home in the dead of night either. I mean, an old couple, at home alone, no soldier boy there to protect them. It wouldn't take much to make quick work of that."

"Yeah," Snapper added. "And household goods are easy to sell. Easy to get rid of."

"And if you're thinking," Ian went on, "that after we've done the drug store, you can just tip off the cops, well, the fact is we'll swear up and down that you helped us. An inside job, you know what I mean? You'll be what's called an accessory. In fact, you already are one."

"You're both awful. Just awful. Let me out of the car. Please, let me out of the car."

"Sure. We'll let you out. And we'll be dropping by the drug store, just to see how you're doing at getting that information."

"Please…let me out now!"

"Just one last thing. You're a smart cookie. Keep in mind that the more we know before we go in, the less likely it will be that anyone gets hurt. If we have all the information we need…then we'll have no need to hurt anyone. We're smart guys. We can play it that way. But, just in case you might be getting the notion that we're all talk, and when it actually gets down to hurting someone…well…that we might not actually do that…"

Snapper took his right hand off Jillian's shoulder, reached around, grabbed her breast and squeezed it so hard she cried out. But her scream never left the car. Ian had quickly clasped his hand over her mouth. Then they both released her. She tried to keep from crying as she sat there holding herself.

"Well," Ian said. "Go ahead and get out. You can walk home from here. It's not that far. And believe me, we'll remember exactly where it is."

Chapter 19

Columbus, LA, Chicago

Virtually every bar in Columbus, Georgia was packed with newly minted paratroopers who had taken the bus from Fort Benning for their last weekend before shipping out. The Red Bulldog was no exception. Soldiers were going through the establishment's alcohol like it was going to be their last for a very long time. It was. Brendon and Riley had elbowed their way to the bar and were wasting no time getting sloshed.

"What'd you call these, again?" Riley asked.

"Boilermakers," Brendon replied. "A shot of whiskey and a glass of beer to wash it down with. How many of these do you think we can knock back and still stay on our feet?"

"Guess we'll just have to find out," Riley answered with shot glass in hand. "Bottoms up."

The fiery liquid caught Riley off guard. He coughed hard and almost choked.

"Take a slug of the beer," Brendon advised. "It's there to douse the flame."

The cold beer soothed his throat and helped his eyes stop watering. "Whew! Kind of takes your breath away, doesn't it?"

"The key is to not go through a lot more whiskey than beer. Of course, after a while, with the beer setting the table, that rye's going to go down a lot easier."

"Kind of like training, huh? Practice makes perfect."

"Practice, practice, practice. That's just what I intend to do."

An hour and a number of boilermakers later, Brendon and Riley decided that a bit of fresh air was definitely in order. They stumbled outside into a balmy summer night and started making their way slowly down the street. Though relatively well oiled, they still had enough reasoning power between the two of them to avoid any overt shows of drunkenness which would attract the attention of the local police or the military MPs who had been assigned to the City of Columbus for the weekend.

Passing a rather grand looking hotel with well-dressed men and women mingling on the veranda, Riley said, "Wow. I guess that's where the swells congregate in Columbus, huh?"

"Suppose so," Brendon responded. "It's okay I guess, for this place. But it can't compare to The Drake Hotel. Now there's a hotel. Did I ever tell you that I was going to take a girl to The Drake Hotel for dinner one night? Gee. That seems like such a long time ago, but it wasn't really, it was—"

"Hey look," Riley interrupted. "Is that who I think it is?"

"Who?"

"That guy in the suit. Just coming out of the hotel. The one about to light a cigarette."

"Just some local swell, I guess," Brendon said.

"No. No, it's Lieutenant Cassidy."

"Hey, I think you're right. Looks different out of uniform. Let's go say hello."

Paul had just walked down the steps of the hotel, shaken out the match he had used and was flicking it on the ground when he saw the two approach. "Well, well. If it isn't airborne troopers Cross and O'Byrne. What are you lads up to?"

Riley said, "Just sampling a bit of the local product, Lieutenant."

"Is that so? Coca-Cola, I take it. You know the fellow who invented Coca-Cola is from Columbus. Name's Dr. John Pemberton, I'm told."

Brendon replied, "Well, truth be told, Sir, we sort of skipped the Cokes and went straight to the harder stuff."

"Boilermakers," Riley said proudly.

"Boilermakers? Well, I am impressed. Surprised you still have your legs under you?"

"Takes more than a few drinks to fell a couple of airborne men," Brendon responded.

"And was it Coca-Cola you were having in that fancy hotel, Lieutenant?"

"Actually it was a rather nice bottle of wine, gentlemen. Rather nice indeed. But enough of this idle chatter. Tell me, did your orders come through?"

"Yes Sir," Riley answered. "You're looking at two members of the 505 Parachute Regiment, 82nd Airborne Division. We ship out Monday."

"Well, I guess you'll just have to continue to put up with me for a while," Paul said. "I've been assigned to the same outfit."

"You don't say," Brendon interjected. "That's swell. Just swell. Hey Lieutenant, you being an officer and all…well, if you have any pull…maybe you can get us assigned to your platoon."

"Guys, a Second Lieutenant has about as much pull as a double amputee. But I'll speak to the company commander and see what I can do."

"That would be great, Lieutenant," Riley said. "Hey, if we're going to be platoon mates and all, can you give us any intelligence on where we're shipping out to?"

"Classified, lads. I don't know myself. And I couldn't tell you if I did. We'll be told after we're on the ship and out to sea."

"Let's have a drink then, and celebrate our last free night," Brendon said.

"Brendon," Riley injected, "you forget. The army doesn't want its officers fra… fra…what's that word, Sir?"

"Fraternizing," Paul replied. "And yes, it's true. The army does not encourage fraternization between enlisted men and officers. They feel it breaks down discipline and can have a negative impact on overall unit effectiveness. However, I think there's going to be plenty of time for both discipline and unit effectiveness when we're back on duty. Tonight gentlemen, we're off duty. So let's go have that drink." Then side by side, taking up much more sidewalk than was appropriate, the three paratroopers strode off to find the nearest bar in the humid Georgia night.

* * *

In Southern California, a warm Santa Anna wind made the night warmer than the ones that had recently preceded it. Felix Pressman and Gwen sat at a secluded table on the patio of a small bistro two blocks from the talent agency.

"It's really nice of you to take me to dinner, Mr. Pressman. This is such a nice place. The weather out here is so much cooler than it is in Texas."

"I'm afraid it's a little warmer than usual tonight, my dear. I hope you're not uncomfortable out here."

"Oh no. I'm fine. In fact I've been wearing light sweaters ever since I've been here. Takes a little time to adjust, I guess."

"Well, speaking of adjustments, you've done a marvelous job in your first weeks at the agency. You seem to learn very quickly."

"That's because Miss Mallory's such an excellent teacher. I just follow her instructions to the letter."

"Yes, Gladys is irreplaceable. I don't know what I'd do without her."

"I know what you mean, Mr. Pressman. I sometimes wonder if she really needs any help at all. I mean I'm very happy to be assisting her with things. Though I'm not sure she really needs the help."

"You're a very perceptive young lady. She doesn't really need a lot of help, does she?" Before Gwen had time to answer, Felix went on. "In fact, what I'm thinking is that you might be of more help to the agency doing something else entirely."

"Really? I'm not sure what else I could do, Mr. Pressman. I've only learned what Miss Mallory has taught me."

"Well, what I have in mind would involve things I can teach you, my dear. Things that could be advantageous to you and to our organization."

"Things like what, Mr. Pressman?"

"Gwen, you have a number of qualities already that can't be taught. A rare, unaffected beauty. A simple and honest way of presenting yourself. A good mind and a capacity for learning quickly. These are all traits that I know we can build on."

"I'm sorry, Mr. Pressman. I still don't quite know what you're suggesting."

"I'm suggesting that you might be of much more value to yourself and to the Pressman Agency as a client rather than an employee."

"A client? But Mr. Pressman, I'm not a model or an actress. And I certainly don't have any money to pay you to help find me those kinds of jobs."

"You misunderstand, my dear. What I'm suggesting is that you sign an exclusive contract with the Pressman Agency. In so doing, I take on the responsibility and the expense of teaching you everything you need to know to make a living in this town as a model, an extra, an actress, or whatever you want to be. In return, you agree that my company alone will have the right to represent you."

Gwen's heart was beating like the conga drum in the band at Ciros. She couldn't believe what she was hearing. "Mr. Pressman, you'd do all that for me?"

"For you and me, my dear. The more you succeed…and I sense you have the charm, the will, and the desire to do so…well, the more you succeed, the more money my agency will make."

"But what leads you to believe I will succeed? You hear so much about girls coming out here and winding up as waitresses, hat check girls, or worse."

"They don't have what you have, my dear. They don't have me. Putting modesty aside, with my experience, my support, and my contacts, I'd be astounded if someone with your beauty and personality doesn't become a fabulous success."

"Mr. Pressman, I'm just…I'm just …I don't know what to say. I feel like I'm dreaming. If it wasn't kind of forward, I'd ask you to pinch me to make sure I'm not."

"You'll need to prepare yourself for lots of pinching in the days ahead, my dear, if we are to embark on this venture together. Some from rather unscrupulous types in the business, I'm afraid."

"Oh, don't worry about that, Mr. Pressman. I know how to take care of myself. Men are just men whether they're in the movie business or the oil fields."

"That's the perfect attitude to take. I'll have the papers drawn up tomorrow. Shall we seal our agreement with Champagne?"

"Oh, let's do. I've only had it once before. But I loved it."

"There is just one more thing, dear. Your living arrangements. Gladys tells me you've been coming to work every day on the bus. All the way from Encino. I'm afraid that just won't do with all the classes, training, and work we're going to have to do. You'll just have to live somewhere much closer."

"But the room I have in my uncle's house is free. I really can't afford anyplace else."

"Well, it just so happens that there's a tiny pool cottage on the grounds of my home. I was hoping you'd agree to live there. Free of charge, of course. Until you begin to make your own money. I'm sure your uncle would understand if I explained it all to him."

"You'd be willing to do that? Please, Mr. Pressman, convince me I'm not dreaming," she said, as she took his hand and put it on her arm.

With his thumb and forefinger, he squeezed ever so gently, and said, "No dear. You're not dreaming. And that's not where you need to worry about being pinched."

* * *

The Chicago night was uncomfortably chilly, as only June can be in the Midwest. Jillian barely said two words to her parents as she passed them in the kitchen and went directly to her bedroom. At that moment, she wasn't sure what to say to anyone. The joy of getting a lifeline to Brendon had been usurped by the fear of being chained to Ian and Snapper. *How had it happened so fast,* she wondered. One day a creepy guy had told her he knew Brendon, and that something awful had happened to him. Days later a guy that seemed like a regular fellow had wandered in and offered to help her get in touch with him. The next thing she knew they were talking about robbing Hightower's, or the O'Byrne's, or even her house, and her parents. And maybe robbing wasn't the only thing they had in mind. Then they were putting their hands on her. *The bastards,* she thought. *The evil, evil bastards.*

But what was she to do, she almost asked out loud. If she went to the police, they were right, no crime had been committed yet. They would simply say they were kidding her all along. If she was able to get the information they wanted, and gave it to them, someone at the store might be hurt, and Mr. Hightower, who had been a good and fair employer, would lose a lot of money. But if she didn't provide the information, they might make good on their threats and take it out on Brendon's parents or even her own. *Damn,* she thought. *Damn. Why are there people in the world like that?*

Then, reaching in her purse and pulling out the address the O'Byrne's had given her, she realized there were other kinds of people in the world too. People like a grinning young Irishman who called her Jilly and who was going to take her to The Drake Hotel for dinner. Wherever he was this night, he would soon be facing a lot more trouble than two rowdy hooligans from the neighborhood. *He shouldn't have to face such terrible things alone,* she thought. He should know that someone back home was thinking about him and wanted him to be okay. Someone wanted him to come back, sit on the stool at the fountain, and make her promises whether he could keep them or not.

Taking a pen and stationery from the drawer in the writing desk beside her bed, she decided to tell him about what had been happening at Finnegan's, Hightower's, with his parents and hers—but only the good things, only the things that might lighten his burden rather than add to it. She'd deal with her own problems herself, she decided. Isn't that what people were supposed to do? Isn't that what her parents taught her? Isn't that what Brendon would expect from… his best girl?

Part 2

Tempest

Chapter 20

The Atlantic

Most of the three thousand and three hundred men packed into the Evangeline had never been on a ship before. She was a converted cargo vessel previously owned by a fruit company who filled her hold with bananas, pineapples, and coconuts on their way to kitchen tables around the world. Now she was filled with soldiers on their way to war.

Heavy Atlantic swells kept the five hundred foot ship rolling and bucking and flipping the stomachs of its human cargo like tossed salad. The men who had scrambled for the top in the six-bunk stacks were the luckiest. They had the most trouble climbing in and out of their racks but they had the least worry of being heaved on from the man above. With so many men in such close quarters, sanitation was virtually non-existent. Stifling, oppressive heat kept soldiers stripped to their underwear when they were below, and constantly on deck whenever they were given permission to be there. Bone-chilling winds, salt spray in the face, and the ability to vomit over the side, rather than into a bucket, became privileges devoutly sought.

None of the enlisted men knew where they were going. Only a few of the highest-ranking officers were privy to that information as well. The cliché was true. Loose lips did indeed sink ships. And with the sea-lanes packed with German U-boats, course and destination knowledge were on the strictest need-to-know basis.

When he couldn't put together a card or dice game, Brendon sat on his bunk in his skivvies playing solitaire. More often than not, Riley occupied his time keeping his rifle oiled and clean.

"Hey, if I didn't know better, I'd think you were falling in love with that weapon, my friend."

"Just want to make sure there's no chance of it ever letting me down, you know?"

"You think much about it?"

"About what?" Riley asked.

"Combat."

"There's not much else to think about on this tub, is there? I mean…that's why we're here. That's why we're going wherever we're going. That's what they've trained us to do. Pretty soon now, we're going to be in it."

"Yeah, I figure that will be soon enough. So I'll just wait. But…isn't the whole idea of all our training that we don't have to think…just react. React like we've been taught."

"You really think it's going to be like that? You really think there won't be all kinds of stuff running through your head when bullets and shells and God knows what else are whizzing by and going off all around you?"

"Don't know, man. Don't know what will be in my head."

"I don't either. But I know what will be in my hands. This rifle. And I'm not taking any chances on it not doing what it's supposed to do."

Brendon looked at the cards spread out on his bunk. It appeared highly unlikely he was going to win this particular game of solitaire. "Maybe you're right, partner. Maybe I'll give mine the once over too. Never know when they might stop this tub and tell us it's time to get off and go to work."

There were two hundred officers on board as well. They were quartered four to a room and spent most of their time in mission briefings and status updates. In the time Paul had to himself, he would generally read or write home. Letters to his parents frequently took the form of asking about their health, assuring them that he was well, and giving a relatively generic account of what he was doing. It wasn't difficult avoiding specifics. He didn't have many. It seemed like junior officers were always last-to-know. By the time official word of anything filtered down to their level, there was a good chance the rumor mill was already carrying the scuttlebutt to noncoms and enlisted alike.

Paul had a number of acquaintances on the ship. Officers he had gone through OCS with, or met in jump school. But none he really counted as close friends. He had taken to heart what he had been taught. A good officer should like and respect the men he takes orders from and gives orders to. But the fact remains; in war there will be casualties. Don't become so emotionally involved with the men around you that you can't continue to carry out your duties when they start to fall, as some inevitably will. Leadership is a lonely profession, he remembered more than one of his instructors saying. A degree of emotional distance is required. *For better or worse,* thought Paul, *that was something I have always possessed.*

The Evangeline crossed the Atlantic, moved through the Straits of Gibraltar and eventually dropped anchor in port at Tunisia. From there, members of the 82nd Airborne would soon be taking part in Operation Husky; the Allied plan to invade Italy. But for now, all the vast majority knew was that they had arrived and they'd soon be enjoying the presence of land beneath their feet and the absence of rough seas and rolling stomachs. Nothing could have made them happier.

Chapter 21

Hollywood

In Los Angeles, Gwen had another benefactor who would be even kinder to her than Felix. That benefactor was the camera. Whether it was a Leica 35mm still or an Arriflex 35mm movie, it made no difference whatsoever. Each lavished her with love and adoration. Cameras brought out Gwen's personality as well as her beauty. She seemed able to instinctively react to them as if they were ardent suitors. From one shoot to the next, Felix made sure she was able to bring more to the party than just her fabulous features. He had her instructed in posture; how to walk, sit, courtesy and more. Diction lessons removed any hint of an East Texas twang. He gave her riding lessons and tennis lessons and even though she already took to the water like sailboats to the wind, he insisted on swimming and diving lessons as well. She was also schooled in dance. From waltzes and minuets to sambas and tangos. She was being groomed like the natural thoroughbred Felix knew she was. And early returns on his investment were not far away. Felix lined up a number of jobs for Gwen that individuals agreed to without ever having seen her in person. Glamour photographs he had arranged began to make their money back with swimsuit, fashion, and catalogue shoots. Extra and non-speaking roles in movies began to get her called to casting sessions where directors were looking for the girl-at-the-bar, the girl-who-walks-by-and-gets-whistled-at, or the girl-next-door, often admired in silence by the aging male lead.

Gwen responded to it all with the enthusiasm of the amateur she was, the dedication of the professional she aspired to be, and the dogged persistence of the loyal subject she had become to the man responsible for it all, Felix Pressman. Felix took it upon himself to make sure Gwen's training included graces social as well as theatrical. He had her accompany him to industry functions and society soirées that gave her exposure to the well-heeled beyond Hollywood as well as within it, even to the point of offering her services to community groups in need of a pretty face for USO shows, political gatherings, and fundraisers. Felix was determined to orchestrate the perfect introduction of his discovery one step at a time. And Gwen was determined to take each and every step necessary to justify Felix's investment of time, money, and faith in her.

The weather had proved accommodating for the cocktail reception being held in the spacious back yard that fronted the ocean. Guests from the business world, the arts, and local government chatted and mingled round the pool like Indians circling covered wagons in one studio or another's current western. Everyone agreed with the sentiment that had motivated their presence, but there were as many additional agendas as there were guests. And there were far too many guests to know who had been invited and who had simply gotten wind of the proceedings and dropped by.

Felix spotted the hosts who seemed to be standing somewhat apart from the crowd. He took Gwen by the arm and adroitly maneuvered his way through the guests without jostling any of the chatterers or bumping anyone into the pool.

"Mr. and Mrs. Cassidy, I wanted to introduce myself. I'm Felix Pressman of the Pressman Agency, and this is my protégé, Miss Gwen Taylor."

"Hello," Charles responded, extending his hand. "I'm Charles Cassidy and this is my wife, Margaret. We're so glad you could attend."

"You have such a lovely home, Mrs. Cassidy," Gwen said. "It's really beautiful here."

"Thank you, dear," Margaret answered. "We're rather fond of it, ourselves."

"As indeed you should be," Felix added.

"The Pressman Agency," Charles began, "is that an advertising firm?"

"No. It's a theatrical agency," Felix responded. "One of the smaller ones in Hollywood."

"Small but exclusive, I'm sure, Mr. Pressman," Margaret volunteered.

"We like to think so," Felix replied.

"Oh, don't mind me not knowing your firm, Pressman," Charles said, "I don't know half the people here. I'm in real estate. The entertainment business is a mystery to me."

"And to many of the people in it, I'm afraid," Felix answered. "We're frequently more concerned with the number of lines in a script than with the color of our bottom lines."

"Black," Charles inserted quickly. "That's the only color you want."

"Mr. Pressman," Margaret asked, "weren't you an actor yourself? Haven't I seen you in one film or another in the past?"

"If you did, dear lady, you had to be perusing the screen intently. I'm afraid all my time in front of a camera was spent considerably behind the featured players and stars."

"Well, I don't know why, Mr. Pressman, you're one of the most debonair men here."

"Merci, madam. You are as gracious as you are lovely."

"And speaking of lovely, your protégé here, Miss Taylor, is simply stunning. Isn't she, Charles?"

"The prettiest girl here by a mile. That's for sure."

"You're both so nice," Gwen responded. "Thank you so much for hosting this event."

"Well, it's for a good cause," Charles said. "It's important to support the war effort, you know."

"We couldn't agree more," Felix said, inserting his hand inside his breast pocket, pulling out a check, and handing it to Charles. "Here's a little contribution for that new USO facility."

Both Charles and Margaret said, "Thank you," simultaneously. Then she continued. "We sincerely appreciate everyone's help. It's rather personal with us, you see. Our son, Paul, is an army officer overseas. So many young men are in harm's way far from home. It's important that organizations have the capacity to support them both here and wherever they are."

"My wife wasn't a big supporter of the war until our son got into it. Now she's raising money right and left."

"I know how she feels," Gwen volunteered. "I knew someone who was called to serve. I think about him now and then. And what he must be going through."

"Our son wasn't drafted," Charles added clumsily. "He volunteered."

"I'm sure they're all very brave," Felix said. "Enlistee and draftee alike."

Somewhat embarrassed, Charles said, "Oh, I didn't mean anything like that. I mean…I know all about draft boards and personnel needs and that sort of thing. I head a division of the War Relocation Authority, you know."

"Oh yes, I've heard of that organization," Felix said. "Each of us lends support in our own way, I suppose."

The conversation drew to a close after that, with Felix and Gwen again thanking their hosts for a lovely evening and saying goodbye. In the car, winding down Sunset Boulevard on their way back, Gwen said, "What is that War Relocation Authority that Mr. Cassidy mentioned? I mean…what…or who do they relocate?"

"Americans, my dear," Felix answered. "Japanese Americans. Who, at this particular moment, find themselves hysteria's offspring."

"What do you mean? Have they committed some crime?"

"Indeed they have. They've committed the unpardonable offence of being the wrong kind of people existing in the wrong place at the wrong time."

Chapter 22

Chicago

The days following her first letter to Brendon, Jillian spent with two unwanted, yet constant companions—fear and angst. She dreaded the thought of those two hoodlums coming back to the drugstore for the information she couldn't bring herself to uncover, much less divulge. And she feared the consequences that might ensue if she didn't do as she was told. There was no doubt in her mind there would be repercussions. They wouldn't think twice about harming Brendon's parents or her own. Especially if she went to the police in advance and foiled their plans to rob the drugstore. And if they decided to commit the robbery with no knowledge of where most of the store's money was, anything could happen. They might rough up Mr. Hightower, or some of the other employees, or even some of the customers. She knew she had to do something, but she wasn't sure the right thing to do was the safe thing to do. And she couldn't bear the thought of good people being hurt.

All through the week she tried to notice things she'd never cared about before. How often Mr. Hightower was at the counter in the front. Whether he manipulated the amount of cash in the register and at what times of day. How frequently he went to the pharmacy counter. What he did when he was there. She would watch as her boss went into the stock room or the back of the store. When he came out she would take her break and go back to see if she could find which of the drawers in his desk were locked. And whether there was any safe in the back she didn't know about. A safe he might have hidden away so that even his workers wouldn't know where to look for it. The more she tried to find out, the worse she felt. Treachery to her benefactor was eating away at her. Fear for her loved ones was making her nauseous. No outcome she could foresee was desirable. And time was running out.

But by the middle of that week, the germ of an idea had begun to form in her mind. At first, it seemed virtually impossible to even consider. But by the middle of the week, she came to some realistic conclusions. The two thugs she had become involved with weren't going away. Simply hoping it would all work out wasn't going to change anything. Wishing someone would step in and solve things for her was simply daydreaming that wouldn't help anyone. For good or ill, this was her problem to solve.

Thursday afternoon, the bell above the front door jingled and something told Jillian it was them. She looked up to see Ian and Snapper walk in, pause to look around the store, then begin their walk back to her counter. They had told her she had a week and now they were here a day early. *It was just like them,* she thought. *You couldn't trust anything they said.* She went ahead and began to make Snapper's root beer float even before they reached the stools at her counter.

"Afternoon, doll," Ian began. "I see you know what he's having. I'll just have a Coke."

Jillian's mind was racing as she gave Snapper the float and pulled down a glass for Ian.

"You said I had a week. You said you'd give me a week."

"Didn't think you really needed that long," Ian said. "What have you got for us?"

Jillian spoke. Slowly at first, then more rapidly as the conversation progressed.

"I…I had a talk with Mr. Hightower."

Ian and Snapper looked at one another. Then back at her. Ian said, "That was not a good idea. Not a good idea at all."

"Yes…Yes it was," Jillian said. "You don't understand. You see I told him that I really wanted to learn more about the store so I could do more for him. I said I wanted to be able to really help out in other ways so that maybe I could work myself up to a higher level…you know? And maybe he'd be willing to pay me more money."

"Hey, that sounds pretty smart," Snapper said.

Not really, Ian thought. With her asking a lot of questions, once the place was hit, Hightower was likely to figure whoever did it might have had inside help. Of course, that was her problem, and they could always take care of Hightower if they had to.

"Did he buy it?" Ian asked.

"Oh yeah, yeah." Jillian went on. "He said he was glad I was so interested in the business. He said that most young people these days don't plan for their future, you know? And that he was glad to see I was not like that."

"Okay, okay, skip the pep talk," Ian injected. "What did you actually find out?"

"Well, you're not going to believe this. But when I asked him about accounting and all…and how he keeps track of the money and that sort of thing…well, he let me in on something that sounded crazy at first…then later when he explained it…it began to make sense."

Ian asked, "What's the crazy part?"

"Well, he doesn't keep a safe, or anything like that, here in the store. Doesn't even keep much of the cash in his desk."

Snapper jumped in. "What's he do with it?"

"Every night, before he closes up, he takes all the cash from the registers and separates the small bills from the large ones. Then he puts just enough back in each register to start the next day. He keeps the rest, and all the larger bills, in one place. And every Saturday morning, he takes it all to the bank to be deposited."

"Where does the crazy part come in?" Ian asked.

"It's where he keeps all the large bills," Jillian answered, "that's the weird thing. He actually keeps them here, in my register. In a hidden drawer underneath the one I work from. I didn't even know it was there. He said he does it because no one would think he keeps most of his money in the soda fountain."

"Why would he tell you this?" Ian wanted to know. "Why now, if he hasn't told you before?"

"I told you," Jillian said. "I've worked here a long time now. He trusts me. He thinks I really can help him more than I have. Maybe even become a manager or something so he doesn't have to do everything himself. He doesn't have any kids or any family. That's why he's always done everything odd and secretly. I think maybe he sees me as the daughter he never had, you know?"

"Very touching," Ian said. "So how much is in there?"

"Gosh, I don't really know. It's Thursday. By the end of the day tomorrow it should be really full of twenties. Even fifties and sometimes hundred dollar bills too."

"Give us a peek," Snapper injected, wiping a dribble of ice cream from the side of his mouth.

"I can't do that now. He's right over there. Anyway, I have to take the whole top drawer out to get to it. I can't do that during working hours. I have no real reason to be getting into it. He'd know something isn't right."

"That's it then," Ian said. "We'll be in tomorrow night, just before your shift ends. One of us will tell you to take the cash out of the drawer. You'll hesitate. Like you don't want to do it. We'll get mad and mess things up a bit. You know, bang the cash registers around and throw them on the floor. Kick 'em around so it looks like they sprung open and we just happened to find that secret drawer. Don't want to make it look like we already knew where to go to get the biggest take."

"You don't have to do this," Jillian said to Ian. "There's still time to change your mind and not do this."

"You've just got pregame jitters, doll. Happens all the time. Hell, we pull this off without a hitch tomorrow night, and chances are you'll be wanting to throw in with us. You'll get a rush. Just wait and see."

"Please, don't hurt anyone," Jillian said. "Be careful not to hurt anyone."

"Now, do I look like the kind of guy that would hurt somebody?" Snapper asked.

Jillian just looked at him. She was incredulous that he'd ask such a question. Then she watched them both as they rose from their stools and walked out of the drugstore without paying their tab.

Sleep didn't come easy that night. She tossed and turned and finally got out of bed, went to her desk and penned another letter to Brendon. It was the only way she had of not letting her thoughts and troubles and plans overwhelm her. She didn't mention any of it to him. She hadn't mentioned anything about it to anyone. Not even her parents. Writing a letter to Brendon was her way of not having to think about it for at least another hour. Though when she finished, fatigue seemed to wash over her. She went back to bed tired, but surer than ever of what she must do.

It was a typical Friday. Lots of people in and out of Hightower's. Lots of dollars changing hands. Bills going in this cash register and that. Jillian stood out on the sidewalk looking in. She had arrived a few minutes before her shift was to start. Now she was having a hard time going inside. Everything looked the same but somehow it was different. Could she do it? Could she go through with it? She had to, she told herself. She just had to.

Near the end of the longest day she had ever spent at work, the store was in the lull that follows the after-work drop-bys. Mr. Hightower was at the front counter. There was one customer in the pharmacy. A middle-aged lady was browsing the perfume aisles. Two high school kids had just left the soda fountain and were walking toward the door to go see a movie. Jillian was ostensibly cleaning up before leaving. Then the bell above the door jangled.

Two men in suits, with kerchiefs over their faces and pistols in their hands, muscled their way in. After turning the OPEN sign on the door around, so that it read CLOSED to people on the street, the first one slammed his gun down on the high school boy's head and the second pointed the barrel of his weapon at Hightower saying, "This is a stick-up! Get those people in the pharmacy to come out here."

Jillian immediately recognized Ian's voice.

Then Ian yelled at the woman in the perfume aisle. "You too, lady! Get over here now." Seeing the pistol in his hand, she didn't dawdle, and did as she was told.

"George?" Hightower's voice creaked a bit, but he continued. "George, please…you and your customer come up here. I'm afraid we're being robbed."

"Do it now, George!" Ian bellowed. Then motioning to the schoolgirl who was helping her date get up from the floor, he continued. "Over here, you two. With the rest of them."

"Do the pharmacy register first," Ian told Snapper. The subordinate responded quickly, racing back to the pharmacy and pulling the bills from the register George, in his haste, had failed to close.

"Not much here," he said. "Just a hundred or two."

"Now the soda fountain," Ian yelled, as the customers and employees continued to stand silently, watching the scene unfold before them.

Snapper charged toward the soda fountain, shouting as he moved, "Open that cash register, bitch!"

Just as he was reaching the counter, Jillian turned and began to hit the keys that would open the register.

"Hey," Snapper half-whispered, "remember, you're supposed to give us a hard time. You're supposed to—"

He never finished his sentence. Jillian opened the register and removed the revolver she had taken from her father's cabinet before coming to work. When she turned, Snapper was so stunned at seeing the gun in her hand that he momentarily froze. A moment was all it took for Jillian to fire one, two, then a third shot into the torso of the astonished robber. He fell headlong onto the counter, knocking over the half-empty glass the high school girl had left behind. Other than pain, the last sensation he experienced was the sweet scent of root beer from the overturned float.

Ian couldn't believe what he had just seen. He couldn't believe what he was looking at now. Here was the cute, perky soda jerk in uniform and apron…the dame he was convinced he had thoroughly intimidated into becoming an accomplice. She was marching toward him like some sort of avenging angel. Her revolver level and ready to fire.

"Hey," he squealed. "Stop! Stop now, or I'll plug the old man."

Jillian didn't stop. She kept walking toward him. The customers started to jump behind aisles and run to other parts of the store. George, the pharmacist, said, "Jillian, put the gun down. He's going to hurt Mr. Hightower."

"No," Jillian responded, never taking her eyes from Ian. "He's not. He's not going to hurt anyone ever again."

She raised her arm and fired. The bullet whistled by Ian's ear, so close he could feel the searing heat. It crashed into the wall sending shards of wood and glass onto the front counter.

"Jesus! Crazy bitch!" Ian shouted, as he pulled Hightower from behind the counter, got behind him and backed quickly toward the door. When he did so, Hightower stumbled and began crumpling toward the floor.

Jillian raised her arm and fired again. Her shot was high this time—blasting the bell over the front door into twisted metal and sending pieces of it onto Ian's hat and shoulder.

"Jesus. Jesus Christ!" he shrieked. "Crazy Mick bitch! Crazy!" That was the last thing he said as he swung the door open wide and bolted down the street without even taking time to pull the kerchief from his face or holster his pistol.

Hightower, George, and the other customers in the store held their positions in stunned disbelief of what they had just seen…of what they were seeing…a young, pretty soda jerk standing before them with the pistol still smoking in her hand. She had killed one armed robber at point blank range and chased the other off screaming in the night.

Jillian looked around the store and saw eyes in faces staring at her. She tried to focus on them. *Who were they? How long had they been there? Why were they looking at her? What had just happened? What is this thing I'm holding,* she wondered momentarily, as her hand began to tremble and she let the offending weapon fall from her fingers to the linoleum floor. Then, it seemed as if all the energy in Jillian's body went rushing out of her as fast as Ian had rushed out the door. She sighed heavily and suddenly felt incredibly weak. Her legs began to quiver and she dropped to her knees. Then Jillian McIntyre, kneeling in front of her amazed boss, her astonished fellow employee, and her stunned customers, slowly cupped her face in her hands, and began to weep.

Chapter 23

North Africa

Since their arrival in Tunisia, the 505 had trained, practiced and conducted maneuvers continuously while American and British planes flew across the Mediterranean Sea conducting bombing sorties over the principle airfields of Sardinia, Sicily, and southern Italy. The Allied bombing missions had two primary objectives—reduce Axis airpower and increase confusion as to where the actual sea-based invasion would come ashore. With a reduced capability to respond quickly and strongly by air, invading Allied forces would face considerably less resistance and dramatically fewer casualties.

As usual, the troops were kept in both a constant state of readiness and of ignorance. They knew they could be going into action at any time but they didn't know where or when. Secrecy was of the utmost importance, and it wasn't until they were marshaled and getting ready to board their aircraft that each platoon learned of its destination.

Just before midnight, Paul addressed the men of third platoon, Bravo Company. Riley and Brendon were in the first squad and listened intently; glad they'd be taking orders from a platoon leader they knew.

"Smoke, if you got 'em, men. This will be your last chance for a while. Once we board that plane, it's all business. I know most of you have been wondering where you're going and exactly what your mission is. Well, I can finally tell you because your role in it is going to be commencing in less than ten minutes. We'll be flying over the Mediterranean, finding our drop zones in southeast Sicily and taking the fight to the Italians and the Germans. Just as we did in maneuvers, once we hit the ground, we'll assemble quickly and move out. Follow your squad leader's signals and do everything in double time. The last thing you want is to be left behind. Our objective is Ponte Grande and the bridge over the River Anape, south of Syracuse. We're to take it and hold it. When our guys and the Brits hit the beaches tomorrow and start moving up, we don't want anything slowing them down."

"Gentlemen, it's time to pay the army back for all the chow, all the discipline, and all the training they've given us over the last few months. It's time to start pushing the Nazis and the Fascists back into the rat holes they crawled out of. And it is now time to let the enemy know that the Americans have arrived…and there's going to be hell to pay. Are you with me?"

The collective reply was instantaneous. "*Airborne*!"

Less than a quarter hour later the troop carrier was thundering down the runway. Once the paratroopers had taken their positions and strapped themselves in, the chattering came to a halt. All the false bravado and feigned nonchalance had been replaced with silence and contemplation. This was the real thing. No training exercise. No maneuvers to be walked away from once they were over. There were soldiers out there—men in different uniforms who spoke different languages—but men whose only goal was to kill, wound, or capture you. And your only defense was to kill, wound, or capture them first. Could you do that? Could you kill another human being? *You had to,* Riley thought. To save your own life or the lives of your fellow paratroopers. *You had to,* Brendon thought. In fact, perhaps this was the penance you had to pay for your transgressions. Transgressions like the little girl in Chicago, and maybe for all the little girls who had suffered in this war. As the wheels left the ground, the men in Paul's plane, just as in all the planes that were taking off with it, had a sense of how very small and inconsequential they were in the universe. They all—churchgoers and non-believers alike—took their last silent moments to try to make peace with their God, their past, or their destiny. Because the one thing they were sure of was...where they were going, there would be no peace.

The flying armada wasn't long off the ground before each plane was buffeted by intense headwinds. Speed was slowed. Human cargo got bounced, bumped, and shaken worse than many had experienced on the choppy Atlantic crossing. The pre-flight weather report had proven faulty. Staying on course became more and more difficult. Winds reached strengths of forty-five miles per hour as the planes neared their drop zones. But aborting the mission was never considered. The order was given to stand up and hook up. Men lurched from one side to the other as they tried to check their equipment and that of the man in front of them. The aircraft was bucking and bouncing so that the impending fear of combat had been replaced by the imminent fear of going down with the ship. No matter what was facing them on the ground, the men of the 505 were more than ready to get out that door.

The red light came on. The door opened. A huge gust of air saved many from losing their dinner all over themselves. The first paratrooper was given the order to stand in the door. He took up his position. The red light changed to green and it began. One by one the men started jumping into the blackness of the night—tearing through the sky as the prop wash blew them like confetti before a fan—then yanking them upward like puppets on a string as their canopies opened. Finally they swung gently to and fro as they began their descent to earth.

Riley saw the tops of the trees coming fast. He got into his landing position—legs and feet together, knees bent. As he paralleled the trees, darkness grew around him and the ground came up fast. He banged down hard, bouncing from his feet to his butt without being able to execute a proper roll. The wind caught his partially collapsed canopy and started to drag him across the earth. He reached up and hit his quick release. One side of his chute cut free and the air went with it bringing him to a stop. He quickly stood up and began to look around for the other men. They should have been all around him, but they weren't.

Where the hell were they, he wondered. His first instinct was to shout, but he knew better. *Think. Think,* he told himself. *Why weren't they here? The plane. The plane was bouncing so the winds must have been too strong. Were we blown off course? Did we miss the drop zone entirely? Where was Brendon…the Lieutenant…the rest of the platoon?*

By now his eyes had adjusted to the dark. He could see that he was standing in some sort of clearing. *Jesus, I'm a target,* he said to himself. *Got to get out of here. Got to get to the tree line.* Without knowing whether he was headed in the right direction or not, he began to sprint toward the dark of the trees. At least there was cover there. He wouldn't be so vulnerable. The ground was rocky and uneven and he stumbled as he ran across it. But he kept going as fast as he could. He kept running toward the darkness of the trees.

Thirty feet from the first row of trees, his eyes started playing tricks on him. The wind had subsided but one branch about twelve feet off the ground was moving while the others were still. It was bouncing and shaking and two long limbs hung downward kicking and twisting. *Limbs can't do that,* Riley thought. *Wait. They're not limbs. They're legs. Someone's in that tree.*

Riley pulled his rifle from over his shoulder and dropped to one knee at the edge of the tree line. He pointed his weapon toward the still shaking apparition, but something told him not to fire. He was hesitant to call out, but he couldn't help himself.

"Who is it? Who's there?"

Brendon recognized the voice. "Riley…Riley? It's you, right? It's me, Brendon. I'm stuck in this blasted tree."

Riley rose from his crouch and started walking forward, still holding his weapon at the ready. "What are you doing up there? Where are the rest of the guys?"

"I don't know where the hell they are. I think we've been

scattered all over the place. And I'm stuck. I came through about two thirds of this damn tree but my chute got caught and I can't get it loose."

"Can't you get your bayonet and cut it away?"

"My arms are pinned. I can't reach my bayonet. You'll have to climb up here and cut me free."

"Climb? You're swinging below the lowest branch. And there's no incline. I'd have to be a squirrel to get up that tree."

"Oh, great! So you're just going to leave me here, huh?"

"No, of course not. Just let me think of something, will you?"

"Sure, take all the time you want. I'm obviously not going anywhere."

Riley looked at the tree trunk. It was too wide to get his arms around. He quickly considered running back to the clearing and trying to find his parachute. Maybe he could somehow throw its lines over the limb and use them to climb up. But it didn't seem a good idea to go back out in the open. Then another thought came to him. He put his rifle down and began to take his pack off.

"You going to…try it?" Brendon asked, still squirming and kicking.

"Had an idea," Riley said, taking his bayonet from his utility belt. "Now, if this works, you're going to be in for a bit of a drop."

"How much worse can it be than the one I've already had?"

"Okay, here goes."

Riley walked to the base of the tree. Standing there, he rose on the tips of his toes, reached high as he could with his arm, and drove his bayonet into the trunk. Then using his feet and legs to grip the trunk—as a rider uses his thighs to cling to the sides of his mount—and with his free arm wrapped as far around the tree as he could manage—he pulled himself up to the level of the bayonet. Extracting it, he reached high and once again plunged it in. Then used it again as a rung to inch himself up. Stab-pull-climb-extract. Stab-pull-climb-extract. Brendon watched in amazement as the lanky Texan slowly made his way up the tree. By the time he reached the branch Brendon was dangling from, Riley was drenched in sweat and breathing hard as a finishing distance runner.

"If I hadn't seen it…I wouldn't have believed it," Brendon said.

"Just let me catch my breath for a minute. Then I'll cut you loose."

"Learn that in Boy Scouts or something?"

"Somebody once said necessity is the mother of invention. Guess he was right. Okay, let's do this." Riley was able to straddle the limb and get far enough out to cut the risers of the parachute holding Brendon hostage. Before slicing though the last ones holding his friend, he said, "Don't forget to tuck and roll. Ready?"

"Airborne."

Riley cut him free and Brendon fell to the ground. Rather than trying to climb back down, Brendon slid his bayonet under his belt, swung his leg over the limb, hung from it, then let go and dropped to the ground.

"Thanks, man," Brendon said. "I owe you one."

"You would have done the same for me," Riley answered.

"Not nearly as well, though."

As Riley was putting his gear back on and Brendon was checking his rifle, they both heard footfalls coming through the grass at the edge of the tree line. Instinctively, they dropped to a knee and raised their weapons.

"Cross? O'Byrne? Cross? O'Byrne?" The trooper kept half-whispering, half-shouting, as he drew near.

"That's Higgins," Brendon said. "I recognize his voice."

"Higgins! Over here," Riley said.

Their squad mate made his way to them. "Oh, both of you are here. That's good. Lieutenant Cassidy sent me back to look for you."

Brendon asked, "Where's the platoon?"

"Just across the clearing."

"On the other side?" Riley asked.

"Yeah...and that clearing's not even our drop zone. Lieutenant said the winds drove the planes off course. And played hell with where everyone came down."

Looking back and forth from Riley to Brendon, Higgins said to the Texan, "You sick or something? You're sweating like a pig."

Riley saw no point in potentially embarrassing his friend. "Nah. Just got a little winded running across the clearing. Packing this gear and all."

"Well, we're about to run back. Lieutenant only gave me ten minutes. Said to be back in ten minutes with or without you."

"Let's make it with," Brendon said. "Riley, you ready to go?"

"Have any trouble coming across, Higgins? See or hear anything?" Riley asked.

"No. Nothing. I think because of the drop foul up...we're actually farther from the action than we're supposed to be. Got a good ways to hump, Lieutenant said."

"Okay," Riley responded. "Let's get started then."

When they reached the tree line on the far side of the clearing, the sentry Paul had posted called for them to identify themselves become coming closer. They did. Then they made their way to where the rest of the men were gathered. Paul was folding the map he had just checked and putting it and his compass back in his fatigue jacket when he saw the three approach.

"Good job, Higgins," he said. "Cross, O'Byrne, you both okay?"

"Yes Sir," Brendon replied. "Sorry to slow things up, Lieutenant. Came down in the wrong place. Cross stopped to help me out. He would have been on time with the others if he hadn't."

Riley started to respond but Paul cut him off. "Don't worry about it. Damn winds spread us all over hell and gone. Lucky it blew us away from the enemy instead of right in the middle of them."

"Is everyone accounted for, Sir?" Riley asked.

"Still waiting on two," Paul replied. "Sergeant Johnson went back to check on Garza and Braverman." Then looking at his watch, he said, "I can only give him a couple more minutes."

"What do we do if he's not back?" one of the other men asked.

"We move out," Paul said. "Johnson knows where we're headed."

Two minutes later, neither Johnson, Garza, nor Braverman had shown. "On your feet, men. And gather round," Paul said. "Here's the situation. We're approximately five miles south of where we should be. We're going to be moving northeast. Mostly through the woods. As far off course as we are, we're going to have to keep a swift and steady pace to reach our objective, the Ponte Grande Bridge, before sunrise. So keep up. Don't fall back or wander off. Since Sergeant Johnson isn't here, I'll take the point. There's a map in my pocket. If something happens to me, one of your squad leaders will take it and make sure you get where you're going. Let's move out."

The platoon sergeant and two men were missing. The lieutenant was talking about what to do if something happened to him. Riley went ahead and said what he was thinking to Brendon. "Not the best way to start, is it?"

"Not sure there is a good way to start something bad," Brendon responded. "Only a good way to end it."

The platoon advanced at a rapid pace. Squads kept enough distance between them to keep from being targeted too easily. From the earliest days of infantry school it had been drilled into every soldier that bunching up was just making it easy for the enemy. One grenade could take out a number of men who were too close together. Hillsides and high grass provided a degree of cover, but a good bit of open land would have to be crossed if the platoon was to achieve their objective in the time allotted to do so. The high winds that had played havoc with their initial assault were now their allies. They kept clouds moving across the sky and moonlight to a minimum. Moving under the cover of darkness enabled them to maintain their greatest advantage—the element of surprise.

They had been moving north for about an hour when they heard the distant sound of gunfire. Paul dropped to his knee and raised his right fist in the air. It was the signal for all to stop. As each man saw the man in front of him assuming the position, he too would follow suit. They quickly became dark objects that pockmarked the hillside like boulders scattered here and there; still, inanimate, part of the landscape. Save for one. One soldier who crouched low and weaved his way through the others until he reached the head of the column and Lieutenant Cassidy. It was Sergeant Johnson. And he was alone.

Platoon Sergeant Vince Johnson was built like a college fullback. But he hadn't earned his stripes on the gridiron. Barrel-chested, blunt, and battle hardened, he was the lone individual with combat experience assigned to third platoon, Bravo Company. And as such, he was the man most depended upon by his lieutenant.

"Are Garza and Braverman in the back with their squads?" Paul asked.

"No," Johnson said, as he reached in his pocket, pulled out their dog tags, and handed them to Paul. "Garza's neck got snapped on the trunk of an olive tree the size of a Buick. Braverman's main chute cigarette-rolled and his reserve wasn't deployed. He either blacked out or freaked out. Either way, he got to the ground long before anyone else."

His platoon's first casualties, Paul thought. *And they hadn't even gotten into the fight.* He realized there was no time to dwell on it. "Thanks, Johnson. Are you winded from catching up with us?"

"No, I'm okay."

"What do you make of that gunfire?"

"Hard to say from this distance. Sounds like small arms, mostly. I'm sure we weren't the only platoon that missed our drop zone and had to scramble for it."

"Well," Paul said, "now the scramble is to get to the bridge in time."

"Want me to take the point, Sir?"

"Yes, Sergeant. I'll make sure the platoon keeps up. We'll move out when you're ready."

"This is as good a time as any, Sir."

Like a chorus line in silhouette, the black shapes on the ground rose, crouched, and moved forward, heading toward the sound of the guns. Half an hour later, squatting in the tall grass that flanked both sides of the river, they could see as well as hear the gunfire that was being exchanged. But they were still too far away to know if the Italians were defending it, or trying to take it back. Johnson suggested the platoon hold while he went ahead to find out what he could. Paul agreed it was the smart thing to do.

As they waited, Riley couldn't help but think to himself that just a few hundred yards from where they were, a life and death struggle was taking place. People were dying. Others were killing. Soon he'd be in the middle of it. He told himself to simply react. *Whatever orders came, whatever he was told to do, just do it without thinking,* he said over and over again. As if repetition and execution could extinguish the fear. As if he could simply will himself forward.

Brendon kept checking his rifle. He knew the eight-round clip was fully loaded and ready to fire. But he kept rechecking it just to be sure. *Should I count,* he asked himself. *Should I count each time I fire? That way I'll know when I only have one round left. But it will stop firing on its own when I'm out. Then I can change clips quickly. Maybe I shouldn't count. Maybe I should just concentrate on aiming and making sure I hit what I'm shooting at. Hit it before it hits me. Jesus. Why didn't I work harder on the rifle range?*

Sergeant Johnson came running back and reported to Paul at the head of the platoon. "The Brits have taken the bridge. Chances are they ran the Wops off pretty quickly. They weren't expected to put up much of a fight. But there must have been Kraut regulars close by. They're counter attacking and they're about to drop some heavy stuff on our Limey friends. It won't take 'em long to set up their mortars and kick into a rapid rate of fire."

"Can we get behind them?" Paul asked.

"Affirmative. They're between the bridge and us. A rifle squad. A mortar crew. There may be more around. I couldn't really tell."

"Alright, you lead the way, Sergeant. Let's get there before they can start a barrage."

Paul gave an arm signal and the men moved out behind him. They were crouched low and moving rapidly. As they hustled through the tall grass, each man met his fear and anticipation his own way. But each kept heading to whatever fate had in store. The sporadic fire and the Germans' own shouted commands as their crews set up their weapons, muted the sounds of Paul's approaching platoon. Sergeant Johnson gave the signal to stop and Paul relayed it to the men. Then he went forward and knelt beside his noncom.

"There," Johnson said, pointing to his right, "about fifty yards up."

"Yes, I see them," Paul said, as he watched the shadows moving up and down. There were two riflemen taking aim at the bridge, while the other two set up the mortar.

"And over there," the sergeant continued, pointing approximately seventy-five yards to his left. "It's a rifle squad. They'll fire first to draw attention their way so the mortars can open up."

"Okay," Paul said. "Hold here while I position the men."

He ran back to the platoon and said, "Germans ahead of us

between fifty and seventy-five yards. First and second squad…when we move out…you go to the left. When you see me stop, do the same. I'll take third squad with me. When we open up on the mortar crew, you fire on the riflemen. Fourth squad…you stay back here in reserve until I tell you to move up. Okay, let's go."

Riley and Brendon moved up with the other members of first squad. Second squad was right on their heels. Third squad followed Paul until he came to a stop beside Sergeant Johnson. Just as Paul was about to give the order to fire, the German riflemen beat him to it and opened up on the bridge. Sparks from the muzzles of their weapons made them even easier targets than they would have been. Across the way, one German soldier was about to drop a mortar down the pipe when Paul, Johnson and third squad let go. Some shots initially missed, ripping up the ground around the crew like kamikaze wasps. But enough ammo found its mark to send all four Germans falling, squirming, and writhing in pain.

The riflemen had been firing from a prone position. Riley had a bead dead center on the back of the trooper in the center of the line. Could he shoot a man in the back? The question raced through his mind. But there was no time for an answer. When they heard third squad fire on the mortar crew, Riley's was the first trigger to be squeezed as both squads let loose on the unsuspecting Germans. Fire was so heavy and the flopping and jerking of bodies so intense that it was hard to tell if you had hit your target or someone else had. But Riley knew for certain he couldn't have missed at that range.

After a few seconds that felt like an eternity to Brendon, he heard Paul shout, "Cease fire." Easing the vice-like grip he had clamped on his rifle, he brought the weapon down to his side and noted that the line of bodies now lay still. He didn't know for sure whether he had hit anyone or not. There were so many shots fired. But he did know he had done as he was ordered. He had engaged the enemy.

"Stay low," Paul shouted. Like Sergeant Johnson had said, he couldn't be sure if other enemy troops were in the area. After a minute, when there was no return fire from either direction, Paul moved the men ahead slowly, telling them to stay ready and reminding them that some of the Germans may only be wounded. As each contingent neared the group they had fired upon, all looked for the slightest sign of life or movement.

"We need to make sure they're dead," Johnson said to Paul. "We're in no position to take prisoners. These are all low level grunts anyway. No intelligence value. And no point in leaving any poor bastard in pain."

Paul began, "How would you…"

The sergeant answered the incomplete question by taking his sidearm and firing point blank into the heart of a German staring up at the starless sky with eyes already incapable of seeing. Then, walking from man to man in the mortar crew, he finished each one. And ended by saying, "We need to do the same with the riflemen, Lieutenant."

Paul froze for a moment. But only for a moment. Then he said, "I'll go with you, Sergeant."

"That won't be necessary, Sir. Why don't you go back and bring up fourth squad. I'll get the squad leaders to help over there."

"I'm not sure that's the right way to do this, Sergeant."

"Believe me Sir, our boys need to get used to it. This is just the beginning."

A quarter-hour later, Paul led his platoon to the bridge. They came in under a white flag so they wouldn't be fired upon by their British allies mistaking them for the enemy. He asked the sentries for the officer in charge and was told he'd find Major Denny at the center of the bridge. Three minutes later he was addressing the man in the black beret giving orders there.

"Major Denny?"

No immediate response. The thin Englishman with the pencil mustache continued giving directions to the men around them until they dispersed. Then he turned to Paul and said, “So, the Yanks have finally arrived.”

“Are you Major Denny, Sir?”

“Indeed I am. Don’t expect me to wear my insignia in combat, do you? And who might you be?”

“Second Lieutenant Paul Cassidy, Sir. Third platoon, Bravo Company, 505 Regiment, 82nd Airborne.”

“And is the remainder of your company about, Leftenant?”

“No Sir. Just my platoon. I’m afraid the winds blew our planes and our paratroopers way past our drop zones. But I’m sure other platoons will be arriving soon…Sir.”

“Yes. Well, until they do, it seems that I’m the ranking officer here. So you and your men are hereby seconded to the South Staffordshire Regiment, 1st Air Landing Brigade, British Eighth Army. How many in your platoon, Leftenant?”

“Twenty-four, Sir…oh, sorry, I mean twenty-one, Sir. We had three casualties in the jump.”

“Damn shame, that. But let’s see, your twenty-one plus our sixty-eight makes…”

“Eighty-nine, Sir.”

“Indeed it does, Leftenant. Eighty-nine. Right, then. Our charge, as I’m sure you know, is to hold this bridge and that’s exactly what I intend to do. The Jerries will soon be reinforcing their Axis mates we recently kicked out and—”

“Sorry to interrupt, Sir, just wanted to let you know we ran into a German rifle squad and mortar crew on the way over and…well…they’ve been…neutralized, Sir.”

“Good show, Leftenant. The fewer the better, if you ask me. But that was probably just an advance patrol. Wouldn’t surprise me if they hit back hard, very soon now. Come, let me show you where to deploy your men.”

Riley and Brendon’s squad were ordered to man the perimeter

near the northwest bridge abutment. There was no time to dig in but they did have the slope of the hill to afford some cover from advancing forces. They took their positions about ten yards from one another with their squad mates approximately the same distance on either side of them. Lying on their stomachs, staring into the darkness of the tall grass that led to the bridge, each new man began to wonder what it would be like to be fired upon. Previously, they had the advantage. They came upon troops who never even knew they were there. It was almost like shooting ducks on a pond, but now they were the ducks, and hunters were coming for them.

"Hey Riley," Brendon grunted, in something between a shout and a whisper.

"Yeah."

"You think they'll come in this way?"

"I don't think we're lying here just for the hell of it."

"Think we'll hear 'em before we see 'em?"

"Not if you keep talking."

Brendon was about to say *sorry, I'll pipe down.* But before he could answer, everyone heard a distant thud, followed by a whistling noise in the sky. Then Major Denny's voice was ringing out loud and clear, without fear, or even any sense of excitement, just a booming, informational, "*Incoming!*" It was followed by momentary silence, then an explosion that rocked the earth half way between the perimeter defense and the bridge. The shell burrowed into the ground, its impact spewing rock, dirt, and grass into the air in all directions, some of the flying debris landing like hail in a rainstorm on the prostrate soldiers waiting for the tornado that was to follow.

"Steady men!" the major was shouting. "No firing until you actually see something to shoot at." Then another thump, and whistle, and silence before another mortar crashed into the embankment near the shoreline, spraying mud and sand and water high into the sky and drenching those who had taken up positions near the bridge itself. Distance and darkness cloaked the aggressors, as one after another third, fourth, and fifth thunderous excavations plowed the ground between the bridge and its forward line of defense. Paul realized the rounds were coming in too close together to be fired by a single battery. He was convinced a large force would soon be counterattacking from multiple directions.

"Sergeant Johnson, make sure the men are ready. They'll be coming soon."

"That they will, Sir," Johnson replied, already on his feet and heading up the hill.

Keeping low, the sergeant gave advice as he ran along the perimeter line. "Be ready, they'll be coming soon….have a target, don't just fire in their direction…if they keep coming, you keep firing…keep your ears as well as your eyes open…no falling back unless you hear a direct order…if they get close enough, use your grenades…this is what you're here for, boys…send 'em to hell."

A few moments after Johnson passed Brendon and Riley, the Germans opened up. Rifle and machine gun fire broke the intermittent silence of the mortars like high-caliber banshees. *Jesus,* Brendon thought to himself as the rounds whistled overhead. *How many are out there? This sounds like the live fire drill, only worse. Much worse. Don't stand up,* he told himself. *Don't run. Hold your position. Hold, damn it!*

Riley was thinking about holding too. Holding his fire until he could see who was firing at him. All the enemy's rounds were passing overhead. *They don't know about our perimeter line yet,* he realized. *All their fire's aimed at the bridge. Well, they'll soon know about us if they come over that hill.* Then they did. A line of German troops walking, crouching, firing. Then getting up to advance again. *Do we wait for a command,* Brendon wondered as he gripped his rifle tightly. *My God, why don't we shoot now?* The answer to his question came instantaneously, with Sergeant Johnson yelling, "FIRE!" Third platoon let go. Riley saw the German rifleman he was aiming at bend in half as his round caught him square in the sternum. He didn't have time to ponder the morality of what he was doing. He was already sighting in on another. The first volley from the perimeter line felled a dozen or more at the head of the advance. But it also gave away the Americans' position. The Germans hit the deck and turned their fire from the bridge to the line of rifles that were firing at them from the dark. All of a sudden the rounds that had been passing overhead were now directed at them. An invisible hornet's nest started chewing up the ground around them. Fear rose like mercury in a thermometer up Brendon's spine as bullets whizzed closer and closer. But he had no time to give in to it. Or no way to get away from it. There was only time to fire back. At a man, a motion, a rifle barrel, anything that moved. Brendon knew there was no place to go. He knew their line had to keep the Germans at bay. But it wasn't objectives running through his mind. It was pure survival. Hope and pray you don't get hit and keep firing. Keep them away.

Riley's fear was just as real. He knew this was at last the real thing. People were on that hill trying to kill him. But somehow he also knew the only thing that would keep that from happening was to concentrate on killing them first. Methodically, he moved from one target to the next, waiting for a helmet to rise above the tall grass, a barrel to extend from behind a boulder, an arm raised to give the signal to advance again. And every time a target presented itself, he'd sight and fire.

Even though the Germans now knew the location of the perimeter defense, they were still unsure of its strength or firepower. And the Allies were just as ignorant of the number of their foes. After what seemed an eternity, but was in fact only a few minutes, the concentrated give and take of fire eventually slowed and then came to a stop, save for intermittent sniping, as each side took stock of their situation.

Paul took this opportunity to scurry down the line of

defenders and see if anyone was hurt. Remarkably, no one in third platoon had been hit. The slope of the hill provided cover and a current advantage. But it was impossible to know whether the size of the enemy force was sufficient to overrun their position if they decided to attack en mass. Paul chattered as he moved past the men. "Good job…way to go…reload while you have the chance…keep your grenades within reach…they'll try it again…we have to be ready."

The mortar barrage had not let up. Shells continued to crash in and around the bridge as its defenders hunkered down in their defensive positions. No serious damage had been done to the bridge yet, but it seemed only a matter of time before one of the incoming rounds found its target. The English major didn't want to wait for that to happen. He found Paul at the perimeter.

"Leftenant, a word please."

"Certainly, Sir."

"Have your men fall back to the bridge. My Sergeant Major Adams will position them."

"But Sir, our boys did a good job of stopping their initial assault."

"No argument there, Cassidy, but right now I'm more concerned with that damned shelling. If the bridge is destroyed, our boys' advance tomorrow will come to a screeching halt. But if Jerry thinks he can get close enough to the bridge to take it back, he won't shell his own troops."

"Good idea, Major," Paul replied. Then an idea formed in his mind and jumped immediately to his lips. "Say, how about a little insurance?"

"Meaning?"

"My platoon will fall back as you say. But while the Germans are moving forward, I'll take a couple of two-man teams and circle behind them. Maybe we can knock out their mortars for good and help with some rear guard action."

"We have no way of knowing what kind of force multiplier

they have there. You could run into more than you can handle."

"If that's the case we'll hustle back down."

"Worth a try, Leftenant. Select your teams and have the rest of your men follow Sergeant Major Adams. And good luck to you."

Paul called the squad leaders over and told them to have their men follow the Sergeant Major back to the bridge. Then he told the first-squad leader to have Cross and O'Byrne report to him. When Riley and Brendon came over, he had Sergeant Johnson join them.

"The platoon's falling back to help defend the bridge. Our job's to decommission those German mortars. Cross, you'll come with me. We'll go around the left flank and take out whatever mortar teams we see. Sergeant Johnson, you take O'Byrne with you, head around the right flank and do the same. If we're lucky enough to take any machine guns, we may be able to get the enemy in a crossfire. They won't be able to go to the bridge or turn back."

Johnson asked, "What if we find more than we bargained for up there, Lieutenant?"

"Then beat it back down and help the guys at the bridge. It's a judgment call, Sergeant. Evaluate the situation and make your decision. We'll make ours."

Turning to Brendon, Johnson said, "You heard the man, Private. Let's move out."

A half-smile and a head nod passed between Riley and Brendon before they headed in opposite directions. Paul seemed to sense the concern between the two friends. As they headed left, he said to Riley, "O'Byrne will be okay, Sergeant Johnson knows what he's doing."

"He's a pro, alright," Riley responded.

"And you're a crack shot," Paul said. "That's why I wanted you with me. This way both teams have an advantage."

"You lead, I'll follow, Sir. I'm with you all the way."

Moving as fast as they could, while making sure they were

taking a wide enough tack to avoid the main force, they headed round and up the hill. The primary assault hadn't begun yet, but it could start at any minute. Each team could still hear the mortar rounds falling. Their silence would likely be followed by volleys of gunfire as the Germans attacked.

Sergeant Johnson and Brendon reached the ridge first. As they did, the repetitive thump, whistle, and explosions stopped. For what seemed like minutes, there was only stillness. Then a shout of "Attakieren!" was followed with a crescendo of small arms fire announcing the assault.

"Stay with me," Johnson told Brendon as he picked up the pace and covered ground quickly, making his way along the rocky hillside. Brendon did as he was told. The last thing he wanted was space between him and the guy who actually seemed to know what he was doing. Then suddenly, the sergeant stopped on a dime and dropped to his knee. Brendon did the same. Johnson reached back with one arm, grabbed his teammate by the shoulder and pulled him up next to him.

Whispering, he said, "Just off to the right there…see them…near that rock."

Peering through the darkness, Brendon was just able to make out silhouettes of two soldiers about forty yards ahead of them. He nodded affirmation that he had made visual contact.

"We go on our bellies from here," Johnson said. "Side by side. I don't want you getting in a hurry to pop them and shoot me instead. When we get close enough, I'll let you know which one I'm taking. You aim at the other."

"Okay, Sarge," was all Brendon could get out before Johnson was on his belly moving out.

As he inched along, moving forward on his elbows and knees, Brendon knew he had to do his part. He couldn't let Johnson down. He couldn't let Lieutenant Cassidy down. He couldn't let himself down. There was no relying on a platoon of men around him. There were only those two silhouettes getting closer and closer. At least one of which he'd have to kill.

The craggy hillside scraped his chest as Brendon moved forward. More than once his elbow landed on a sharp rock and it was all he could do to keep from uttering an involuntary expletive. But he held it in, and he managed to keep up with the sergeant who seemed to slither like a snake up the rocky grade. When they were within twenty yards, the stock of Brendon's rifle clipped the side of a boulder he was passing. It made an unnatural sound.

"Wie bitte?" one of the silhouettes uttered, turning in their direction. He was reaching out to get his rifle when the first of Johnson's two rounds struck him mid center. Brendon immediately raised up on his elbow and leveled his weapon on the other soldier. Before he could squeeze the trigger he saw his target fly straight back, felled by two more rounds from the sergeant's rapid fire.

Johnson was already on his feet and moving toward them when he said, "Off your ass, soldier. You just gonna lay there all night?"

Scrambling to his feet, Brendon hustled behind the sergeant wondering if he had indeed frozen at the last minute or whether Johnson was simply out of his league when it came to soldiering. When he got to the Germans he found out.

"You make sure they're dead, private, I'll take care of the mortar."

Brendon stood over one of the fallen soldiers staring intently at the downed man. Staring too long for Johnson's comfort.

"I don't want you to examine them, I want you to put a bullet in each of their hearts. And do it quickly. We're moving out of here fast."

Earlier in the night, Brendon had watched members of the other squad take on the same task. Now it was his turn. He went to the first soldier who was lying face up. *Just looking, the guy appeared seriously dead,* Brendon thought. But he put his rifle just above the German's heart, held his breath and fired. No movement. But he had done as he was told. The second man was lying face down. Brendon was about to take the barrel of his rifle and roll him over when Johnson grabbed him by the arm.

"Don't turn him over, Private. If he's lying on a pistol and he ain't all the way dead, you could be. Just put one there. Right there below his helmet, in the back of his neck. If that doesn't kill him then he doesn't deserve to die. Do it, now!"

He did. And the German's gullet splattered over the tops of Brendon's boots. He didn't have time to wipe them off.

"Good shot, Private. Now let's get the hell out of here. I'm about to drop a grenade down that mortar pipe. And we don't want to be here when it goes off."

On the far side of the hill, Paul and Riley took longer to reach their objective. They spotted a mortar crew about fifty yards from where they were crouching. But these Germans were neither reloading nor taking a defensive position. They were obviously embroiled in a heated argument about something. Standing and facing each other, one was using his index finger to poke the other in the chest while jawing like an angry mule.

"I can take them from here, Lieutenant," Riley said.

"Are you sure, Cross? We're looking at their profiles and it's still pretty damn dark."

"I can drop them, Lieutenant. I'll take the one on the right. When he falls, the other man will probably pause in shock before bolting. I should be able to get him too."

"I'll take a bead on the other one," Paul said. "The one on the left. We'll get ready, and I'll fire when I hear your retort."

"Okay," Riley answered, "but if you miss, miss to your left. When the one on the right goes down, yours will try to run away in the opposite direction. He may run right into your shot."

"Okay, tell me when you're ready," Paul said.

"Take aim, now," Riley answered. "And get ready to fire when you hear me say one. Got it?"

"I'm ready," Paul responded.

Riley aimed and said, "Three...Two...One."

The rifle went off in perfect synchronization with Riley's last word. His bullet knocked the man on the right off his feet. The other German froze for just an instant, then turned to run away from his fallen comrade. Paul anticipated his motion by too much and his shot zipped past the soldier's face. He turned on his heel quickly and started back in the other direction like a tin duck in a shooting gallery. When he did, Riley's shot felled him.

When they reached the two, one was obviously dead and one was breathing heavily, blood darkening his gray tunic. Paul looked at Riley and almost spoke. Then he pulled his sidearm from its holster and fired one round point blank into the dying man's heart. After which, they quickly destroyed the mortar and started back down the hill.

Neither team found a machine gun emplacement they could overcome or a weapon they could commandeer to get the Germans in a crossfire. But they didn't need to. Halfway back they saw the enemy begin to take fire from their flanks as well as from the bridge across the River Anape. The cavalry had arrived in the form of the remaining platoons from Bravo Company. The Germans, caught in the open, were taking a terrible shellacking from fire on three sides. They quickly realized the futility of their situation and retreated in haste back up the hill. The bridge at Ponte Grand was now securely in the hands of Allied forces. With the coming of the sun, it would stand ready to help the Allied invasion make its way north. A key objective had been achieved. An important battle had been won. A virgin group of GIs had tasted their first blood. But as Sergeant Johnson had said prophetically, it was only the beginning.

Chapter 24

Los Angeles

Opportunities are what you make of them. That's the way Felix saw it. He hadn't really made the most of his when he was in front of the camera, but he earnestly believed that Gwen just might. And this was an opportunity from which much could be made. It wasn't a starring role. Far from it. It wasn't even a major supporting role. But it was a role ripe with scene-stealing possibilities. Who could possibly keep looking at the older male character actor when a young, voluptuous beauty was slinking across the screen?

It was however, far from a sure thing. The part required an actress as well as a figure. An important director was at the helm. The casting profile called for a strikingly beautiful young woman, wise to the ways of the world yet not embittered by them. A girl who knew her place and wasn't embarrassed by it. An angelic seductress, who roused male passions simply by walking across a parlor and stretching out on the sofa to read a magazine. Understated, understanding, undemanding. Without ever asking, she'd cause her aging provider to plot abandonment of his loving, but chronically ill wife. The woman he knew in his heart he should be committed to. And of course, it would be his undoing.

The bleached Los Angeles sky had turned a turquoise twilight as Felix waited for Gwen to emerge from the pool house. After tanning in the late afternoon, she had taken a quick swim and dashed inside to change quickly and join him for white wine on the patio.

"I've gotten them to agree to a screen test," he said rather offhandedly.

"A screen test. For a couple of lines, a tight dress and high heels?"

"It's a good deal more than that this time, my dear. It's a potential role in *The Concrete Caverns.*"

"*The Concrete Caverns*? That cops and robbers movie the columnists have been writing about? The one that Jules Hobart is supposed to direct? I thought it was mainly an all-male cast. Tough guys, mostly."

"Mostly. But not entirely. One of the supporting characters is an older lawyer who appears accomplished and successful to the outside world, but who, in reality, is virtually broke. He agrees to act as a go-between for the thieves and their fence. In reality, he's planning to pocket the ill-gotten gains himself."

"I don't think I'd be very convincing as an older lawyer," Gwen joked.

"The part is his mistress. It could be a breakthrough for you."

"Are there a lot of lines?"

"Enough. Just enough for the right person."

"And you really think I could be the right person, Felix?"

"Potentially, my dear. Potentially."

"When's the test? What do I need to do to prepare?"

"How much do you want this part, Gwen?"

"Well, I guess I really want it. I mean…if you think it's right for me. You know so much more about these things than I do."

"I think it just might be the culmination of what we've begun together, dear. It might very well be the springboard to major roles. Perhaps, even leading roles."

"Then I want it, Felix. I really want it. For you, as much as me. I owe you so much."

"You asked when the test is. It's in two weeks. You also asked what you'd need to do to prepare. Quite a lot, I think."

Gwen put her glass of wine down. "I'm up to the challenge. What do I need to do?"

Felix put his glass down as well. "My dear, have you ever

made love to an older man?"

"What?"

"I assume you've had some sexual experience. A woman as lovely as you. Has it all been with boys, or young men?"

This is it, Gwen thought. It had been in the back of her mind ever since she became a fixture in Felix's pool house. Everything he had done for her, all the ways he had helped develop her and bring her along, it had all been leading up to this, she thought. *Nothing is free in life,* she told herself. *We all have to pay for what we get in one way or another.* But was this some sort of blackmail? Was he merely dangling this opportunity in front of her to see if she'd submit to him for what might lie ahead rather than what he had done for her already? Confused, and after a pause more pregnant than it should have been, she replied.

"I'm not a virgin. If that's what you're asking, Felix. Who I've been with is really my business. Isn't it?"

"Gwen, I want you to listen closely to what I'm going to say to you. Let me finish before you respond. Can you do that?"

"Yes. I can. Go ahead."

Felix reached over and took both of Gwen's hands in his. Then he began to speak slowly, softly, directly. "Gwen, physically, you possess everything that is needed for this role. Your beauty, your natural grace, the charm you exude by simply being yourself... it's perfect for what this role demands. But it also demands an understanding of life, and what goes on in life...what really goes on...between men and women. Whatever sexual encounters or relationships you have had up to this point, have only shown you one facet of life. The woman who plays this role, needs to have experience in her eyes, her smile, the way she touches a man's shoulder or refills his glass. She needs to convince audiences that she knows the difference between passion for a younger man and compassion for an older one. If she hasn't experienced both, she'll never be able to pull it off."

Gwen started to say something, then realized she didn't know what to say. But Felix had only paused for a moment. He wasn't finished.

"Gwen, for the next two weeks, I want you to live here as my mistress, not just my protégé. I want you to experience what a more mature man brings to your life and your bed. I promise never to hurt you, and never to make you feel less than you are…an incredibly beautiful, desirable woman. And I want you to experience what your feelings are for me. Whether they're kindness, pity, repulsion or regret, I want you to soak them in and examine everything you feel within yourself. You should also know there are no strings attached whatsoever. After the screen test, whether you get the role or not, we can go back to life just as it has been up to this point. I will continue to do everything I can to advance your career in any way I can."

Felix let go of her hands. "Now, you may respond."

A tear was wavering at the corner of Gwen's eye. For now, it was holding fast. But it might not for long. She reached over, picked up her wine glass, and took a drink to steady her nerves. Then she spoke.

"Felix…you didn't say what would happen if I said no."

"If you say no, my dear, nothing will happen. We will continue just as we are. Your career will continue to progress. As to where it will lead eventually, I know not. You can even take the screen test without my suggested arrangement. But you won't get the role. You won't be ready for it."

The tear lost its footing and trickled down Gwen's cheek as she said, "It seems unfair, Felix. It seems…I don't know…a bit like blackmail, you know. You dangle an exciting possibility in front of me…then you tell me it comes with a cost. A cost that might make me feel so much less of myself."

"Life is seldom fair," he responded. "And all our decisions are eventually paid for one way or another."

"But…why didn't you just come out and ask me to marry you?"

"Your question is an example of why you wouldn't get the role, Gwen. It reveals you're still looking at life through an unfinished prism."

"Two weeks? And after the test we can go back to the way it was…I mean…the way it's been?"

"If you desire."

A flood of emotions careened throughout Gwen's mind and heart. She had felt this day would come, but now that it had, and the way that it had, she was unsure what to do. She had never really been sure. Like a child, she had hoped her dream would continue to unfold the way it had. But like a woman, she knew that was a fantasy. Gwen steadied herself as best she could.

"A minute ago…you said I'd be able to examine what my feelings are for you. You mentioned kindness, pity…I think you also said repulsion and regret. But you never mentioned love, Felix. Why not?"

"I harbor no illusions that you could love me, dear. Not now or in the future. The younger women you see with older men in Hollywood…they're only baubles. The young girls know it. Even if the old men don't. I'm a realistic man, Gwen."

"So…what you're telling me…is that you're doing this for some…I don't know…some educational purpose. Instead of acting lessons, you'd be giving me life…or mistress lessons. Is sex all that clinical to you, Felix? Does it have nothing to do with how you feel about me?"

"It has everything to do with how I feel about you. That's why I suggested it. That's why I say it can end with the screen test. That's why, whatever happens, it will never stand in the way of your future."

"But, I can't help it, Felix. If I'm to do something like this…even if it's for only two weeks, I have to know. I have to know how you really feel about me."

"Why, my dear, I thought it would have been patently obvious by now. I've loved you from the moment I first laid eyes on you."

Chapter 25

Chicago

For some time now, Hightower's business had been booming. It wasn't that the drug store had made a radical change in their prices, their décor, or their advertising. It was undeniably due to the press coverage they received since their own Jillian McIntyre had been splashed across virtually every edition of Chicago's newspapers as the pistol-packing soda jerk who served fire and brimstone to gun-toting crooks on the south side. People came pouring in every day wanting to meet and shake the hand of the heroine who had blasted the bad guys and saved both customers' and employees' lives. At least that's the way the fourth estate so picturesquely put it.

Mr. Hightower was so impressed with what Jillian had done, and with all the new business the publicity was bringing in, that he immediately gave her a raise, though not a bonus, and promoted her to Assistant Manager, a position that didn't even exist before the attempted robbery. He also insisted on taking a picture of Jillian posing as if she were blowing smoke off the barrel of her father's revolver. Then he had it framed, autographed, and displayed prominently above the lunch counter. Everyone who came in the drug store and saw the picture, asked if Jillian was there. Hightower had given all his counter staff specific instructions to say that Jillian was now a member of management and while she wasn't available to meet customers, an autographed eight by ten glossy photo, like the one residing over the counter, could be purchased for a mere twenty-five cents. The number of takers was amazing. It was safe to say that Jillian and Hightower's Drug Store now rivaled the White Sox as the number one attraction on the near south side. It was also safe to say that the only member of Hightower's staff who wasn't predisposed to continual promotion of Jillian's derring-do was Jillian herself.

Since the dramatic event unfolded, she had thrown herself into the new duties and responsibilities with which Mr. Hightower had entrusted her. Organization of inventory, juggling of staff schedules, and general oversight of the drug store's operations became not only her daily routine but also her way of coping with all that had transpired. When her father had asked why she happened to take his gun to work that fateful day, she simply said she had a premonition that something bad was going to happen. He, being a religious man, took it as divine intervention and accepted her response without question. She led her coworkers to believe that she always packed heat in her purse and based on the outcome of that particular evening, they found no reason to believe otherwise. When the police questioned her regarding any knowledge of the inept hooligans, she merely replied that she thought she might have seen them in the store once or twice prior to the holdup. This too was accepted as gospel since it was then much easier for them to quickly close the case.

Keeping everything bottled up inside, however, can be a prescription for paralysis, especially in one as naturally communicative as Jillian. She needed an outlet and she found it in Brendon. While she felt she couldn't tell anyone else about what had truly gone on prior to the confrontation, she freely unburdened her soul in letter after letter to her soldier far away. She had no way of knowing when, or even if, he'd ever receive the letters she wrote. But sharing her innermost secrets provided a catharsis that was badly needed.

She told Brendon the whole story. How she met the two and how they took her to Brendon's parents so she could get his address. Their subsequent attempt to blackmail her into helping them with the robbery. Her determination to solve the problem she had gotten herself into. She told Brendon she didn't really know what she was going to do that night. She just reacted, and it all happened the way it did. It seemed like a dream to her now, she told him. Just something she'd never wholly remember, yet something she'd definitely never forget.

She also said the police had her look at some mug shots to see if she could identify the robber who got away. She didn't see anyone she recognized and they told her not to worry about it. They said chances are—since he reacted the way he did that night—it was highly unlikely she'd ever see or hear from him again. He showed what he was made of when he took off and ran.

Jillian wanted to believe that. She wanted to believe that Ian Donovan was out of her life forever. But for some reason she couldn't seem to shake, she didn't believe it. She was sorry her other shots had missed him, and she had a nagging feeling at some point in the future, she'd have to deal with him again. But she didn't tell Brendon that. She was determined she'd never send him a letter that didn't end on a positive note. She'd never say anything that might cause him to worry about her or things back home. Surely he had more than enough to worry about, wherever he was.

Chapter 26

Apennine Mountains

After a less than stellar beginning, the Allied Campaign in Italy was beginning to go as the generals had envisioned. The Italian government agreed to an armistice, and most of their armed forces surrendered immediately. The Germans did not. They were prepared to defend the country without assistance from their timid Axis partners, even though only three divisions were available to immediately oppose the entire Eighth Army. The rest of the German forces in Italy were busy disarming the Italians and making sure Axis stockpiles of weapons didn't fall into the invaders' hands. So the Americans were able to move up the eastern coast relatively quickly. They soon took the port of Bari and key airfields around Foggia.

But what appeared easy when measured in miles and days, was expensively purchased with the blood and sacrifice of soldiers in the field. Generals may have been fixated on campaigns and battles, but these conflicts had no meaning to the dogfaces that had to win them. The enlisted man's only concern was the firefight he was in, or the combat to come. His goals were infinitely less strategic and much more primal. Shoot before you get shot. Kill them before they kill you. Do whatever you have to do to stay alive.

After the bridge had been secured, Bravo Company joined the main force moving toward the central part of the country where natural conditions provided more advantages to defenders than aggressors. The Apennine Mountains formed a spine along the Italian peninsula. Crests and peaks, some over three thousand feet high, provided easily defendable positions. Difficult terrain slowed the pace of the Allied advance significantly. Hills and mountains would have to be taken on foot with the enemy dug in and waiting. The element of surprise was no longer in play. Victory or defeat was now about who wanted Italy the most—the Allies or the Nazis.

There's a reason it's called infantry, Brendon thought. *We sure as hell do a lot of walking.* Since landing in Sicily, third platoon had humped it from the wrong drop zone, through woods, over hills, to the river, and now along a rutted road barely wide enough to contain two vehicles passing in opposite directions. Vehicles, Brendon noted, like deuce-and-a-halfs full of soldiers getting a bumpy, but relatively easy ride while his outfit had to tramp up the seemingly endless grade.

"I don't get it," Brendon squawked, "we're supposed to be the elite unit around here and we walk while those guys ride. Doesn't seem right, if you ask me."

"They'll be dodging bullets a lot sooner than we will," Riley reminded him. "Can't believe you're in a big hurry for that."

"A valid point, my friend. My brain agrees with you but I'm not so sure about my feet."

"Just keep walking. We'll get where we're going soon enough. Then we'll probably wish we were all out hiking again."

Complaining about their situation, whatever it happened to be, was more than a way to pass the time. It was a substitute for talking about what was really on all their minds, but on none of their lips. Who would survive? There had been too much to do the night they jumped into Sicily to give much thought to their comrades who had never gotten past the drop zone. Garza and Braverman hadn't been what Brendon considered close friends. But they were guys he had trained, eaten and lived with. Then, just like that, they had each bought it in the initial drop. *Maybe that was better,* Brendon thought. Maybe it was better to have gone that way than the way Allison went at the bridge. Allison had been their squad leader. He hadn't asked for the job. But he took on the responsibility without trying to duck it. Brendon remembered that when he and Sergeant Johnson eventually scrambled back to the bridge and found Lieutenant Cassidy and Riley had beaten them back, they were standing over Allison as the medic worked on him. He had caught two rounds in the chest. Blood was bubbling from his mouth as he tried to breathe, speak, and keep from crying all at the same time. *He was a regular fellow,* Brendon reflected. Just your average Joe from Indiana who had his insides shot out trying to pick up ammunition for the rest of his squad. It took him a while to die. *Too long,* Brendon thought. *Quick. Quick was the way to get it, if it had to happen.* One moment your lights are on, the next they're out. Then you're out of it. Out of the anxiety, the fear, the ridiculous idea of trying to live moment to moment as if you weren't in the middle of a world gone insane. Yes, Garza and Braverman had it better than Allison, the lucky bastards. Good for them. Maybe they never even realized what happened. Realizing where you were and what you were doing would drive you nuts if you dwelled on it. That's why you tried to stop thinking about Garza and Braverman and Allison. That's why you never talked about them. You never brought up the ones who weren't there anymore. You just found something to squawk about. Anything at all. Like walking up a hill when others were riding. *That's what I'll think about,* Brendon decided. *That's what I'll think about for now.*

Bravo Company made camp mid-afternoon three miles south of the Volutuno Line, Germany's first and southernmost placement of four heavily manned defensive positions that had been set up to halt the Allied advance toward Rome. Riley, whom Paul had promoted to squad leader after Allison's death, had been right. They could hear the sounds of battle already underway as they set up mess tents, a field hospital, command headquarters, and personnel bivouac areas. There was no way the enlisted men could know when they'd be sent up to the front line, so they busied themselves with card games, equipment cleaning, heated conversations about arcane baseball statistics, or anything and everything that would keep their minds off what they'd be facing in the hours to come. One activity was head and shoulders above the rest when it came to taking their thoughts away from impending danger, but because of time, distance, and logistics, soldiers never knew when they'd have the chance to participate in it. Luckily, this was one of those times, heralded by the shout that sent them swarming like locusts descending on a wheat field toward the GI who sang out, *"Mail Call!"*

Letters, packages, and boxes were torn into with the eagerness of men starved for proof that the world they remembered still existed. The ink-stained lines, crumpled paper, and crushed cardboard were proof positive that there were still places where people wore clothes that weren't only green or gray, where your history with those around you went much further back than boot camp, where the human beings you met round the next corner weren't waiting there to kill you.

Connecting men on the move with their mail was an inexact science at best. Soldiers would often get four or five letters at once from the same person. They quickly learned to check the postmark of each so they could read them in the order they were written. And while any missive from home was enthusiastically opened, there was always the momentary anticipation of bad news rather than good. The hardships faced by those at home, the dissolution of a relationship, the passing of a loved one. That's why most read their letters in what little privacy they could find. Spontaneous emotions were hard to hide.

Brendon couldn't believe his luck. In addition to a letter from his parents, there were at least three from Jillian McIntyre. Jillian? Jilly? His Jilly? The soda jerk of his dreams? *It must be,* he told himself. *But how did she find out he was in the service? How did she learn where to write him? Oh,* he paused. *Does she know why I'm in the service? Does she know what I did? But wait,* he thought. *There are three letters from her. If she knew what happened...if she was shocked by it...if she was as disappointed in him as he had been in himself...surely she wouldn't have written multiple times.* Knowing the enlisted men's mess tent was empty this time of day, he hurried there to devour every word.

Riley opened the letter from his mother without apprehension. She had been a faithful and consistent chronicler of events, or the lack thereof, in Pilot Hill since he left for boot camp. She always began her letters the same way. *How are you, Riley? We are fine.* But this one started differently. As was her way, she got right to the point.

Dear Riley, your father had an accident. He fell from an oil derrick. He has been in the hospital for some time now. There was a question as to whether he'd ever walk again. But he's able to stand now, and move slowly forward with the help of a cane. The doctor has said he will never be able to work in the oil fields again. Or perhaps anywhere else, for that matter. He says it is virtually a miracle your father can stand and walk on his own. The high school was kind enough to give me a job in the cafeteria. So we'll have some income to sustain us. I guess we should thank heaven that he's even alive. The Lord works in mysterious ways. I hope this letter finds you well. I pray each night for your safety and for the safety of the young men you are with. I know he'll take care of you. He has plans for you, son. Plans for a life far different than your father's and mine. That's how I know he'll protect you. Try not to worry. We'll get by. It's what people like us do. We both miss you and long for the day you return.

Your loving mother.

* * *

In the officer's mess, Paul sat alone, drinking a cup of coffee. The letter from his parents, unopened, half in and half out of his breast pocket. There would be time to read it later, he thought. For now he wanted to concentrate on the briefing he had just received. He wanted to be sure he knew exactly what to do, what to say, and how to act when he told his platoon they'd soon be moving up to the front.

Chapter 27

Los Angeles

The Concrete Caverns was a verifiable hit. Not only did it have the studio bigwigs bragging about their box office returns, it also had the critics handing out plaudits left and right. A gripping, taught melodrama in the classic tradition, one said. Another lauded the director's sure hand at the tiller. While still another waxed poetic about the exceptional performances of the actors who freely gave themselves to the ensemble rather than chewing the scenery when each had the chance. There seemed to be something for everyone to like about this hardboiled look at tough guys in tense situations. Something for each viewer to find exciting in his or her own separate way. But there was also something that struck a collective chord in all who sat in the audience. Something that fans and critics and even cast and members of the crew couldn't deny. That girl…that blonde who played the aging lawyer's mistress…wow, was she something!

Gwen was on cloud nine. She had never received such notices before. Of course, she had never really received any notices before. All the other walk-ons and one-liners and pretty-girl-in-the-crowd roles she had done previously never rated mentioning at all. Now, she was the blonde everyone was talking about. Who was she? Where did she come from? Why could no one remember seeing her before? These were the questions the fan magazines and critics wanted to know. Pressman had been right. The role wasn't really that big. But it was big enough to launch a real career if it were done well. And Gwen had nailed it.

True to his word, Pressman had volunteered to return to their initial agent/client relationship at the end of their two-week arrangement. But Gwen had told him she was happier together.

Their lovemaking wasn't passionate, but it was tender and warm and in a way, loving. It helped ease the loneliness of being far from home and the fear that she wouldn't live up to the confidence Pressman had shown in her, or the demands of actually being an actress, and not just another pretty face. With her work on the film, and the continuing publicity and promotional engagements that were arranged for her, she had little time to question the morality of her choice. She was building a career. They were giving each other kindness. No one was being tricked or hurt. Surely there were far worse ways to live a life. At least for now.

As the war neared its third year, support for America's men in uniform remained high. All wanted to do whatever they could to lend assistance and support. Hollywood was no exception. In addition to making movies encouraging patriotism and perseverance, studios also made their contract players, even their stars, available for special films and personal appearances. Pressman knew this kind of participation was not only the right thing to do, but also good for one's career. That's why he volunteered Gwen's participation at the opening of the newly completed Hollywood USO Center. Coming on the heels of Gwen's recent cinematic success, it was an excellent opportunity to get even more positive press for the up and coming actress and to mingle with Los Angeles high society simultaneously.

In addition to serving coffee and soda to the servicemen who had been lucky enough to be detailed to this community event, Gwen also posed for pictures with each sailor or GI who requested one—which was basically every soldier, sailor, and airman. While she worked with the servicemen, Pressman worked the crowd.

"Mr. and Mrs. Cassidy, hello. I'm Felix Pressman. We met at the fundraiser for this facility. The one you so graciously held at your home."

Paul's mother remembered. Paul's father acted as if he did.

"Oh yes," she said, "Mr. Pressman. You remember Mr. Pressman, Charles. He's an agent. A talent agent."

"Pressman? Oh yes, sure, Pressman. We meet so many people at events like this, you know."

"I do know. I also know that without the kind philanthropy of individuals like you and your lovely wife, there wouldn't be nearly as many fine facilities for our young men and women in uniform to relax and enjoy themselves when they have some time of their own."

"Well, we do what we can," Paul's mother said. "Our son's serving overseas, you know."

"Yes, I believe you mentioned that when we met. Have you heard from him?"

"He writes when he can," Paul's father said. "Of course he can't say much. Nothing about where he is, or what he's really doing. Their letters get censored, you know. To make sure no secrets are revealed inadvertently."

"Well, if he takes after his parents, I'm sure he's doing a fine job. As are they all."

"Mr. Pressman," Paul's mother said. "Weren't you with a striking young lady at our home?"

"Indeed, I was, Mrs. Cassidy. Gwen Taylor, a protégé and client of mine. In fact, she's here tonight…making a personal appearance in support of the USO."

"Didn't we just see her in a movie that came out recently? Wasn't she in that gangster picture?"

"*The Concrete Caverns*. Yes, she was."

"Didn't I tell you, Charles? Didn't I say, we know that young lady. We've met her."

"Did you, dear? I really can't recall," Paul's father replied.

"I'll ask her to stop by and say hello," Pressman volunteered. "Just as soon as she's finished taking pictures with the servicemen."

"That may be a while, from the looks of things," Paul's mother said.

"Yes, she's quite popular with the young men, isn't she?"

"And she was very good in…uh…that picture you mentioned," Paul's father added.

"Yes. Thank you. She did a marvelous job. Not only has she gotten excellent reviews, by the way, but a lot more scripts with larger roles are starting to come her way too."

Involved as they were in the conversation about Gwen, they paid no heed to the little man who had entered the USO hall moments earlier. Neither did anyone else, for that matter. He was the sort of fellow people see without seeing. Slight, stoop-shouldered, dressed in a suit that had seen far better days, scuffed shoes, and a battered fedora pulled low on his head—he was someone who never garnered a second glance. The first seemed to tell you more than you really wanted to know.

The man wound his way through the crowd more like an apparition than a flesh and blood human being. He would step this way and that to avoid conversations that were ending and people who were moving quickly away without really watching where they were going. He was watching, however. As he moved toward them, he was watching the older couple and the elegant man still apparently deep in conversation.

"Say, Pressman, did I tell you that I was involved in the war effort beyond just this sort of thing?"

"I believe you did, Mr. Cassidy. I think you mentioned something about an organization…now what was the name of it again?"

"The War Relocation Authority. I'm the head of a District you know, and—"

"I know," the little man said, now standing within arm's reach of the trio. The voice bore the hint of an accent as he repeated, "I know."

All three turned to look at the individual who had just spoken. Of course no one seemed to know him. He didn't appear to be the type of person any of them would ever know.

"Did you say something, Sir? Were you addressing me?" Paul's father asked.

"I know who you are. I know what you do."

"My work with the War Relocation Authority? You're familiar with that, are you?"

The man's left arm came slowly up and removed the fedora, revealing close-cropped gray hair that once was black. The salt and pepper look matched the mustache above his lip. His small nose and black eyes revealed a not unpleasant face. A not unpleasant Japanese face.

"I am very familiar with your work, Mr. Cassidy. I corresponded with you. I even spoke with you during my interview. Later I tried to correspond again, but you never replied."

"Well, look here, fellow…you can't expect me to remember everyone I meet, now can you? So…what are you doing here, then? Is there something I can do for you?"

"You've already done a lot for me, Mr. Cassidy. You helped me lose my job, my home, my garden, my friends, my privacy too. One doesn't really think about losing one's privacy, until it happens. Then you think about it all the time."

"Well," Paul's father started to answer, a bit unsure of exactly what to say. "You know, Sir, that in these turbulent times…these dangerous times…we all have to take measures…temporary measures, you know…temporary measures for the safety of—"

The little man interjected before Cassidy could finish. "You helped me lose my wife too, Mr. Cassidy. A loss that is in no way temporary. She became sick in the camp where we were assigned. Very sick. The camp doctor said only an operation in Los Angeles could save her. We petitioned the camp personnel. We petitioned our elected representatives. We even petitioned you, Mr. Cassidy. You never responded."

"Listen, my good man," Paul's father began. "There are rules and regulations for this sort of thing. This is hardly the time or place to be airing any grievance you might think—"

"She died, Mr. Cassidy. She died. Death is not temporary, Mr. Cassidy. Death is permanent."

Paul's mother was saying, "Can't someone just get security, please?"

Pressman turned to look for a policeman or an MP or whoever was supposed to be on duty. When he did, the little man drew his right hand from his coat pocket. The hand held a gun. He brought his left arm across quickly and covered the gun with his hat. Then he fired two shots that actually set his hat aflame before entering Charles Cassidy's abdomen. The flames frightened him so that he threw it to the floor as if in fear of being burned. An action that would later strike Pressman as odd when he replayed the scene in his mind. Why would a man committing suicide be concerned with slightly burning his hand? Reflex perhaps, the agent would conclude.

Before his hat hit the floor, the little man brought the gun up to his temple and fired. Blood sprayed from his head and spattered Paul's mother's shoulder and cheek. Her screams could be heard in the street. It was some time before they could quiet her. Some time long after the big man and the small one lay dead on the floor.

Chapter 28

Chicago

It was prematurely chilly, even for Chicago. Jillian had a shawl over her shoulders that she kept in her office for those times when it was a bit drafty. This was one of those times. She was totaling the day's receipts as she always did before closing and going home for the night. It had been a typical day. Lots of people in and out of the drugstore. Mr. Hightower in his usual genial mood. The rest of the staff performing their duties with varying degrees of pleasantness. It had been the kind of day that ordinarily would quickly be forgotten. But it would not be an ordinary night.

Her final task finished, Jillian put on her coat, took her purse from the bottom drawer where she kept it, turned off all the lights and locked all the doors. She had a three-block walk to the stop where she always caught the number six twenty-five bus that dropped her off another three blocks from her home. Jillian enjoyed walking at night, especially when the air was crisp as it was this evening. *Chilly is okay,* she thought to herself. *Cold is not. Oh, you get used to it, sure. Living in Chicago you have no other choice. But nobody really liked the cold,* she reasoned. Even the people who had lived here all their lives.

The bus had several people on it this time of night. Kids on dates. People like her, going home from work. People unlike her, older women, who were on their way to work in the big office buildings where they'd spend the next eight hours scrubbing floors, cleaning lavatories and emptying trash. When she looked at women like that, she felt sorry for them. Unlike her mother, who still had a husband who provided for her, they apparently had no one, she assumed. She also felt grateful that she had such a good job and the ability to take care of herself. Independence was a very valuable commodity, she knew. Especially in wartime. As the bus rolled past countless row houses and apartment buildings, Jillian stared at the lights in the windows and wondered how many of the women inside were waiting for their husbands, and brothers, and fathers to come home from the war. How many of them were living hand-to-mouth on only their spouse's military allotment each month. *It must be so hard for them,* she thought. *I do indeed have a lot to be thankful for.*

"Did you say something, dear?" the woman sitting across from her asked.

"Oh, no. It was nothing, sorry," she said, feeling a bit embarrassed about talking to herself. Aloud, apparently.

The bus made its routine stop at the corner and Jillian stepped down carefully as she always did. The three blocks to her home took her past Saint Michael's Catholic Church, Faraday's Hardware Store, and two apartment buildings before spilling onto her quiet tree-lined street of modest houses. There were never very many people out this time of night and even though she was alone, she always felt safe because she was so close to home. But just as Jillian was walking past the alley by the church, her peripheral vision caught sight of some sort of dark blur. There was no time for her head to turn toward it before she felt the force of the blow. It was as if some sort of boulder had been dropped onto her skull just behind her left ear. Heavy and hard, the knife-point pain ricocheted from the spot of impact to just above her eyes, and she immediately felt her knees turn to jelly as dizziness overwhelmed her. She thought she might be sick as she struggled mightily to stay on her feet. Suddenly, she felt herself tumbling forward and then something or someone caught her beneath each arm, steadied her, and pulled her away from the glow of the street lamps and into the darkness of the alley.

Jillian tried to speak but it was hard to form thoughts, much less words. The pain was still crashing through her head and the dizziness hadn't abated. She felt herself roughly leaned against the side of a building, but she couldn't stand by herself. Her legs crumpled and she slid slowly down the wall until she sat on the pavement. Her hand instinctively rose to the point of the most intense pain behind her ear, and when her fingers touched her hair they felt wet and sticky. She tried to bring her hand back in front of her eyes to see what she had touched, but it was too dark and too difficult for her to focus. Then some form that had been standing in front of her, looking tall as a tree trunk in her addled mind, squatted so he was eye to eye with her.

"Hello, sweetheart. Feeling a bit under the weather, are we?"

In the darkness, she still couldn't focus on his facial features, but she recognized the voice. And she knew in her soul it was Ian Donovan.

"Better let me have a look inside that purse, before we get too far along here," he said, wrenching the bag from her hand that had gripped it like a vice when she was first struck. Jillian tried to hold it, but it was no use. There was no longer any strength in her fingers.

"Well, well. No gun this time. Isn't that something? Did you think that enough time had passed, was that it, love? Did you think you didn't have to worry about me anymore?"

She had a hard time making out what he was saying. The ringing in her ears was now matching the pain above her eyes.

"All we wanted was a nice, clean job, you know? A quick in and out. But no, you had to go all Annie Oakley on us. And you killed my friend. Now granted, he was no great shakes as human beings go. But at least, he did what I told him."

His comments were long enough for her to understand this time. And she mumbled, as best she could, a reply. "Shh…should have killed you…too. You…coward."

Ian swung the sap and caught her across the mouth, splitting both lips and sending blood onto her chin and down her throat.

She cried out weakly, unable to muster a scream.

"Still got a smart mouth, huh? Well, now you got a fat one too. Seems like you're getting less and less pretty with each passing second."

Her teeth had cut the inside of her mouth. She bled as she talked through the new wound and the pain still throbbed in her head from the initial blow.

"You…waited. Didn't you? You waited…and…you watched me."

"Sure, I waited," he said. "I waited while I hid out. I had to make sure you weren't going to give my name to the cops. And you didn't, did you? No, you didn't. Cause you didn't want me telling them you were in on it all the time and you just freaked out at the end. You didn't want that, did you?"

"You…ba…bastard!"

"Sticks and stones, my pretty. And yes, I watched. I watched how you went to work every day. And how you came home every night. Hey, consider yourself lucky. I could have done your parents like I said I would. But I figured…maybe this would be better."

Jillian's head was pounding. She was still woozy and now both of her busted lips began to swell. "I'll tell…the cops. This time…I'll tell them. I might not get you…but they will."

"Tell them whatever you want, sweetheart. I'm blowing this town anyway. Got myself some new mates. No cops will be crossing state lines to track me down."

Even with the pain making it feel like her head was about to burst open, even with the taste of her own blood hot in her mouth, Jillian sensed a ray of hope in what Ian had just said.

"You mean…you're not…going to kill me?"

"I should, you know. I should kill you because you killed my friend and you tried to kill me. But I'm not going to do that. I'm just going to leave you with a little something to remember me by."

Then Ian reached up to Jillian's collar with both hands. He dug his fingers along the top of her blouse and yanked hard as he could. It all ripped open. She could feel the chilly night air on the bare skin above her bra. Unable to marshal the voice to cry out, and with her head feeling as if it was on the verge of exploding, Jillian began to cry and pray simultaneously. "Hail Mary, full of grace, the lord is with thee." But when Ian jerked and pulled her skirt and underwear down to her ankles, Jillian felt that faint glimmer of hope, that had surged within her only moments earlier, turn to stone.

Chapter 29

Monte Cassino

Paul had outlined the mission to the men of his platoon. When they reached the front, they'd be just below the village of Monte Cassino. The Germans held defensive positions at the top of the hill leading into town. Those positions would have to be knocked out if the Allies were going to pass through and continue their march toward Rome. Air strikes had been pounding the hill for the last couple of hours but the Germans had not been routed, nor had they retreated. As usual, the final push would have to be made by troops on the ground.

Hiking to the embankment that would mark the start of their assault, Brendon couldn't get Jillian's letters out of his mind. *My God,* he thought, *she actually shot Snapper and killed him. And Ian got away, that son of a bitch!* He didn't want to believe he had been involved with thugs like those two, but he knew all too well he had. He couldn't believe Jillian cared enough about him to write and share everything with him—particularly after he left Chicago without telling her anything. *What an incredibly lucky guy I am,* he thought. Then he thought, *what am I saying? I'm walking into a fight for my life. I could be shot, wounded, even blown to hell and gone. God, I hope my luck, if I really do have any, continues to hold.*

Riley felt bad about his mom and dad's situation but he quickly put it out of his mind when orders were given to move up. He knew he couldn't do anything about their situation. He was already sending most of his pay home every month. And if he didn't concentrate on what he had to do during the attack, the next thing his parents received might be a letter from the war office beginning: We regret to inform you.

At the embarkation point, Paul broke the platoon into squads and gave each their own assignments. They'd be moving up the hill in staggered intervals, each sixty seconds apart. There were rocks and craters along the way to provide some cover. But the basic strategy was for each squad to provide cover fire for the squad in front and at the back of it. This meant that the first squad up the hill would be on its own, at least until support moved up behind it.

Sergeant Johnson hurried over to Paul and said, "Want me to take the first squad, Lieutenant?"

Paul didn't hesitate. "No Sergeant, I'll take the advance squad."

"Uh…it might be better, Sir, if you were to stay back here and make sure each squad gets off when it's supposed to."

"That's your job, Sergeant. A platoon leader's job is to lead. If anything happens to me along the way, you'll need to make sure the men keep moving up the hill."

"Whatever you say, Lieutenant. I was just thinking—"

Paul cut him off. "My thinking, Sergeant, is that your experience is more beneficial to these men than any Second Lieutenant's. That's why I want to keep you with the bulk of the platoon. Understood?"

"Understood, Sir."

"However, I'd be more than happy to take any advice you might have for me?"

"Keep your eyes up and your head low, Sir. The second you come under fire, hit the deck and give it back to them. We'll be moving up like clockwork right behind you."

Paul's heart was beating like a toddler turned loose on a Chinese gong, but he managed to keep it from showing when he said, "Will do, Sergeant. See you at the top."

Once the order was given, Riley and Brendon's squad moved out with Paul in the lead. They moved as swiftly as they could, but the incline was steep and their serpentine movement to avoid presenting too easy a target slowed their ascent. A third of the way up the hill the Germans opened fire. Machine gun bullets tore up the earth around them and sent them scrambling for whatever boulder or branch they could get behind or whatever blast crater they could roll into.

"Return fire!" Paul yelled. And each man began to train his fire on the pillbox the Germans had constructed near the top of the hill. The slit in the earth housed a thirty caliber and it was now spewing lead, fire, and hell all around them.

Between bursts, Paul scanned the men in the squad. Riley was behind a boulder, rolling from one side to the next and firing from the prone position each time he'd clear the rock's edge. Brendon had dived into a shell crater that had enough of a lip to provide some measure of defense as he focused his fire on the machine gun nest. One soldier was behind the remains of a tree stump being continuously splintered by fire from atop the hill. It looked like Atkins, Paul thought, but he couldn't be sure. Another squad member, Richardson, Paul believed, was sprawled face down on the hillside. He wasn't moving at all and his weapon was protruding from underneath his body. *Poor bastard,* Paul said to himself, *he must have bought it when they opened up on us.* Morales was the remaining squad member, Paul remembered. *Where the hell was he? Morales had the bazooka, damn it! Where was he?*

"Hold your positions!" Paul yelled, between sporadic strafing from the enemy machine gun. He knew it was too dangerous to try advancing further before the next squad arrived to provide cover. He yelled to Riley, who, at fifteen yards or so, was the closest to him.

"Cross! Cross! Have you seen Morales? Can you see him from where you are?"

Riley rolled to the center of the boulder and looked around. "I think that's him, Sir. I think that's Morales in that crater over there."

Paul looked in the direction Riley was pointing. A soldier was sitting up in the crater. His back was against the dirt wall the shell had excavated. He wasn't moving. Paul couldn't tell if he was alive, dead, wounded, or what.

"I'm going to try to get to him," Paul yelled to Riley. "We need that bazooka. Shout at the other men and let them know. Then count to ten and give me some cover."

Riley did as he was told and when word had been passed, Paul counted then made his break for the crater. Even with the rest of the squad firing on the gun emplacement, rounds came ripping down the hill all around Paul as he scrambled on his belly to get over the edge of the crater as quickly as he could. He anticipated feeling burning pain at any second, but it did not come. He was not hit. Morales was not so lucky. Even though he was sitting up, his torso was soaked with blood. His eyes had rolled back into his head and he simply sat there, holding the bazooka in his lifeless hands.

Staying low, Paul rolled him over on his side, removed his dog tags and pocketed them. Then he pried the young Mexican's fingers from around the wide barrel of the bazooka. This was the weapon they had to have. With no tanks to back them up, they would need the firepower from the high explosive warheads in the shoulder-mounted weapon.

Enemy fire had paused for the moment, but Paul knew the minute he tried to roll out of the crater and hustle back to his position, he'd be the target again. There was no alternative, however. They weren't in range yet for the stovepipe to do its job. He yelled to Riley again.

"Cross, on the count of five, I'm coming out. Cover me again."

"Will do, Lieutenant. Get ready guys, open up on the count of five."

Paul began to count to himself. "One…two…three."

Then a volley of rounds opened up over his head. Not at him, but towards the fortified bunker. It was the next squad, moving up and covering just as they were supposed to. Paul rolled over the side, bazooka in tow, and quickly made his way back to where he had come from, the tip of the initial squad's spear.

Diving behind the rocks that stood as sentries between him and the enemy, Paul hit the ground with heart pounding and chest heaving up and down like pistons in an eight-cylinder engine. He didn't know if it was actual fatigue or acute adrenalin swirling through his system. But whatever it was, he had to pause for a moment to catch his breath. As he lay there, trying to keep from hyperventilating, he realized that the squad he was leading was now short two men, and they still had to get at least a hundred yards farther up the hill for the enemy's machine gun to be within range of the bazooka. Lying on his back, momentarily looking down at his troops moving up rather than the Germans in front of him, he spotted one soldier outdistancing the others. The man was bobbing, weaving, and moving up the side of the hill nimbly as a mountain goat. The closer he got, the more Sergeant Johnson's features came into focus.

"I thought I told you to oversee the rest of the platoon, Sergeant."

"You did Sir. And I did. They've staggered their advance just like you told them to."

"What are you doing here, then?"

"The guys are in good shape. The squad leaders know what they're doing."

"You didn't answer my question."

"Guess I just don't care for bringing up the rear, Sir. The view there never changes."

"We're two men down, Sergeant. Richardson and Morales."

"Only lost two? That's pretty good soldiering, Sir. Know how to use that thing?"

"The stovepipe? It was covered in OCS weapons training, Sergeant."

"Yeah. Well that time you didn't answer my question, Sir."

"I know how to point it and fire it. I don't know how proficient I am," Paul said.

"Let me hump it a while, Sir. You look a little winded. And we still have a ways to go."

"Alright. But pass the word down the line to Cross, O'Byrne, and I think that's Atkins behind that tree stump. Once we have second squad fully in position and ready to lay down cover fire, we're moving up."

"You got it, Sir."

For the next hour, Bravo platoon snaked their way up the hill rock-by-rock and tree-by-tree. They'd dart from one cover position to the next. Each time praying that the rounds exploding around them wouldn't take an arm, or leg, or worse. Brendon managed to reach the cover of a huge oak just as bullets from the German thirty-millimeter tore the bark off it. A shower of shards and splinters sprayed down his arm, two of them impaling themselves in the side of his hand. A shudder ran through Brendon as he realized how close he had just come to buying it. With his good hand shaking as badly as his wounded one, he pulled the wood from his flesh and wrapped his hand with a bandana that had previously been around his neck. *It might not be sanitary,* he thought, *but at least it would stop the bleeding until there was an opportunity for a medic to take a look at it.*

Riley made it a point to move when Paul and Sergeant Johnson did. He figured they knew what they were doing and that it would be harder to be singled out as a target if more than one man was moving at the same time. He still found himself burrowing into the earth like a groundhog when shells started blowing chunks out of the rocks he would hide behind. But doggedly, relentlessly, they kept moving up. Until finally they were within the bazooka's range.

"Cross!" Paul yelled. "Have you got a shot at that gun emplacement from where you are?"

"I can put some rounds in there, Sir. But I'm not sure if they'll hit anyone."

"That's okay. We just need some cover fire to use this."

"Okay, Sir. Let me put in a fresh clip first, alright?"

"Right. We're getting set here. Shout when you're ready."

"Better let me take the shot, Lieutenant, I'm pretty good with one of these things."

"Whoever takes the shot will have to move from behind this boulder to do it, Sergeant."

"That's why they call it war, Lieutenant."

"Ready!" Riley yelled back to them.

"I'll take the shot, Sergeant. You and Cross cover me when I give the go."

"I wouldn't trust that M6 shell, Lieutenant. Those things are pretty unreliable."

"We've only got one M10-A4. White phosphorus."

"Go with that," Johnson said. "If you get it in, the bastards will light up like a Roman Candle. Even if they're not on fire, they'll feel like they are. And if you miss, we'll still have a smoke screen we can move up behind."

Paul yelled to Riley. "Cross, get set. When you see my signal, open up."

Johnson put his hand on Paul's shoulder. "Sir…blow 'em to hell and gone."

With the stovepipe loaded, Paul signaled to Riley. He opened fire and Johnson followed suit. Paul bolted from behind the rock, dropped to one knee and aligned his sights on the German pillbox. Sweat pouring and heart pounding, he let one go. The back blast scorched grass and weeds behind him and the rocket raced forward through the distance like destiny come to call. It smashed into the pillbox, ignited and exploded simultaneously, and sent a white cloud of dust, debris, and God knows what else into the sky. Dense smoke hung in the air denying a clear field of vision to both attackers and defenders. Johnson didn't wait for orders. He sprung from behind the boulder and started running toward the blast scene. Riley, Brendon, and Atkins followed him up the hill. Before he knew it, Paul was on his feet and running too. He was also yelling, "Keep your heads down, damn it! Keep your heads down!"

Johnson came up the left side of the hill and signaled Paul and Brendon to stay to the right. Through the smoke he saw the hole that the shell had torn away in the cement fortification. Then he heard coughing and choking inside. "Stay low," he yelled to Riley and the others. Random pistol fire came from the burning chasm. Muzzle flashes were visible in the dark. Johnson quickly grabbed a grenade from his utility belt, pulled the pin and tossed it through the center of the opening. Seconds later it exploded and belched up another serving of mud, sand, metal and blood.

When the smoke cleared, Paul had caught up with the others. He said, "Keep your weapons ready and your eyes open. That team has had it, and the others are on the run. But they might leave a sniper or two behind. So don't bunch up. Find some cover until the other squad moves up."

As each looked for a measure of protection, Riley said, "Pretty good shot, Lieutenant."

Brendon followed, saying, "Damn good shot, I'd say. What would you say, Sergeant?"

Johnson, whose back was to the others, turned slowly. His hand was at his neck and blood was running between his fingers, the result of a Luger fired wildly by a desperate German choking on phosphorus fumes and fear. "Hell of a shot, I'd say. Almost as good as that damn Kraut's." They were the last words Platoon Sergeant Vince Johnson ever uttered.

Chapter 30

Los Angeles

The Times headline shouted the news in bold letters. HOLLYWOOD CANTEEN MURDER SUICIDE. The article beneath it went on to lament the death of Los Angeles real estate magnate, Charles Cassidy. Tributes from the Chamber of Commerce and the Kiwanis Club extolled the virtues of the civic leader who had been a boon to the community both as an accomplished businessman and a munificent philanthropist. Editors deemed his affiliation with the War Relocation Authority inconsequential in the overall scheme of things, and therefore judiciously left it out of the article.

The perpetrator of this heinous crime, *The Times* went on to say, was identified as Myakka Hiroshi, a one-time professor of economics at the University of California at Los Angeles. Much was made of his Japanese ancestry, through there was no mention that he was, in fact, an American citizen. The article went on to say that he had apparently escaped from a relocation center in Arizona, made his way back to Los Angeles, and committed this random act of savagery mere seconds before taking his own life. The label *madman* was used more than once. And since the individual had dispatched himself, thereby saving the county the expense and scandal of a trial, no further exploration was done, nor mention made, of any other potential motive for his dastardly act.

For weeks following the tragic event, Paul's mother had been in seclusion. Felix Pressman had done his best just after the bloody encounter to help spirit her away from the scene, but she was violently inconsolable, weeping and wailing at ever-rising decibel levels and throwing her body across that of her dead husband until medical personnel engaged bystanders to help restrain her. Felix blamed himself for not reacting more swiftly, or for not recognizing impending violence, or for simply being immobile when faced with inexplicable horror. Logically, he knew the act had been so sudden and devastating that there was really nothing he could have done to stop it. Yet emotionally, he couldn't help but feel a better man might have somehow intervened. Perhaps that's why he continued to follow Mrs. Cassidy's progress—even going so far as to have a personal nurse check in on her daily.

Word of his father's death reached Paul after Bravo Company helped take Monte Cassino. Since the event had occurred at a location with military connections, various chains of command moved the information along swiftly and got it to the Second Lieutenant as quickly as possible. Still, there was no chance of getting leave to return to the States for the funeral or to console his mother. Parents of men in uniform were dying every day somewhere. The business of death in one part of the world couldn't be stopped for the finality of death in another. It simply became one more burden to endure. A burden Paul chose to endure alone.

After some weeks had passed, Felix began calling on Mrs. Cassidy and taking Gwen along. He felt the need to do what he could to revive the socialite's spirits, to any degree possible. And Gwen didn't mind accompanying him as she remembered the Cassidys fondly and she felt Paul's mother enjoyed having a woman to talk to, even if the woman was more a daughter's age than a friend's. She talked about their family constantly and would make Gwen look through their old photo albums that had become her lifeline now. Proof positive that once there had been happier times, and hope that there might one day be again.

On one such occasion, Felix brought along a camera to snap shots of Gwen and Mrs. Cassidy together. The older woman insisted on changing into her best finery. She wanted to look good for the photos. Some, she told them, she'd send to her son. To let him know she was doing well and that she was being comforted by new and glamorous friends. Friends who would help take her mind off her loss. Friends she couldn't wait to introduce to her Paul, when this awful war was over and they were reunited once again.

Chapter 31

Chicago

Crying and virtually stumbling the rest of the remaining blocks to her house, Jillian couldn't decide what she was going to say to her parents. Fortunately—*as if anything could ever be considered fortunate about that dreadful night,* Jillian said to herself—she didn't have to make that decision. They weren't home. They had left a note on her door saying they had gone to the movies. A double feature, they pointed out. They'd be home late. She shouldn't wait up, they counseled. Perhaps even in the worst of times there are small favors, Jillian realized. She could be cleaned up and in bed before they returned home. She wouldn't have to deal with the rapid-fire questions, the frantic pleas to rush to the hospital, or the unwanted advice to call the police. At least not tonight.

The only thing Jillian wanted at this moment was to crawl under the bed covers and stay there as long as she could. But she knew even that wasn't possible until she made some attempt to look to her wounds, remove her now-tattered clothes, wash herself of the dirt and grime of the street, and to cleanse herself of the scent and memory of Ian Donovan.

When she looked in the mirror, she almost cried out, more in shock than in pain. Her lips had swelled to more than twice their size. There was a mark, already turning blue, just above her chin. Her mascara-streaked eyes seemed too far back in her head. They were red from tears and rimmed beneath with dark circles. The blood had matted her hair on one side and it stuck to her head as if flattened by a stone rather than a sap. No longer the heroine, she looked and felt like the victim she was. It took all her strength to run the water and step haltingly into the bath. Once in, she let the warm water engulf her as she slid completely below the surface before rising to wipe her eyes. Then she began to rub the soap over her battered face. Gingerly, she began, letting the smoothness of the bar slide softly over the bruised and swollen lumps. With a washcloth, she wiped the soap from her face but not the pain from her heart. As she moved down her body, lathering herself first, then removing the soap with a squeeze of the cloth, her strokes became more and more tentative until she knew she had to clean where he had been. Reaching between her legs the tears began again. She rubbed softly at first. Then harder. Then harder still as she fought to smear every possible vestige of him away and into the quickly darkening water. Finally, she stopped, unable to continue. The cloth dropped from her hand and sunk below the surface. Then Jillian slid her feet together, raised her legs, wrapped her arms around them, and bent forward to let her head rest on her knees. It was time to let the tears flow unabated. Time to cry until she could cry no more. Time to get out all the pain and the sorrow and the pity. She wanted it gone. All gone. She couldn't stand the thought of having any of it in, on, or around her anymore.

The following day she faced the same reactions from her parents she had so dreaded the night before. But by then she had her story ready. She had been attacked by a couple of ruffians. Schoolboys, really. They had tried to take her purse and there had been a scuffle. She managed to thwack them both with her bag and the headlights of an oncoming car frightened them away before they could do more harm or take what they had been after. Yes, she'd report the incident to the police so they could keep a more watchful eye on the neighborhood, and at her parents' insistence, she'd check in with the doctor just to make sure no bones had been fractured and to secure pain medicine strong enough to keep the physical hurt at bay. Her parents, just like her coworkers, believed her immediately. The tale certainly fit the image of the Jillian they had come to envision since the thwarted robbery attempt.

While the bumps and bruises were subsiding, the painkillers prescribed by her doctor and filled by her very own drugstore, kept her feeling relatively free of both pain and angst. She earnestly believed she had now seen the last of Ian Donovan. Even if she had paid an awful price to do so. Weeks went by and as her face and head healed, the glow came back into her cheeks, though not into her soul. She didn't seem to smile as much as she once did. Nor, thought her friends and family, was she as outgoing as she once was. But it was probably to be expected, they all rationalized. She had been through so much with the shooting and the attack and all. The stepped-up patrols of the neighborhood proved of no particular benefit. Just boys high on beer and hormones, the cops reasoned. Things seemed to get back to some degree of normalcy. Papers and radio reports were still filled with news from both fronts of the war.

Jillian had decided that this time she would not share what happened to her in any letters to Brendon. There was certainly no point in adding to his worries with something he could do nothing about, wherever he was. And she really had no idea of where that might be. The army had become quite expert at censoring any mention by any GI of where they were or what they might be doing. This was a burden she'd carry on her own.

Weeks after the initial drug prescription had run its course, and the second prescription Jillian had asked for was exhausted as well, she still found herself in the doctor's office asking for even more medicine and wondering out loud if perhaps something else might be wrong.

"Well, doctor, my bruises have all healed and everything. And it's not like I'm in pain…I mean not really. Well the thing is…you see I was wondering if I might have sustained some injuries that weren't obvious, you know. Maybe internal injuries…like to my stomach or my organs…or something like that."

"Why do you ask, Jillian? What have you been experiencing?"

"Well, I've just been feeling a bit sore…well, not sore really, but sort of bloated, you know. And frankly a bit nauseous too, sometimes in the mornings. I just wondered if there was anything we might have missed when you examined me following the incident."

"You know, Jillian, I certainly don't want to offend you, or anything like that. I mean there might very well be something stemming from your encounter with these hoodlums that wasn't apparent to you or me at the time. However, I also have to ask…I mean it's part of what we doctors must do with female patients who describe the sort of symptoms you've described…so, please don't take offense. I'll just ask you outright. Jillian, is there any possibility at all that you might be pregnant?"

Chapter 32

The English Channel

Everyone in Paul's platoon took the loss of Sergeant Johnson hard. Riley and Brendon were no exception. They had experienced other soldiers dying beside them. Men they had known, trained and fought with. But this was different. Johnson had been the best of them. The top soldier. The one who seemed to know instinctively what to do regardless of the situation. If he could be killed, blotted out in an instant, by an enemy who wasn't even aiming at him, just firing wildly as he choked on the smoke and fire around him—if Johnson could lose his life in such a haphazard way, what chance did they have of keeping theirs? None expressed their feelings to one another, though. You didn't talk about the ones you left behind. But they all felt the same way. Vulnerable. More vulnerable than any of them had ever felt.

After Monte Cassino, the road to Rome was open. But Bravo Company wouldn't be taking it. Along with the other companies in their battalion, they were pulled from the field and reassigned. None of the enlisted men, and only a select few of the officers in their regiment knew the reason why. But those deemed trustworthy soon found out. The entire brigade was being sent to England, where plans were afoot to cross the English Channel and invade France. If all went as planned, Paul Cassidy, Riley Cross, and Brendon O'Byrne would be joining one hundred and fifty-six thousand of their allies in what was codenamed Operation Overlord. Its logistics were staggering. Its planning, encyclopedic. Training and practice, to the degree possible with such an enormous force, was methodical. All the Allies needed to unleash the largest gathering of men, planes, and ships ever assembled, and to flawlessly execute the most massive invasion the world had ever known, was a little cooperation from the weather. They didn't get it.

For weeks, ships bulging with human cargo sat at English docks. Warehouses bursting at the seams with men and equipment kept doors closed against the wind and rain. The greatest armada and the largest landing force in the history of the world twiddled their thumbs and bided their time because Mother Nature simply wasn't following orders. If the inclement weather didn't let up, the channel crossing could prove disastrous. If the wet beaches bogged the tank treads down when the Shermans came ashore the entire assault could be compromised. If the winds were too strong and the paratroopers missed their drop zones, the casualties would be unconscionable. But if the Allies waited too long to begin the arduous journey from the shores of France to the heart of Germany, winter could overtake them, slow their advance, and give the Nazis even more time to shore up defenses, plan counter attacks, and keep their boots on the millions who had been suffering under the yoke of their oppression since the war began.

Bravo Company's role in the grand plan once again put them in the thick of things. They and thirteen thousand other paratroopers would be making a night drop behind enemy lines prior to the main assault on Normandy the following morning. They were, in essence, a massive diversionary force, designed to make the Germans move troops from their beach fortifications to deal with the invaders from the sky. If they didn't, the Nazis could lose vital bridges they'd need for their retreat, which would surely come after some degree of coastline defense. This tactic was essential, the Allies believed. Without it, the German defense forces on the coast could focus entirely on repelling the invasion. Were that to happen, the cost in human lives of those coming ashore could be monumental.

Paul, who had been promoted to First Lieutenant after the battle of Monte Cassino, was called into a briefing around midday on the fifth of June. His company commander informed the platoon leaders that while the weather hadn't completely turned, there was a window expected that evening where the rain would end for at least twenty-four hours. The conditions would be far from perfect, Paul's captain said, but the waiting was over. It was a go.

A few hours later, paratroopers were assembled on tarmacs in preparation to board the C-47s that would be taking them over the English Channel and into the heart of Nazi-occupied France. Some smoked. Some prayed. Some wrote letters they folded and stuffed into their fatigue jackets. Letters they hoped would be sent to their loved ones in the event they were no longer around to send them. Riley and Brendon sat beside each other as they waited. Their conversation was minimal. Even though they were tried and tested combat veterans now, they knew this was different. A massive jump of such size and scope had never been attempted before. While the weather was calm for the moment, no one could guarantee it was going to stay that way. A sense of dread kept finding its way into whatever false bravado they could muster.

"Think the ground in France will be softer than the ground in Italy?" Brendon asked.

"I doubt it," Riley answered. "Just try to stay out of the trees this time, okay? I don't look forward to climbing another one."

"Bet the ride over's gonna be bumpy, huh?"

"Have we been on one of these things yet that wasn't?"

"Say, Riley, you know…just in case we don't…I mean if I shouldn't—"

"Stow it." Riley cut him off. "I don't plan on making the hike to Paris by myself. Don't have your gift of gab. I'll need you along to say the right thing to all those femmes."

"Got a point there," Brendon tried to chuckle. But his throat was so dry it came out more like a grunt.

Less than an hour later they were onboard and on their way.

The weather report proved partially correct but overly optimistic. While the planes in the first wave executed the channel crossing with relative precision, they started to run into all manner of difficulties over the Cotentin Peninsula. Lack of navigators on more than half of the planes caused tight formations to loosen. Radio silence kept pilots from hearing that the weather was turning more adverse than predicted. Winds picked up dramatically. A solid cloudbank obscured virtually half of the peninsula and there was heavy ground fog. Flying beneath German radar to avoid detection enabled ground observers to spot the assault and anti-aircraft fire began filling the air with flak. The transponder radar system used to guide the planes to their drop zones performed poorly and emergency efforts to correct it actually jammed the system. Many of the C-47s wound up either above or below the seven hundred foot drop altitude, in excess of the one hundred and ten mile per hour drop speed, and some even needed second or third passes over areas to find their drop zones. But the effort was too gigantic to do anything but press forward. On every aircraft, regardless of where they were, or what the altitude was, when the green light came on, paratroopers filled the black night sky.

Riley had been directly in front of Brendon when he exited the aircraft. But the blast of the prop wash and the darkness surrounding him made it impossible to find his squad mate in the sky. In the far distance, he could barely make out lights rising from the ground and the outlines of canopies as they drifted toward them. He had no way of knowing the lights were coming from the village of Sainte-Mere-Eglise, and the paratroopers there were descending into enemy gunfire.

As Riley hung in the harness, the wind was so strong it seemed to whisk him more laterally than downward. The night was so black it was virtually impossible for him to gauge the top of the tree line and he knew that at any minute he could be crashing into the earth. Pulling down hard on his risers he assumed a landing position and hoped the speed of his descent wouldn't result in a busted ankle or leg. Prepared for impact, he waited tensely for his feet to feel the hard ground. But what he felt instead, was something altogether different.

Squish…squash…splat…came the sounds that accompanied Riley's plop into the muck and mire of grassy swampland. Rather than the jolt he was expecting, he felt his boots sink deep into the mud and his momentum carried him over onto his side, which immediately felt a cold chill as he was soaked with dark water. His canopy had immediately collapsed and he knew he had to get up lest the mud and the water and the reeds swallow him. Struggling to his feet, he banged the quick-release and let his parachute fall away. It was difficult for him to move his legs and feet but he knew he must if he didn't want to sink even lower into the bog. Pulling each leg up slowly, he held his rifle aloft, as much to keep his balance as to keep it out of the mud. In this way he tramped to what he hoped was dryer ground. Ground further from the lake that was now visible through eyes that had finally adjusted to the dark.

It was then that a strange feeling came over Riley. A feeling he hadn't experienced for a very long time. Looking around, he suddenly realized he was alone. There was no one else around. Just moments ago he had been surrounded by hundreds of fellow soldiers on the plane. For months on end he had been in the middle of a mass of male humanity wherever he went. Now, just like that, he was here. Wherever *here* was. Totally alone in the dark night in a country foreign to him. A country occupied by the enemy. *You miss your privacy so,* he thought, *when you constantly have other soldiers around twenty-four hours a day*. Now, he thought, he'd give anything to be back in the middle of all of them. Rather than where he was. Seemingly in the middle of nowhere. With no support, no help, no one to give him orders and tell him what to do. For a moment, the feeling was paralyzing.

Then reality clicked in. It came with the sound of movement

somewhere to his left. Riley crouched low in the high reeds surrounding the marsh. *We must have missed the drop zone,* he told himself. *Or been blown beyond it by the high winds. I can't believe we were supposed to land in the middle of a bog like this.* Again there was movement. He could hear the rustling of the grass. Someone walking, he guessed. But friend or foe, he knew not. He held his position and waited cautiously. Perhaps whoever was out there would speak, and he'd know how to react. But if it were an enemy patrol, there would be no talking. *Stay quiet. I should just stay quiet,* he said to himself. *That way they'll pass by without even knowing I'm here. But if it is my guys, they'll maintain silence too. They'll walk right by me and I could be left totally alone. Have to do something. Have to find out who it is.* Then he remembered, and reached inside the pocket of his fatigue jacket to pull out the toy cricket all the paratroopers had been issued. Each platoon leader had handed out the little metal gadgets and spent time drumming their use and their importance into each soldier. Paul's words came back to him. "If you get lost or separated from your unit...and you're not sure who's around the corner or behind a hedgerow...one click is to be followed by two clicks. If you don't get two clicks in response, assume it's the enemy."

The sound of footsteps grew closer. *Jesus,* Riley thought. *What if the Germans have captured some of our guys already? And what if they found these stupid things on them and figured out what they're for? I'll be playing right into their hands. I'll be setting myself up. But I have to do something. I have to.* Suddenly, his internal debate ended abruptly. In addition to footsteps, he heard voices.

"Lieutenant, I really want to thank you, Sir. You saved my life."

"If you keep talking, it just might have been for nothing."

Riley couldn't help himself. He recognized both voices and responded excitedly with a kind of loud whisper. "Hey, guys! Over here. It's me."

"Riley?"

"Cross? Is that you?"

"Yes," Riley answered, rising and moving briskly toward the sound of their voices.

"Get down," Paul said as Riley reached them, and they all dropped to one knee in the tall grass.

"Why didn't you use your cricket?" Paul asked.

"I was about to Sir, when…Jesus, both of you are soaking wet. What happened?"

"Lieutenant Cassidy saved my life," Brendon answered before Paul could respond. "I came down in the lake and was all tangled up in my chute. Would have drowned for sure if the Lieutenant hadn't come in the water and cut me free."

"Forget it," Paul said. "Anyone would have done the same."

"Yeah, but anyone might not have reacted as quickly as you did, Sir. I'm just lucky it was you."

"Well, I'm afraid our luck quotient is probably all used up, Private."

"What do you mean, Sir?" Riley asked.

"I've got a feeling we landed way beyond our drop zone," he answered. "If this is the marsh I think it is…the one mentioned in the briefing…that means we're way east of Merderet. Ten miles or more."

"And the other guys in the platoon?"

"God only knows, Cross. They could be scattered all over the place."

"So, should we just wait here, Lieutenant?" Brendon asked. "To see if any of the other guys turn up?"

"It's just as likely a German patrol could turn up. And we didn't come over here to sit on our backsides in some swamp. Let's move out."

Paul assumed those who had landed on the drop zones they were supposed to, were on their way to take the bridges at Chef-du-Pont. He hoped that by heading in that direction, he, Cross, and O'Byrne might meet up with other stragglers from their platoon or barring that, any members of the 82nd Airborne at all. He knew the jump had been massive and he assumed there were Americans strung out all over the place. But he also realized that the three of them were so far east of where they should have been, it was entirely possible large contingents of enemy soldiers were between them and Allied forces on their way to the bridges. Paul knew he wasn't responsible for where the aircraft and the winds had taken him, but he did feel responsible for getting himself and his platoon mates back to his unit to join the fight as soon as possible.

The going was slow. Every time they'd take one step forward they'd sink into mud up to their knees. It was imperative, though, that they keep their balance. Falling might result in dropping their weapons. And rifle barrels full of muck were more dangerous to them than to the Germans. Mosquitoes circled them relentlessly and they continually ran their hands in front of and behind their faces to ward them off. It was all they could do to fight their instinct to slap and kill as many as they could. But they knew they could scarcely afford to make that much noise not knowing who was within earshot.

It took almost two hours to reach the edge of the swamp. When they finally got to dry ground Paul suggested they take a break. Both Brendon and Riley fell to the earth to stretch and regain their wind. The adrenalin of the jump itself and its aftermath had kept all three of them moving through a difficult environment at a pace most men couldn't sustain. They had been immune to the effects of fatigue. But very quickly a sense of weariness engulfed them.

Between deep breaths, Brendon said, "Tell me we don't have any more of that to get through…will you, Lieutenant?"

"I don't think so. But it's still a long haul from here," Paul answered.

"As long as it's a dry one," Riley commented. "As long as it's a dry one."

They rested for ten minutes. Then Paul got them up and moving again through a forest dense with oak, beech and poplars. The three did their best to move as silently as they could, but with each step onto a rotted tree branch too dark to see, or a dry twig that would snap beneath the weight of an ill-placed boot, their hearts would leap into their throats hoping they hadn't just informed an unseen enemy that prey was close at hand.

A half-hour after they entered the forest, Paul raised his hand as a signal to stop. All three stood in place like statues frozen amid the tree trunks. Paul then put both hands to his ears so Riley and Brendon would listen to see if they could pick up whatever Paul thought he was hearing. In the stillness of the night, muffled sounds began to waft back to them. Just muted noise at first. Then came the unmistakable sound of human laughter. Followed by mumbles. Mumbles and the occasional raised voice. A voice, like the rest that could be heard but not understood. Because it was in German.

Paul motioned for the two to move up beside him. When they did, he whispered softly, "We're going to move quietly to the top of that rise. From the sound of things, I think they may be in the ravine that's below it."

"Don't want to just go around?" Riley asked.

"We need to know how many there are. Stay within arm's length. And keep quiet. Once we can see them, I'll let you know what to do."

Before they could move, another unmistakable sound sliced through the night air. A sound that chilled all three. It was a scream. A scream of agony. Followed by even more laughter. Paul gave the signal to move forward.

Reaching the rise, and lying prone on the edge of the hill, they could see the campfire below and the men around it. One squad, Paul noted mentally. Six enlisted, but also one officer. Probably an outpost for a larger contingent, he reasoned. But another individual was there as well. An American soldier who was on his knees. He had been stripped to the waist and his hands were tied behind his back. The officer towered over him shouting questions. When the American refused to answer, the German would shove the barrel of his Luger into a dark black and red wound on the prisoner's shoulder, causing him to cry out.

"Fucking bastards," Brendon mumbled involuntarily.

"Quiet! Now listen. Here's what we'll do. Cross, switch places with me. Get in the middle." As they quickly exchanged places, Paul went on. "You're the best shot, I want you to take the ones in the center. This way there's less chance of our guy being hit. Start by wounding the officer if you can. He's worth taking prisoner. We need to know how big a unit these guys are part of. I'll go for the Krauts on the right. O'Byrne, you take the ones on the left. We'll open up on your shot, Cross. Fire when ready."

Riley raised his M1 and sighted on the officer. *I'll put a round through that son-of-a-bitch's shoulder,* Riley thought to himself, *and let him see how hot lead really feels.* Just as he was squeezing the trigger, the German swung his arm down hard, raking the Lugar's barrel across the face of the American. The blow was delivered with such force it swung his body around and Riley's shot tore into his upper bicep sending him crashing to the ground. Paul let loose with his Thompson. The automatic weapon cut into both of the Germans on the right. Brendon's first shot dropped a burly soldier who had been standing up. By the time he took aim at his second target, the enlisted man had rolled over behind a log and grabbed his own weapon. Riley had quickly moved from the officer to the two Germans sitting nearest the fire. The first man caught it square in the back, and when the second one grabbed his rifle and turned to fire, Riley's shot tore into his heart.

The American prisoner was so shocked when the firing began that he simply kneeled there for a moment unable to contemplate what was happening. Then reality sent an alarm bell to his brain and he immediately dropped to the ground and tried to crawl away. With his hands bound behind him and in immense pain, it was all he could do to move inches at a time. The German officer had fallen only a few feet from the captured Allied soldier. While the burn in his arm was excruciating, he could look down and see that it wasn't a lethal wound. Rising on one elbow, he picked up the nearby Sturmgewehr 44 and tossed it over to his comrade behind the log, shouting, "Mich decken!" The German soldier picked up the assault rifle and wasted no time debating whether he should cover his officer or not. He quickly began firing bursts that sent dirt, rock, and leaves exploding across the top of the hill.

The three Americans ducked and turned away from the incoming rounds. With fire from the hill momentarily stopped, the officer picked up the Luger in his left hand and fired point blank into the bound prisoner's head. "Mich decken! Mich decken!" the officer yelled again to his subordinate. Then he struggled to his feet. With his right arm hanging limp and lifeless, he began to run as fast as he could away from the campsite and into the darkness. Bullets continued to rip across the top of the rise sending debris splattering in all directions around the Americans. Then, just as suddenly, the blast of incoming rounds went silent as the German soldier's gun jammed.

"All of us," Paul said. And the three rose as one concentrating their fire on the lone German behind the log that virtually disintegrated in a hail of bullets that tore it and him to pieces.

"He's had it," Riley said. "But the officer's gone. Should we go after him?"

"Check the prisoner, first," Paul answered. "O'Byrne, you and I will make sure these others are done."

Moments later Paul and Brendon were walking over to where Riley was kneeling by the American.

"He's dead, Sir. That bastard shot him. He moved just as I fired. If not…maybe…"

"Don't blame yourself, Cross." Paul said. "It wasn't your fault. Let me just get his dog tags and we'll get out of here."

"But shouldn't we try to bury him…or something?" Brendon asked.

"No time," Paul said. "That officer is on his way to a larger unit that may have heard the firing already. They may be heading this way. The Germans will take him when they take their own men away. Cross, you and O'Byrne check the bodies for side arms or grenades. Anything we can take with us that we might be able to use later."

As they turned to follow the orders they had been given, Paul dropped to one knee to remove the dead man's dog tags. Pulling them free, he read them before putting them in his fatigue pocket. The shock was palpable. He looked back at the dead man to see if it could be true. It was. Paul found it almost impossible to believe, but the compatriot lying as his feet was the same young man who had taken him to task so very long ago. The schoolmate who had chided him for being rich, out-of-touch, and immune to the plight of others. The fallen comrade was Lev Goldman.

As the three moved out of the camp and back into the woods, hoping to find their unit and not the enemy's, Brendon said, "I thought they weren't supposed to torture prisoners like that. I thought they said prisoners would be treated okay. Not great, maybe. But okay."

"He wasn't a prisoner to them," Paul responded.

"What do you mean?" Riley asked.

"He wasn't a prisoner to the Nazis," Paul replied. "To them…he wasn't even a man."

"Why not?" Brendon asked.

"Because he was a Jew.

Chapter 33

Hollywood

Gwen Taylor's career was in high gear. She had been featured as an "up and comer" in *Photoplay Magazine*. The article was short on copy but long on pictures of Gwen in a bathing suit, Gwen in an evening gown, Gwen in a negligee. What few words there were, talked about her all-American beauty, her vivacious smile, and her alluring measurements. This girl was going places, the article gushed. Why not come along for the ride?

Felix masterminded the whole thing of course. He convinced the magazine's editor that Gwen was a virtual shoe-in to be nominated for a Supporting Actress Academy Award for her performance in *The Concrete Caverns*. And with publication of the magazine preceding the nomination announcements by only a few days, Felix convinced them that the magazine would look prescient and be immediately recognized as a star maker of the first caliber. The nominations were announced a few days after the spread on Gwen appeared and it turned out she was not one of the nominees. However, the Hollywood Foreign Press Awards were presented shortly thereafter and Gwen was named "Best Newcomer Female," which allowed Felix to soothe the ruffled feathers of *Photoplay's* editor and open contract negotiations with Harry Cohn for Gwen's services at Columbia Pictures.

While Gwen's contract called for her participation in at least six films, Felix made sure a clause was included allowing her to be loaned out to other studios for at least two movies over the course of her contract. He knew the quality of the screenplays at Cohn's studio was mediocre at best, but he realized she needed the experience to help her improve as an actress. And he was content to let Columbia make Gwen far more recognizable to a broader audience, leaving him free to pursue more prestigious vehicles for her.

Felix's artful manipulation of the press and the industry was not lost on Gwen. She knew she owed an enormous debt to him for his skillful direction of her career. It was a debt she felt obliged to pay, in bed and out. She wasn't bitter about it. She simply looked upon it as the way things were. The way things worked if you wanted to better yourself and have a chance of becoming something you might never have become on your own. That's why she was a bit surprised with what Felix spoke to her about over lunch at one of Hollywood's busiest midday restaurants, Musso and Frank's.

"After dessert, my dear, I'll drive you over to your new place on Franklin. It's not far from here."

"My new place? What are you talking about?"

"A lovely little bungalow has been rented in your name on Franklin in the hills. It's quite appropriate for a rising young starlet."

"But…I mean…well, what about us?"

"Our relationship won't change, dear. Not unless you want it to. It's just that with your profile increasing, it's not best to have your address at my place. Your new residence is really only a stone's throw away. And with the contract we've just signed, you'll be extremely busy."

"But what about transportation? I mean…how will I get back and forth to the studio?"

"There's a red coupe in your driveway. But it's just for your personal use. The studio will send a driver for you on the days you're required to be there. I negotiated that as part of your contract."

"Felix, I'm really not sure what to say. I mean, I really don't know exactly how to feel."

"You should feel that your career is progressing as it should. Here's the checkbook," he said, handing it to her across the table, "for your bank account and to handle your expenses. A complete record of your income, as well as the investments I've made for you, is on record at the office. You need only ask Gladys any time you wish to see it."

"A place of my own. I can't believe it, Felix. Is it really mine and the account too?"

"Indeed it is, my dear. You've earned it. And it's all yours as long as you pay your bills. And you can more than afford to do that. Particularly if you keep working hard and continue to apply yourself as you have."

Gwen was giggly. And she'd only had one Champagne cocktail. "I'm an independent woman. I can't believe it."

"Well, not too independent, dear. I trust you'll continue to listen to my counsel and advice as it relates to your career."

"I'll listen to your counsel and advice as it relates to my life, Felix." She reached across the table and squeezed his hand. "I owe you so very, very much."

Before Felix had a chance to reply they were interrupted by a man who had left his party in their red leather booth and walked across the clamorous room. "Felix…I thought that was you. Hello. How have you been?" Then, leaving no doubt he had zero interest in the answer, he immediately asked another question. "And who is your stunning companion?"

With no effort to disguise his annoyance, Felix replied. "Etiquette dictates, I suppose. This is Gwen Taylor, a fine young actress I'm fortunate to represent. Gwen…this is David Hammer, an unexplainably successful actor I'm fortunate to no longer represent."

Without waiting to see if Gwen was the least bit embarrassed by Felix's barb, Hammer said to her, "Don't mind, Felix, Miss Taylor, he's always looked upon me as the one that got away."

Felix responded, "I'd much rather think of you, David, as the one who stays away."

It was obvious to Gwen by Felix's tone, as well as his words, that there must have been a good deal of unpleasantness between the two in the past. She would have liked to add a witty bon mot either to intercede or support Felix in his apparent disdain. But she found herself momentarily unable to speak, and just sat there staring into the eyes of the most gorgeous man she had ever seen.

Chapter 34

Chicago

Jillian sat in the front pew at Saint Michael's Catholic Church three blocks from where she lived. It was the church in which she had been baptized. It was where she had received catechism instruction from the nuns, where she made her first confession and received her First Communion. Saint Michael's was the church where she received Confirmation. It had been like a second home to her for most of her life. With her parents, she attended Mass there every Sunday. She frequently took part in Catholic Youth Organization activities and often volunteered to help in food drives for the poor and destitute, or the collection of toys for the underprivileged at Christmas. But it was also the church by the alley where she had been beaten and raped. In her heart and in her mind, she had been a good Catholic girl. Why then, she wondered, had God forsaken her?

Looking up at the ornately decorated stained glass windows with renderings of the stages of the cross, she wondered if she, like Jesus, was being made to suffer for the sins of others. *Why had this happened to her? What had she done to deserve it? What had she not done that she should have, to go through such pain and torment?* In comparison of course, it was nothing to what He had to endure. But then He was the Son of God. She was merely a hard working Irish lass who found herself in a situation she had no idea how to cope with.

The wooden Rosary beads draped around her interlaced fingers had been a gift from her parents when she was a child. She had kept them and found strength in them for longer than she could remember. But this day they seemed somehow insufficient and bereft of their powers. She had come to the church this day for solemnity and contemplation and guidance as to what she should do. But as she sat seeking insight and direction within the walls that had sheltered her all these years, she felt more alone than she had ever been.

Jillian had chosen not to speak with Father Fitzsimmons about the questions that were now her constant companions. She knew what his answers would be. Though he was kind and caring, he never seemed to stray from orthodox interpretations of right, wrong, sacrilege, and sin. Her questions touched on all of those, but they were not easily answered. At least by her. Can anything good come from such an evil act? Can an exposed liar ever truly be believed? Is it possible to do something you know is wrong, then try to make up for it for the rest of your life? Will the one who means the most to you ever be able to understand the decision you have made? Can you give up your dreams and ever be truly happy? Are you capable of loving that which came from the opposite of love?

Suddenly, Jillian felt strangely warm, and a little dizzy. Even though the ceiling of the church towered high above her, she felt as if the entire building were closing in and she was about to be crushed by the weight of the wood and the glass and the statues and the candles. She rose quickly from the pew, genuflected and made the sign of the cross, then hurried down the aisle and out the doors into the sunlight.

Across the street a park bench was nestled beneath a huge mulberry tree. There was an elderly man sitting on one end of it. Even though Jillian was in no mood for company, she still felt woozy and hurried across the avenue to take a seat on the opposite end of the bench. As she sat there for a moment, a cool breeze from who knows where picked up and drifted across her face. It seemed to calm her.

The man spoke. "I see you've just come out of the church."

"Yes," Jillian answered, simply to be polite.

"Always go to church in the middle of the day?" he

questioned.

"No. Not really. I've got to get back to work in a minute or two."

"People go to church in the middle of the day...generally having problems...or maybe don't have nowhere else to go."

"Well, I have to get back to work in a minute."

"You got a place to work...you got a place to go. So you must be having problems."

Gee, Jillian said to herself. *The nerve of this guy.* But he was so old and fragile looking, she couldn't bring herself to be rude to him. "Everyone has problems, I guess. I was just trying to come up with some answers."

"No point in that."

"Really? Why do you say that?"

"Whatever's happened in the past was meant to happen. Can't change the past. Can't really influence the future. Whatever's gonna happen is gonna happen."

"Really? What about the decisions we make? What about free will?"

"Free will's got nothin' to do with it. There's a flow to life, missy. A flow to everyone's life. You can go with it. Or fight against it. Either way, you're gonna end up where you end up."

"That sort of sounds like giving up to me."

"It's not givin' up. It's lettin' go. Lettin' go of the notion we can control everything that happens to us."

"We really can't control what happens to us? Is that what you're saying?"

"That's what I'm sayin'."

"But what if...what if something really bad happens...and you know you have to do something about it...but you're not sure what to do."

"Best thing to do is just get on with your life. Put one foot in front of the other and let the chips fall where they may...as the poets say."

"Is that what the poets say?" Jillian asked, smiling.

"Some of them…I guess."

"I'd like to think I have some control over my own life. I'd like to think the decisions I make matter."

"Oh, I didn't say they didn't matter. I just said whatever's gonna happen, is gonna happen. Like talkin' to me right now. You didn't plan on that. Did you?"

"No, I didn't."

"That's what I mean. You just have to let life happen. And make your decisions when life decides it's time to make them."

"But how do you know when it's time?

"You'll get a sign, missy. You'll get a sign."

Jillian had no idea why. But somehow she didn't feel quite as overwhelmed as she did when she ran out of Saint Michael's. She looked over at the elderly man and asked, "Are you a sign?"

"I'm just a fella' waitin' for the bus. Make of it what you will, missy. Make of it what you will."

Chapter 35

Near Flamanville, France

As the three soldiers went deeper into the woods, the night became even darker. They had to move slowly and cautiously to avoid tripping over a stump or losing an eye to a low hanging branch. Paul had taken the point. As he came to a limb that might snap back and whip into Brendon's face, he would hold it until Brendon took it from him. Then Brendon would do the same for Riley who was bringing up the rear. Paul couldn't keep from thinking of the nursery rhyme, Three Blind Mice, as they started, stopped, grasped, and inched their way through the dense foliage.

He also couldn't keep from thinking about the fact that fate had dealt him a rather lousy hand. Somewhere, his platoon, his company, even his battalion, were doing what they were supposed to be doing. Engaging the enemy. Securing bridges. Creating havoc that would pull German forces from their beach fortifications to deal with the insurgents from the air. They were getting on with their mission while he was leading two other blind mice he knew not where. His compass had been smashed when he landed. He prayed he wasn't walking his fellow soldiers around in circles.

And there was the image that seemed to keep reappearing as they walked. The image of Lev Goldman with part of his skull blown away. *God*, he thought, how long ago it seemed that he and Lev and his other school chums sat in the campus diner and argued about the war, anti-Semitism, and the internment of Americans of Japanese descent. That brought back thoughts of his father. He couldn't help but wonder if what happened to him wasn't some sort of karma. Some sort of crazy revenge for the role his dad had played in treating particular individuals as something less than the Americans they were. He knew his father had done it out of concern for his community, and love of country. But still, was there ever justification for deciding that some people were somehow less patriotic, less loyal, less human that other people? Wasn't that exactly what the Nazis were doing?

They decided that German Jews were somehow not German at all. A sub-human race that didn't deserve to exist in Germany or any other European country for that matter. And wasn't that how the Japanese were treating American prisoners in the Philippines? Like something less than human. Like animals, who didn't deserve even the most basic rules of fair treatment as prescribed by the Geneva Convention. At least those were the stories that filtered back through the officers' clubs. Then Paul would quickly be brought back to reality by walking into a tree limb that he hadn't seen. All that stuff, the philosophy, the debates, the mental gymnastics…it was all for some other place and time. This night was a lot more primal. It was simply about staying alive.

Brendon followed closely behind Paul. He gave no thought to whether or not they were heading in the right direction. Lieutenant Cassidy was his platoon leader. Of course he knew what he was doing. His wet uniform still hung heavily on him as a reminder than the lieutenant had saved his life. He would have surely drowned were it not for him, Brendon knew. He remembered the shock of hitting the flat surface he thought was ground, and then crashing right through to the cold waters below. He recalled how his canopy had fluttered down on top of him and how his risers got tangled in the cords and how he began to sink while seeming to be gripped by unseen tentacles that made it impossible for him to free his arms and hit his quick release. He remembered too struggling for breath below the surface and beneath the weight of his equipment and helmet and weapon. And how as if from nowhere a force was grabbing him and pulling him upward. Upward to where his chest wouldn't burst and he could pull cool, fresh air into his aching lungs. The recognition that it was his platoon leader who pulled him from certain death only made him that much more determined to follow his orders quickly, perform his assignments without hesitation, and do whatever he could to help the lieutenant accomplish whatever mission was called for. *It's a heavy debt,* he thought to himself as he followed Paul through the brush, *to know you owe your life…your very existence…to one particular individual.* It wasn't something that Brendon was going to put out of his mind any time soon.

As best he could, Riley scanned the terrain around him while they walked. He knew there was just as great a chance of them being overtaken from the rear as running into trouble ahead. And he knew that Lieutenant Cassidy knew it too. That's why he arranged the three of them as he had. It was no slight to Brendon's courage or fortitude. He had both in spades. But the simple fact was, Riley was the better marksman and woodsman. He'd react quicker and more effectively to peril. And whoever walked point would be facing the most danger. Riley couldn't help but be impressed that Lieutenant Cassidy would take that role for himself. *It's the kind of thing Sergeant Johnson would have done. It's the kind of thing real men do.* Riley thought to himself that if he had to be lost, stumbling around in the dark behind enemy lines, not knowing whether he was going to walk upon his own troops or the enemy, he was glad to be doing it with an officer like Lieutenant Cassidy.

Paul raised his right hand as a signal for them to stop. They were near the edge of a tree line. A few feet beyond it, there was a clearing of about thirty yards. In the dark it was impossible to know if it was natural or manmade. The point was, they'd be a lot more visible crossing it than beneath the canopy of the trees they had been traveling under, assuming there were eyes out there to see them. Paul signaled for Brendon and Riley to come forward to his position. They moved up quickly.

Paul whispered, "We have no idea what, who, or whether anyone's on the other side." He started to say that he believed they ought to keep going in the direction they were headed. Then he realized that might imply he wasn't sure. And the implication of indecisiveness might create a lack of confidence in his leadership. That was a problem he didn't want to create at this time. "So we're going to crawl across below the tall grass. It will be slow going. But it will be safer."

Both Brendon and Riley nodded their understanding.

"When we move out," Paul continued, "stay close enough so you can see the man's boot in front of you. We don't want to bunch up, but we don't want to get separated."

Again there was nodded agreement. Then all three dropped to their bellies and Paul started the slow crawl from the cover of the trees.

If the trek through the trees had been cautious, which it had, this crossing made the former look like a Sunday afternoon stroll. Paul was cognizant that moving too fast would rustle the top of the grass like a wave rushing toward shore. If there were prying eyes on the other side of the clearing, he didn't want to signal that something was out there and moving unseen on their location. So from heels, to knees, to stomachs, to elbows, they moved at a crawl that would lose a race with a pygmy slow loris.

Half an hour out, and about half way across, all three heard it distinctively. The metallic click meant to simulate the sound of a cricket. Riley and Brendon knew the instructions that had been drilled into them. One click was to be followed by two clicks. But they both looked toward Paul to see how he was going to respond. Paul put a finger to his lips to caution both of them not to make a sound. Then he pulled his own toy from his fatigue jacket and responded with "click, click."

Immediately, about fifteen yards to his right, a soldier

unfolded himself from the grass, brushed the dirt from his uniform, and began talking as he took a step toward them.

"Boy, am I glad to see—"

The explosion was deafening. The ground literally shook beneath them. The soldier that seconds before had started their way burst apart like a ripe tomato, sending arms, legs, and internal organs in different directions. Shrapnel sprayed in a three hundred and sixty degree circle whizzing over the crawlers like red-hot locusts come buzzing from hell. Paul felt a hard blow to his thigh like he had been kicked by an angry mule with a sawed off hoof. Dirt, grass, and blood rained down on Brendon. Moments after the blast, a tree limb fell from the sky and plopped on Riley's back. Only it wasn't a tree limb. It was the leg of the soldier who had been so happy to hear the two-click confirmation.

They all lay there frozen in place. Aware that at any moment the enemy could open up on them from across the clearing. But no firing came. No shouted orders in German or any other language. When the dust and debris finally settled, they all waited to hear what might happen next. But it seemed that nothing was happening. There was apparently no one around, Axis or Allies, to respond to what had just occurred.

The initial blow that Paul felt in his leg turned quickly to pain. It began to burn like fire. He knew he had to look down to see what had happened, but he feared doing so. Summoning his will, he turned his head and looked at his thigh. Half of the soldier's bayonet, still affixed to a foot of the M1 barrel, protruded from Paul's leg. For a second, he thought he might faint. Might blackout right there. But he knew he must not. He knew he had to keep himself together.

Brendon had raised his head and was staring at the hideous shard sticking out of Paul's leg. He could see his lieutenant wincing in pain. But he held his position, knowing what movement might cause.

Riley reached behind him to pull the tree limb from his back. When he felt the combat boot in his hand he jerked it in front of his eyes to see what it was. Upon recognition he flung it from his hand like a hot coal, and barely kept himself from retching.

They were all in some degree of shock, but Paul knew he had to take charge. Still there was no sound from the other side of the clearing. He gritted his teeth, trying not to let the intense pain in his leg find its way into his throat. Looking back at his two men he said, "Don't move. Don't move at all. We're in a minefield. Are you both alright?"

"I'm okay," Brendon quickly answered.

Regaining his composure, Riley replied, "Me too, Sir."

"But Lieutenant," Brendon said, "your leg. Are you alright? Are you sure you're alright?"

"I'm okay for now, Private. Just hold your position, okay? And let me think for a minute."

"Yes Sir," Brendon said.

"Will do, Sir." Riley echoed.

The only thing Paul could think about was the stabbing pain in his leg. He could feel the wet blood around the wound and he hoped he wasn't losing enough to make him pass out. He had to tell them what to do. He had to.

"Guys, listen to me. We're in a minefield. They could be anywhere. There doesn't seem to be anyone else around….or we would have heard someone coming after the blast."

"Did you know that guy, Lieutenant?" Brendon asked.

"No…no I didn't. Just a straggler…lost like us, I guess. But listen. Here's what we're going to do. We have to stay here. It's too dangerous to try to get through here in the dark."

"How long do we stay?" Riley asked.

"We stay put until morning. We don't move at all. Do you understand? Not even to take a leak. If you have to do it, just do it where you lie. In the morning, when we can see what's ahead of us…we can use my bayonet to detect what's ahead of us. You guys will crawl exactly where I crawl, and we'll get out of here."

"But your leg, Sir. Your leg. Riley? Can you see the Lieutenant's leg? He caught it bad."

"Don't worry about the damn leg," Paul shot back. "We aren't going anyplace anyway tonight. We're here for the duration. So try to get some rest. And don't move, okay? Don't move. Got it?"

"Got it, Sir," Brendon answered.

"Airborne," Riley said.

"Airborne, guys," Paul answered back between clinched teeth.

He knew he was in a fix. But he also knew there wasn't a lot he could do about it. There was no point in trying to remove the bayonet and barrel from his leg. That would only increase the bleeding. He kept pressing on his groin to slow the rate of blood loss as much as he could. But he knew if he had to lie there all night, eventually he'd tire and be unable to maintain pressure. And if the pain became too intense for him to stand, he was afraid he might cry out, causing O'Byrne or Cross to leave their positions to come to his aid, which could be fatal for all of them.

Paul's mind was racing, he knew he needed to calm down and control his breathing more, but he couldn't seem to keep from mentally searching for alternatives. Then it hit him. He remembered that he had followed his commanding officer's suggestion for all of the platoon leaders to secure two morphine syrettes from the medic, in case they were separated from one another or the medic was killed in battle. *Well,* he told himself, *they were definitely separated, and he had to do something to keep the pain at bay.* He was loath to do it though, afraid he might become so groggy that he couldn't function when first light came. But there seemed to be no other choice. He opened his fatigue pocket and took out one of the two small tubes of morphine attached to a hypodermic needle. Then he tried to pull his leg up so it would be easier to reach, but the piercing pain made him stop immediately. He'd have to try to sit up so he could bend over and inject close to the wound. Moving slowly, he laid his weapon beside him. He slid his elbow around so it could support him. Reaching down, he pulled back a piece of his trousers that had been torn in the blast. He wanted to simply plunge it in, just to get it over with, but he knew the proper way was to insert the needle into the skin at a shallow angle. He did so and winced with even more pain. Then he squeezed the small tube allowing the morphine to flow through the needle. Once that was done, he lay back down to let the drug take its effect.

"Are you sure you're okay, Lieutenant?" Brendon asked.

"Yes. I'm…okay. Now get some…shuteye."

For Riley and Brendon, what was left of the night seemed to drag on forever. Trying to sleep on cold, hard ground, without moving for fear of rolling over on a German Bouncing Betty, made their joints ache with stiffness. Paul was out cold for most of the night. As the sun began to peek over the horizon, it didn't immediately occur to any of them that while they passed the night lying beneath the tall grass, seven thousand Allied vessels were crossing the English Channel and a hundred and sixty thousand men were starting to come ashore on the beaches of Normandy. Perspective is sometimes difficult to maintain even in the best of times. When it's battling for attention with survival, it always comes in a distant second.

Once Paul was fully awake, the detection process began. With his bayonet, he probed the ground in front of him slowly, and ever so carefully, being sure to maintain a low angle that would not accidently depress any pressure sensors. Dragging his leg behind him as he crawled, with the shard still protruding from it, he meticulously explored the ground in front of him. The pain was now greater than it had been the night before. Sweat poured down the front of his face, as much from fear as from fatigue. But he kept going. And Brendon and Riley kept following directly behind him. It took them an hour to cross the remaining twenty yards of ground. But they all got there in one piece.

Riley and Brendon rose right away, stretching and bending

over to loosen up. Paul made an attempt to stand, but the minute he put the slightest pressure on his leg, the pain was so intense he fell to the ground. The other two rushed to his aid.

"Help me over to that tree and lean me against the trunk."

After they sat him there, he spoke again. "We're going to have to get this thing out. When we do, it may start to bleed a good deal. There are a couple of bandages and some gauze in the first aid kit on my utility belt. Get those ready."

Brendon did as he asked.

Riley asked, "How should we go about this, Sir?"

"One of you hold my foot still. The other one will need to pull it out. And once you start, don't stop. In fact, make it as straight and fast as you can. Then we'll need to get pressure and the bandages on there quickly. Okay?"

Brendon said, "I'll take the foot, if you don't mind, Riley."

"Okay. I'll do it." Riley responded. "Why don't you count to three, Lieutenant. I'll pull it out on three."

"Alright," Paul replied. "And listen guys, don't panic if I pass out or anything. It sometimes happens with pain and shock, you know."

"We'll take care of it, Sir, no problem. Brendon, hold his foot steady. And let me get a good grip on this thing."

Just the slight movement of Riley gripping the barrel that the bayonet was affixed to, caused Paul to gasp in pain.

"Sorry, Sir," Riley said. "I'm ready now. When you're set, Lieutenant, start your count."

Paul was dripping with sweat. He knew it had to be done, but he knew it was going to hurt like no pain he had ever felt before in his life. He took a deep breath, then said, "One…tw—Arghhhh!"

Riley pulled the barrel and bayonet out in the middle of "two". "Brendon, it's out. Let's get those bandages on…now!"

Paul's chest was heaving. Tears were running from both of his eyes. "God…that hurt," was all he could say.

"Believe me, Sir, it would have hurt a lot more if I had waited for three."

"You're probably right, Private. But damn that hurt!"

After the bandage was applied, Paul managed to get himself upright with their help. With one hand still on the tree, he tried to put weight on his leg to see if he could walk. The cautious half step he took sent a jolt of pain through him that he couldn't stand.

"Jeeze...I think you guys may have to leave me here. I can't put my weight on this."

"Begging your pardon, Sir, but that's not going to happen," Riley said. "We're not going to leave you."

"Right," Brendon added. "If you stay, we stay."

"We can't stay here." Paul said. "If that minefield's there, that means there are Germans around somewhere. We can't just wait for them to find us."

"I've got an idea," Brendon said. "Sir, why don't you give me the Tommy gun?"

"You know how to use this, Private?"

"Yes Sir. And it will probably improve my chances of hitting what I'm shooting at. The chamber's empty and I've taken the clip out of my M1. You take it, Sir, and you can use it like a crutch or a cane. You'll still have your forty-five if we run into any Krauts."

"Let me try that, Private."

"You are sure it's unloaded," Riley added.

"I'm sure," Brendon answered.

Paul took the rifle, pressed it against his side, gripped it hard, and took a step. There was still pain, but it was pain he thought he could handle. "I'll be moving slow, guys. But at least I'll be moving."

Riley said, "Then let's get to it, Sir. If you like, I'll take the point. Brendon will cover the rear. We'll stay close and go at your speed."

"Thanks, fellas. I'll try to go as fast as I can."

"We're in no hurry," Brendon said. "I'm sure the war is more than willing to wait for us."

The going was slow. With every step, Paul winced with pain. But he kept going, and he kept hoping he was directing the trio toward Chef-du-Pont. He had noticed where the sun rose that morning, and he used that knowledge to begin their hike. But in the woods, shade hides the sun. Twists and turns to avoid impassable ground complicate matters exponentially, and navigating by landmark or site point becomes almost impossible. Were they going in the right direction? Paul couldn't be sure. But he was sure that the longer they walked, the more his leg ached. By mid-afternoon they stopped to rest under the canopy of a cluster of oaks atop a sloping hill. It gave them both cover and some degree of visibility. Plus some few seconds of warning should danger approach.

"How's the leg, Sir?" Riley asked.

Why lie, Paul thought. "Hurts like a son of a bitch."

"Well, just stay off it a while," Brendon injected. "This is as good a place as any to hole up for a while."

"Okay, but just for a while. The sooner we get to Chef-du-Pont and connect with our unit, the better off we'll all be. I don't fancy sitting out the war in some half-baked POW camp."

Riley thought for a moment. Then he asked, "You really think they'd take us prisoner…if they got hold of us, Lieutenant? I mean, if they're an army in retreat…well…would they want to slow that retreat with prisoners?"

Paul knew his thinking was reasonable. But he was in no hurry to blacken an already darkening mood. "They might not want to initially…but I'm sure their officers are as smart as ours. They'd know prisoners might just provide information they need…or be useful in negotiations if they got in a fix with our guys."

"Don't know as I'd want to be a prisoner," Brendon said. "Not after I saw how our guy got treated back at that German camp. Of course, like you said, Lieutenant, he was a Jew."

"Jewish prisoners have it tougher, that's for sure," Paul replied. "But I don't plan for any of us to be prisoners. That's why we're not going to stay here very long. Fifteen minutes at the most. Then we're on our way again."

Afternoon turned to dusk. The setting sun confirmed they were still on a westward track. Paul had become so used to a sharp pain with every step that he had virtually willed himself to accept it. *That must have been it,* he thought. *Mind over matter.* That must be why as he walked now, there was a virtual numbness there. Like he was dragging a leg along with him that was simply asleep. He had managed to put the pain somewhere so deep in the recesses of his mind that he couldn't even feel it anymore. He hoped that was a good thing.

Night came. The sky was alight with stars. So bright they were visible through the tops of the trees. All three were looking up at them when they heard it. A muffled sound at first. Some sort of slow rumble. Then the sound grew more intelligible. Engines. A lot of them. Somewhere off to their right.

"Hey, Lieutenant," Brendon said. "That's a convoy. And a big one at that. Think it's ours?"

"No way to know," Paul said. "But the road must be close. The sound's coming from over there."

"I'll go check it out," Riley volunteered. "You guys follow. Don't try to rush. I'll double-time it, and let you know if they're ours."

"Give it a go, Private. We'll trail you."

Riley took off, dodging tree branches, stumps, and bushes as he ran. Paul tried to move faster than he had before, but it was no good. It was like he was hauling a ball and chain. Brendon resisted the urge to hurry forward. He kept pace with his lieutenant, continually scanning to make sure they were the only ones trying to follow Riley.

Less than five minutes after they started, though it seemed infinitely longer, the duo saw Riley making his way back to them. He was holding up one hand as a signal for them to stop. Plus a finger in front of his lips to keep them from shouting.

"It's the Germans," Riley said. "At least three companies, I'd guess. Trucks, armored cars, vehicles like our Jeeps…I even saw a couple of staff cars."

Paul injected, "They're in retreat. They must be. They've got to be moving away from our guys advance."

"Great," Brendon cut in. "That means all we have to do is wait near the road. And come out when our boys show."

"It's not that straightforward, Private."

"What do you mean, Sir?"

"We don't know if this is the front end or the back end of a retreating army. We don't even know if it's an army at all. It might just be a unit redeploying."

"Well…okay… I understand that. But doesn't it make sense to just stay near the road and see what we can see?"

"It makes sense for a while, Private. But only for a while. If there's not a larger contingent behind this one, then they're only redeploying. Maybe getting ready for a counter attack, or going to reinforce or try to retake the bridges at Chef-du-Pont if our boys have secured them."

Riley queried, "How long do we wait, Sir?"

"An hour or two, no more. Let's get close enough to see. But not close enough to be seen, okay?"

"Sure, Lieutenant." Riley said. "I know just the spot."

One hour came and went, but the road stayed quiet. No additional German units. No Allies on their tail. To pass the time, they swapped stories about home, sharing some things, keeping others to themselves. Brendon talked about the letters he received from his girl in Chicago. A girl in a drugstore he couldn't wait to see again once this crumby war was over. Riley mentioned his father's accident, and said he was glad for the few extra dollars he received as a paratrooper. Extra dollars that would help out at home while his dad was recuperating. Paul chose not to mention what had happened to his father. That wound was still a bit too tender for him to open it again. Nor did he share much about his home or neighborhood in Pacific Palisades. He knew his particular rung on the social stratum was a good bit different from the two men he had trained and fought with. He didn't see any point in reminding them of that. It did occur to him though, that they might enjoy one of the things he had been sent by his mother. A photograph of her and some actress she had recently met through USO activities. He pulled the small photo from the folds of the letter in his pocket and tried to show it to them. But it was so dark they could hardly make out the two women's features.

"So, which one's your mom?" Brendon asked in mock seriousness.

"Very funny," Paul replied.

"Can I take a closer look at that, Lieutenant?" Riley asked. "It's so dark here, it's hard to see." *There was definitely a resemblance,* he thought to himself. He simply couldn't be sure in the dark.

"Wait until we get someplace we can see better, Private. I'll show you then. She's a looker alright."

"Your mom didn't mention her name, did she, Lieutenant? I only ask because she kind of reminds me of someone I knew…or someone I've seen before…or something."

"She did, but I don't really remember her name. And it's too dark here to try and find it in the letter. I'll let you know later. Think we better move out now. I don't believe anything else is coming down this road. And wouldn't you know it…it's starting to rain."

"Sure, Sir," Riley said. But he couldn't get the thought out of his mind. *Could it really be her? An actress…in Hollywood? No,* he told himself. *Must just be someone who looks like her.* Someone who looks like the girl he had loved and been loved by. The girl he didn't ask to wait for him…so very long ago.

They moved back into the woods to continue toward Chef-du-Pont. The road was too dangerous, Paul told them. There was too great an opportunity of being spotted by a German column or troops using the road to move men and equipment. The hour they spent waiting, had caused Paul's leg to stiffen. And the rain didn't help. Once they started moving again, the pain came back with each step forward. He kept as much weight off of it as he could, using Brendon's rifle as a crutch. But the going was even slower than before.

The three had been walking for close to an hour and a half, in what had turned out to be a downpour, when Riley, still on point, spotted a yellow glow through the trees. *Far too low to be the moon,* he thought. Then he realized, it was a light.

"Lieutenant. Look Sir, there's light up ahead. Just beyond the break in the tree line."

Paul limped up to Riley, wiped the water from his eyes that continued to drip from the rim of his helmet, and looked in the direction he was pointing.

"You're right, Cross. I think it must be a farmhouse. Yes, it must be. Look, over there. It's a field that's obviously been planted with something. Not sure what at this distance."

Brendon spoke up. "You don't think it's been planted with more of those Bouncing Betties, do you, Sir?"

"I doubt it. Don't think the Jerries would want to blow up something that might help feed their troops."

"Think there's anyone in there, Sir?"

"Yes. I do. Otherwise, I doubt that the light would be on."

"Sure would be nice to spend the night somewhere with walls and a roof, Lieutenant. Rather than out here under a tree. I don't know how your poncho is holding up, but I'm pretty damned soaked."

"We need to know who's in there," Paul replied. "Here's what we'll do."

Paul laid out his plan to Riley and Brendon. They would make their way across the field. Paul would stay behind at the tree line because of his inability to move quickly. He wanted them to get close enough to the farmhouse to see in without being seen. Once they determined just who, and how many, were inside, Brendon would come back to report. If the place was full of Germans, they should both come back. No need to engage the enemy if they were outmanned.

Both of the soldiers darted from the woods and into the field. Paul waited just out of sight as the rain continued to fall. He could see them moving from row to row in the field, until eventually, he lost sight of them. There was nothing left for him to do but wait.

Five minutes later, he saw Brendon break from the field and head back to his position.

"What did you find out?"

"You're not going to believe this Sir…but it looks like the only one in the house is a woman. A pretty good-looking woman at that, Lieutenant. We watched her for a few minutes…and managed to see most of what's inside. She appears to be alone in there."

"Where's Cross right now?"

"He's positioned beside the porch…on the front side…like you said, Sir."

"Okay, let's head over," Paul directed, wincing as he stepped forward.

"I'll be right beside you, Sir. Oh! By the way…that field's a vineyard. Grapes everywhere. Lots of wine bottles inside too. Can you believe our luck?"

"We won't know for a while if our luck's good or bad, Private. Let's move."

They headed toward the back of the house and got close enough for Paul to take a look in the window. He saw a woman cross from one side of the open room to another. She appeared to be putting wine bottles in crates and stacking them against the wall. He scanned the room as best he could and saw no one else. Then he and Brendon went around to the front where Riley was waiting.

"She came out a couple of minutes ago," Riley said. "When Brendon went back for you. Had a few drags on a cigarette and went back inside. I didn't hear her lock the door behind her."

"Okay," Paul replied. "I'll open the door, then you two move in fast. It looks like a pretty tiny place. But if there are other rooms, check them out and be ready, just in case. Let's get on the porch."

Riley and Brendon had to help Paul up the steps. The pain in his leg was now like a knifepoint jabbing him every time he moved. And even when he was still, he could feel it throbbing. The two privates positioned themselves on either side of their officer. Paul was just about to reach for the handle when the door opened toward him and almost knocked him over.

She stood in the doorway silhouetted by the light. Her arms were folded across her chest as she leaned against the frame. She said not a word, but she didn't have to. It was evident she was neither afraid of them nor surprised to see them.

"Do you speak English?" Paul asked.

"Oui." The one word reply was followed by a pause intended to make him uncomfortable for having asked, Paul thought. Then she added, "Lucky for you, n'est-ce pas?"

"I don't speak French." Paul said quickly. "Are you alone?"

"Oui. I am alone."

"We have to check. I'm sorry. We have to check." Then he motioned for Riley and Brendon to move in and search the house.

Inside, Paul and the woman stood in the open room that included the kitchen and a small table, a fireplace with a rocking chair in front of the hearth, and in a far corner, a small bed. Riley and Brendon went to the one door within the room that apparently led somewhere else. They kicked it open quickly and rushed inside to find an empty room, save for a double bed, and a chest of drawers.

"Bedroom," Riley reported back to Paul.

"Empty," Brendon added.

"How big is the bed?" Paul asked.

"Big enough for two," Riley answered.

Turning to the woman, Paul asked, "Where is your husband?"

"Les morts."

"English, please," Paul said.

"Dead. My husband is dead! Killed by the Germans."

Then, motioning toward the smaller bed, Paul asked, "And your child?"

"Also dead," the woman replied. "Drowned before my husband went off to fight this stupid war."

"I'm sorry," Paul replied. "We're Americans."

"Oui. Very loud Americans. I saw you in the field. And heard you on the porch. You have tobacco? Cigarettes? Yes?"

Paul was about to say he didn't smoke, when Brendon reached in his pocket and tapped out a couple of Lucky Strikes from his pack. He handed them to her and she put one behind her ear while lighting the other one.

"Merci. Thank you, Joe."

"Brendon. The name's Brendon, not Joe."

"I thought all American soldiers were named Joe."

"None of us are," Riley said.

"I'm Lieutenant Cassidy. This is Private Cross and O'Byrne. What is your name?"

"Colette Auteuil. But why do you ask?"

"We're hoping, Miss Auteuil, you'll let us stay here tonight."

"The Germans would not ask. If they wanted to stay…they would stay."

"We're not like the Germans," Paul quickly responded.

"Men are like men. Have you just come from a battle?" she

asked.

"We can't tell you anything about that," Paul answered. "But you needn't be afraid of us, we're here to get the Germans out of France."

"I only ask," she said, "because you are bleeding all over my floor."

Paul looked down and saw the liquid on the floor wasn't just rainwater. Fatigue and nausea hit him all at once. He almost swooned and toppled over.

"Put him in the chair," she said to Brendon and Riley. "And take his trousers off."

"What?"

"Take his trousers off. We must clean his wound."

They did as they were told and hustled him into the rocking chair while pulling his fatigue pants down. Both men gasped as they saw the bandage that was virtually black with blood. Paul's head was starting to spin and he was sweating profusely. "Sorry, I'm just," he began, but never finished. His head tipped over on one shoulder causing his helmet to come off and bang down on the floor. At least for the moment, he was out.

"Keep him in the chair," she said, already pumping water into a bowl and pulling cloth from the shelves beneath the basin. The two soldiers steadied him as she knelt and began to pull away what was left of the bandage. She had to rub hard to remove the blood that had dried and caked around the wound. When she did, the pain brought Paul back to consciousness. He twitched involuntarily.

"Be still," she said. "I know it hurts. But it must be done."

As she worked, Paul bounced back and forth between pain and pleasure. The pain from his wound and the pleasure of soft, feminine hands moving over his inner thigh. He was glad when she finished, but also a little sad.

"Thank you," Paul said. "I really appreciate it."

"The wound is bad," she said. "A doctor should see it."

"I'll have it looked at tomorrow. Now about—"

"Stay if you must. What can I do about it?"

"Thank you."

"Are you hungry? I have some bread."

"That's very kind of you."

"And you might as well have some wine to go with it," she said, "a gift from France…for liberating us."

"I'm not sure we should—"

"But what is bread without wine? You are not fighting tonight. There are no Germans near." She pulled two bottles from one of the cases she had been filling earlier and put them on the table. Then she brought the bread from the cupboard. When the bottles were open, she poured a glass for each of the men and one for herself. Raising her glass, she said, "Vive la France!"

"Vive la France!" the three echoed, and all took a drink.

She followed that toast with another. "Vive l'Amérique!"

"Vive l'Amérique!" they repeated, and drank again.

"You continue," she said. "I must retire. There is much work for me tomorrow. I am happy you have come. France is happy you have come."

The three looked at her, but none knew exactly what to say. So they just nodded. As she walked to the bedroom door and shut it behind her, Riley shouted after her, "Thanks again for the food and drink."

"Can you believe this?" Brendon began. "Imagine what the fellows would think if they saw us now."

"I'm not sure they'd think much of us," Paul said, "having wine and bread while they have to choke down C-rations."

"They'd be doing the same as us, Lieutenant," Riley replied. "If they had the chance."

"I guess you're right, Cross. I guess you're right."

"How's that leg, Sir?" Brendon asked.

"Hurts like hell, Private. I've got one morphine syrette left. But I hate to use it."

"Save it, Sir," Brendon answered, "and have some more of this wine. I bet it will help."

Paul acquiesced, for medicinal purposes, he said. He knew he needed something to help blunt the pain, and there was always the chance they'd need that last bit of morphine before they made it back to their unit. So they ate and drank and actually talked of things other than orders and tactics and missions. For an hour or so, they were no longer simply an officer and two infantrymen. They were three friends realizing they were experiencing a night they'd probably never forget. Three men knowing there were things they had seen already, and more things they were likely to see, that they would try very hard to put out of their minds in the future. But here was a night they would be glad to remember. A night they wouldn't mind telling their friends and family about. A night where kindness, comradeship, and at least for a few hours, a quiet shelter had shut out the fear, chaos and insanity of war.

When the bread was gone and the bottles were empty, fatigue finally overwhelmed them.

Riley volunteered to take the first watch. But Paul reminded them their benefactress had said there were no Germans in the area. He believed her. And he knew they were all so dog-tired that, at least this one time, the best thing for them was sleep. Let's put out the light, he told them, and get as much shut-eye as we can before morning.

At dawn, the sunlight crept silently through the farmhouse window bending a ribbon of light across the brown wooden floor and over the olive drab leg of the soldier with his back to the closed front door. Riley, still somewhere beneath consciousness, felt the heat on his shin and involuntarily pulled his knees higher, away from the beckoning finger of morning.

Brendon was half in and half out of the smaller bed that sat in one corner of the room. Colette had said it belonged to her drowned son. Brendon knew he'd only be able to get part of his frame into the bed. But he reckoned a few hours on even part of a mattress was preferable to the hard floor.

Paul was still in the chair he had been helped into the previous night. It seemed as good a place as any to rest and keep weight off his leg. He too was having trouble shaking off the sleep that had overwhelmed them all the night before. Groggily, he willed his hand off the arm of the chair and up to his head where he ran it through his hair, then he rubbed the tips of his fingers across non-complying eyelids. Finally they opened slowly and he surveyed the room around him. Neither soldier was awake yet. They had all apparently slept longer than they should have.

"Cross…O'Byrne," he said loudly, "time to get up. Come on, it's time to get up."

Both men stretched their arms and legs as far as they could, put their steel pots on their heads and struggled to their feet, stretching again once they were upright.

"Have you seen Miss Auteuil?" Paul asked.

"Haven't seen anything, Sir. I've been dead to the world," Brendon answered.

"Same here, Sir. I was out like a light."

"Funny she didn't wake us up," Paul said. "She must have thought we really needed the sack time."

"She was probably right," Brendon cracked.

"Cross, knock on that bedroom door, and see if she's in there?"

Riley ambled over and tapped on the door with the barrel of his rifle. "Hello…good morning…you awake in there…anybody home?"

When there was no answer, he turned the doorknob, and opened the door slowly saying, "Sorry, just checking to see if—"

Both Paul and Brendon noticed his abrupt halt in mid-sentence.

"What is it, Cross?"

"Sir, you'd better come here."

"What's the matter, Riley?" Brendon added.

He didn't answer. He just stood there at the door, staring.

"Help me up, Private," Paul said to Brendon, who hustled over and helped lift his lieutenant from the chair. Still using the rifle for a crutch, Paul hobbled over and Brendon followed. Now all three stood in the doorway, staring in silence.

Colette Auteuil lay face up on the bed. She was naked, save for the blue scarf that was wrapped around her neck. The blue scarf that had apparently been used to strangle her. Paul limped closer saying, "Miss Auteuil…Miss Auteuil." But the closer he got, the more he knew there would be no answer. Her face was an odd purple and there was dried blood around her mouth and nose. The scarf had been pulled so tightly around her throat that a small bone appeared to be broken in her neck.

"God," Brendon said, "what happened?"

Pausing before answering, Paul replied. "I think it's obvious what happened. That's not really the question."

"You mean, how?" Riley questioned.

"I mean…who," Paul answered.

"Hey, Lieutenant, don't look at me," Riley said. "I was out all night."

"Me too," Brendon quickly added. "Me too."

"And I was slumped in a chair all night," Paul said. "Could anyone have gotten in?"

"I slept against the front door," Riley answered. "There's no way someone could have gotten past me."

"The windows don't open," Brendon said. "They're just for seeing out."

Paul took one of the blankets on the bed and quickly threw it across her body. "This woman was kind to us," he said. "She took us in…gave us her food."

"Look, Lieutenant," Riley began. "You can't believe one of us had anything to do with this. There's no way I could…and

Brendon's not capable of something this…this horrible."

"That's right, Lieutenant. I could never…I mean never. And I can't believe Riley would ever do anything like this."

"So…are you implying that I got out of my chair last night…virtually crawled in here on one leg…then raped and killed this woman?"

"No…no, Lieutenant. We don't believe you could do anything like this either. Do we, Brendon?"

"No. No way, Sir. But…but…you said raped…you said raped and killed. How do you know she was raped?"

"I don't know for sure," Paul shot back. "But for God's sake man, look at the way we found her. Naked. What do you think happened?"

"I don't know," Brendon answered. "I don't know."

"Maybe…I mean do you think it's possible," Riley said haltingly, "that…maybe she killed herself?"

"No, Cross. I don't think she killed herself. I don't think she took her clothes off, wrapped a scarf around her neck and tried to hang herself. Do you see any beams in here…no. Did you see any signs of a woman last night that was about to kill herself? I didn't. And what about before we came in. What about when you two were looking in the window. You didn't say she looked depressed. You didn't say she looked suicidal. You said she was working. And smoking a cigarette. Does someone do their work before they kill themselves? I don't think so."

Brendon asked, "What are we going to do, Lieutenant?"

"Look…one more time," Paul began. "We all had too much to drink last night. Particularly for not having had anything to drink in so long. None of us have been around women for a very long time either. It's understandable…if something got out of hand. If something got started and went wrong…and turned bad. It may not have been intentional. It may have just gone too far."

"Sir, I swear…I had absolutely nothing to do with this. I was sound asleep," Riley said.

"I swear too, Lieutenant. I swear too. Nothing. Nothing at all," Brendon added.

"That only leaves me…doesn't it? And you know what, I had nothing to do with it either."

Riley asked, "So…what are we going to do…Sir?"

Paul thought for a moment before he spoke. "We're going to finish our mission. We're going to find and rejoin our unit."

"But what about her, Sir?" Brendon questioned.

"We'll leave her here. There's nothing we can do for her now. Someone will find her. Just like we found this place. Whether it's the Germans or our guys. Someone will find her and bury her. We have to move out now. We have to get back to Bravo Company."

"Yes Sir," Riley said.

"Right," Brendon added.

"Help me straighten her in bed," Paul said. "And let's pull these covers up around her. So when she's found…well…she won't be found like we found her."

The three soldiers moved Colette Auteuil to the head of the bed. They pulled the blanket up until it covered her completely. Then they just stood there for a moment looking down at her. As bad as it was, it was easier than looking at each other.

"Should…should you say something, you know, something religious, Sir?"

"Yes, Cross. I probably should. But right now, words to her and to you two, fail me. Let's just move out."

Chapter 36

Hollywood

David Hammer was six feet five inches tall. He had broad shoulders, a thin waist, and the face of a Greek god. His dark black hair was full and his eyes were blue as the Caribbean. High cheekbones framed a long, straight nose. When he smiled, a mouthful of gleaming white teeth shone like pearls. From the first moment Gwen met him at Musso and Frank's, she was smitten. And it was obvious he was taken with her, Gwen knew. He couldn't take his eyes off her. There was something electric between them, she felt. Some sort of animal magnetism drawing two beautiful people together.

She did her best to hide it from Felix that first day at lunch. She could tell he was antagonistic toward his former client. There was obviously bad blood between them. At least from Felix's point of view. He was particularly sarcastic with Hammer who had approached their table and said hello. But the tall, striking man didn't seem to be the least bit affected by the agent's barbs. He was pleasant, polite, and as gracious as he was handsome. "Hope to see you around town," he had said to Gwen when he left their table. "With someone as lovely as you though, I'm sure I'll have to stand in line."

"A former client," Felix said after Hammer had departed. "All looks and no talent."

"Oh?" Gwen responded. "I hadn't really noticed."

"Come now, my dear. I could see your bodice rising and falling like waves breaking on the shore the moment he said hello. He tends to have that effect on people. That's why I signed him."

"It didn't work out? Why not?"

"Because Mr. David Hammer's middle name is Judas. I secured top modeling assignments for him with all the best publications. The moment he was noticed by enough of the right people to land a movie offer, he dumped me for a competitor."

"Well, that certainly wasn't loyal, was it?"

"The only thing he's loyal to, my dear, is himself. He uses people and discards them like yesterday's newspaper. Keep your distance, love, keep your distance."

The bungalow and car Felix had arranged for Gwen with the earnings from her recent contract with Columbia gave her a wonderful feeling of freedom and independence. A feeling she had really never had before. She loved making herself coffee and enjoying it in the small, but manicured lawn that was her back yard. The little white house, with purple bougainvillea spilling from the windows, felt like the first thing she could really call her own. Felix would come over once a week. Sometimes he would spend the night. Often he wouldn't. Their sex had become infrequent. And when they made love, it seemed more out of responsibility than desire. On both their parts. It was a far cry, Gwen sometimes thought, from the urgency she had felt with Riley.

The six-picture contract Felix had negotiated for Gwen definitely kept her busy. The parts weren't the best, nor were the pictures, but every day she was gaining more experience and learning how to handle herself more professionally. Her outgoing personality made her a favorite among casts and crews. Acquaintances were becoming friends. As beautiful as she was, she was constantly being asked out, but she had become adept at letting suitors down easily without revealing too much about her relationship with Felix. As a contract player, she was required to attend various functions the studio was involved with, often on the arm of this upcoming actor or that. Harry Cohn believed it was good publicity to have his unmarried leading men seen in the company of beautiful girls. And Gwen certainly filled that bill. She didn't mind though. She simply saw it as part of the responsibilities required to live the life she was living. A life she might have dreamed of, but never really thought she'd be experiencing when she left the pine woods of East Texas for the palm trees of Los Angeles.

On the soundstage one morning, her director had just released her and her fellow actors for lunch, when a tall man stepped from behind the lights and rigging and took her gently by the arm. The man was David Hammer. "Remember me?" he asked. "We met at Musso and Frank's."

"Yes. Mr. Hammer, isn't it?"

"Call me David. I'd love to call you Gwen."

"Alright, David. What are you doing here?"

"Well, I could tell you that I came to the studio to meet a friend today…a friend I was supposed to have lunch with. And that he was called away unexpectedly, so I found myself wandering around the soundstages and just happened to happen upon you."

"You could tell me that?"

"Yes, I could. But I won't. You see it's absolutely not true. The truth is I've been wanting to see you since that day we met. I made some inquiries, found out where you were working this morning and took it upon myself to ask you out to lunch."

"Is that what you're doing? Asking me to lunch?"

"Am I making that big a mess of it? Sorry. Yes. Would you care to have lunch with me?"

"I only have an hour. No time really to leave the lot."

"No problem," he said, "I have it on good authority that the food at the commissary is absolutely delicious."

"It's not. But it's cheap."

"How wonderful. I'll buy."

Incredible, Gwen thought. *Breathtakingly handsome and charming to boot. What could it hurt,* she told herself. *It's just lunch with an acquaintance on the studio lot. It might be fun.* And it was. Not just that lunch, but all the lunches that followed for the next week. The week after that, David jokingly said they'd gone through everything on the canteen's menu, so the least they could do was jump in his car and go out for a quick bite. A quick bite turned into a long afternoon at a seaside restaurant in Santa Monica. The sun was warm, the wine cool, and the conversation light, breezy, and fun. They stayed much too long but David made a phone call to someone who made another phone call and he was then able to assure her that her tardiness in returning to work would be forgiven. It was.

At first, Gwen thought about telling Felix she had become friends with David Hammer and that they occasionally shared a midday meal. The "occasionally" was her idea. But even with that qualifier she couldn't bring herself to mention it. She knew Felix disliked David intensely and she was afraid he'd ask her to stop. Which she simply didn't want to do. He was just too much fun. And what was the point of life if it couldn't include a little fun now and then?

David began a picture of his own, so the regularity of lunching became irregular. But he compensated for that with the occasional dinner. Virtually always at some secluded spot far from the bright lights of the Brown Derby and other venues where people went as much to be seen as to be fed. Gwen knew she was betraying Felix by not telling him about her relationship with David. And she knew that she was betraying David by not being honest about the extent of her relationship with Felix. But she just couldn't find the words or the strength to tell either. And the more she fretted about doing so, what started as jokes and handshakes progressed to endearments and handholding. Then to arms around shoulders and waists and goodnight kisses. Eventually to heavy petting and rapid breathing and steamy car windows. But David never once went farther than allowed. And Gwen kept finding it harder and harder to summon the will to stop. Until one night, parked in an isolated alcove off Mulholland Drive, with tongues intertwined and David's hand firmly caressing her breast he said, "Gwen I love you so."

"And I love you, David."

"You're too fine, Gwen. Too precious. I don't want you to be just another conquest. I want you to be my wife."

"Marry you? But David…there's so much I, I haven't told you."

"I don't want to hear it, Gwen. I don't want to hear anything about your life before us. And my life doesn't matter either. Nothing either of us did before we met means anything at all. Be my wife, Gwen. Let's get married. Let's get married tonight."

"Tonight?"

"We can drive to Mexico. We can be there in just a few hours. We'll be married and we can make love for the rest of our lives as man and wife."

"But David, it's…I mean it's just so sudden. And marriage. What about your commitments, your career?"

"Career be damned! Hell, for that matter, it will probably help both our careers. Two young people in love, romantically elope—we'll probably be the toast of the town. The gossip columnists will have a field day."

Gwen was short of breath. She wanted to answer. But she really wasn't sure what to say.

She looked deeply into those big, beautiful eyes of his and was about to respond when the glare of headlights pierced through their back windshield blinding them in a sea of light.

"God, who is that? Do you think it's the police, David?"

Shielding his eyes against the glare, but still looking backward, he said, "There would be flashing lights if it was the cops. Stay here. Stay in the car. Let me handle this."

David opened the door and unfolded his six foot five inch frame to its full height. Holding one hand in front of his face, he said, "Who's back there? What do you want? And turn those damn lights off."

The lights went out, revealing a single figure behind the

steering wheel. The silhouette of a man in a fedora. He just sat there for a moment. Waiting.

"Who the hell are you? What do you want?"

The man opened the door and stepped out. He stood momentarily, then began walking slowly toward David. The moon above and the glow from the lights of the city below provided enough illumination for David to see that the man walking up to him was Felix Pressman.

"Felix? What the hell are you doing here?"

"I'm protecting my investment, dear boy."

"I can't believe you followed us."

"I've actually been having you followed for some time. Tonight, I thought I'd do it myself."

Gwen recognized Felix's voice. But she wasn't sure what to do. And she was even less sure of what they might do. She got out of the car and came round as David was saying, "You may be her agent, Felix, but you're not her master. She can do as she wants and see who she pleases."

"Whom. See whom, or whomever she pleases," Felix corrected.

"Felix," Gwen began, "I was going to tell you about David and me."

"Of course you were, my dear. But the more important question is when. I finally decided you would probably wind up telling me too late."

"Too late? Too late for what?"

"Oh it's not what you think, love. I wasn't worried about your appetites. I can understand those. It's your decision making I was most concerned about."

"What is all this claptrap?" David said. "Gwen, get back in the car and let's get out of here."

"No, Gwen, don't get back in the car," Felix said. "I'll take you home."

David fired back. "Like hell you will, Felix."

"Please...please," Gwen said. "This is all my fault."

"It's not your fault, Gwen. It's his," David said. "He's a manipulative s.-o.-b. who thinks he can make you do whatever he wants you to do just because you're his client."

"Is that what she told you, David? That she's merely my client?"

"I was trying to tell him tonight," Gwen interjected.

"Don't," David said. "Don't say anything. Just get back in the car."

"And what did he tell you, my dear? Did he tell you that he loved you? More's the point, did Mr. Hammer ever show you that he loved you?"

"He does love me, Felix. He's asked me to marry him."

"Yes...no doubt he has, dear. But I ask again...has he ever showed you he loved you? Has he ever actually made love to you?"

"That's none of your damn business!" David shouted.

"You need not answer, Gwen. It was a rhetorical question. I already know the answer. And I have a feeling that Mr. Hammer's marriage proposal involved some sort of elopement. Did it not?"

"How did you know that?" Gwen asked.

"Shut up. Just shut up, Felix. You're going too far!"

"No David, I'm afraid I should have gone farther earlier. But I'll remedy that now, so we need not continue this charade."

"What...what are you talking about?" Gwen asked.

David quickly said, "I'm warning you, Felix...keep your damn mouth shut."

"Gwen, darling," Felix said. "The reason Mr. Hammer asked you to elope...in whatever form he did...is so a marriage could be recorded and therefore not quickly overturned."

"Don't listen to him, Gwen. He's a manipulative liar."

"And the reason Mr. Hammer hasn't made love to you is that he's a homosexual, dear. It's probably stretched his acting capabilities mightily to make you think he's actually in love with you."

"Gwen, this is stupid. Please, get back in the car."

"You see, it would prove disastrous to Mr. Hammer's career if it became common knowledge that he prefers boys to girls. His potential as a romantic leading man would be virtually nil. However, if he was to announce that he was married to a young, beautiful, voluptuous woman...well then...anything that came out after that...he could just deny as scurrilous rumor and innuendo. Believe me, dear, no one would like to see a female bride on Mr. Hammer's arm more than his studio."

"Gwen...don't believe any of this. He's lying to keep you under his wing."

"You were the perfect choice, Gwen. An emerging talent...with a recent hit...the kind of woman every real man would want. And of course, you were new enough to our rather insular community...to not be acquainted with the various peccadilloes of all its inhabitants."

Gwen was stunned. She wasn't sure what to believe, or how to react. She just stood there looking back and forth between the two men.

"Come, my dear," Felix said stepping toward her. "I'll take you home."

David stepped quickly between them saying, "She's not going anywhere with you."

Felix spat back, "Out of my way, you preening fairy."

David reached back and threw a right cross he had learned from the boxing instructor on his last film. But this time he didn't pull the punch. It smashed into Felix's face and sent him careening over the front fender of his car.

Gwen shrieked, "Felix!" Then turned and slapped David as hard as she could before rushing over to help the older man.

"Felix...Felix...are you alright?"

Still flat on his back, he managed to get out in short breaths,

"Never better." But when he tried to sit up, he quickly brought his hand to his heart. "Is this where he hit me?"

"No...no...he hit you in the jaw."

"How odd," Felix said, wincing. "It hurts...hurts like the devil...right here."

"David...David," Gwen yelled. "I think something's wrong with Felix."

"Oh God," Felix said, now with both hands on his chest. "Oh merciful God."

"David...David...I think he's having a heart attack! Come help me get him up. Come quickly!"

But David didn't come. In fact, he didn't even hear her. He was already behind the wheel and backing around Felix's car.

"David...David, I need you to help us!" Gwen screamed, but her screams were drowned out by tires spinning on gravel and the roar of David's engine as he peeled out of the alcove and sped away into the night.

Slumped on the ground, cradled in Gwen's arms, Felix moved his mouth to speak, but no sound emerged. She pressed him to her bosom, crying, "Felix...don't...please don't go. It's going to be alright. You're going to be okay. Felix...please say something...say something, please...answer me, Felix. Please answer me."

But Felix was beyond answering.

Chapter 37

Chicago

Jillian could no longer wish away the fact she was pregnant with a rapist's child. Ian Donovan's parting gift to her had been far more than the degradation he set out to inflict. There was a life growing inside her. A life that might forever evoke a vision of the beast she'd always remember, and the night she would never forget.

It was no longer enough to bemoan her fate, and question why God had let this happen to her. *Perhaps he never lets anything happen,* she thought. *Perhaps people everywhere are the ones who make everything happen. Then it's up to even more people to deal with the cards that have been dealt. There was too much to think about,* Jillian concluded. Too many questions that couldn't be answered. Too many what ifs, and if onlys. There was no point in trying to find the eternal why. There was only the what. What was she going to do about it?

For the last few days she had continually stared at herself in the mirror—naked, turning sideways to see if she was beginning to show. She dressed to draw as little attention as possible. But she couldn't avoid the fact that a decision was imminent. She couldn't bring herself to speak the word aloud. Each time she tried it would sour in her mouth and make her sick to even think about it. Abortion. Who creates such a word? Such an appalling word.

Every time she was alone, she would wind up weeping. Not really feeling sorry for herself. She had gotten beyond that. She would just cry for no other reason than the fact she was alone. No one to talk to. No one with whom to share the burden with. No one with which to anguish over a decision that could never be reversed.

Jillian couldn't bring herself to talk to her parents. They had lived too long and worked too hard to be thrust into a situation that could only fill their hearts with sadness for their daughter and her dilemma. And she couldn't ask for Brendon's advice. By the time he received her letter…if he ever received her letter…she would have reached a point of no return, one way or the other. And why should he have to face this too, with everything he had to bear. No girlfriends were close enough to help. She simply hadn't made that many friendships. And most of the girls she knew prattled on about whatever was told to them. No matter how much the teller asked that they keep it to themselves.

No. The decision was hers. And hers alone. It hadn't happened to anyone else. It had happened to her. And only she could bear the weight of how she would deal with it. The time had come for her to decide. And she did.

A knock, faint, but definitely a knock, caught Mr. Hightower's attention. "Yes. Come in."

Jillian stepped inside his office. "Mr. Hightower. Do you have a moment?"

"Certainly, Jillian. Come in and sit down."

Since the aborted robbery, and Jillian's subsequent rise to assistant manager, Mr. Hightower always made time for her. And why not? Business at the drug store had done nothing but grow since he increased her responsibilities. "Is there something with the accounts I should know more about? Or is it the pharmacy? Running low on anything, are we?"

"No, Mr. Hightower. It's not about any of that. It's about me. I have to talk to you about me."

"Oh? Having problems with the other employees, is it? Are they jealous of your advancement?"

"No Sir. It's not that."

"Not one of my competitors trying to steal you away is it? I know I should have reviewed your salary some time ago and—"

"No Sir. It's not that either."

"Well Jillian, if it's not about any of that, what's it about?"

"Well Sir, I'm going to need to take some time off soon. Some time away from the drugstore. To deal with some personal problems I'm having."

"Hope you're not sick, girl. You don't look sick. Still got that glow in your cheeks. You've always made this place look better, you know. People always happy to see you."

"Well, Sir. That's sort of what I wanted to talk to you about. You see I'm…I'm going to start looking a little different…pretty soon."

"Different? How do you mean different?"

"Please, Mr. Hightower. Please don't say anything for a minute, okay? Just let me say what I came to say. Before you speak again. Alright?"

"You have the floor, my dear. I'm all ears."

Jillian began by telling her boss that the mugging she had recently endured wasn't only a mugging. She said she had been less than honest with the police and everyone else about what had really happened to her. The more she talked, the more tears began to well in her eyes and run slowly down her cheeks. But she didn't stop until she got it all out. She didn't stop until she had mentioned the rape, and the pregnancy, and the fact that she had decided to keep the baby.

"And…I know, Mr. Hightower…how important it is to you…for the drugstore to reflect a business-like atmosphere. For the drugstore to be a place where people know they're dealing with upstanding people in the neighborhood. And…well, I'm afraid a woman that's obviously with child…a woman that so many people know is not married…well, I'm afraid for how it might look…how it might make some people talk and maybe even keep others away."

"I see," Hightower said.

"And I just don't see any other way around it, Sir. I think the only thing for me to do...well...is to leave when it starts to get obvious...you know."

"And just when do you think that might be?"

"Probably in a month or less...I guess...I'm not really sure. I've never been through this before."

"Well, you know, Jillian...there might just be one other way to deal with this. One way where you wouldn't need to leave...and you wouldn't need to share with others what you've just shared with me...and you wouldn't have to worry about being ostracized...or out of work...or anything."

"Oh, Sir...what's going to happen...is going to happen. I've made up my mind to that. Someone told me the other day that you can't change life. You can only deal with it."

"That's what I'm suggesting, Jillian. I'm just suggesting a different way of dealing with it."

"I'm sorry, Sir. I really don't understand. What do you mean?"

Then, Mr. Hightower, a widower of some fifteen years, did the most remarkable thing. He asked Jillian to marry him.

Chapter 39

The French Coast

After the bridge at Pont-du-Chef had been taken, a field hospital was set up to handle the wounded. That's the first place Riley and Brendon brought Paul when they finally reached Bravo Company. The last few miles before arriving, each private took turns carrying their lieutenant, via a fireman's lift, on their backs. He had been incapable of walking. Two days later he was sitting up on his cot in the infirmary, writing a letter to his mother, when Brendon and Riley came in to see him.

"Well, look at that," Brendon joked, "malingering again. Wouldn't you know it, Private Cross?"

"Looks pretty healthy to me," Riley responded. "Pretty healthy, indeed."

"Hey, fellows," Paul said. "Thanks for coming by. And thanks a lot more for getting me here. Sorry I kind of let you guys down."

"No way you let us down, Sir," Riley said. "You pointed the way, we just followed."

"Well, if it wasn't for you two, I don't know what I would have done."

"You'd have hobbled your way over here like Long John Silver," Brendon said. "We just didn't want to take that long."

"What did the sawbones say?" Riley asked. "You going to be coming back to the platoon, in a day or two?"

Paul paused before he spoke. Then he put down the letter he had been writing. "Afraid not. Wouldn't be able to keep up with you. According to the doc, I'm never going to do much more than lean on a cane from here on out. Some nerves sustained damage that simply aren't going to get better. I get to keep the leg. But officers who can't run can't lead men into battle. Looks like it's a desk job for me from here on out."

"That one of those million dollar wounds you hear about?" Brendon asked. "The kind that get you sent back stateside?"

"I suppose it is."

Riley said, "Sort of bad news, good news…isn't it, Sir?"

"All in how you look at it, I suppose," Paul answered.

"Well I'd look at it like I don't have to worry about dodging any more Kraut bullets," Brendon said. "That's the way I'd look at it."

"Sorry you won't be putting us through our paces, though, Lieutenant," Riley added. "You got us through some tight scrapes in Italy and here. We owe you a lot. It's going to take a bit longer to win this war without you."

"You'll get the job done."

"Look, Lieutenant…" Brendon began, his tone turning decidedly more serious, "both of us wanted to say again…that we're convinced neither one of us…or you either…had anything to do with that woman's death. She must have killed herself. Somehow. She must have."

"That woman had a name. Colette Auteuil."

"I know we can't figure it out, Sir," Riley said. "But it's just seems impossible to believe any of us is that kind of man. That's the kind of thing we came over here to stop…isn't it?"

"Whatever we think," Paul answered, "once something like that is done…it can never be undone. But I believe justice eventually prevails. In this world, or the next."

"Well, we don't want to keep you, Sir," Brendon interjected. "We know you must be tired from all those painkillers they're pumping into you."

"Yes Sir, we'll let you get some rest now," Riley added.

"Listen, both of you…I think you should know. I submitted an After Action Report regarding our separation from the unit and our subsequent return. I felt it was my duty. It includes the night we spent at the farmhouse."

"What did you say happened, Lieutenant?" Brendon asked.

"I simply included what we found. And what the situation was. I didn't speculate on how it happened. I simply reported on what you told me and what I told you…that none of us profess any knowledge of what transpired."

"Won't that raise more questions than it answers, Sir?" Riley said. "Won't it lead to some sort of investigation?"

"I don't know…Riley."

"Hey, that's the first time you've used my given name."

"Well, who knows when…or if…we'll be seeing each other again."

"So where does it go from here, Lieutenant? The report I mean. What will happen next?"

"Brendon…I can't really say. That's up to the army. I just didn't feel it was right to act like nothing happened. I felt there should be some record of her passing. Even if that record was inconclusive. After what she did for us, I thought it was the least we could do."

Riley looked at Brendon, then at Paul. He said, "It's a hell of a thing. A hell of a thing for three…friends, to always have between them."

"Yeah," Brendon replied. "A hell of a thing."

"I wish it hadn't happened," Paul said. "I wish a lot of things hadn't happened. And I wish you both…good luck."

Part 3

Reckoning

Chapter 39

Berlin, Germany 1952

The war had been over for seven years. Across Europe, cities were slowly rebuilding. The speed of their recovery, however, was often dependent on the amount of devastation that had befallen them in the war and the amount of American economic aid they received from The Marshall Plan. Berlin had been a recipient of both. Allied bombing during the war, and the Russian assault at the end of it, had destroyed nearly one fifth of all the buildings and virtually half of the inner city itself. Monetary infusions from the United States went a long way to start the process of rebuilding. At least in West Berlin. The eastern zone, which was controlled by the Soviets, chose not to be a recipient of such American largesse. To have done so, the Russians believed, would have given the West too much control over Communist economies; something they were loath to contemplate.

Immediately after the war, Berlin became a divided city. Under the London Protocol of 1944, the United States, United Kingdom, France, and the Soviet Union each bore responsibility for a different sector of the city. Both military and civilian personnel from each country became involved in the restoration of what the Third Reich had envisioned as the Welthauptstadt Germania, or World Capital Germany. Rather than becoming the center of the world, Berlin had become a center of homelessness, hunger and fear. A city that depended more on the benevolence of strangers than the strength of its people for renewal.

One of those strangers was a young, thin, bespectacled Frenchman who had spent his educational years immersing himself in the mountains of minutiae and oceans of archives that chronicled the Second World War. While still in school, he talked his way into an unpaid apprenticeship in the French ministry charged with locating, cataloging, and housing both the Free French and the Vichy Government's documentation of Germany's occupation of France during the war. He threw himself into the myriad of tasks he was asked to perform with such verve and gusto that upon graduation he was immediately offered a full time position in the records division. There he continued to prove diligent, conscientious, thorough, and industrious to the extreme—always willing to volunteer for assignments that others would shy away from. No task, regardless of how formidable it was, or how challenging it might be, or how long it might take, did he ever turn down. He showed what one supervisor noted as an obsession for detail, knowledge, and information that dwarfed his peers as well as vastly more experienced coworkers. Not surprisingly, he soon found himself in demand from bureaucrats at virtually all levels with all sorts of personal agendas. The lazy wanted him to do the work for them. The earnest wanted the best individual they could get for the job. The ambitious wanted to loan him out to others so they would look good for recommending such a clerical phenomenon. And he, never content to stay too long in one place, continued to accept any and every assignment that would allow him to feed his unquenchable thirst for detail about everything relating to the war, the occupied, and the occupiers.

This particular morning it was misting rain as he walked past the Hotel Kempinski on his way to the singularly unattractive office building that had been inexplicably untouched by Allied bombs during the war. As was his habit, he stopped by the outdoor newsstand to quickly peruse the multitude of newspapers and magazines on display. Fluent in English and German, as well as his native French, he scanned the various publications quickly and found nothing worthy of turning his attention away from the work that awaited him. Turning his collar up against the rain that was starting to fall harder, and pulling his hat lower and tighter on his head to keep the rising wind from blowing it off, he leapt over a puddle at the curve, crossed the street and entered the building.

An official in the French government had seconded the young man to an American military liaison office. He had arrived in the city shortly after the Berlin airlift had begun and he was seemingly quite taken with the Americans' ability to throw whatever resources were necessary at whatever problem needed solving. He was especially enamored with the voluminous files the Yanks kept within the building. Since few of them were of a highly classified nature, they had no problem with him perusing documents on his own time to increase his insatiable appetitive for all things war related. In fact, they were actually flattered that he frequently voiced his admiration for the U.S. role in liberating the continent, as well as his obvious desire to learn more about American operations in France and Germany. The young man was at his desk when his superiors arrived in the morning and still at it when they left at night. In their minds he possessed the sort of gung ho attitude that was all but absent in most Europeans. This endeared him to them even more.

His day ended, like most, with him alone at his desk smoking a cigarette and finishing a cup of coffee long after everyone else had left for drinks, dinner, or whatever else the evening held. He exhibited no particular interest in socializing, preferring interesting files to itinerate friendships. This night, there were a number of folders he wanted to wade through that he had pulled aside. But leafing through one while reaching over to set his cup of coffee down, he inadvertently sent the top of the stack flying off the corner of his desk. The files crashed to the floor like firebombs over Dresden, spilling papers in every direction.

The young man was much too fastidious to leave them lying about or to put them back in mere random order. So he began to scoop the scattered papers off the floor and place them back on his desk where he could more easily re-alphabetize them. Scanning each rapidly as he sorted, his heart suddenly stopped. Stopped cold. His eyes froze on the paper in front of him. The supervisor who had referred to his attraction to folders, files, documents, words and letters on paper as an obsession, was more correct than he knew. And now, at this very moment, the young man realized he potentially held the object of his obsession in his hand.

There, between his fingers, on a single sheet of paper, was quite possibly what he had been looking for as long as he could remember. His glance had caught her name near the bottom of the page and he stood transfixed. Had he really seen it? Was it an apparition? If he removed his thumb from atop her name would it fly from the paper like a butterfly taking wing? He could not bear to chance it. So he held his thumb firmly in place as his eyes darted to the heading and he began to read from top to bottom.

HEADQUARTERS 505TH REGIMENT 82ND AIRBORNE
SUBJECT: Report After Action Against Enemy
To: Bravo Company Commander

1. In accordance with paragraph 10 (c3) AR 345-105, the following report after action against enemy for the period of June 5 to June 8, 1944, is hereby submitted.

2. On the night of June 5, 1944, along with Bravo Company, I participated in a parachute assault over Contentin Peninsula, Southern France. Upon landing, I was separated from my unit.

3. I joined fellow platoon members, PFC Riley Cross and PFC Brendon O'Byrne who were also separated. Determining that the proper course of action was to link with Bravo Company, we set out for our mission objective, Chef-du-Pont.

4. En route, we engaged an enemy patrol at approximately 22:30 HRS and overcame same. Later, we encountered a minefield where I sustained a wound. We remained in the field the night of June 6.

5. The night of the following day, June 7, we took refuge from a storm at the farmhouse of French citizen, Colette Auteuil. She, Privates Cross, O'Byrne, and I, were the only ones present in her home. Due to the weather conditions and the severity of my wound, we accepted her offer to stay overnight. The following morning, we discovered Miss Auteuil dead by apparent strangulation. Neither PFC Cross, PFC O'Byrne, nor myself, profess any knowledge of how her death occurred.

6. We proceeded to Chef-du-Pont where we rejoined Bravo Company at approximately 17:30 HRS, June 8, 1944.

Paul C. Cassidy
1st Lieutenant
Bravo Company
505th Regiment

It was real. It existed. He was actually holding in his hand the information he had been seeking for the last seven years of his life. The years that took him from a child of ten to a young man of seventeen. Years that never came close to diminishing his resolve. If anything, the years had strengthened it. The years of searching and reading and thinking he was on the right trail, only to find the trail led nowhere. The years of accumulating and processing and rethinking information that might lead to some other piece of information that would put him in a position to dig further and further. There was always the possibility that nothing existed. In a conflagration that consumed over sixty million lives, who could know for certain that the death of one particular individual would be noted. Yet he always believed he would find something. Some scrap of information that would give him insight into a day that had been burned into his memory forever. He hadn't known what form it would take. But he knew in his heart it would be there. Now, it was not only in his heart, it was in his hand.

He put the paper down long enough to reach inside his valise and pull out the framed photograph of his mother and father in Paris. Setting it beside the After Action Report, he said to himself, "Ma mère, I have their names. Your son, Rémy Auteuil, has the names of those who turned you from a flower...to that creature you became. It will not be difficult to track down their 201 Files...their personnel records. Then I will find a way to get to America. No matter how long it takes, I will find them. Find them wherever they are. If I can find this," he said, "I can find anything. You will have your vengeance, ma mère...je te promets."

Chapter 40

Los Angeles, 1944

Paul had been reassigned to the States before the war ended. His leg made it impossible for him to serve in a forward position. The army, realizing the public relations value of having a young, decorated veteran available for publicity assignments, sent him back to Los Angeles to serve as administrative officer for the Hollywood recruitment center. His mother was thrilled to have him home, though she wept openly when he stepped off the train at Union Station and limped toward her leaning on his cane. She protested that hers were tears of joy simply to have him back, but she couldn't fool herself. A ramrod straight young man left her orbit to serve his country. The country sent back something less. It failed to cross her mind that so many sons were not returning to their mothers at all. Still, she mustered the courage to dry her tears and avoided the temptation to stare too long at his leg or the cane that was its constant companion.

Paul moved in with his mother at their Pacific Palisades home. He told her he planned to move closer to the city the first opportunity he had. She didn't argue, but she never missed an opportunity to tell him how wonderful it was to have him with her. How it eased the loneliness of no longer having his father there. Paul's sense of responsibility, as well as his love for his mother, made it impossible for him not to give priority to her feelings.

One weekend soon after he returned, the dry cleaners returned his dress uniform, which he had recently sent to be cleaned and pressed. They attached a small packet to the garments that the delivery boy explained held the contents of his pockets. Among the assorted loose change and railroad ticket stubs, Paul realized he had also left the photo there that his mother had sent him in one of her letters. The photo of his mother with the young film actress. He took it with him when he joined his mother for lunch on the patio.

"Say, Mother…what did you say this girl's name was?"

"Let me see that picture, dear. Oh. Yes, that's the actress, Gwen Taylor. Actually I haven't seen her for some time."

"Why is that?"

"Well, she was involved in some rather scandalous business."

"Oh, really? Well, don't hold back. Tell me all about it."

"Well she used to come here quite often…with her agent. That Mr. Pressman. Felix Pressman. You remember, I told you about him. How we were speaking with him the night your father was…"

Sensing his mother was about to get emotional, Paul jumped in. "Yes. You told me about that. But let's get back to the scandalous part."

"Well, Mr. Pressman suffered a heart attack and died."

"Nothing very scandalous about that."

"No, but you see it was the manner in which his heart attack occurred. Apparently, he and Miss Taylor and another actor…Hammer, yes, David Hammer was his name. Well, apparently they all got into some sort of row and Mr. Pressman wound up dead."

"What was the row about?"

"I'll get to that. But you see the whole thing happened on some shady lover's lane…late at night, out on Mulholland Drive."

"Ah ha! The plot thickens."

"Indeed it does. There was a trial and everything. The district attorney's office charged this Hammer fellow with manslaughter."

"But I thought you said Pressman had a heart attack."

"He did, but it happened right after Hammer struck him. Struck him with his fist. And Hammer was both a much larger and younger man."

"So...did Hammer get convicted? And just where does Miss Taylor come in?"

"No. Hammer was acquitted. The jury said there was no way he could have known about Mr. Pressman's heart condition. Gwen testified she didn't even know about it. Hammer received a lesser conviction of simple assault. And he even got a suspended sentence for that. I think those Hollywood people have the courts in their pockets. Like when Errol Flynn got off for...well you know."

"Yes, that one, I do know about mother. His statutory rape case was in the old papers we got overseas. In Like Flynn became the expression for getting away with things. But I'm still waiting for the really scandalous part."

"Paul...the entire affair was all over the tabloids and the gossip columns. A younger woman and an older man. Another man as well. Mulholland Drive late at night. Fisticuffs. A death. I mean the whole thing is just all so tawdry, isn't it?"

"If you say so, Mother. Certainly is a lovely girl though, isn't she?"

Paul didn't give their conversation much thought after that. Until he received a request from Columbia studios to attend a pre-production meeting they were having regarding an upcoming war movie. The studios often made requests of the army for technical advisors. More often than not the military was happy to oblige. Especially when the script was considered beneficial to morale and the war effort. During the meeting, Paul found much to take issue with in the script. He made several suggestions regarding tactics, operations and the like. Of course, he had no idea whether his suggestions would be implemented or not.

After the meeting ended, he was walking across the studio lot to where he had parked his car. "Incredible," he said to himself in response to the myriad types of costumed characters who were going in and coming out the long row of sound studios. There were cowboys, centurions, Arab tribesmen and Vegas showgirls. There was also a woman walking his way who stood out from all the rest even though she was simply clad in a tailored business suit. The way it clung to her Coke-bottle figure had Paul transfixed. When he got past that and saw the face atop it all, he was even more impressed, and delighted to realize he had actually seen it before.

"Oh, pardon me, Miss."

"Yes. Can I help you? I believe they're shooting the war picture on Stage 8."

"Oh, no…I'm not in uniform…well, I mean I am in uniform…but it's not a costume."

"I'm sorry. I assumed you were an extra or something. But you're a real soldier, huh?"

"I suppose I am. You see I recognized you and—"

"You'd like an autograph. Sure, no problem. Do you have a pen?"

"No. I mean I do have a pen. But I didn't stop you for your autograph."

"Oh…I'm sorry."

"No. It's my fault, really. I mean it's not that I wouldn't like your autograph. It's just that, well, you see, I think you're a friend of my mother."

"Your mother?"

"Yes. Mrs. Cassidy…from Pacific Palisades?"

"Why, of course. And you must be Paul. The Paul she talked so much about. Is she okay?"

"Yes. She's fine."

"I'm afraid I haven't seen much of her lately. Of course, I haven't seen much of anyone, really. I've been very busy you know…with roles…and, well, other things."

"No, listen I understand completely. And believe me, she's fine. I just wanted to stop you to introduce myself."

"You need no introduction, Lieutenant Cassidy. Your mother's told me all about you. Paul Cassidy, First Lieutenant, United States Army."

"And you're Gwen Taylor. Actress. A quite beautiful actress, I hope you don't mind me saying."

"No girl ever minds a compliment like that, Lieutenant Cassidy."

"No, please. Call me Paul."

"Certainly, Paul. And you call me Gwen. So, what are you doing here on the lot?"

Paul went on to explain why he was there and what he had been doing. And the fact that he recognized her from one of the photographs his mother had sent him.

"I wonder, Miss…I mean, Gwen…I wonder if you might like to have dinner with me some evening?"

She paused before she answered. "Well, Paul, that's a lovely invitation…it's just that I'm really busy with a movie at the moment. And, to be honest…well, I haven't actually gone out with anyone in quite some time. Not since the…well, not for a while now."

"That makes us even," Paul said. "I haven't been out with a member of the opposite sex in…well, I couldn't tell you how long. But I'd very much like to take you out, Gwen. Whenever your schedule allows. Oh, of course, if there's…I mean if you have a—"

"No, Paul. There's no one. I mean, I'm not seeing anyone right now or anything like that."

"Well, I could tell you that if you accepted, you'd really be helping the war effort," Paul joked. "But the truth is, this is a purely personal request."

Gwen looked into his eyes. *They were nice eyes,* she thought. *Honest eyes.* The kind of eyes she hadn't seen for a long time. "Sure, Paul. I'd love to have dinner with you. Can I ring you once I know more about what the call times are going to be for the picture I'm doing?"

"Absolutely. I'll be waiting by the phone. Both of them. Let me give you my office number and my home number. Use either one. I'll look forward to hearing from you."

Paul took a pad, jotted down the numbers, and gave them to her. He tipped his cap when they parted. As they walked away in opposite directions, Gwen heard the sound of the cane on the cement and looked back over her shoulder to see him limping toward his car. *What a shame,* she thought. *Hopefully, it's only temporary. Such a nice looking guy.*

Connections were made and schedules worked out and dinner happened at a hillside restaurant overlooking the Pacific. Gwen was happy to be away from the studio and spending time with someone who wasn't a card-carrying member of the movie establishment. Paul was happy to be in the company of such a gorgeous young woman who seemed relatively free of the affectations Hollywood starlets put on like lipstick. The dinner was filled with expected conversation about what it was like to work in the movies and what it was like to go to war. Both touched on the banalities of each with neither getting into what it was really like to land a role or take a hill. Polite decorum reigned and when Paul dropped her off at her bungalow, both seemed a bit uneasy about the appropriateness of a good night kiss.

Gwen broke the ice by taking Paul's shoulder in her hand and saying, "Thank you for a lovely evening, Paul." Then she leaned forward to give him a peck. When their lips touched, there was a mutual feeling of warmth and pleasure that surprised both of them. They held the kiss a little longer that either had expected.

"Gwen, I had a wonderful time. I do hope we can do it again soon."

"Yes. Let's," she said. "Please call me when you can."

"I will. I will definitely call you," Paul answered.

He wanted to kiss her again, but he felt it probably wasn't right. So he said goodnight and they parted. Then each spent the rest of the night before they fell asleep thinking about each other. Paul contemplated how lucky he was to have survived the war and met someone so beautiful. Gwen wondered if perhaps a life outside stage sets, false fronts, and klieg lights might actually offer more satisfaction that the frequently counterfeit culture of Hollywood.

Many dinners followed. Many lunches too. As well as Sundays at the beach and visits to different Los Angeles art museums, concerts, and plays. Their conversations progressed to much more personal areas. Gwen talked about her short and silly infatuation with David Hammer. Though Paul never asked, Gwen also opened up about her relationship with Felix—his guidance of her career and the ways she repaid him. She said she had loved him but she had never been in love with him—if that was understandable. Paul said it was. He spoke of past girlfriends, his time at college, he even got into more specific details of action he had seen in the war. Though he kept to himself the night at the farmhouse in France. The sharing of their experiences was soon followed by the sharing of the bed at Gwen's bungalow. Paul had never known such ecstasy. Her body and what it yielded was everything he had dreamed it would be. Gwen loved the way Paul was both gentle and strong with her. When she took him inside her, she felt his warmth of love for her as well as her body. They made love long into the night. And held one another long after the morning light had washed across them.

* * *

On May 8, 1945, the announcement was made of Germany's unconditional surrender. Japan's surrender would follow approximately three months after that. Which was then followed by the wedding day of Gwen Taylor to Paul Cassidy. Paul's mother was less than thrilled with the pairing. She still felt the hint of scandal was not something she wanted the Cassidy name associated with. But there was no denying Paul's feeling for Gwen. So she did nothing to stand in the way of their happiness.

Once the war ended, the army was obliged to scale back to peacetime personnel levels. This was fine with Paul since he no real desire to re-enlist. He had accomplished his goal of serving his country and doing his part. Now he was eager to get on with the rest of his life, although he wasn't completely sure about the best way to do that. He made no effort to encourage Gwen to give up her career. He felt she should work as long as she continued to enjoy it. She let him know that was what she wanted as well. At least until they had children, she said.

Paul knew he had to make a decision about his father's real estate business. It had been overseen by one of the firm's longtime employees since his father's death, even though Paul's mother retained actual ownership. She wanted Paul to take over, but he was hesitant to make the commitment—knowing deep down that wasn't really how he envisioned his future. He suggested they look into selling the business, telling his mother he thought they could probably make enough to keep her in her home and comfortable for the rest of her days. She hated the thought of Cassidy & Company taking on some name other than her late husband's, but she didn't want to chain Paul to something he didn't really want. She felt he had more than earned the right to live his life his own way. So Paul told the firm's lawyers to look into potential buyers. He added the stipulation that any buyer must agree to keep the firm's current personnel employed for no less than two years. He didn't feel they should have to suffer simply because he didn't want to spend his days with surveys, appraisals, and escrow accounts.

Gwen's career continued to move forward. The long term deal Felix had secured for her at Colombia saw to it that she'd stay in the public eye at least for the run of the six pictures she was contractually obligated to make for the studio. But with Felix no longer around to find opportunities for her, the ability to be loaned out for great roles at other studios simply didn't develop like she hoped they would. Still, she was happier than she'd even been with a job she loved and a husband she loved even more. All of the pictures she was involved with were being made at the studio rather than on location, so she was home every night at a reasonable hour. And she loved the role she was able to play day in and day out as Mrs. Paul Cassidy.

"Will we be going to your mother's for lunch this Sunday, Paul?"

"Actually, this coming weekend you get a reprieve."

"Now, Paul, you know I don't mind it. I think your mother may even be getting back to the way she felt about me before Felix's death."

"She thinks the world of you. Even if she won't admit it to you, me, or herself."

"Then why aren't we going over, Sunday?"

"We've been invited to a garden party. It's being given by a fellow who just might turn out to be a potential buyer of dad's business."

"Do we know him?"

"Not yet. That's why we're going to the party. The attorneys set it up."

"Does this fellow have a name?"

"Yes. It's Zellenski. Herman Zellenski, I think. Some foreigner who recently moved to Los Angeles. Apparently, he's very well off. The lawyers say he's been snapping up real estate in LA and surrounding counties too."

"So…is this so-called party really pleasure…or business?"

"Come on, darling. You're in the movie world. You know there isn't really any difference between the two."

"Right. I simply ask so I'll know what to wear. Dangerous, demure, or dowdy. What do you think?"

"I think…talented as you are…even you aren't a good enough

actress to pull off dowdy. And with your assets, well, demure would be a hard sell too. Might as well go for the gusto and make it dangerous. I like the idea of showing up with a wife on my arm that looks totally unattainable. Might cause him to start his bidding for the company higher."

Gwen joked, "So…I'm just a bauble to be used, huh?"

"Sure," Paul kidded. "Why don't you come over here now and let me shine you up."

The drive to the party took them high into the hills of Benedict Canyon. There were other homes near where they were going but they were all hidden behind towering Live Oaks, Eucalyptus trees, or massive stucco walls that imprisoned their wealthy inhabitants in luxurious cells of green leaves and blue sky. A twenty-foot iron gate halted their ascent just shy of Zellenski's property. The guard stationed there checked their invitation, pulled the latch free, and pushed the gate open granting them access to a winding lane lined with soaring Italian Cypresses. A circular drive fronted the main Spanish style house and ringed a fountain surrounded by honeysuckles, hummingbirds, pink Manzanita, and yellow monkey flowers. The butler greeted Paul and Gwen at the door and showed them to the back of the house where people were strolling past the long, rectangular swimming pool, grazing at a table filled with fruit and canapés, or accepting glasses of Champagne from waiters who wove between them. Looking around to see if they recognized any of the guests, and finding that they didn't, Gwen and Paul accepted the offer of Champagne from the first waiter to walk by. They were just sharing a toast to one another when the butler, who had escorted them to the back, stepped up and said to Paul, "Mr. Zellenski is so glad you could attend. If you and Mrs. Cassidy will follow me to the study, please?"

They did as they were asked and allowed themselves to be led back through the house past hand-carved furniture and over heavy oriental rugs, by walls draped with tapestries, swords, and armor, and through rooms that looked more like movie sets than living quarters in someone's home. Arriving in the study, where heavy red velvet drapes covered the walls not containing bookshelves, the butler excused himself saying Zellenski would be there momentarily.

"Can you believe this place?" Paul asked Gwen.

"Looks like the first reel of a Douglas Fairbanks swashbuckler," Gwen responded.

Peering over Paul's shoulder toward the study's open door, Gwen added under her breath, "And here comes the hero or the villain…I'm not sure which."

Paul turned and saw a thin man walking toward him. His stride was formal and he was clad in tall brown boots, riding pants and a white shirt with a red bowtie. A camel hair blazer was buttoned at the waist, highlighted by a white silk handkerchief in his breast pocket, and the right sleeve of his coat was tucked into his jacket pocket indicating there was no arm there to fill it.

Extending his left hand as he approached Paul, Zellenski said, "I'm so pleased you've come."

Paul set his drink on the desk, switched his cane to his right hand, and reached out awkwardly to shake hands. "It's our pleasure to be invited, Mr. Zellenski."

"This must be your lovely wife, the talented actress, yes?" Then, bowing, he said, "Vous grace ma maison avec votre beauté."

"Your words are as lovely as your home, Mr. Zellenski. Unfortunately I don't understand them," Gwen said.

"I said you grace my home with your beauty. And indeed you do."

"That was French, wasn't it?" Paul asked. "I understood you were Polish."

"That is correct, Mr. Cassidy. However I am relatively fluent in five languages—Polish, French, German, Spanish, and English.

I'm afraid I couldn't help but show off, as you say, in front of such a beautiful lady."

"Yes. She has that effect on most men," Paul responded. Gwen simply smiled and accepted the compliment silently.

"I see you have a cane, Mr. Cassidy. A recent accident perhaps?"

"No, just something to remember the war by," Paul answered.

"Ah, yes. I heard you served very heroically."

"Just served like many others," Paul said.

"He's very modest, Mr. Zellenski," Gwen added. "Paul received the Purple Heart and the Bronze Star." She was a bit annoyed that their host had brought up Paul's condition. So she added, "Pardon me for asking, but was your…was it a result of the war too?"

"Yes and no," he answered. "I was not in the military. Like a few fortunate others, I was able to get out of Poland. But not before the Nazis saw fit to deal with me rather harshly. I'm sure your husband, like myself, is simply happy to have survived and prospered. So many did not."

"Indeed I am," Paul interjected. "But why dwell on the past. That's not what parties are for, is it?"

"Certainly not. Come let me show you around."

For the next half hour Zellenski walked them through his house pointing out particular paintings and artifacts and sharing occasionally interesting details of their history and lineage. At the end of the tour he finally got around to mentioning his interest in Paul's father's company.

"I am an investor, Mr. Cassidy. I invest not only in art and real estate, but also in businesses, as I'm no doubt you're aware. That's why I wanted to meet you, Mr. Cassidy. Similar to my art…I'm always interested in knowing a bit about the individuals involved in my potential acquisitions."

"Well, the company was really run by my father, I've had very little to do with it."

"Yes, but it is said the apple does not fall very far from the tree, correct?"

"Some people say that, I suppose," Paul answered.

"Well...suffice to say that my people are looking into your firm and I am sure there will be further discussions about it. But as you said earlier, this is a party. You two should go enjoy yourselves."

On their drive home, Gwen said what she was thinking. "Well, that was sort of creepy, wasn't it?"

"What do you mean?"

"I mean the whole thing. The party...I got a feeling no one really knew anyone else there. The house...a bit of a mausoleum opened for the day...you know. And Zellenski...well, he just seemed a bit odd to me."

"Have you known very many European aristocrats?"

"Including him...one. But...I don't know. Can you trust him, do you think? For such a talkative fellow, he didn't give many details about himself or his wealth."

"Who knows," Paul said. "That's what lawyers are for. They'll check him out, just like his people are checking us out."

"I'm sure you're right, Mr. Cassidy. You know, for someone who professes to be a non-businessman...you're pretty businesslike."

Mocking Zellenski's thick European accent, Paul said, "Perhaps it is because the apple does not fall very far from the tree."

They both laughed, as Gwen slid across the front seat and Paul put his arm around her. He thought to himself that somewhere in the world there must be someone who was happier than he was. Somewhere there must be a man who loved his wife more or felt more content than he ever had in his life. No, he reconsidered. Maybe there wasn't.

Chapter 41

Pilot Hill

Riley and Brendon had marched into Paris with their comrades. They were received as liberators amid the cheers and adulation of the French people. But they never made it to Berlin. Their fighting ended in the south of Germany as Supreme Allied Commander Dwight Eisenhower made the decision to leave the assault of the German capital to the Russians, while the western Allies sought to mop up the other pieces of the Wehrmacht and keep escaping members of the Nazi government from reforming in the Alps.

Both soldiers mustered out of the service within a year of the German and Japanese surrenders. They exchanged addresses and vowed to keep in touch with each other, though somehow each suspected it was unlikely they'd do so. They had both sworn to one another that neither had anything to do with the death of Colette Auteuil. And both said they found it impossible to believe their lieutenant could have been involved either. Yet the simple fact remained. They had been alone in the farmhouse and she was dead.

Upon returning to Pilot Hill, Riley planned to take advantage of the G.I. Bill, which provided a range of benefits for World War II veterans. He hoped to continue his education by going to college with tuition and living expenses provided through the bill. But once he was home, he realized that wasn't to be. His father, injured in a fall from an oil derrick years before, had been physically unable to go back to work. His mother still had a job in the school cafeteria, and did occasional seamstress work whenever she could, to bring in extra money. They had barely gotten by with the financial help Riley sent when he was on active duty. Now, he couldn't bring himself to leave them to fend for themselves while he lolled about some college campus. So he resigned himself to a life he had always hoped to avoid. A life virtually every other adult male lived in Pilot Hill. A life in the oil fields.

Riley made an appointment with the line boss at one of the service companies that sold equipment to various drilling operators. He was on his way to meet him, but realized in his haste not to be late that he was going to be early by forty-five minutes. So he decided to stop for coffee with a side order of killing time. The decision as to where to stop wasn't difficult. Rosalie's was the only café in Pilot Hill. So he pulled into the gravel parking lot and went inside.

Nine-fifteen was after most working people had breakfast, and long before any of them had lunch. So the place was virtually empty when Riley came in, except for the two men having coffee in one of the booths by a window. Riley recognized one of them right away. He had seen his county car outside. It was Deputy Sheriff Ward Andrews. Ward was the deputy for the southern part of Chambers County. The part that included Pilot Hill and a whole lot of not much else. He had been the deputy for as long as Riley could remember. County government wasn't particularly partial to change in that part of Texas. Riley didn't recognize the man with Ward.

Halfway through his second cup of coffee, Riley watched out of the corner of his eye as Ward got up and walked over to where he was sitting.

"Say, you're Cross, ain't ya? Tom Cross's son?"

"Yes Sir. That's right."

"Back from the war, huh?"

"Yes Sir. I am. Most of us are now, I guess."

"Heard you saw a lot of action over there. Got in some real shootin' scrapes, I understand."

"Hard to avoid, Sir," Riley answered, not really wanting to go into details.

"Wonder if you might have a minute. Someone over here I'd like you to meet."

"Well, I've got an appointment in a few minutes. Got to see a man about a job."

"You don't say," the deputy replied. "Well you just might kill two birds with one stone this mornin' son. Or maybe you won't need that second bird. Come on over."

Riley went with him to the booth and was introduced to Ward's boss, Harris Totter, the Sheriff of Chambers County. Totter was a raw boned, rail-thin man of considerable height, with red hair and a mustache to match. Riley assumed he was probably in his late forties or early fifties. After introductions were exchanged, Riley soon found out the Sheriff was not a man to mince words. He told Riley he had three deputies who worked for him in different parts of the county. And he was about to lose one.

"I got the cancer," Ward said. "No gettin' around it. Just can't be relied on to perform my duties, like I should. Gonna have to retire."

"I'm really sorry to hear that, Sir," Riley said. "But what does it have to do with me?"

"I understand you got sand," Totter said. "And you know your way around firearms. Ward says your old man's in a bad way. That true?"

"He had an accident…Sheriff. Fell off an oil derrick. Can't really do any work now."

"He can't work. Ward can't work. You're out of work. Seems like the whole damn country's going to hell in a hand-basket."

"It's not my dad's fault. Not Deputy Andrew's either from what I can see. And like I told him, I'm on my way to see a man about a job."

"Now don't get your back up, son. That's what you're seeing me about. I need someone to replace Ward. You know this part of the county. You're young and strong. Ward says you come from a good family. And you proved your grit in the war. I think you might make a damn fine deputy."

"But…Sheriff…I don't really know anything about…you know…law enforcement."

"Hell, I can teach you all about that in a day, son. And Ward can give you the ins and outs of his routine."

"It's just that I never thought about this kind of work before."

"You think about busting your back lifting drill pipe, and maybe lose a finger or worse in the process? Think about that, son."

"I just didn't have anything like this in mind, when I came in here…you know?"

"I know this," Totter said. "When fate deals you a pat hand, you play it. Now I'm only going to say this once. Do you want to be a Chambers County Deputy Sheriff? A man respected by the community. A man of authority. A man who makes his living helping the good people he lives with. Or would you rather be just another grease-soaked, back-bent, oil field roustabout?"

"I feel like I have to ask one question before I answer that, Sheriff."

"Okay. One question. What the hell is it?"

"How much does the job pay?"

"You were right, Ward. He's smart too."

Riley Cross took to the job of Deputy Sheriff like cutting horses take to calves. First, he looked the part. His long, lean frame in starched khakis, white button-down shirt, and wide-brimmed Stetson, exuded authority. And the forty-five holstered on his hip helped make up for any questions his youthful mien might have raised in that regard. Second, his time in the army had given him a sense of himself. He knew who he was and what he could do. There was no gnawing need to prove anything to himself or others. Third, he was neither ambitious nor slothful. He believed doing a job well, and being adequately compensated for it, was about as much reward as a workingman could ask for.

Ward took Riley through the majority of his duties before he left to deal with his declining heath. Patrolling was the major one. The streets and roads that ran through Pilot Hill, the gravel trails in and out of the oil fields, in fact all the ranch and farm to market roads throughout the southern section of Chambers County were his responsibility. Riley was basically to look for anything that didn't look right. Like unlocked doors on commercial buildings at night. Cars or trucks where they shouldn't be at times when they shouldn't be there. Ward told Riley one of the main reasons for patrolling was simply showing the flag. Letting citizens know that someone was out there keeping an eye on things. The crime rate in and around Pilot Hill was virtually nil. But there were other responsibilities as well. It was Riley's job to serve as escort for high school athletic teams going to and coming from ball games. He was also expected to be at all the home games to make sure rivalries on the field didn't turn into altercations in the grandstands. Plus he was expected to be the initial responder to any traffic accidents on county roads within his jurisdiction, and to be available to assist the highway patrol if wrecks on the state highway occurred in his area.

True to his word, Harris Totter took a day to brief Ward on the particulars of dealing with citizen requests and complaints, breaking up bar fights, the rudiments of traffic safety, and how and when to report back to him, seek assistance, or simply handle things on his own. Totter told him the weapon he'd have to rely on most often to deal with the policing of southern Chambers County was common sense. "And if I'm as good a judge of character as I think I am," he added, "I'm betting you have a head full of it."

Routine is habit forming. At least it was for Riley. He got into the cadences of his job and gave little thought to getting out of step. There became a sense of security to the place he held in his world that he never sought, but found comforting. People liked him and the way he did his job. They liked the way he stuck teenagers' heads under hydrants to sober them up before taking them home, rather than putting them in jail. They liked the way he never acted high and mighty regarding his particular status in the community. They liked the way he actually looked into personal or neighborhood disputes when he said he would. Even if they didn't always agree with how those disputes were resolved.

One who seemed to like everything about Riley Cross was Sharon Tanner. She came to town a year after Riley became Deputy Sheriff. Just out of Southeast State Teachers' College, Sharon was a willowy redhead with green eyes, a wide smile and a sharp mind. Pilot Hill High School wasn't used to young, pretty teachers. She stood out in the faculty break room like a cactus flower in the desert. It didn't take long before head nods and pleasant greetings between the new teacher and the deputy at football games turned into dinner dates and long drives whenever Riley was off duty. Six months after they met, they were married. Two years after that Sharon gave birth to their son. They named him Dwight, after Riley's former Supreme Commander and the new President of the United States, Dwight D. Eisenhower. Who was also born in Texas, Riley was fond of reminding everyone.

The days, weeks, and months came and went in Pilot Hill, with more and more people moving into Chambers and surrounding counties. The post-war economic boom was on, and energy was needed at ever-increasing rates. It took more employees and more employers to keep the oil fields and refineries operating at peak capacity. Riley's responsibilities increased as the population did. He found himself involved in more complex law enforcement situations than ever before. The county paid for him to take some criminal justice courses at the new Junior College. He did so on his nights off so they wouldn't interfere with his primary duties. And even though his job was taking up more of his days and nights, he always found time for his family. He and Sharon enjoyed taking Dwight, who was a toddler now, on picnics to the lake. There he could walk, run, stumble and fall to his heart's content. Dad or mom were always right behind, to pick him up, dust him off, and stand him back on his feet so he could take off on his next adventure.

Once every other month or so, they'd have a babysitter watch Dwight while Sharon and Riley enjoyed a movie or dinner. At one such outing, Riley was returning to his seat from the concession stand just after the credits had rolled and the movie was starting. He had handed Sharon her popcorn, kissed her on the cheek, and turned to the screen when he saw a blonde and heard her say, "Hello, I'm Belinda Jones and I'm new in town." But Riley knew in an instant she wasn't Belinda Jones. It was Gwen Taylor. The Gwen Taylor he had left behind when he was drafted. The Gwen Taylor he had almost gone AWOL for. The Gwen Taylor he thought he might have recognized in the photograph his lieutenant had shown Brendon and him that dark, rainy night in France. The night he could never get completely out of his thoughts.

My God, Riley said to himself. *Gwen Taylor…an actress in the movies.* A pang of nostalgia momentarily swept through him and it was all he could do to keep the tear in the corner of his eye from moving down his cheek.

"Something wrong?" Sharon whispered.

"No. Nothing," Riley responded under his breath. "Just got some salt from the popcorn in my eye."

Sharon went back to watching the movie. And he watched her as she did. Watched as her bright emerald eyes surveyed the huge black and white screen. Gazed at the cheek he loved to touch with the back of his hand. Stared at her thin, delicate fingers as they gingerly reached in the bag and brought a kernel to the lips that were his, and his alone.

When he looked back at the screen, someone was coming up

behind Gwen…or Belinda…or whatever she said her name was…and surprising her with a kiss on the neck. Then Riley thought…*she's okay. She's really okay. Everything turned out alright for her. Better than alright. She's a big time actress. A success. She has a life of her own and she's obviously living it. Maybe things do work themselves out eventually, one way or the other.*

On the drive home, Sharon said, "You seem awfully quiet tonight. Didn't like the movie?"

"Oh, it was okay, I guess."

"Then what's on your mind, Mr. deep-thinker? Not keeping secrets from me, are you?"

Riley had never lied to Sharon. He didn't want to now. "Not secrets really," he began. "Just things I've always kind of kept to myself."

"Well, I won't pry if you don't want me to. But I'm also a good listener…if that's what you want."

It just seemed the right time, Riley thought. The right time to talk about a girl he had loved a long time ago, and a night in France when he had come upon a farmhouse in the rain.

Chapter 42

Chicago

Brendon mustered out of the service at Fort Benning. The long train ride from Georgia to Chicago gave him plenty of time to think. So much had happened since a Cook County judge gave him a choice between enlisting or facing trial for manslaughter. He knew he had made the right decision, even though there had been times over the last two years when he experienced more fear than he ever thought he could handle. But he survived. He had come out of the war in one piece. In his heart, he wasn't sure that was the outcome he deserved, when so many others didn't come back at all. But he was glad it was behind him. Glad he could lock the war away somewhere in a dark cave, a deep cavern of his mind. It was just something that happened. Something he became a part of but could never fully understand. Like that night in the farmhouse. The one night that plagued him the most. He thought he would have put it behind him by now. But it was still there. Visions of the night, the vineyards, the rain. Visions of the following morning and the bedroom. He wished those scenes would go far back in his mind too. Maybe they would, he hoped. Maybe they would now that he was going home.

As the steel wheels carrying him home rattled and clanked along the rails, thoughts in Brendon's head kept rolling across the tracks of his brain. Thoughts about the place and people he had left years ago. Why had Jillian stopped writing? He knew she didn't have to write him in the first place. Most girls wouldn't have after he left like he did. Just disappearing without a word. But she did write—sharing so much and sounding like he was the most important person in the world to her. Then, nothing. For weeks that turned into months, not a word. He knew it seemed to always take forever for mail to reach guys in the thick of things. He even wondered if all the mail was being held up near the end of the war. But when all his mates received letters time and time again, and he didn't, he had to accept the fact she had simply stopped writing. Maybe, he thought, she was saving him the pain of receiving one of those "Dear John" kiss-offs so many of the guys in his outfit got. But that didn't seem like the Jilly he had known. Or the one who had risen from the ink-filled pages of letters that often kept him going when the going was incredibly tough. What had happened? Why had she stopped? For good or ill he was determined to find out.

Brendon surprised his parents. They knew he was coming home but they didn't know which day he'd actually arrive. There were hugs and kisses and tears of joy. And Brendon's dad broke out the Irish and they all shared a glass at the kitchen table. Brendon gave them the gifts he had brought back with him. A cream and gray scarf from Paris for his mother, and a vintage Black Forest wood pipe from Germany for his dad. They could tell how happy Brendon was to be home. So they said they understood completely when he said he might drop into Finnegan's and see if any of his old chums were about. *Why not let him enjoy himself,* they thought. Their boy was now a man. Perhaps he had been for a long time. And he was safe and home at last.

Finnegan's looked and sounded remarkably like Finnegan's always had. *Gee, it's good to know that some things don't change,* Brendon thought, as he walked through the relatively thin weeknight crowd and up to the bar. Harry, the bartender, didn't recognize him immediately. Just another soldier in for a drink, he assumed. Then Brendon took off his cap and said, "Don't suppose you can make the first one on the house…can you…for an old customer?"

"What…well, as I live and breathe…if it ain't Brendon O'Byrne. In the flesh, as they say. Still got all your fingers and toes…and all your other parts, do ya?"

"I do," Brendon answered. Then bringing his left hand up with his middle finger extended, he added, "Of course this one's a bit paralyzed in a rather unfortunate position."

Both laughed, and Harry said, "Put that away before I break it off, lad. You bet, first one's on the house. What's it going to be?"

"Make it an Irish…a double I think."

"There you go lad, stretching your luck. But then you always did as I recall."

The two jawed for a bit with Harry asking about the war and Brendon asking about the old crowd. Brendon said whoever coined the phrase, "War is Hell," was right, and left it at that. Harry said a lot of the old regulars still came around. He even pointed out Beetle Hearne who was in the booth on the telephone. Beetle was a little bit older than Brendon and had been exempted from military service because of his clubfoot. Brendon remembered he always seemed to have the latest scuttlebutt about things going on in the neighborhood, so he buttonholed him when he came out of the booth and offered to buy him a beer.

"No way," Beetle said. "I'll buy you one. For sticking it to those Nazi bastards."

They took their drinks over to a table in the corner and reminisced for a bit about old times. Eventually Brendon brought the conversation around to the main thing on his mind.

"Say, you know that girl that worked at Hightower's…behind the lunch counter. Jillian, I think her name was. Whatever happened to her?"

"Jillian…Jillian…oh yeah, the pistol packer. The one who dropped that Snapper creep and ran his partner off in the night. Man, was that something."

"Yeah," Brendon said, "I heard about that. That was really something. But I mean what happened to her after that? Is she still around here? Do you know?"

"Oh yeah, man. She's still in the neighborhood. Still at Hightower's. But in a very different capacity."

"What do you mean?"

"I mean she's not behind the counter jerking sodas anymore. She's in the front office, you know. Counting the proceeds."

"No I don't really know what you mean, Beetle. Does she have a different job, or what? What are you talking about?"

"She did it the American way, my man. She married the boss. She's now Mrs. Hightower's Drug Store."

Brendon was stunned. Married Hightower? He had to be twenty…maybe thirty years older than her. "But…what…I mean when…when did this happen?"

"A while back, I guess. Some time ago. Long enough for them to have their own little Baby Snooks crawling around the joint."

"A baby! She and Hightower have a baby?"

"Yeah, can you believe that? Who would have thought the old pill pusher still had the guns and ammo to get the job done, huh? Guess she lit a fire in the old boy. In fact, there's some around who keep up with such things…that say the baby arrived a might sooner than it should have…if you get my drift."

Brendon got his drift, but he didn't reply. He just sat there dumbfounded. Beetle had to ask him twice if he wanted another beer. *No,* he said. Then he made an excuse about having to be someplace and quickly strode out into the Chicago night.

Hightower, he kept saying over and over to himself. An old guy like Hightower. It just didn't add up. And a baby. That seemed even harder to believe. Especially coming on the heels of her letters and all. He lit a cigarette, took a drag, and then let it dangle from his lips as he stuffed his hands in his pockets and took off down the sidewalk trying to make some sense out of what he had just heard. *Maybe,* he thought…if like Beetle said and a baby was already on the way…maybe that explains the marriage. But how did the baby get on the way? Well, he knew how babies came about. But he just couldn't reconcile Jilly and

Hightower that way. He certainly didn't want to conjure that image in his mind. *Could she have planned it,* Brendon wondered. There were some girls he knew who trick guys into marrying them that way. But Jilly wasn't like that. She couldn't be. And there were the letters. The letters that made him believe she couldn't wait for him to come home from the war. Of course, the letters stopped, didn't they? They simply stopped coming.

The more he walked and tried to figure things out, the less sense it made. But whether he could figure it out or not, there were two undeniable facts staring him in the face. They were married, and they had a baby. The reality of that dwarfed everything else. What difference did it make why or how it happened. The fact was, it had. And there was simply nothing he could do about it. When he took the last pull from his cigarette, flicked it into the gutter and looked up, he realized he was standing across the street from Hightower's Drug Store. Had he been walking there unconsciously, but on purpose? Had it just been coincidence? What difference did it make? It was late and Hightower's was closed and shut tight. Too dark to see inside the building. Were there eyes in there? In the dark, peering back at him? Her eyes, maybe. *Don't get any more stupid than you already are,* he told himself. He had vowed to figure out why she stopped writing, and now he knew. He had hoped for a different outcome, but it was what it was. There seemed nothing else to do but move on.

The next day, Brendon asked his dad if there was anyone he knew who might be able to help him find work. The trouble he had gotten into and out of before the war…the incident with the little flower girl…the kind of men he had lived and fought with in the war…all made him realize there were no real shortcuts. If a man wanted a better life, he'd just have to work hard for it. And that's what Brendon intended to do. His dad knew a couple of representatives in the Teamsters' Union, and he said he'd definitely talk to them. The Teamsters had been active in the war effort at home and abroad. They were the only union to guarantee members who had served in the war their seniority status when they returned. And while Brendon hadn't been a member, they were looking to swell their ranks by signing up as many returning servicemen as they could. A week later, Brendon was behind the wheel of a one-ton Ford truck hauling produce between Illinois, Wisconsin, Indiana, and Missouri. He stayed behind the wheel and on the road more than he was off for the next five years. All that walking he had been forced to do in the infantry made him partial to covering miles on a padded seat behind the wheel of a big rig.

By the autumn of 1953, Brendon had built up enough seniority in the union that he could get time off for the occasional holiday. Like most truckers, he knew quite a few women in quite a few truck stops throughout his four-state territory. But none he was necessarily committed to. Plus his parents were getting on in years so he decided to spend Thanksgiving with them in Chicago. After the turkey, dressing, mashed potatoes, and cranberry sauce had been pretty well depleted, Brendon decided to walk off his meal with a late afternoon stroll. A light snow was falling. Light enough to see the flakes fall individually and melt when they hit the back of your hand. But it had been snowing for a number of days, so there was still a bit of white frosting on the limbs and hedgerows in the park outside Saint Michael's church where Brendon stopped for a smoke.

As he sat on the bench enjoying his cigarette, he watched a few children kicking a ball and playing nearby. They were all covered from head to toe in coats, scarves, earmuffs, or hats. It wasn't quite winter yet, but it was Chicago after all. A chill was definitely in the air. After a few minutes, Brendon finished his smoke, dropped the butt on the ground, mashed it out with the sole of his shoe, then picked it up and tossed it into the trash receptacle beside the bench. He then reached into his pocket, pulled out the pack and began tapping out another when she spoke.

"You aren't going to have another, are you?"

Without looking up, Brendon replied, "Nasty habit, I know, but enjoyable."

"Better than chocolate milkshakes?"

Those words did it. He should have recognized the voice initially. But now he knew even before he looked up that he'd be staring into blue eyes. Jilly's eyes.

"Jilly? I mean…Jillian," he said, rising. "I'm sorry I didn't notice…I mean I didn't look—"

"And I wasn't completely sure it was you," she said. "Not from across the park. But I thought it might have been. I came over to make sure I wasn't just imagining things."

"You...you look great. I mean you look very pretty. That's a very nice coat. Is it cashmere?"

"Yes. It is. But do you really care about that?"

"No. Not really. It's just that…well…I'm not really sure what to say."

"You never seemed to be at a loss for words before."

"Yeah. I had a pretty quick mouth, didn't I?"

"I always liked your mouth…I just wouldn't admit it."

"Well, look…why don't we sit down? I mean…do you have a minute?"

"Yes, I do," she said, as they both sat down on the bench.

Jillian asked Brendon how long he had been out of the service and what he had been doing. He talked about his job and how much traveling he had to do. How he had gotten used to living on his own and constantly being in different places. They both spoke of their elderly parents and how they were getting along. It was all preliminary chatter leading to the main event, and they both knew it. Eventually, the real conversation began.

"I understand you got married…and had a child."

"Yes, I did," she replied. "That's my little girl over there," she said, pointing to where a group of three children were playing together. "The one in the red coat."

"What's her name?"

Jillian paused before she answered. Then she said, "Her name is Brenda."

He was stunned. "My God, Jilly, why would you do that?"

"I guess it was my way to be sure I'd always love her. That way…every time I'd speak her name or look in her face, I'd think of the father she should have had."

"Jesus, Jilly. What a thing to say. And if you felt that way…why did you even get married at all? And have a child? It all seems…I don't know…it just all seems so strange."

"Brendon, I want to tell you about it. I've been wanting to tell you about it for so long."

"When your letters stopped with no explanation or anything…I couldn't imagine why."

"It was just something I couldn't bring myself to tell you in a letter. Not with all the awful things that were going on around you. There was nothing you could possibly do about it. So I just stopped writing. I'm so sorry. But I want you to know, Brendon. I want you to know it all."

As the snow continued to fall lazily about them, Jillian unburdened her soul. She told Brendon that she had been raped by Ian Donovan, and that she had become pregnant. She told him of her internal struggle over whether to maintain the pregnancy or not. And how her Catholic faith had finally made her unable to go through with an abortion. She explained Hightower's incredibly kind proposal. A proposal that kept her from having to suffer the humiliation of being an unmarried mother. She told Brendon that Hightower was the kindest man she had ever known and that she had buried him six months ago. A stroke had left him paralyzed for over a year, she said. In many ways, his passing was a blessing, she confided. And his kindness didn't end with his death, she added. She told Brendon that he had left her and the child everything. And that now she was the proud owner of Hightower's Drug Store.

Brendon was overwhelmed. The revelations were the polar opposite of what he had assumed. He felt swamped by the emotions that washed over him. But there was one emotion he couldn't shake. Rage. Rage at Ian Donovan.

"Where is he?" Brendon asked.

"We laid him to rest in the cemetery behind the church," Jillian answered.

"No. Not your husband. Not Hightower. I mean, Ian. Where is Ian?"

"He's gone, Brendon. Gone from Chicago…and gone from my life. For me, he doesn't exist anymore. Today is the first time I've spoken of him in all the years since."

"I'll find him," Brendon said.

"No. No, Brendon, you mustn't. Don't you see? Trying to find him will just bring him back. Bring him back to me as well as you. You have to forget him, Brendon. Forget him like I have. Please do that for me. Please promise me that you won't ever try to find him. That you'll let him stay out of my, and Brenda's, and your life forever."

Jillian was crying now. Brendon found it impossible to do anything other than try to stop her tears. "Alright…I promise. I won't try to find him."

She reached across and took his hand in hers. "Thank you. Thank you for listening and understanding."

He put his other hand on top of hers. "No. Thank you, Jilly. Thank you for being honest with me. And I've never had the chance to thank you for the letters you sent me. They kept me in touch with the real world…with home…with you. They meant everything to me."

She leaned forward, kissed him gently on the lips, and said with a smile, "Okay, then…so when are you going to pay up?"

"Pay up? What do you mean?"

"As I recall, Mr. Brendon O'Byrne, the last time we talked, you invited me to dinner at The Drake Hotel. So when are you going to come through?"

The years, the miles, the oceans he had crossed, and the battles he had fought, melted away like the snow that was dissolving on the park bench. Suddenly he was back at the soda fountain staring into the eyes of Jilly McIntyre, the prettiest girl in the neighborhood. Suddenly the world seemed right again.

"I never meant to stand you up, you know. I was just too ashamed to get back in touch with you. But you're right…what's past is past. How about tomorrow night? You and me…and Brenda if you like…for dinner at The Drake Hotel."

"I think I know of a good babysitter who can watch Brenda tomorrow night. You've got a date, Mr. Brendon O'Byrne. Here," she said, reaching into her purse for a pen and a piece of paper, "let me give you my address."

They kissed again as they parted. Not a passionate kiss, just the kind of kiss one friend might give another in a public place. But when their lips touched, each felt a spark of warmth and excitement that had been missing from their lives for a very long time. Brendon watched as Jillian walked over and took Brenda by the hand. They turned and waved as they were leaving the park. When he waved back, Brendon was no longer thinking about the past, he had the future in mind. A future that now seemed infinitely brighter.

* * *

Old habits die hard. The following day, Brendon decided to get dressed early and stop off at Finnegan's for a couple of drinks before picking up Jillian to take her to dinner at The Drake Hotel. He had donned a blue double-breasted suit, and put a gleaming shine on his dress shoes even though the snow was continuing to fall. When he entered Finnegan's and stepped up to the bar, he ordered an Irish. "Just a small one," he said.

"Well, don't you look like the cat's meow," Harry said, getting the bottle to pour him his drink.

"Big night," Brendon replied. "Wanted to look the part."

"Hope she's worth it, lad."

"Oh, she's worth it alright. No doubt about it."

"Say, Brendon," Harry began. "Take a look at that one...over at the far table."

Brendon looked and saw a man shooting pool by himself. He was young, thin, wore wire-rimmed glasses, a suit that was a half size too big for him, and he still had his hat on. A brown fedora that came close, but didn't quite complement his suit.

"Funny little guy," Brendon said.

"You don't know him?" Harry asked.

"No. I don't know him. Why?"

"He was asking about you. Asked if you ever came in here?"

"Really? What'd you tell him?"

"I told him the truth. Told him you come in here all the time when you're in town."

"What'd you do that for? The guy might be a bill collector or something."

"Or something is more like it. The guy's a foreigner. A Frenchman I think."

"What makes you think that?"

"Got a pretty heavy accent. And he put a nickel in the jukebox and played that frog tune, you know. That *La Vie en Rose* thing."

"Well, like I said, got a big night tonight. Don't want anything getting in the way of that. I'll just finish my drink and be on my way. If he asks again, tell him I'll be in tomorrow afternoon, around three. I'll see what he wants then." With that, Brendon downed his shot of whiskey and turned on his heel.

"Sure thing, lad. Probably just some snail-eating reporter or something. I'll—"

Harry was interrupted in midsentence by a couple of tipsy patrons starting a row at the other end of the bar. He quickly headed their way to break it up. Brendon paused for a moment to see what the fracas was about. The Frenchman heard it too. When he looked up to see what the trouble was, he saw Brendon looking their way. He recognized him immediately from the photograph he had been studying in Brendon's 201 File.

"Chowder-heads," Brendon said to himself, grinning. Then he turned and walked out of Finnegan's. When he did, the Frenchman put down his pool cue and followed him. Harry was too busy corralling the drunks to notice either one of them.

It had snowed a little harder during the day, and a layer of white now covered the sidewalks. Brendon wasn't wearing an overcoat, so he turned his suit collar up as he started to walk the three blocks to the nearest cabstand. The Frenchman closed fast. By the end of the first block he was close enough behind for Brendon to hear him when he spoke.

"Monsieur O'Byrne! Monsieur Brendon O'Byrne!"

Brendon turned and looked at him. "Yeah, I'm Brendon O'Byrne. I thought Harry was going to tell you I'd be in Finnegan's tomorrow."

"You are Brendon O'Byrne, who was a Private First Class in Bravo Company, 505th Infantry, 82nd Airborne?"

"Yeah…that was my outfit. Look mister, I have to be someplace. I'll be in Finnegan's tomorrow afternoon. We can talk then, okay?"

"You were with Private First Class Riley Cross and First Lieutenant Paul Cassidy on the night of June 7, 1944 in the home of Colette Auteuil?"

"Jesus…who are you? What is this about? I really have to be—"

The Frenchman put his hand in his pocket. When he brought it back out he was holding an automatic pistol. "Step in the ruelle…the alley."

"Hey, now wait a minute. Something's wrong here."

He raised the gun saying, "Now! Step in the alley now!"

Brendon did as the man with the weapon ordered. His mind

was racing. *Who is this guy? Why is he asking about that night? How does he know who was there?*

After they had walked a few feet into the alley, away from the street, Brendon turned and said, "Please…listen to me…I don't know who you are, or—"

"I am Rémy Auteuil. My mother was Colette Auteuil."

"But…but she said her son was dead. That he had drowned."

"You and the other two. You killed her. You left her naked and dead. She was a flower and you turned her into something hideous."

"No…listen, you don't understand. I had nothing to do with it. Nothing. I don't know what happened. Riley and the lieutenant…I don't think they…they couldn't have—"

The first shot struck Brendon square in the chest. He jerked back and involuntarily brought his hand up to the wound. The second and third shots knocked him back into the wall of the building. One bullet shattered the wrist he had raised. The other entered his stomach. His legs buckled and he slid down the wall until he was on his side lying in the alley. He wanted to speak but he couldn't. Nor could he stop the visions racing through his mind. He saw the farmhouse again…Colette Auteuil on the bed…he saw Jilly—not as he saw her yesterday, but behind the counter handing him a milkshake…he saw the blood seeping from his wounds and leaving red blotches in the white snow…red blotches that became red rose petals…the red rose petals he had seen when he stepped around the car and found the little flower girl crumpled on the sidewalk. Red rose petals in the white snow. Then the final shot turned everything black.

Chapter 43

Oklahoma / Texas Border

The rapidly aging DeSoto had already come quite a distance, and it looked it. Layers of dust made the sedan more gray than black. It hadn't been washed since its three occupants left Kansas City, where they had done okay for the last few years. Jocko, who was driving, generally served as the wheelman. Kelly, riding shotgun, was the muscle. The man in the back seat, perusing the map he had unfolded on his lap, was the owner of the car and the brains of the outfit, Ian Donovan. Since leaving Chicago, KC had been his base. A town where he made his living pimping, breaking and entering, running numbers, collecting protection money from shopkeepers and other businesses under the thumb of the local mob bosses, and serving as go-between for politicians and local authorities who were on the take and in the pocket of the city's hoodlum hierarchy.

When Ian's bosses got a request from their west coast affiliates for a team to help out some new foreigner who had bought his way into their Los Angeles operations, Ian's trio was selected. Not because they were effective, rather because they were expendable. Frankly, the Kansas City crowd was glad for the opportunity to be rid of them. While there was no honor among thieves, there was occasional camaraderie. Except where these three were concerned. They were the proverbial bad apples. Either screwing up completely or making easy jobs hard. So they told Ian that he and his men had two weeks to get to LA. How they did that and what they did along the way was up to them. While his two cohorts mistakenly assumed this was a reward for their exceptional service, Ian recognized the fact he and his mates were being cast off to some naive outsider. So he decided to use the journey as an opportunity to line their pockets as they went—provided they were smart about it. So far he had seen to it that they were.

Initially they drove from Kansas into Oklahoma and swung onto Route 66 to make their way west. But since time was on their side, Ian made a habit of changing course often to knock over whatever small town gas station, motel, café, or bus stop provided an easy target. Then he'd cut north or south for a while before turning west again to keep the direction of his trek less obvious. He also went out of his way to make sure Jocko, and especially Kelly, didn't get too carried away with their designated roles. He reminded the heavy-handed thug that the cops were a lot less likely to put together an all-out manhunt for a few robberies as opposed to multiple assault and batteries or murders. Ian had no misgivings about the intellectual quotient of his partners.

Ahead of schedule, and with a number of jobs already behind them, when they crossed into Texas, Ian decided to make a steep dip south before starting west again. He thought if they could make a much bigger score, they'd have no need for capers in New Mexico and Arizona, and could make a cleaner, quicker run all the way to California. He had heard stories about how some of these small town banks in and around the oil fields were flush with payroll cash and potentially ripe for the picking. And now seemed as good a time as any to pick one clean.

The reservoirs around Pilot Hill had proven particularly productive over the last few years. So much so that the burgeoning population of welders, pipefitters, roustabouts, roughnecks, drillers, geologists, engineers, and assorted others, grew tired of taking their pay ten miles or more to the nearest bank in the next county. It was only natural that one of the larger, more metropolitan financial groups would respond to demand and open a branch in the growing oil field community. It was also only natural that viewing this secluded one-story fiscal edifice on the corner of four roads surrounding it, Ian Donovan pronounced it not only a prime target, but even better, a sitting duck. He advised his partners in crime that they'd hit it Saturday morning, following the Friday that most of the working men in town would have deposited the lion's share of their pay they couldn't afford to drink or waste.

When Saturday morning came, Riley was on patrol covering the north side of the county for one of the deputies who was in bed with the flu. The only cars in the bank's parking lot belonged to the three employees on duty that day—one assistant manager and two tellers. Ian's DeSoto was parked across the street at the Donut Shop next to the gas station.

"Alright," Ian said, "let's go over it one last time. Jocko, you pull into that parking space closest to the front door. You sit there with the motor running."

"Got it," Jocko answered.

"Kelly, you go in first, I'll be right behind you. Wave your gun…don't fire it. The three people we saw go in earlier aren't about to give us any trouble. Then you keep an eye on them while I clean out the teller-drawers and the vault."

"Check," Kelly said. "But how do you know there's not some bank guard who maybe slept there overnight?"

"There are no other cars outside except the ones we saw the three people come in."

"But how do you know they don't have a time-lock vault, or some alarm system set up to call in the Texas Rangers or something?"

"This isn't Chicago or Kansas City," Ian countered. "It's Bumfuck, Nowhere. And there aren't any Texas Rangers waiting to come riding over the hill. Hell, for that matter, there isn't even a hill. It's flatter than a frozen lake out here. Just don't forget…before we leave, you go around and pull the phone cords out of the wall. Go it?"

"I got it…I got it!"

"Okay," Ian said. "Let's get this show on the road."

But just as Jocko was pulling out to drive across the street, a Ford turned the corner, entered the bank's parking lot, and pulled into the spot Ian had told Jocko to take.

"Never mind," Ian said quickly. "Looks like it's just a woman and a kid. Take the spot right beside it."

Jocko had to wait for a pickup truck to pass before he could cross the street. While they were waiting, Sharon was getting out of the car, walking around to the passenger side, and saying to Dwight through the slightly cracked window, "Just stay there, sweetie. Mommy will be right back. I just have to cash this check. It will only take a minute and I'll be right back."

She was already walking through the door when the DeSoto pulled up and parked beside the Ford. All three men looked over at the toddler inside the car. "Nothing changes," Ian barked. Then he wrapped a scarf around his face to serve as a mask and the other two did the same. "Just as we planned. Let's go!"

With Ian behind him, Kelly burst through the door, gun in hand, shouting, "This is a stick-up. Everybody get your hands in the air! Hands high, where I can see them."

The two female tellers quickly did as they were told. The assistant manager, a young bespectacled man of twenty-five whose eyesight was so bad it kept him out of the service, started to say, "Now see here, you can't—"

"Shut up four-eyes!" Kelly screamed. "Before I blow those glasses through your skull."

He now did as he was told. But Sharon didn't. She started for the door.

"Where do you think you're going, sister?" Ian said, grabbing her by the arm.

"Please, my child's in the car. I just want to make sure he's okay. I won't go anywhere."

"Right," Ian answered. "And as soon as you're out that door, you'll be in your heap and peeling out of here. No dice.

Everybody stays put. We won't be long."

"But he's just a child…please!"

"Our buddy's watching him," Ian said. "Now get over there and keep your hands up."

He shoved her toward the counter then went around the other side of it to start emptying the cash from the teller drawers into the bag he had brought with him. As he was doing so, he yelled to Kelly, "Get on those phone cords!"

Kelly began to walk around the inside of the building looking for telephones and ripping their cords from the wall. Ian had moved on to the assistant manager and was forcing him toward the vault that was already slightly open. With both men engaged, and terrified for Dwight, Sharon broke from the counter and simultaneously reached into her purse for her keys. Ian heard the commotion and saw her movement out of the corner of his eye. *My God,* he thought, *it's happening again!* A vision leapt into his mind. A vision of the drug store and Jillian squeezing off rounds as she came toward him firing. Before he knew it, he had raised his arm…and fired.

The bullet struck Sharon in the back, passed through her lung, and opened a gaping hole as it exited her chest. She immediately fell forward, landing face down on the cold stone floor as her car keys slid into the blood sprayed in front of her.

Ian blinked twice involuntarily, then quickly regained his faculties, and pushed the assistant manager toward the vault shouting "Get me the cash…all of it!" Less than a minute later, with bag in hand, he was racing past Kelly toward the door. "Make sure you're gotten all the phones," he yelled.

Kelly took one last look around, then headed for the door. As he was opening it and preparing to step outside, the assistant manager let loose with the shotgun that was kept behind the file cabinet for just such occasions. He thought he was pointing squarely at the big thug's back, but his exceptionally bad eyesight and his adrenalin-stoked heartbeat caused him to aim low. The blast tore through both of Kelly's legs dropping him half in and half out the door.

"Jesus!" Jocko screamed. "Kelly's down. We have to help him."

"No time," Ian countered. "We've got to get the hell out of here."

"But…we can't just leave him."

"We're screwed if we take him with us…the way he's shot up…we've got to go…now!"

Jocko threw the car into reverse, backed up just far enough to turn toward the street, then peeled out. Kelly, lying on the ground in excruciating pain, saw the car pulling away and shouted, "You fucking assholes!" But then he heard the sound of the assistant manager's heels clicking on the stone floor behind him. He tried his best to roll over and get a shot off, but he couldn't. His shredded legs and knees had left him immobile. "Stop!" he yelled, to the man he knew was behind him. "Stop…or I'll shoot that kid in the car."

The assistant manager was afraid he would. So he stopped…aimed…and fired. Even though he was closer, he missed Kelly's back again. This time the load of buckshot blew away the big man's gun and most of the hand that was holding it. The thug looked over and saw the smoking stump at the end of his arm. He tried to scream…but he passed out with the squeal still in his throat.

Chapter 44

Los Angeles

After the sale of his father's business, Paul began to give serious thought to what he wanted to do with the rest of his life. He had already acknowledged that real estate, his father's trade, wasn't for him, and his initial forays into public relations—first as an intern in college, and then with his stateside role in the military—proved interesting but not necessarily what a man ought to do for an actual career, he reasoned. There was no financial pressure to make a decision. The proceeds from the business sale had set his mother up nicely and left him with considerable funds in his own bank account. Plus Gwen's career was continuing to provide income. So he had the luxury of time to come to a conclusion.

Oddly enough, Paul's thought process was given an injection of excitement in the unlikeliest of places—one of his mother's charity soirées. He and Gwen had agreed to attend and put the arm on various socialites for a children's Recreation Center. The Pacific Palisades Good Works Organization was raising money to construct it in one of the underdeveloped economic areas of east Lost Angeles. None of the members of the organization would ever be caught dead there, but they were more than happy to generate funding for something that would keep disadvantaged youth in an East Side gymnasium rather than a West Side neighborhood.

During the gathering, after Paul had already secured checks from a banker and a stockbroker, he was approached by a group of four men. Two of the four were the aforementioned contributors. The other two looked like good bets as well. The banker spoke first.

"Paul, now that we've...at least some of us, so far...have

supported your mother's fine project, we wanted to see how supportive you'd be of something that we need help with."

"And just what might that be?"

Avoiding Paul's direct question for the moment, the banker went on. "Paul, did you know that Los Angeles now assembles more cars than any other city than Detroit?"

Paul was about to say, no, he didn't, but the banker had only paused to take a breath.

"We make more tires here than any city other than Akron…more furniture than Grand Rapids…we even stitch more clothes than any city other than New York."

"I must admit I did not know any of that, of course—"

"Paul, we're the nation's capital for motion picture production, radio programs, and it's quite possible that television's going to be bigger than all of them."

"Well, my wife would probably know more about that than I would. She's an actress you see and—"

"We know, Paul. We know. In fact, we think she can be very beneficial in gathering support among the theatrical community and the movie industry."

"Support for what, Sir? I'm afraid I don't follow you."

"Why…support for your candidacy, son. As the next Congressman from the State of California, district of Los Angeles."

Paul stood there speechless. In fact, even before trying to speak, he determined that a slug, rather than a sip of his Chardonnay was in order. Finally, he responded.

"You have to be joking."

"Far from it, son. Let's step over to this table, take a seat, and we'll tell you just how serious we are."

The banker and his friends outlined their thinking to Paul. Postwar Los Angeles was growing by leaps and bounds. They needed representation in Washington that understood the opportunities for even more growth. There was no reason the city shouldn't continue to expand toward the ocean, the east, and the San Fernando Valley. Representatives from General Motors had already talked to the banker's group about the disadvantages of light steel rail and streetcars. They advised, as one who gave it any thought might expect, that superior growth opportunities were more readily achievable with bus systems, and the expansion of local, state, and federal highway systems that could make the burgeoning California city the nation's model for urban mobility. Of course, they also advised, the right representation in Washington would be needed to secure the kind of federal funding necessary.

Paul pushed back initially, saying he had never even considered going into politics—explaining that he had no experience whatsoever in any level of government. Perfect, his tablemates replied. He was a clean slate. Someone who couldn't be tripped up by things he had written or said in previous campaigns. What's more, they continued, he was a candidate right from central casting—a handsome, young, decorated war veteran with a beautiful, extremely photogenic wife. He was the son of a longtime California businessman and patriot, they said, who had lost his life at the hands of, in effect, the nation's enemy. With the right management, they all enthusiastically agreed, he'd be a natural. Finally, as an escape device, Paul agreed he'd at least give the idea some thought.

Later that evening, after they had left the event and returned home, he half-jokingly told Gwen about his conversation with the businessmen. He expected her to laugh uproariously. She didn't.

"Paul, I think that's a wonderful idea."

"What? You can't be serious."

"But I am. I think you'd make a great Congressman."

"Gwen, I don't know the first thing about politics."

"So what? You're honest and fair. You know a lot about leading men. You were saying yourself that you didn't know exactly what you wanted to do? Well, here's something you could do for the time being…then decide later if you want to make a career of it."

"I just can't see myself as a politician. It seems silly somehow."

"Look…I couldn't see myself as an actress. I thought it was impossible too. But with the right guidance and support, it happened."

"Yes, but I get the feeling they have a lot more in mind that just guidance and support. I get the impression they're looking for someone who simply knows how to take orders."

"Well, too bad. You know how to give orders. You gave them in the army. You could give them as a Congressman. I think," she said, taking both of his hands in hers, "you should at least think about it. Ask your mother what she thinks. And meet with them again to let them know that if you were to do this thing…and get elected…then you'd be your own man. And you'd only vote for things that you really believe in. And that they can just take it or leave it."

Paul moved her hands around his waist, then put his arms around her saying, "I know one thing I could never leave…you." They came together and kissed. Then Paul said, "You know…if I were to get elected…I'd probably have to spend most of my time in Washington…might even have to move there."

"You mean we might have to move there. Where you go, I go, my love. That's what this marriage thing is all about, you know."

"I know I'm going to bed," he said.

"Oh, lovely. Can't think of any place I'd rather go with you," she said, kissing him again.

Over the next week, Paul did give it some thought. He thought about how the right man in the right position might really be able to do some good in Congress. It was a form of service, really. Similar to the military. He might actually be able to help people in ways he'd never realized before. But he wouldn't be just a front for this business group or that. He'd never do that. The backers would have to accept him on his own terms or not at all. A tinge of excitement was starting to come over him. His mother had been all for the idea. Gwen was certainly willing for him to put his foot in the water. And like she said, even if he got elected and realized it wasn't really for him, he could simply not seek a second term and turn to something else. There seemed to be too many pros and not enough cons. He met with the bankers' group again and told them up front he'd only support what he truly believed in. They said they would expect no less from a man of his character. And that they believed in him. Two weeks later, Paul Cassidy was a candidate for the Congress of the United States.

Chapter 45

Pilot Hill

The crowd at the funeral for Sharon Cross exceeded the capacity of the Pilot Hill Methodist Church. Many of those who had come to pay their respects had to stand outside during the service. Townsfolk, students, teachers, and more, all felt that their tiny center of the world had somehow been torn asunder. What a terrible tragedy, they told one another. She was so young and pretty, and a mother too. The Lord works in mysterious ways, some would offer, hoping to remind that some events in this world were beyond understanding. She's gone to a better place, others would say, attempting to blunt the pain of irreparable loss.

Providing traffic coordination for funerals was usually one of Riley's duties. How he wished that were his job this day. Instead, his fellow county deputies and even Sheriff Harris Totter were on hand to move the procession from the church to the graveyard, and to show support for their fellow lawman. Six seniors from the high school served as pallbearers. The gravesite ceremony was as overcrowded as the funeral because so many wanted to say goodbye. The preacher was sincere but thankfully short. He knew that grief can only contain itself for so long. And sometimes the best thing to do is to simply move on.

Riley had tried his best to give Dwight some understanding of what had occurred. But the toddler was too young to grasp the finality of it all. *Maybe that's a blessing,* Riley thought. Yes, he would be sad and cry and miss his mother and wonder why she wasn't around, but quick as a wink his mind would be distracted by a toy, or a sound, or a hug from a grandparent and he'd be back in his child's world where it was not only okay to laugh, it was even encouraged. Riley wondered how long it would be before he could laugh again.

Both Sharon and Kelly had been taken to the same hospital the morning it happened. One of the tellers had run across the street, called the authorities and told them of the robbery and shooting and that an ambulance was needed. When Riley got the call from his dispatcher, he was only told that two people had been shot. He didn't know Sharon was one of them until he arrived at the bank and saw them putting her in the emergency vehicle. He quickly got in with her and sat holding her hand as the ambulance sped along. She never regained consciousness. He knew she was gone long before they arrived at the hospital.

Kelly survived but was heavily sedated for a couple of days. When he came around enough to be questioned, he had no qualms about giving answers. *Screw them,* he thought. The bastards left him lying there in his own blood. He wasn't about to do them any favors. Kelly gave them Ian's and Jocko's names, told them that they had been in a 1938 DeSoto with Kansas plates, and that they were on their way to Los Angeles. He had forgotten the name of the man they were going there to work for. If he remembered, he said he'd give them his name too. The sons of bitches, he snarled. He hoped they'd get what was coming to them.

Witnesses had confirmed that it was the other one in the bank who shot Sharon. The man Kelly identified as Ian Donovan. That was the only answer Riley really cared about. The day after the funeral, he took Dwight over to stay with his grandparents. They didn't have to ask where he was going.

On his way out of Pilot Hill, Riley saw Sheriff Totter's car parked on the side of the road. He pulled up beside it and rolled down his window. The Sheriff's window was already down.

"Don't suppose I can talk you out of this."

"No," Riley responded.

"Well, if it was my wife, guess I'd do the same."

"I suspect you would."

"Why don't you call in each day," Totter said. "That way I can let you know if we've received any information from police departments along the way."

"I'll do that, Sheriff. But chances are they'll ditch the DeSoto and get another car as soon as they can."

"Probably. But if we know where they leave it, we'll know where they've been."

"Appreciate your help, Sheriff."

"Riley, if the law finds these bastards…it will have to be handled through the legal system. You're still a young man…with a son to think about. You don't want to do something that's going to foul up the rest of your life."

"How long is the rest of a life, Sheriff? You think Sharon had any idea how long she had left?"

"I'm just saying you should be careful. You still have a little boy who's going to need you for a long time."

"I know that, Sheriff. That's why the sooner I get this done, the sooner I'll be back."

"Guess you're right. Then I'll say, adios, amigo."

"Goodbye, Sheriff."

"I'd add vaya con Dios. But I suspect you're not too keen on the Lord's ways right about now."

Totter couldn't tell if Riley heard his last comment or not. The younger man had already rolled his window up, pulled back on the road, and started heading west. He turned his own engine over and was just about to take off when he got a call on his car radio from the dispatcher back in his office.

"What is it, Hazel?"

"Have you seen Riley Cross this morning, Sheriff?"

"Why do you ask?"

"Well, there's a fella here says he's looking for him."

"What's he want with him?"

"Don't rightly know, Sheriff. He's been kinda closed-mouth about that."

"Well, I'm heading back to the office. I'll talk to him when I get there. What's the guy's name?"

"I wrote it down. Let me see. Here it is. It's Rémy Aut... Auteu...oh hell, I can't pronounce it, Sheriff. It's some kind of French name."

Chapter 46

Los Angeles

The group backing Paul's candidacy had set up a suite of campaign offices in the Bradbury Building on the corner of Third Street and Broadway. Relatively non-descript on the outside, the interior was a spectacle of design and engineering. Its vaulted ceiling with a central skylight let in sunshine from all directions. Twin open-grille elevators rose through floor after floor of ornate ironwork banisters that rimmed exceptionally wide stairways. Once visitors moved from the central core of the building into the corridors, things got a lot more businesslike. Floors were narrow and doors and windows of frosted glass kept those in the hall from seeing into the offices. The old man who had come to see the candidate this morning checked the name etched into the glass of each door as he passed it. Finally, he came to the one that read PAUL CASSIDY CAMPAIGN HEADQUARTERS.

After only a few weeks of campaigning, Paul had already begun to do things that rubbed his backers the wrong way. They wanted him to concentrate on speaking engagements in front of large groups such as Chambers of Commerce, Kiwanis Clubs, union meetings, and major corporations. The candidate didn't avoid such venues, but he was constantly scheduling time for local community associations and church organizations, as well as education and military groups. But what really perplexed the assorted political pros that had been brought in to run the campaign, was Paul's insistence on setting aside time to meet with individuals from different walks of life. The pros could understand if these one-on-one meetings were with presidents of large companies or high-ranking military officials, but they were often apoplectic when they found out time had been set aside for sit-downs with tradesmen, factory workers, even cab drivers. This morning was no exception. Somehow an old man named Solomon Goldman had secured a half-hour appointment with the candidate. Paul's handlers hoped the septuagenarian was the head of a large Jewish congregation that could be turned into a voting block. Paul was less interested in Goldman's ability to deliver votes, and more interested in his ability to share what was most important to the man and his neighbors.

The elderly man looked every bit his age, but his voice was strong and clear. "I want to thank you for seeing me, Mr. Cassidy. I know you must have a very busy schedule."

"Thank you for coming in, Mr. Goldman. Frankly, I find I learn a lot more about what's important to people by talking with individuals rather than talking to audiences. And, to be honest, when my secretary showed me your request, I was intrigued by the name of the group you represent. The League of Reckoning…what exactly is that?"

"We are a small but growing organization, Mr. Cassidy. Our members are mostly Jewish, like me, but not all. There are others who share our aspirations."

"And what exactly are those aspirations, Mr. Goldman?"

"We seek two things, Mr. Cassidy. One is to do whatever we can to make sure people never forget what happened to Europe's Jews in the war. And the second is to not allow the perpetrators of that evil to go unpunished."

"Those are definitely worthy goals, Sir. As to the first…I can certainly entertain the idea of using a public pulpit to remind people there were unspeakable horrors perpetrated on individuals solely because of their religious beliefs. The second was addressed directly by the Nuremberg Trials. I'm not sure how a candidate for office in the U.S. could help in that regard."

"Mr. Cassidy, you're not naïve enough to believe that all of the German criminals were rounded up and put on trial…are you?"

"Like other people, Mr. Goldman, I've heard stories of some

Nazis and members of the German high command escaping to places like Argentina and other areas of South America."

"They aren't just stories, Mr. Cassidy. And it isn't only South America that is harboring war criminals."

"Well, be that as it may, Sir, I still don't see how I can be of help on this issue."

"Consider a hypothetical, Mr. Cassidy. Just for the sake of discussion. What if you were to find that one of the people supporting your campaign....a large supporter, let's say...was actually a war criminal. What would you do?"

"Well, hypothetically speaking, I think I would disavow his support and if I was dead certain about his past...I'd probably report him to the authorities."

"That's the sort of thing I hoped you would say, Mr. Cassidy. In fact, I said to some of my fellow members that I thought that's what you would do. They were not so sure. They are generally not as optimistic as I am."

"But why would you even be talking with your fellow members about such a hypothetical?"

"Because it's not a hypothetical, Mr. Cassidy. It's not a hypothetical at all."

Paul was taken aback. "What? You can't be serious. I'm certainly not aware of anyone like that supporting my campaign. In fact...to be honest...I have no firsthand knowledge of any German-influenced support at all."

Goldman stared into Paul's eyes. He was trying to see if subterfuge was hiding there. He decided perhaps it wasn't. "I believe you're telling the truth, Mr. Cassidy. At least, the truth as you know it. Might I ask you a question or two?"

Paul was beginning to believe he had made a mistake accepting this meeting. The old man meant well, obviously, but perhaps he was just some zealot who accosted all candidates with such tales. "If you make the questions brief, Mr. Goldman...you see I have another meeting scheduled directly."

"Do you know a man named Zellenski? Herman Zellenski?"

"Well, yes I know Mr. Zellenski. Or, at least I met him. That's probably closer to the truth. In fact I sold my father's business to him. But that was all done through intermediaries. But why do you ask? Mr. Zellenski isn't a supporter of my campaign."

"Mr. Zellenski is a rather large supporter of your campaign. Members of my organization have already discovered that. If you doubt it, check with your banking friends. We have financial connections as well. This sort of information gets around."

"I will look into it," Paul said, perhaps more indignantly that he initially intended. "But what if he is? What has that to do with what we were discussing?"

"Mr. Herman Zellenski is actually Herr Frederick Zell. He is not Polish. He is German. He is not a Jew. He is a Nazi. Rather than escaping from Poland with his life…as he is fond of telling people…he escaped from France with millions in ill-gotten gains hidden from the German high command and purloined from Jews sent to their death."

"That can't be true," Paul said. "My lawyers assured me he was a Polish industrialist who came to this country to escape the Nazis."

The old man clasped his hands together in front of him and a line-thin, yet understanding smile crossed his lips. "If he could fool the German Wehrmacht and outwit the Gestapo, Mr. Cassidy, it's not surprising he might hoodwink a cadre of well-intentioned but gullible real estate attorneys."

Paul was reeling. He wasn't sure what to believe. "I suppose you have proof of what you're saying. And if you do, then why don't you go to the authorities? Why come to me?"

"We don't have the sort of documentation that would be deemed admissible in a court of law, Mr. Cassidy. Our evidence is gained by putting bits and pieces together here and there. Along with eye witnesses who have seen Zell…or Zellenski as you call him, here in Los Angeles…and have shared their knowledge with us."

"But why don't these witnesses go to the police?"

"Most are Jews who suffered terribly and wound up losing everything…including the mental stamina to stand up under questioning."

"Then how can you believe them?"

"People seldom forget their tormentors, Mr. Cassidy. Over time we lose touch with many things. But we never forget that which we can never forgive."

Paul let out a huge sigh. It was as if from out of nowhere, the wind had been knocked out of him and he wasn't sure how to react. "Well, what exactly is it that you want me to do, Mr. Goldman?"

"Just what you said you'd do, Mr. Cassidy, when we discussed the hypothetical. We would very much like for you to remove Zell's influence from your campaign. We would ask that you look perhaps even more closely than you already have into any issues or positions he or his minions are encouraging you to take. We do not ask you to make any of this public at this time. We know that becoming embroiled in potentially scandalous associations could lead to your defeat at the polls. And that is not what we're seeking. In fact, we believe you to be a man of honor and good faith. Many of us intend to vote for you. We only ask that you separate yourself from this cancerous association before you become tainted with it…or so deep in its debt that it becomes impossible for you to extricate yourself. We will continue to pursue the information we need to bring this man to justice. It may take a very long time. But we have very long memories."

"Mr. Goldman, you should know that I will indeed look into this personally and promptly. Would you mind very much if I have one of my…as you said…well-intentioned but gullible lawyers, come over and look into any documentation you might have supporting your claims? The attorney I'm thinking of has no association whatsoever with the campaign and he's a loyal, and trusted friend. He's served my family for a number of years."

"We'll be happy to share what we have with him, Mr. Cassidy. And the best of luck with your campaign. I think you'll make the kind of congressman California can be proud of."

"I appreciate your confidence, Mr. Goldman."

They stood up, shook hands, and the old man turned to go. But just before exiting Paul's office, he said, "Oh…Mr. Cassidy, I wonder if you might entertain just one more query. Rest assured it has nothing to do with what we've discussed. This is more in the nature of a personal question."

"Certainly. What is it?"

"I noted in your biography, that before joining the army you graduated from UCLA. I know there's little chance of this…but I just wondered as an old man does…if perhaps you knew my son…who also went to school there?"

Paul was about to ask what his first name was…then it hit him…as Goldman was volunteering it.

"Levi…Levi Goldman was his name…but everyone called him Lev."

My God, Paul thought. *Lev's father.* Before he could respond, the old man spoke again.

"He served in the military too, you know. Not an officer like you, of course. But he served with distinction, I believe. That's what they said in the letter. The letter they sent that told me he was killed in France. I'm not sure how it happened. They never give any details. One always wonders, you know. One always wonders."

The old man had lost his train of thought for the moment. He wasn't even aware that Paul had not answered his question. But Paul was aware. And he couldn't believe it. He couldn't believe that the soldier he and Cross and O'Byrne had tried to rescue from that German patrol…had been this man's son.

"I did know Lev, Mr. Goldman. I knew him at school…and, as it turns out, I knew him in the service. If you have a minute, I'll tell you about it."

So Paul took a few moments to tell Solomon Goldman how his son died in France. He didn't mention the captivity. He didn't speak of the brutality. Instead he wove a tale of heroism. A tale of how the Jewish GI gave his life leading an assault that wouldn't have been successful save for Lev's sacrifice. The old man wept with pride. And Paul had never been so glad in all his life of telling a lie.

Chapter 47

Near Van Horn, Texas

Riley was driving the black, 1950 four-door Ford sedan he had bought just before Dwight was born. This time however, the car wasn't filled with diaper bags, a playpen, toys, an oversized purse, a child's laughter, and the smile of a pretty young woman. Other than Riley, the only things in the car now were clothes in the duffle bag he had kept from the army, a forty-five automatic that was strapped to his hip, and his jacket that covered the stock of the Winchester twelve-gauge pump that was facing barrel down beside him in the front seat. He knew Ian Donovan and his flunky, Jocko, had at least a three-day head start on him, but he was determined to make up as much ground as he could. It would take twelve hours of hard driving to make El Paso by nightfall, but Riley never considered doing a mile less.

About half way from the Piney Woods of southeast Texas to the state's western tip, one begins to encounter a whole lot of nothing. Nothing like flat earth, brown dirt, prickly pear cactus, fire-ant hills the size of Galapagos tortoises, and mesquite trees that suck whatever water might be available out of the cracking ground and into their pointy thorns. But it made no difference to Riley. Sightseeing wasn't on his agenda. Now and then he'd turn on the radio just to break the monotony. More often than not the only thing that would come in clearly would be a country and western station. He'd stick with it for a few songs. Then one would hit a little too close to home. When Webb Pierce warbled the chorus of "There Stands The Glass", and the lyrics became—I'm wond'ring where you are tonight…I'm wond'ring if you are alright—Riley would get a catch in his throat and turn the music off in favor of the sound of the wind whipping by the open window. *Why her?* He couldn't help from asking. Why someone who never did anything bad to anyone? Such questions have no answers, he knew. But he couldn't stop asking them.

When Sheriff Totter returned to his office, he had missed the Frenchman. He asked the dispatcher what had transpired. She was more than happy to report.

"Oh he's gone, Sheriff. Left some time ago."

"I thought you said he wanted to see Riley. That he was here asking about him."

"That's right, Sheriff. But I took care of it."

"And just how did you do that, Hazel?"

"Well, I told him all about what had happened to poor Deputy Cross. About his wife being shot and all. And how their little son doesn't have a mother anymore. And how it was all just so awful. The way she was killed and whatnot. And how Deputy Cross has taken off to Los Angeles, California to find that murderer and bring him back to justice."

"Hazel…I thought you said this man was stranger. Why did you tell him where Riley was going?"

"Well, Sheriff, he just seemed like such a nice little foreigner. Kind of out of place so far from his home, you know. And he said how he really wanted to see Deputy Cross. And I figured…well, I figured everyone in town knew where the deputy was going. And if he didn't hear it from me, well, he would definitely hear it from the next person he asked."

"Look…did he ever tell you why he wanted to see Riley?"

"Well, yes and no, Sheriff. He started to tell me that he might have known him from the war. And now that he was here in America, he was looking up some soldier friends he had made back then. American soldiers, you know. Anyway, that's kind of the gist of it. He was pretty hard to understand with that accent and all."

"Listen…Hazel…don't be so free to hand out information to any Tom, Dick, or Pierre who might walk in here. Okay?"

"Not Pierre, Sheriff. His name was Rémy. I still can't pronounce that last name."

"I don't care if his name was General Charles By-God de Gaulle. You don't give out personal information about department personnel without my authority. Got it?"

"Well, you don't have to get so huffy about it!"

Totter simply shook his head and mumbled as he walked into his office, "I'll tell Riley this guy was looking for him…when he calls in." Stopping at his office door, he turned and said, "And Hazel…if Riley does call in, it will probably be collect…so be sure to accept the charges. Okay?"

"You don't have to tell me my job, Sheriff. I think I know my duties pretty well and—"

The Sheriff's door slammed ending the conversation.

Chapter 48

North of Marfa, Texas

Rémy Auteuil had never seen such vast emptiness. The miles and miles of nothing but miles and miles on either side of him was what he imagined Mars might look like. As he sped down the black asphalt ribbon that intersected the flat brown landscape and stretched out to the far horizon, he hoped his prey wasn't too far ahead of him. It made him nervous to think he might have to spend the night in such a desolate place. Surely there were terrible creatures that haunted such a lifeless environment, he imagined. Creatures that pulled and tore their victims apart, and dragged their carrion off into the deep arroyos on either side of the highway.

He had taken the train from Chicago to Houston, where he rented a green 1950 Chevrolet Coupe to drive to Pilot Hill. After hearing that Riley Cross was driving to Los Angeles, he decided to keep the car in hopes of catching up with him along the way. Chicago had gone so well that he was now more committed than ever to finishing his mission. He would track down and kill the Américains who had violated his mother and turned her into something so foul it could never be expunged from his memory. If he was lucky enough to dispose of Cross in Texas or New Mexico or Arizona, he would continue to California to do away with the man who had actually signed the After Action Report that had made his quest possible—First Lieutenant Paul C. Cassidy. *To hell with the automobile,* he thought. He'd simply leave it at the airport when he flew back to the Continent. If they traced it there later, so what? By then he would be back in Europe and they would not continue to look for him. Américains didn't have the will, the stamina, or the perseverance to see something through to the end. They were too well off and too content in their land of plenty, Rémy fixated. They simply had too much food, too much money, and too little honor. Américains were merde. He had convinced himself of that long ago. And he continued to dwell on it as he drove on through the emptiness.

Chapter 49

South of Socorro, Texas

The moon was round and yellow and high in the sky. A soft azure hue fell over the landscape as if it shone from heaven's light bulb. *You could almost drive without the headlamps,* Ian thought, as he looked over at the sleeping Jocko next to him. *The little bastard,* Ian said to himself. *What the hell good is he? All he can do is drive. And now he says he's too tired to do that.* He had been ruminating on Jocko's inadequacies for the last hundred miles, and the little man's stock was continuing to fall.

They were still in the DeSoto and they had been driving all out, with only stops for gas and nature. Fatigue and exhaustion had been crawling over Ian for hours. His nerves were raw as uncooked steak. The more he drove, the more he talked to himself, muttering under his breath just to stay awake. And the more he muttered, the madder he got. "He's a fucking idiot that's what he is. I don't know why I listened to him. Let's keep the car until we're out of Texas. That way it will be harder to trace. Dumb bastard. Why the hell didn't he know that fucking Texas goes on and on and on forever? Let me keep driving. I'm okay. I'm okay. Sure, he's okay driving through the daylight, but when it gets dark, then the little asshole isn't okay. Then he has to rest. Has to get some shuteye. So I have to do the driving at night. How did I get stuck with this numbskull? What's he doing for me? Nothing. That's what. Not a damn thing. And now…I'm supposed to share the take with him. Hell, we only got a few thousand dollars from that one-horse bank. That's not going to last all that long…especially if I'm supposed to split it with him. He'll probably want fifty percent, the little creep! What the hell for? Kelly and I did all the work. All the real work. Why give away half of what I worked for?

What I risked my neck for? That could have been me lying back there instead of Kelly. But not Jocko. No. Not little Jocko. He was safe behind the wheel with the motor running. Probably would have run out on me too if he hadn't seen the bag I was carrying full of dough. Now…in the middle of the night, when I ought to be the one getting some rest…the bastard makes me drive. And I'm supposed to share the take with him…with that ridiculous excuse for a human being! Not on your life."

The DeSoto was clocking sixty-five miles an hour when Ian took his foot off the accelerator. He reached across Jocko's body and opened the latch on the passenger door. Then he raised his right leg and used it to shove Jocko out of the speeding car. The little man disappeared into the night.

Ian hadn't gone a hundred yards up the highway when he pulled to a stop. There was nothing but emptiness for miles in front of him, and behind. "I bet the little bastard survived," Ian said. "I bet he was so damn limber from being asleep that the fall didn't even kill him. Why won't he give me any peace?"

He turned the car around and headed back. Even though moonlight was flooding the area, Ian turned on his high beams so he could scan the roadside. Driving slowly, no more than ten miles per hour, he peered into the night looking for a lump on the side of the road. Suddenly, something struggled, half crawling, from the ditch thirty yards ahead of Ian on his left. With his window down, he heard it speak.

"Ian? Ian? Was there an accident? Did we have an accident?"

Ian didn't answer. He simply slammed his foot down on the accelerator and headed straight for the weaving Jocko. The little man raised his hand as if to wave just before the DeSoto smacked him. The force drove his legs backward and he flipped onto and over the hood of the car—landing face up in the middle of the highway. Ian went a quarter mile down the road he had already driven. He turned the car around again. By the time he got to the body in the road he was doing sixty.

Chapter 50

Texas/New Mexico Border

Riley hadn't called when he arrived in El Paso. It was much too late. But the next morning he was on the phone to Sheriff Totter just after finishing breakfast.

"This is Riley. Just checking in."

"Yeah, Hazel said you were on the line. Hey, where are you, anyway?"

"El Paso. Plan to head out soon as we get off the phone."

"Well listen, there's been a development. Let me look at my map here. Looks to me like you're only about forty miles from Las Cruces."

"Is that New Mexico?"

"Yeah. Not all that far from you. Seems they found the DeSoto there that Kelly told us about."

"Traded-in or abandoned?"

"Abandoned, I'm afraid. Know what you're thinking. If they had traded it in, we'd know what kind of car they took off in."

"Yeah, our bad luck I guess."

"Well the bad luck wasn't all ours. The car wasn't all that was found. Just outside of Marfa, the highway boys found some road kill that turned out to be one of our suspects."

Riley's heart raced. "Was it Donovan?"

"No. It was the other one. Jacob Palmira. Alias Jocko Palmira. Still had his identification on him. Seemed it was about the only thing that wasn't squashed flatter than Aubrey Hepburn's chest."

"When did they find the body?"

"Day before yesterday. But we didn't get the call until late yesterday afternoon."

"That means I might have made up a day on him."

"Maybe. Probably also means he's going to hightail it straight to LA…now that he's got a vehicle we have no way of identifying unless we get a stolen car report from Las Cruses."

"Okay, I'll run up to Las Cruces, have a look at the DeSoto, and see if anything's been reported. Then I'm going west with the hammer down. Anything from Kelly on that name of the guy Donovan's supposed to get with in LA?"

"Not yet…but we ask him about once every hour…so maybe something will come to him. I don't think he's holding out. I think he'd like to nail this Donovan son of a bitch almost as much as we would."

"No, Sheriff," Riley said. "It ain't even close."

Riley had taken the phone away from his ear and was about to hang up when he thought he heard Totter saying something. "Sheriff, I missed whatever you just said. Was there something else?"

"Yes. Well maybe. I don't know. Just thought I'd ask since I have you on the phone now."

"What is it?

"Before you left, there was some French guy who came to the station looking for you."

"French guy?"

"Yep. Said he was French. And apparently sounded a lot like it too, according to Hazel."

"I don't know any French guys."

"Said he might have known you back in the war. You spend any time in France?"

The rain and the night and the farmhouse came back to him. It had never completely left. He paused before he answered. "Yeah. I was in France for a bit. But I never really met any French guy I remember. What's the story?"

"Don't really know. But he asked where you were going, and Miss Blabbermouth Hazel told him you were headed for LA. Haven't seen anyone in your rearview mirror lately…have you?"

"No, Sheriff. But it wouldn't matter if I had. The only thing that matters to me right now is what's ahead of me."

"You take care, son. And keep calling in. That's the only way I have to get hold of you. Riley? Riley?"

The phone was back in its cradle. And Riley was headed for Las Cruces.

Chapter 51

Los Angeles

The conference room within Cassidy Campaign Headquarters was small and private. There were no windows and only one table that would seat no more than six comfortably. This morning, all the seats were taken. But no one was comfortable with the conversation that had been brewing for weeks now.

"The research people tell us that we actually have a chance to win this thing," the banker said. "Now is not the time to rock the boat, Paul." His three minions nodded their heads approvingly.

"You'll recall that before I agreed to run, I said I'd only support what I truly believe in."

"What has that to do with the matter at hand?"

"I no longer believe we should accept any financial support from Herman Zellenski."

"Paul…every campaign has multiple supporters. If this Zellenski…or whatever his name is…supports your campaign, that's neither here nor there."

"I think you know very well what his name is. And I think you know that's he's been one of our biggest supporters."

"Paul…you did business with the man. You sold him your father's company. Why wouldn't you accept support from such a man?"

"Had I known more about him, I wouldn't have sold him the company. And believe me, if what I've heard is true…I don't want to be associated with him. And I wouldn't think you would either."

"If you're referring to those malicious rumors being spread by that Jewish organization…well, I wouldn't put much stock in that. They are a bit extreme, you know."

"We've been picking up more and more support from individuals and neighborhood groups. I think we can get along without Mr. Zellenski's support."

"Individuals and neighborhood groups don't write six-figure checks, Paul. A good candidate should know that."

"A good candidate should let people know what his principles are and stick to them. That's the ethical thing to do and that's what I'm doing."

"Good losing candidates do that, Paul. Good winning candidates learn situational ethics."

"Oh, really…situational ethics…well, here's a situation I'm sure you're likely to find ethically challenging. I'm not sure I can continue to support a number of those highway expansion projects."

The banker, who had been sitting back in his chair during the earlier verbal joust, leaned forward, put his elbows on the table, clasped his hands together and said, "This is something perhaps better discussed just between you and I."

The banker's minions took their cue, gathered their papers, and rose to leave. Paul turned toward the sixth person in the room, his secretary, and suggested she go back to her desk. When they were alone, the banker spoke again, quietly and slowly.

"Paul…from the very beginning…this campaign has been about the growth of Los Angeles and California. Growth is what provides prosperity for everyone. Highway expansion is part of that growth. I thought you understood that."

"I do understand it. And I agree with it…in general. But there are some specifics that frankly I have to question."

"Which specifics would those be?"

"I understand there are plans for links from the city to the valley that would require acquisition of property which would displace whole groups of citizens and virtually level entire neighborhoods."

"The key word you used, Paul, was acquisition. The citizens

would be compensated."

"No...actually the key word I used was displace. These are people who have lived in these neighborhoods for generations. Who's to say they want to leave? Or that their compensation will be enough for them to find something better elsewhere?"

"Paul, this is a local city and county matter. It's not something that a candidate for state or national office should become embroiled in."

"It can't be avoided. Newspapers, radio and television reporters will want to know where all candidates stand on this."

"I don't think it will be an issue to anyone other than the citizens involved."

"Well...they're voters too, are they not?"

"Those are not the kind of votes we want or need, Paul. And I hardly think there will be much public sympathy for their situation."

"You mean...principally because many of the neighborhoods involved are Asian...and many of the people are Japanese."

"I would think that you, Paul...of all people...would have little sympathy for the plight of our former enemies. Considering what happened to your father."

Paul took a breath before he spoke. "First...they are not our former enemies. They are our fellow citizens who were uprooted from their homes and interned like criminals. Second... yes...what happened to my father was awful. But it was the unintended consequence of a public policy based on fear that led to loss, sorrow, and eventually despair. Is that something we really want to consider again...this time under devotion to growth?"

The banker began gathering his own papers. He picked up his pen and placed it inside his breast pocket, signaling the meeting had come to an end. But before he rose to leave, he looked Paul straight in the eye and said, "Growth is a fact of life, Paul. When anything stops growing, it withers and dies. I meant what I said earlier. There's a very good chance we can win this election. You must decide if you really want to win. And, if you do…whom you really want to help. There are powerful people who support you. People who have a good deal invested in your candidacy and your eventual influence as a Congressman. Consider your positions carefully before you walk away from such people, Paul. They are not fond of bad investments."

It had taken most of the day, but by late afternoon Paul had almost managed to put the morning's unpleasantness behind him. He wasn't precisely sure what his final position on the highway access issue would be, but he knew there was no way he'd come down on one side or the other without knowing all he could about the human costs as well as the civic benefits.

That evening he and Gwen took Paul's mother to dinner. He was actually looking forward to it. His candidacy had seemed to re-energize her. She was constantly putting together fund-raisers and putting the bite on the well-heeled of Pacific Palisades. But talk turned the tiramisu sour when Paul's mother brought up his potential support for the Asian community position on the highway issue. Someone among the banker's coterie had obviously contacted his mother. And she proceeded to launch into a condemnation of those awful people and their impediment to progress. She finally went too far when she said Paul's father would roll over in his grave and forever hide his face in shame at the mere thought of trading his legacy for the votes of people who never really deserved suffrage in the first place. Paul stood up and stormed away from the table and it was left to Gwen to put Paul's mother in a cab that would take her home.

A bad day was on its way to concluding with Paul and Gwen sharing a nightcap at home before retiring. She had calmed him down by asking Paul to consider his mother's advancing age. And by going on to point out that her blaming an entire race for what one man had done was certainly ridiculous, but at least somewhat understandable under the circumstances. Gwen said she might even feel the same way if something like that happened to Paul. He didn't believe her and said so. But at least they were smiling again and committed to changing the subject. Before they could, the telephone rang. Paul picked it up and said, "Hello."

There was no reply. But Paul could tell the line was open and someone was on it. "Hello!"

"Mr. Cassidy...so nice to hear your voice again."

There was a distinct accent Paul knew he had heard before, but he couldn't remember where. "Who is this?"

"Why, it is Herman Zellenski. I hope I am not disturbing you. We Europeans tend to forget that you Americans keep earlier hours than we do."

Paul couldn't believe it. He couldn't believe the man would call his home. "One second, please. Just hold on for a moment."

Covering the mouthpiece of the phone with his hand, he said to Gwen, "Darling, this is campaign related. It may take a moment or two. Why don't you go on up to bed and I'll join you shortly."

"Okay, Mr. Candidate. But don't be long. I could doze off. And that might spoil a very pleasant end to the evening."

"I won't be long."

Paul waited until Gwen was out of the room. Then he brought the phone back up.

"Why are you calling me?" Paul asked rather brusquely.

"I see…another American trait. You choose to forego the pleasantries. Very well. I am calling you, Mr. Cassidy, because I was told some things today that frankly, I find hard to believe."

"Told by whom?"

"That is neither here nor there, as you say. But the fact is, I was given some rather unpleasant information about your attitude regarding my support of your campaign."

"Ex-support. That's ex-support of my campaign. I'm instructing my campaign finance staff to no longer accept contributions from you, or your company, and to return any funds that we might have received from you previously."

"Mr. Cassidy, you don't seriously believe I would have my name or any of my companies names attached to any donations I might have made. Do you?"

"Up to now, I haven't really given it any thought. But if that's the case…and since you've chosen to call my home…let me just tell you that your contributions are no longer sought, required, or for that matter…appreciated."

"Rather ungrateful of you, I must say, Mr. Cassidy. I was hoping that what I heard was false. However, based on your tone, I must assume it to have been correct."

"Assume whatever you want. Just don't send any more support in any form and do not call my home."

"Mr. Cassidy, I think it is altogether possible that being new to politics, you may not appreciate the gravity of your situation."

"Gravity? I assure you, Mr. Zellenksi, I'm abreast of my situation. And I don't think it's grave. In fact, I think I'm in a position to quite possibly win this election."

"And how do you think you got into that situation? Whose financial support do you think made it possible for you to get your face and name before the public? I don't know how closely you've looked into your campaign financing, Mr. Cassidy, but if you did, you just might find that it is considerably deeper than it is wide."

"What are you trying to say?" Paul asked.

"I am trying to tell you that the only reason you are where you are today…is because I have made it possible. Your mother's pathetic fund-raising efforts are laughable. And your consortium of bankers and businessmen and industry leaders are only viable as long as everyone agrees on the issues. Issues I've heard, Mr. Cassidy, that you seem to be re-thinking."

"There's also the public. Have you forgotten them?"

"Ah yes, the masses, as it were. Masses that are really no more than unconnected groups of special interests who are concerned more with marshalling enough money to pay the rent rather than marshalling the political will to put the right man in power."

"Your observations on the body politic, Zellenski, are less than fascinating. But thank you for sharing them with me. And now that you have, I'll take my leave of—"

"Mr. Cassidy," Zellenski raised his voice, "if you like I shall be blunt."

"By all means," Paul said. "And brief too, if you will."

"Let us see if this is sufficiently blunt and brief enough for you, Mr. Cassidy. As of this moment, you will cease and desist all efforts to change or even monitor the oversight of your campaign financing. The people who are doing that now will continue to do it. You will also halt any and all public opposition to the proposed highways projects under review by local and state government. If asked by the press…you will enthusiastically voice your view that they are vital to the continued growth of both Los Angeles and California. You will then go on to win your election, make sure matching federal funding is approved, and then you will be free to continue your political career as you wish…or retire from public life and become a private citizen with a beautiful wife and a bank account the size of which you cannot now comprehend."

Silence ensured on both sides of the line. After it became apparent the pause was more than pregnant, Zellenski said, "I take it that was blunt and brief enough."

Paul waited just a moment before answering. He gathered himself and said, "Now that you've made it perfectly clear that you have absolutely no idea of who I am… or what kind of man I am…what could possibly make you believe that I would agree to do as you ask?"

"I believe you will do it, Mr. Cassidy, for the very reason that you consider yourself a man of honor and character. You sincerely believe you can help all the people of California by becoming a Congressman. That is why you agreed to run in the first place. And it is something you can in fact do…once you are elected. I am only suggesting that you do it after you pay your debt to me and others for getting you elected."

"And what if I fool you…and others…by getting elected without you?"

"That will be impossible, Mr. Cassidy. Would you like to know why?"

"Enlighten me."

"If you do not do as I ask, your war record will be leaked to various members of the press and your chances of being elected will become nonexistent."

"My war record? It's already public knowledge. I've been told countless times that it's one of the reasons people will want to vote for me."

"Not when they learn of what transpired on the night of June 7, 1944, in the home of one Colette Auteuil."

Another silence. This one longer. Paul knew Zellenski was waiting for him to reply. "How could you possibly know about that?"

"How is unimportant. What happened is all that matters."

"Well…I mean if you know…well…then you must know that I submitted a report about that…that night. I made it clear to my company commander that neither myself, nor my men knew anything about what happened…what happened to her."

"Three men…alone in a house with a woman. A woman who is viciously killed. You were the officer. You were in charge. And your public explanation will be that you simply don't know what happened? Who do you think will believe that? Who do you think would vote for a man who could do such an evil thing? Or be so cowardly as to refuse to admit…that he couldn't control his own men? Who exactly would vote for a man like that, Mr. Cassidy?"

Paul didn't have an answer.

Chapter 52

Arizona

Riley's detour to Las Cruces proved unproductive. There was no information in the battered DeSoto relating to Ian Donovan's LA connection. A search through the personal effects of Jacob, alias Jocko, Palmira provided nothing either. And there had been no recent reports of stolen vehicles. Riley thanked the local authorities for their help, filled his Ford with gasoline, and headed for Los Angeles.

Rémy, who had spent the night in El Paso, but was unaware of his prey's diversion from the main route to California, was on the road early. He passed through southern New Mexico and into Arizona checking the license plates of every car he would catch and pass. None were from Texas. Undaunted, he kept driving, cognizant of the fact that even if he didn't catch up with Cross, Los Angeles was the home of one of the other men on his list, Lieutenant Paul Cassidy.

Just west of Phoenix, the Frenchman's attention was diverted to a hillside of giant Saguaros. He had never seen anything like the colossal cactuses before. When he looked back, a roadrunner made a mad dash in front of his car. Startled, Rémy jerked the steering wheel instinctively to the right. The Chevrolet skidded off the pavement and rumbled over the rocky shoulder before he could right it again. He was able to regain his composure and his direction. But after going about a mile down the highway, he was certain he could both hear and feel a distinctive thump on the right side of the car. Slowing down, he pulled off the road, and got out to see what damage had been done. After walking around to the passenger side of the car, he saw that his right front tire was now flat. Apparently something had punctured it when he ran off the road. "Merde!" he shouted to the rocks, the horny toads, the snakes, and the cactus—as they were the only ones around. Then he peeled off his jacket and set about the task that was ahead of him.

After securing the lug wrench, the jack, and the spare tire, Rémy was just about to begin when he saw a car coming down the road he had already traversed that morning. In hopes of getting a fellow traveler to help him, he stopped what he was doing, walked to the back of the car, and stood beside it waving.

Still a hundred yards away, Riley could see the vehicle and the man on the side of the road. Had it been any other day, he would have slowed, asked if he could help, and done so if requested. But it was no other day. And the man who had killed his wife was probably in LA by now. The motorist would just have to fend for himself. Or wait for the next car to come by whose driver wasn't obsessed with the task before him.

The bespectacled man on the side of road continued to wave his arms, but it quickly became apparent to him that the driver wasn't going to stop. The car sped closer and closer, never cutting its speed. It became larger and larger in Rémy's field of vision, then whizzed past and moved down the highway as rapidly as it had approached. But it had not passed too quickly for the Frenchman to recognize that the speeding Ford, and the momentarily crippled Chevrolet had one thing in common. A Texas license plate.

Chapter 53

California

By mid-afternoon Riley had crossed into California. He planned on waiting until he reached Los Angeles to check back with Sheriff Totter to see if Kelly had remembered the name of the man Ian Donovan was going to California to work for. As he was approaching Indio, his laser focus on finding Donovan was momentarily interrupted by the sight on a huge billboard on the side of the road. The fact that a billboard was there was not that unusual. With the burgeoning increase in automobile travel across America, advertisers of all stripes had rushed to get their messages alongside dirt roads, gravel paths, asphalt turnpikes, and state highways from one end of the country to the next. On this particular billboard, it was the message itself that caught Riley's eye, along with the photograph that accompanied it. The message was short and to the point. It said, CASSIDY FOR CONGRESS. Beside it, there was a picture of the candidate.

By the time the communication from the billboard had actually lodged itself in Riley's mind, he was hundreds of yards past it. "Did I just see what I thought I saw?" he asked himself. Then he answered his question by pulling over to the side of the road, executing a U-turn, driving back beyond the billboard, then turning his car back around to face it again. "Wow," he said. "It's Lieutenant Cassidy."

Reflections of the war started to wash over him in waves. Their time in jump school together…the Italian campaign…the minefield…that night at the farmhouse…seeing him for the last time in the field hospital. And now here he was, larger than life, staring down from a gigantic sign. *Incredible,* Riley thought. Then he recalled that the lieutenant had told him and Brendon that he was from Los Angeles. Why hadn't that occurred to him earlier? He knew why. He had been so fixated on catching Donovan that it never occurred to him he actually knew someone in Los Angeles…his fellow airborne trooper and former platoon leader, Lieutenant Cassidy.

For the next two hours, Riley saw at least four more billboards with the same message and photo. By the time he got to the eastern outskirts of Los Angeles, he had the beginnings of a plan. Stopping at a gas station to fill up, he asked the attendant if he knew of a public phone nearby. The kid mentioned a diner just down the road. Ten minutes later, Riley was in their phone booth thumbing through the Los Angeles directory. He had never seen a phonebook with so many names. And so many Cassidys. There were at least twenty Paul or P. Cassidys. He didn't know where to begin. Then a thought came to him and he called the operator.

"Operator, I'm trying to call Paul Cassidy, the man who's running for Congress. Is there any way you can help me find the right number?"

"One moment please….let me see…you said Cassidy, right? There is a Cassidy for Congress Campaign Headquarters number here. Would you like that?"

Moments later, Riley heard the receptionist say, "Cassidy for Congress. May I help you?"

"I'd like to talk to Paul Cassidy."

"Do you have an appointment with Mr. Cassidy?"

"No. I don't actually have an appointment, but—"

"I'm sorry Sir, candidate Cassidy is very busy and if you don't have an appointment, then—"

"Wait…wait…you see I'm an old friend of Lieutenant…I mean Mr. Cassidy, and I'm sure he'd want to—"

"I'm sorry, Sir. The procedure is that you leave your name and number. Then if Mr. Cassidy agrees to an appointment we will call you back and—"

"You don't understand. This is important. It's...well it's a police matter and if Mr. Cassidy is there, it's important that I speak to him now."

"Police? What did you say your name was, Sir?"

"My name is Riley Cross. Tell him it's Private Riley Cross."

"Private? I thought you said this was a police matter?"

"Well, it's actually Deputy Riley Cross. Tell him it's Deputy Riley Cross who used to be Private Riley Cross. I'm sure he'll want to talk to me." Actually Riley wasn't at all sure, but he thought it was worth a try.

"Please hold Deputy...I mean Private...I mean Mr. Cross....oh...just hold, please."

Less than a minute later there was a man's voice on the line. "This is Paul Cassidy?"

"Lieutenant? Lieutenant Cassidy? This is Riley Cross. Private Cross. Do you remember me, Sir?"

"Cross...of course I remember you. How are you? Where are you? And why are you calling?"

Five minutes of conversation tore through seven years of separation, and within that time, Riley laid out what he was doing in Los Angeles and why he was on the trail of a bank robber and murderer. Paul listened with sympathy to what happened and said he'd do whatever he could to help. He also asked if Riley had a place to stay in LA. When Riley stumbled with an answer, he said, "Look, you should stay with me. With us, I mean. My wife and I. We have plenty of room."

"I can just get a motel room, I wouldn't want to—"

"I wouldn't hear of it, Cross. You're staying with us. Look, things are crazy here, right now, so I'm going to put my secretary on the line. She'll give you my address and instructions on how to get to my house. My wife is home today, she's not shooting...at least I think she's not shooting today. Anyway, I'll call her and she'll be there when you arrive. I may be a little late getting home this evening, but I'll see you tonight. Alright?"

"I really don't want to put you out…Sir. I mean—"

Paul cut in, feigning a tone he hadn't used since he left the service. "Private…this is an order!"

Riley smiled and responded with, "Airborne, Sir."

Chapter 54

Benedict Canyon

Ian Donovan had seen some big houses in Chicago—from the outside, of course. He had been in some spacious and ostentatiously decorated mob homes in Kansas City. But he had never been near, or in, anything like the Benedict Canyon house where he now found himself as he awaited an audience with his new employer. Seated in an antique Portuguese throne chair of tufted leather and hand-carved oak, he imagined himself the lord of the manor rather than the lackey waiting to meet his new master. *This was the way to live,* he thought. These were the kind of surroundings he belonged in. There would be no more terrible Midwest winters to suffer through and no more Wop cretins to take orders from. He had made the big leagues, he told himself. He had finally arrived.

The butler retrieved Ian and led him to the study. "Mr. Zellenski will see you now," he said, opening the door to let Ian in and then closing it behind him.

Zellenski was seated at a massive, intricately carved Spanish desk. His head was down, perusing the papers in front of him. Ian walked across the room and stood in front of the desk as he said, "I'm Ian Donovan. Pleased to meet you, Sir." Then he extended his hand.

Zellenski looked up at him and his gesture with thinly veiled contempt. It was only then Ian realized there was no right hand to shake. He jerked his hand back to his side, saying, "Sorry."

"There were supposed to be three of you."

"Yes Sir, well you see those other two were really unreliable…plus we had a bit of bad luck on the trip and—"

"Where are the other two?"

"Well, as it turns out, Sir, they're both…well, they're both dead."

"Explain. Quickly."

"Sure…I mean certainly, Sir. You see Kelly, well…he got a bit greedy on the way over and tried to stick up this gas station in Texas and he got himself shot. Yes Sir, shot dead. I didn't even know he was planning to do anything…I thought he was just going inside to pay for the gasoline you know, and then the shooting starts—"

"And you left him?"

"Well, there was no point in me and Jocko sticking around, you know. I mean we couldn't help him. I saw that gas station owner put a bullet right in the back of Kelly's head as he turned to walk out."

"Did the police get a description of your car?"

"No…oh, no Sir, I mean. We got away before that station owner could get a good look at us. We even switched cars along the way. Just to be sure, you know."

"And the other man…this Jocko?"

"A terrible traffic accident, it was. I couldn't believe it. Somewhere near Arizona or New Mexico, we were, and Jocko…well…he gets the call of nature you know, so we stop the car and he gets out to relieve himself. On the driver's side he was…because he was driving…and as he steps out of the car…well this huge truck just barrels him right over. Awful it was, Sir. Truly awful."

"You left him as well?"

"Well, Sir, there was absolutely nothing I could do for the poor soul. I mean he was way beyond any earthly help… and…and I didn't want to have to explain to the police or anyone about who we were and where we were going. I mean…I certainly didn't want your name brought up, Sir."

Zellenski found Ian's explanation incredulous. He was annoyed that he had only gotten one third of what he had ordered from the Kansas City contacts. But he reasoned that if the other two had been of the same quality as the man standing before him, perhaps he was better off.

"There are rooms above the garage. The butler will take you to yours. He will give you a street map of the Los Angeles area. Study it. Tomorrow morning I will have an assignment for you."

"Ah…good. Thank you, Sir. I look forward to working for you, Mr. Zellenski."

"Donovan…there is one more thing. You Americans have a saying. It goes, we all make mistakes. You have heard this saying, yes?"

"Yes, Sir. I have heard it. And to be honest, I have to admit I've probably said it myself once or twice."

"Never put yourself in a position to say it again. Here, in my employ, we do not make mistakes. Do precisely as you are told. Excuses are not tolerated. Do I make myself clear?"

"That you do, Sir. That you do."

Chapter 55

Los Angeles

Riley had jotted down the address and the instructions he received from Paul's secretary on how to get to the candidate's home. They proved to be excellent. He pulled into the circular driveway in front of the house less than an hour after getting off the phone. As he looked around at the neighborhood of two-story Spanish stuccos, flowering gardens, and manicured lawns, he thought how very different this environment was from the tiny houses, vegetable patches, and rock-strewn yards of Pilot Hill. For the first time since he headed west, he was now concerned with his own appearance too. He glanced in the rearview mirror and rubbed his hair over with his hand. He slipped the shotgun down into the floorboard of the Ford, then took his holstered forty-five and put it in the glove box. He decided to leave his Stetson in the car as well. It seemed even more out of place than he felt. But he pulled his western-cut jacket out and put it on before locking the car, walking to the front door, and ringing the bell.

A few seconds later, when the door opened, Riley was dumbstruck. There, standing before him, was the somewhat older but no less beautiful girl he had loved and lost track of years before. The beauty he had recognized on the giant screen. The woman who had brought a tear to his eye as he watched and listened from the darkness of the audience. There she was. The face he thought he had only imagined in the wrinkled photograph Paul had tried to share so many years ago in France. There was Gwen Taylor.

Gwen, even though she had the advantage, paused before speaking as well. When Paul had called to tell her that he had invited a mate from the war to spend a few days with them, she automatically asked his name. When he answered Cross...Riley Cross...she almost dropped the phone. He was in such a hurry to get off the line and attend a meeting that she didn't try to hold him to get more information. But somehow...as impossible as it seemed...she knew, without a doubt, who was soon to be knocking on her door.

"Riley...it's me...Gwen."

"Gwen...my God, Gwen. You look more beautiful than ever."

"And you...you're still...still as tall and handsome as ever." Her eyes misted over and she stepped forward and gave him a hug saying, "Oh, Riley...Riley."

He returned the embrace warmly, but cautiously. The scent and feel of her within his arms was almost overwhelming.

"Gwen...did you know? Did you know it was me that was coming?"

"I asked Paul the name of our impending house guest. When he said, Riley Cross, I was so shocked I couldn't get any other questions out before he had to get off the phone. And you...did you know...about me?"

Paul hesitated before answering. "No...yet maybe yes...but really no. It's sort of a long story."

"Well, for heaven's sake, don't stand out here to tell it," she said wrapping both of her arms around his. "Come on inside."

For the next two hours, the house echoed with their conversation. There was so much to say on both their parts. They started with what was most recent. Riley explained why he was in Los Angeles, the loss of Sharon, and that he had a son, back in Pilot Hill. Gwen shared how she met Paul, their marriage, and his decision to run for Congress. The more they talked, the more they kept turning the pages backward. Gwen told Riley about Felix Pressman, and all that he had done for her. She left out the details of their personal relationship, but her obviously intense regard for him was hard to hide. Riley talked about how he and his good friend, Brendon O'Byrne, had met Paul in jump school, and how they subsequently went through Italy and France together. He left out any mention of the night, and the farmhouse, and Colette Auteuil. He didn't know if Paul had talked to her about it or not. He wasn't sure what he'd say if she brought it up. The words kept carving a path back in time. It was inevitable the path would lead all the way back to them.

"Do you ever think about those times, Riley? Those times back in school and everything?"

"I guess everyone does…don't they? At some time or another. They say no one ever forgets their first love."

"Were we in love, Riley? Were we really in love? Or just sort of…I don't know, overwhelmed with each other?"

"I don't know, Gwen. We were both so young. Neither one of us had much experience with the world outside Pilot Hill. Not then, anyway."

"I like to think we were in love. I like to think that's what it was. That's what it always seemed like to me."

"Gwen, there's something I want you to know. Something I'd feel better about you knowing."

"What is it, Riley?"

"I remember when I was still in basic training. I got this letter from my mom. She used to write and tell me about everything that was going on in Pilot Hill. You know how small towns are, Gwen. I mean...you know how they talk. Well…one of the letters from mom told me about when your family left town. She indicated that maybe there was a reason you all left. Like you didn't want people to know that you were…well…"

"Riley," Gwen said, "there are good things and bad things about small towns. One of the bad things is that people always assume the worst."

There was just no point, she told herself. *No point in telling him now, all these years later.* She was the one who made the decision. She hadn't talked to him about it then. She saw no need to now.

No need to burden him with the memory of something she had never been able to forget. So she lied.

"I wasn't pregnant, Riley. It was just small town gossip. Nothing more."

"Well…I just wanted you to know...that it wasn't like I didn't care. It wasn't like I was just going to leave you to deal with everything on your own. I couldn't get away. I even tried sneaking out once…going AWOL. Just because I didn't want you to have to be alone with all that. Of course, I never really heard from you directly…so I couldn't really be sure what the situation was."

"Riley, like you said earlier…we were both so young. You were about to go off to war. So many young men weren't coming back. I didn't want to add to your burdens. It was probably wrong of me. But that's why I didn't write. I was just young…and couldn't bring myself to say how I really felt in letters. I actually thought maybe it was best for each of us to go our own separate ways. Like we eventually did…right?"

"Gwen, there's no need to apologize for anything. Life always works out…well…the way it works out. I just wanted you to know that back then…way back then…I just didn't forget you."

Gwen reached out and took Riley's hand in both of hers. "You're a good man, Riley Cross. I hope you understand me saying…that even with the terrible thing that happened to your wife…she was a lucky woman for being able to love and be loved by you."

"I'm glad your life has worked out so well, Gwen. You deserve all of this. The house, your career, and a man like Paul. They don't come any better in my book."

She smiled and said, "I think we've been reading the same book. Oh, my! Look at the time. I think the next Congressman from the state of California is going to be walking through that door pretty soon now. Better make sure there's something good for him to eat. Come on…let me show you the kitchen. It's Paul's favorite room."

Once Paul got home, over cocktails, Gwen and Riley revealed the astonishing coincidence that they were both from the same tiny town in Texas, and had once known each other, slightly, in school. The small world cliché was used a number of times. Over dinner, the three shared bottles of wine and war stories fit for mixed company. Along with tales of jump school, two hundred and fifty feet towers and old mates like Brendon.

"You ever hear from O'Byrne?" Paul asked.

"No. I'm sorry to say I haven't. Once we mustered out, I went home to Texas and he went to Chicago and...well...you know how it is? We just never kept in touch."

"Yeah," Paul said. "We always plan on doing things that we never seem to find the time to do. I bet he's tearing the Windy City up, though. There was a guy who always had a wise crack and a laugh. You and O'Byrne were two of the platoon's best," he said. "Sure wish I knew someone who could tell me how he was doing."

Outside, just down the street from his house, in the front seat of a green Chevrolet, was the man who could have done that for Paul. He was a young, thin man in glasses and a brown fedora. And even though he would be spending this particular night in his car, he was a lucky man. He didn't have to keep driving to the homes of the other P. Cassidys listed on the phone book page he had torn out and put on the seat beside him. Fortunately, the first house he drove by turned out to be the winner. Because parked outside in the circular driveway, was a black Ford sedan with Texas license plates.

Chapter 56

Outside the Cassidy Residence

The day broke chilly and wet. A low-pressure system had moved across the Pacific and paused along the California coast turning normally sunny LA skies gray, and dropping more rain on the city than it had seen in the last three months. Big, round drops drumming on the roof and hood of the car woke Rémy Auteuil from a miserable sleep. He had tried a number of different positions to get comfortable during the night but it seemed that all of them simply added to his cramped neck and sore shoulders. After stretching his arms and his back to the degree possible in the front seat of an automobile, he looked over to make sure the cars he had been watching the night before were still in the driveway. They were.

He checked his watch. It read six fifteen. They would be stirring soon, if they weren't already. Though he was hungry and badly in need of a cup of coffee, he was hesitant to leave for fear whomever was in the house might leave before he got back. Being this close, he wasn't going to take a chance on getting separated again.

The Frenchman's plan had always been equal parts inspiration and improvisation. His inspirational devotion to a meticulous multi-year search had enabled him to uncover and locate the Américains. But he knew his disposition of them would always have to be improvised based on the circumstances in which he found them. He realized he had been lucky in Chicago. Both in spotting O'Byrne, and in having an available alley in which to isolate his subject. The fact that the two remaining targets were together could complicate things immensely. He thought it unlikely he could overpower and dispatch two men if they recognized their situation and decided to put up a fight. Yet it was paramount that each indeed recognize his situation. Before they died, it was imperative they know what they were dying for…that they realize retribution for their atrocity was at hand. He was determined that the last thought on their minds be fear and self-loathing for the venality that brought them to their doom.

At seven o'clock the rain was still falling, though not as intensely as it had been earlier.

Rémy had removed his glasses to wipe them with the handkerchief he had just pulled from his pocket when he glanced over and saw the front door open. Quickly, he put them back on. A figure in a mackintosh emerged from the vestibule and closed the door behind him. He carried a briefcase and walked briskly even though he was using a cane. The hair color didn't look quite right for Cross, he thought, as he hurriedly scanned the photos from his copies of the 201 Files that were also on the seat beside him. *No. No,* he thought. *This wasn't Cross. This was Cassidy.* Paul C. Cassidy, the candidate on the billboards. Lieutenant Paul C. Cassidy, the officer in charge on that hideous night. His assumption was confirmed when the sandy-haired man opened the door of the Oldsmobile rather than the Ford with the Texas plates. As a plume of exhaust belched from the tailpipe into the morning rainfall, Rémy realized he had a decision to make. *The Texan must still be in the house. But this one is leaving. Should I stay here and wait for Cross? Should I follow Cassidy?* "A bird in the hand," he muttered. And when the Oldsmobile pulled out, the Frenchman started his car and followed.

When Paul reached the corner of Third Street and South Broadway, he turned into a public parking lot. Rémy found a spot on the street and pulled over near the curb. The neighborhood had already come to life. People were walking past each other on the sidewalk, stopping at the corner newsstands, going in and out of the diner with the flashing sign. *Too busy. Too crowded,* the Frenchman told himself. He watched as Paul left his car with the attendant and walked to the corner to cross the street. Afraid he might lose sight of him, Rémy turned his engine off, got out and locked his car. Then he fell in behind people who were heading in Paul's direction.

The light changed and they all crossed the street. Rémy stayed close enough behind Paul to keep him in his eyeline. He watched as Paul passed by the large picture window of Bridal City, and stepped into the main entrance of what appeared to be the same building. When Rémy got to the entrance, he noted the address, two hundred four, South Broadway, and the sign that read BRADBURY BUILDING. Then he quickly realized the wedding shop only occupied the ground floor corner. Once inside, he saw Paul and two other people step into one of the two open-grille elevators. The vaulted design of the building enabled him to watch the elevator's ascent. He noted the floor on which Paul exited the elevator and he kept watching to see which interior door he was using. When the elevator came back down, the Frenchman got in it.

The sign on the door read PAUL CASSIDY, CAMPAIGN HEADQUATERS. Rémy wondered if perhaps Paul had gotten to the office ahead of everyone else—in which case he'd have him alone. He opened the door a crack and peeked in. No such luck. The offices were abuzz with people on phones, others typing, some sharing conversation with coffee cups in their hands. No opportunity here, he told himself, and quickly closed the door. *Best to wait,* he thought. *Wait and watch.* He went back downstairs to the lobby, found a coffee stand, bought a cup, and cursed its inferior quality. Then he found a bench to sit on with a view of the office door he had opened only moments earlier.

Chapter 57

Cassidy Residence

Riley finally stirred. His head rolled off the pillow and his eyelids felt like they weighed a hundred pounds each. He brought his hands up to his eyes and used his fingers to pry open the anvils on either side of his nose. Slowly a diffused and glassy image in front of him turned into a clock on the bedside table. It read two-twenty. Incomprehensible. *Can't be,* he thought. *We stayed up until midnight. Surely I've been asleep more than two hours.* Then it hit him. *Jesus! It can't be two…in the afternoon!* Flinging the sheets back, he scrambled out of bed, pulled on the pants he had left on the chair, then stumbled to the window and looked outside. The rain was still coming down. But it was definitely not night. Still barefoot and shirtless, he walked over to the door of the guestroom and opened it.

"Hello," he shouted.

From somewhere downstairs came back Gwen's reply, "Hello yourself. Finally decide to get up, sleepyhead?"

"Tell me it's not two in the afternoon," he yelled.

After a pause, she yelled back. "It's not two in the afternoon…it's two-twenty-five."

He walked to the edge of the stairway and said, "Why did you let me sleep so long?"

She stuck her head out of the kitchen and replied, "Because you were exhausted. Grab a shower and come on down. I'll fix you some eggs."

Gwen was right. Riley had literally exhausted himself. He probably hadn't slept more than an hour or two a night since the hold up, the funeral, and his sixteen hundred mile dash from Texas to California. He had finally relaxed enough with Gwen and Paul to let his emotions go for a few hours. When he did, it was as if a steam valve had been released and all the strength and energy he had been hoarding over the last week spewed out into a roaring, all-consuming tsunami of sleep.

After he'd showered and changed clothes, and over eggs and lots of hot coffee, he found himself apologizing for hibernating like a bear in winter.

"Don't be silly," Gwen said. "If anybody deserved to crash like that, it was you. You were literally out on your feet. You just didn't know it."

"I guess you're right," he answered. "But now, I've got to get some things done before this whole day gets away."

"Is there anything I can do to help?"

"Actually, there is. Let's see…what's the time difference between here and Texas?"

"Two hours. So now," she said, looking at her watch, "it's almost five o'clock there."

"I need to use your phone. Can I do that?"

"Sure. The closest one's in the hallway. Take your coffee with you."

Moments later, he was hearing Harris Totter say, "Been off the radar for a while, haven't you son? Hope you got some rest."

"I did, Sheriff. I just wanted to let you know I'm going to call back to Las Cruces and see if there's any new stolen car reports, then I'm going to check with the county law here and—"

"Yeah, well that's all well and good, lad, but you're flapping your gums so, I haven't had a chance to tell you the best news of all."

"What's that, Sheriff?"

"Our guest with legs full of lead and a lot fewer fingers than he used to have…came up with the name of that fella Donovan was going to Los Angeles to work for."

"He did? What is it?"

"Let's see…now where's that note I made. Oh yeah, here it is.

Listen Riley, you better get a pencil and paper. You're going to need to write this one down."

"Okay, just a minute." Putting his hand over the speaker, he said, "Gwen, do you have a pencil, or a pen, and something I can write on?"

"Sure thing," she answered, pulling open the drawer in the occasional table the phone was sitting on, then retrieving a notepad and pen from inside it.

"Okay," Riley said, "let me have it. Wait a minute…just a second…better give it to me a letter at a time and I'll read it back to you. Go ahead. Z-E-L-L-E-N-S-K-I. Zellenski."

"What?" Gwen blurted.

"How about a first name?" Riley asked. "Did he remember the first name?"

Totter replied, "He wasn't a hundred percent on that. Said he thought it might be Harry…or Henry…or Herman…or Harley…something with an H is the best he could do."

Riley was jotting down the names as Totter was saying them and Gwen was looking at Riley's notes with widening eyes.

"That's great, Sheriff. Great. I'm going to get on this right away. I'll check back with you tomorrow."

Totter tried to respond but Riley banged the receiver down before he got the chance.

"Riley," Gwen said, "can I see that paper?"

"I really need to get on this, Gwen. I can tell you about it later. Now I—"

"Riley…I know that name."

"What? What are you talking about?"

"Well, if it's the same person…the H is for Herman. Herman Zellenski."

"What do you know about him? How do you know him?"

"Well…not much really. I know that he's some kind of European. Polish, I think. Paul actually sold his father's business to the guy. We went to a party at his home. Boy, is that a weird place. The guy struck me as a little creepy, if you want to know the truth."

"You know where he lives? You've been there?"

"Yeah. It's up in Benedict Canyon."

"Is that far from here? I've got to go see this guy."

"Well, how do you know…I mean, how do you know it's the same Zellenski?"

"I don't know for sure. But he's as good a one as any to start with. Can you give me directions, or do you have a street map you can show me?"

"I can do better than that. I can get in the car and go with you."

"No…listen, Gwen. I appreciate the thought. But no. If this guy is associated with Donovan…it could get…well, it's just potentially too dangerous. You can't go."

"Riley, I could wait in the car and—"

"Gwen…I just lost someone who…well, you heard me talk about that yesterday. Let's just say now…I'm not going to put anyone else I care about in harm's way."

"But if you think it really might be dangerous you ought to—"

"It's not dangerous, Gwen. It won't be dangerous. I'm just being cautious, okay. But, I need those directions…or a map…or whatever you can give me."

"Sure. I guess if you got through a war and all…you probably know what you're doing, huh?"

"That's right. I know what I'm doing. So can you—"

"Yes. I'm on it. I think there are maps in Paul's study. And I can mark one for you."

"Thanks, Gwen. And thanks too…well, for everything…you know?"

"I know, Riley. I know."

Chapter 58

The Bradbury Building

Rémy sat and watched patiently. Patience had become second nature to him. A condition rooted in childhood trauma and forged over years of the unending obsession to destroy the ones who had destroyed his mother. People went in and came out the CASSIDY FOR CONGRESS door, but Paul did not. It made no difference to Rémy. If he had to sit there all day and all night, he would. There was nothing he had to do that was as important as this. Around noon, a crowd of people came through the building's main entrance. As they dispersed to go their separate ways, one man in a suit and hat bumped into the Frenchman's foot dangling from his left leg that was crossed over his right.

"Hey, buddy…watch your big feet, will you," Ian Donovan said as he bent over and brushed his trousers.

"Désolé, monsieur," Rémy responded without thinking.

"Lousy foreigner," Ian muttered under his breath, but loud enough to be heard.

Then he walked over to the elevator, got in, and rode up to the floor Rémy had been watching all day. When he stepped inside, Rémy flicked the bottom of his chin with the backs of his fingers and said, "Stupide imbécile."

"Which office is Cassidy in?"

"That's Mr. Cassidy's office," the receptionist replied. "Can I take a message for him?"

"I'll deliver the message myself, sweetheart."

"I'm afraid that's impossible unless you have an appointment."

"He's the one who's got the appointment," Ian responded, "only he doesn't know it yet."

Ian started for the office door and the receptionist rose quickly to her feet. "Sir, you can't go in there without—"

"Hold your water, sister," Ian said, cutting her off with both his reply and his right hand. With his left he opened the door and barged in.

"Mr. Cassidy, I'm terribly sorry…I told this…this man…that if he didn't have an appointment he couldn't see—"

"Is there some problem, Sir? What's the meaning of this?" Paul asked.

"She's the one with the problem. Me? I'm fine myself. Mr. Zellenski sent me."

There was a moment's pause before Paul spoke. "Ah…it's alright, Doris. I'll see him. Go back to your desk."

She left, closing the door behind her as Paul said, "I don't appreciate you giving my receptionist a hard time."

"Oh, believe me, Mr. Congressman…of course, I guess I shouldn't call you that yet…but just to show my respect, I will. Anyway, believe me, Mr. Congressman, that was not a hard time…not at all."

"Look…who are you? And what are you doing here?"

Ian took a seat, leaned back in the chair, and put his feet up on the edge of Paul's desk. "My name's Donovan. But that's not important. What is important is that Mr. Zellenski would like you to come see him…now."

Paul took his cane and shoved Ian's feet off the desk. Almost tipping over, the thug managed to keep his balance, but not his dignity.

"And just what's so important about seeing him now?" Paul asked.

Recovering his machismo to some degree, Ian answered, "He said to tell you it's time to resolve this thing now. You are to come with me and not tell anyone where you're going."

"And just why would I do that?"

"Mr. Z said to mention…that he knows both your mother and

your wife's address."

"Is that some sort of veiled threat?"

"I don't wear no veil. But if I were you, I'd do as the man says."

"You know what," Paul said, "maybe it is time to get this whole thing settled once and for all. Let's go see your Mister Z."

On the way out, he said to the receptionist, "Doris, I'm going to be out of the office for a while. Take the number of anyone who calls and say I'll get back to them."

"Where should I say you've gone, Sir?"

Paul didn't answer, he just turned and followed Ian out into the hallway.

Rémy, whose eyes were still glued to the office door, saw Paul exit and walk with that rude fellow who had bumped into him, toward the elevator. They rode down then headed out the main entrance. Rémy trailed at a distance, and watched as the two men got in a car by the curb. The rude man got behind the wheel. Rémy hustled over to his car. There was a parking ticket inserted behind the driver's side windshield wiper. The Frenchman pulled it out and tossed it on the ground. Then he quickly got in, started his engine, and when Ian pulled away from the curb and into traffic, Rémy followed.

Chapter 59

Benedict Canyon

The rain was less intense than it had been earlier, but it hadn't stopped. It was as if the heavens were having a good long cry, and all those beneath its falling tears would simply have to deal with it. When Ian and Paul reached the main wrought-iron gate, the guard recognized Donovan, and allowed them entry. Tailing at a discrete distance, Rémy saw them turn in, and decided to drive slowly by. He followed the winding road as it curved around, keeping his eye on the high concrete wall that he assumed ringed the property. A quarter mile from the gate, he spotted a huge live oak just outside the wall, and once again inspiration gave way to improvisation. He drove past the tree, then made a U-turn and came back. When he was close enough, he pulled off the paved road and drove the Chevrolet right up to the trunk. By climbing on the hood of the car, he could grab the lower branches and swing himself up and over the wall. Any passerby seeing the car at the tree would simply assume someone ran off the road in the rain. And if he were found inside, he'd simply say he got lost, had an accident, and wandered onto the grounds to see if he could call for help. Being considered, as the rude man had muttered, a "lousy foreigner," the Frenchman believed his story was apt to be accepted.

Once over the wall, Rémy saw he was half way between the front and back of the property. Seeing the car he had been following parked in front of the house, he chose to go for the back. The charcoal skies and continuing rain helped mask his movement from the wall as he dashed from manicured shrub to trimmed topiary to poolside cabana. From there, he could see through the glass French doors on the back of the house.

Someone was on the other side...pacing back and forth...and using a cane. It was Cassidy.

Rémy's heart began to pound in his chest. Perhaps this was the time. He could race to the doors, throw them open, fire, and make his escape. *But no,* he thought. He needed more time. He needed to make sure the Américain knew why he was dying. Before he could debate with himself further, another man entered. They spoke for a moment. Then they walked toward the right side of the house and he lost sight of them.

Dripping wet now, reservations began to dart through his mind. He had overplayed his hand. Why had he come over the wall and onto the property? Why didn't he just wait for them to come out? The rude man would have to take Cassidy back to his car eventually. Why hadn't he thought of that before he did this stupid thing?

The Frenchman broke from the cabana and ran toward the right side of the house. He'd go round. Go round and find a way out. This was not the time or place. He had made a mistake. But as he swung round, he caught sight of a stairway. An outside stairway that ran from the ground to the second floor. *Perhaps a servants' entrance,* he thought. A way inside the house where he wouldn't be seen entering. *Why not,* he told himself. *Why not? I can say I thought it was a servants' entrance. I was trying to find a servant to tell them of my accident.* His mind was leapfrogging from why he should keep going to why he should turn back, and he seemed incapable of evaluating either. Without really knowing why, he broke for the stairs and climbed them at a run. All the while, he was thinking, *I'll tell them I was looking for a servant to report my accident...that's what I'll do...they'll believe me...a stupid frog...isn't that what these Yanks call us...frogs. Perfect for a day like today. A frog in the rain.*

He reached the top of the stairs, looked through the glass window in the door and saw a long corridor. It appeared to be empty. The knob turned in his hand. The door opened and he stepped inside. For a moment he simply stood there. His clothes were soaked. He began to drip on the carpet running down the hall. Both of Rémy's hands were thrust in his jacket pockets. He could feel the automatic in his right but he dare not take it out. It would not serve his story well. At the end of the corridor, the space opened into a semi-circle with doors on either side. He wasn't sure which way to turn. What an idiotic thing he had done. Why had he come in? There was no time for an answer. He heard footfalls and voices ascending the interior staircase. Quickly, he bolted to his left, opened the door and stepped into the room. *What luck,* he almost cried out. *It's empty. I can rest for a moment. Collect my thoughts. Decide what I should do and—*

"Let's talk in my study. It's quieter there."

The words had come from just outside the door. There was no more time to think. Only time to act. Ahead of him, behind the grand desk, he saw floor-to-ceiling red velvet drapes. *Do it,* he told himself. And he did. He pulled one back and jumped behind it just as the door opened and the men walked in.

Zellenski motioned for Paul to take the seat in front of the desk as he walked round and sat behind it.

"I'm so glad you could see me on such short notice. Thank you for coming."

"Let's get something straight up front," Paul said. "I won't have my family threatened."

"Did my man say something untoward? Do forgive that, please. He's a new man and frankly a bit of an oaf. It is difficult to get good help these days."

"Look…why have you summoned me here?"

"Ah yes, right to the point as always. Fine, then. I asked you here today…Paul, I hope I can call you Paul…because frankly time is growing increasingly short. The election is not that far away and it is imperative that my associates and I know exactly where you stand."

"Where I stand on what?"

"Let's not play games, Paul. Our conversation ended abruptly the other night and I never got a definitive answer as to whether or not you are going to do what is expected of you."

"You brought me here for that?"

"I like to look a man in the eye when he answers my questions. I have an innate ability to know when a man is lying."

"Have you been lied to often?"

"Never more than once by the same man, I assure you, Paul."

"So, you want to know if I'm going to support everything you and your people want regarding the highway projects. Prior to the election…after the election…and whether or not I'll do everything I can to get federal funding as well. Basically, you want to know if I'll work for you when I'm supposed to be working for all the people."

"A crude summation perhaps, but essentially, yes."

"Before I answer…I think it's only fair if you answer a question or two for me?"

"I agree that it is time you and I are completely open with one another. What would you like to know?"

"Why did your people…and I assume you…approach me to run in the first place?"

"For reasons you have heard, and reasons you may not have heard. You are young, attractive, you have a beautiful wife, you have a history in the community, you have a war record that is enviable…assuming we leave certain parts of it out…"

Paul interjected. "You're right. Those are the reasons I heard. What about the ones I may not have heard."

Zellenski opened an ornate gold cigarette case that was before him on the desk. He picked it up and offered one to Paul who shook his head, declining. Zellenski put the case down, selected one, put it in his mouth and used an Evans table lighter with an embossed eagle to light it. All with one hand of course. After taking a long drag, and releasing the smoke from his lungs, Zellenski finally said, "The other reasons were…that you are ambitious yet naïve…you present a brave exterior but are essentially weak, and therefore an excellent prospect for blackmail."

Paul said, "And that brings us back to Colette Auteuil. Does it not?"

"I suppose it does."

"How do you know anything about that? Did you see my After Action Report?"

"No."

"Then how do you know? Damn it…tell me!"

"Paul, I am a student of human nature. And of human response. Your aggression leads me to believe you are not going to do what is expected of you. Am I correct?"

"I'll tell you what's correct. You are not Herman Zellenski. You are Frederick Zell. You aren't Polish either. You're German…an ex-Nazi who got out of France with millions stolen from Jews you incarcerated or killed. And if you think…in your wildest imagination…that I would ever subjugate my ethics for your money…then you're as witless as you are evil. I don't care what you do with whatever information you think you have. I'm going to tell people the truth and whatever they decide is okay with me. My character is not for sale. I won't be a hostage to you or anyone else…for any price."

Zell continued to smoke his cigarette. He showed no signs of anger, or for that matter, any emotion at all. After a few seconds, he spoke.

"I would give you a round of applause, Paul, but as you can see that's not quite something I can manage. What I can do however, is to be as honest with you as you have been with me. Shall I begin?"

"Suit yourself."

"Now…as you and I speak…I am Herman Zellenski, a Polish Jew. No one can prove otherwise. No matter what those radical Zionists tell you. Then…in the war…I was indeed Frederick Zell. A German officer. There was nothing better to be at that time. In fact, there was nothing better to be for a very long time. But all things end, as you know, Paul."

"Why won't you tell me how you knew about Colette Auteuil?"

"If you insist, Paul, certainly I will tell you. Now that we've come to this impasse, I see no reason not to. Perhaps it will enlighten you. Perhaps it will finally make you see how petty and inconsequential you and your mongrel American race really are."

Rémy was virtually holding his breath—trying to make no sound whatsoever. His right hand was still in his pocket gripping the gun. But he was mesmerized by the conversation he was hearing. And the voice he was hearing it from. There was something about the Pole, or the German, or whatever he was. Something about the quality of his voice that teetered in the far reaches of Rémy's mind. He hung on every word.

"You see, Paul, like you I was a soldier. Though it is quite absurd to compare a German officer to an American. It is a bit like comparing an eagle to a vulture. Both hunt, but one kills while the other feasts off the killing someone else has done. You and your countrymen feasted on what we started in Europe. You have recently subjugated the continent with your money. We subjugated it with our might."

Unimpressed, Paul replied, "As I recall, yours is the country that surrendered."

"The unavoidable result of numbers," Zell responded. "By 1944, you had more troops, more planes, more ships, more bombs, more supplies, more food, more of everything. I knew…though many of my comrades did not…that once you invaded, the war would be lost. So I put plans in motion to make sure my postwar life would be a profitable one."

"By stealing everything you could get your hands on."

"The spoils of war."

"Look, Zell…what does all this have to do with Colette

Auteuil?"

"Ah yes...you see, even in defeat...the superior species can find a way to inflict appropriate revenge. The story of Colette Auteuil is a story of my revenge on both the conquering heroes and the miserable rabble that, in hindsight, wasn't worth mastering in the first place."

"Zell, will you—"

"I was ready to make my way out of France, but before I could, I was seconded to a unit in the field. They needed officers skilled in interrogation and that was one of my specialties. You can imagine my chagrin when I found myself tramping through the woods looking for potential prisoners from advance forces the Allies assumed we'd know nothing about. The patrol I was leading managed to snare a hapless American. A pathetic Jew who had gotten himself lost. I was in the process of interrogating him when we were attacked by small arms fire."

No. No, it can't be, Paul thought.

"I was hit in the first volley. I knew at that instant my arm was lost. So I executed the Jew dog and managed to escape."

"That was you? That was you that killed Goldman, and ran away?"

"I did not run away. I escaped. Escaped to exact my revenge somewhat later."

"What do you mean?"

"I found my way to a farmhouse. The house of Colette Auteuil. I persuaded the French bitch to give me food, and nurse my arm as best she could. Though I knew there was no way to save it."

"You were there? There before we were?"

"I was there before you...when you arrived...and when you left."

"But...but how, I mean where—"

"There was a root cellar below the floor. Many French farms have them. This one was covered by a rug beneath the table you ate on."

"But why would she hide you? Why didn't she tell us? Why would she help you like that?"

"My powers of persuasion consisted of holding a Luger to her son's head."

"Her son? But she said he was dead. That he drowned."

"Of course she did. That is what I told her to say if she wanted to keep the little bastard alive."

"But…I still don't—"

"No…you do not know anything. So keep quiet for a moment and I will tell you how inept you were."

Paul sat back in his chair. He wanted to hear it all. Almost as much as Rémy, who was now hanging on every word.

Zell couldn't keep from adding editorial comment. "You Americans are as clumsy in implementing a plan as you are in preparing it. We saw and heard you coming when you first reached the vineyard." Then he went on with the details. "Her son was asleep in his bed when I arrived. She had given him codeine for his cold that had effectively rendered him unconscious. I had her quickly bind and gag him to make sure he wouldn't wake while you were there. Then I had her carry him down to the root cellar with me. She knew that if she betrayed me in the slightest, I would not hesitate to kill him. I also had her put some of the codeine in the wine she would later offer you. Being Americans, you would likely never notice the difference in taste, and being hungry and exhausted, you would likely go…what is the expression…out like a light. You did."

"That's why none of us woke up. That's why we slept so long."

"Exactly."

"But…that still doesn't explain…well…so many things. Why didn't you just escape when you had the chance? Or, for that matter, why didn't you kill us while we slept? And…for God's sake…why did you kill her?"

With Paul's question, Rémy began to weep silently. The different language had slowed his memory of the voice. Now he knew. The man talking was the man who had led him from the root cellar to his mother's bedside.

"I knew I could escape when I wanted. I was in no hurry. As I told you earlier, I knew the war was lost. But here, before me, was an opportunity for an unparalleled victory over the victors. If I had shot you while you slept, all three of you would be dead, but the dead take nothing with them. The living…on the other hand…carry the mind's valise of guilt, distrust, disappointment, and eventually despair, all the days of their lives. Poisoning four lives forever seemed a far more fitting revenge than a quick bullet to the brain. That's why Colette Auteuil had to die."

"Zell…I find it impossible to grasp the depth of your depravity."

"Of course you do. That is why your mixed-breed race is so inferior."

"But wait a minute…you said four…you said poisoning four lives forever. Unlike us, you killed her. Why? If she was dead, her life couldn't be poisoned."

"No…but her son's could. You see…I convinced the little French bastard that you Américains killed her."

Chapter 60

Outside The House

The map Gwen had marked for Riley laid the route out precisely enough, but the traffic and the rain extended his journey. It took him almost twice as long to get across town, up Benedict Canyon and to Zellenski's main gate as he thought it would. But while the delay slowed his progress, it didn't dampen his zeal to get Donovan, the man who had murdered his Sharon.

Riley realized that whomever Donovan was working for, would have little regard for the law. So he set his mind to the task at hand. Along the way, he retrieved his holstered forty-five from the glove compartment and strapped it to his belt. His coat would cover it on his hip. He picked up the twelve-gauge shotgun from the floorboard and put it on the seat beside him. He even reached over, grabbed his Stetson, and put it on.

When he reached the main gate, he got out of the car with the forty-five in his hand, but his arm behind him—out of the sight line from the guard he was approaching.

"Howdy," Riley began. "Sorry to bother you, but I'm looking for a friend of mine. Does a guy named Donovan work here? Ian Donovan. And might he be on the grounds?"

"Yeah," the guard replied. "He just started working here. In fact he and another guy came in a little while ago."

"Good. Well, if you don't mind then, just open the gate here and I'll run up and see him."

"I'll have to call up to the house first…to get the okay. What's your name?"

Riley swung his arm from behind him and stuck the forty-five between the bars and in the guard's face. "My name's drop-the-goddamned-phone-and-open-the-gate-now. I don't need to be announced."

The guard, recognizing sincerity when it came from the barrel of a forty-five, did as he was told. Riley then walked the guard around to the back of the Ford.

"Does Donovan stay in the main house?"

"No," the guard said. "Those of us who work here, live in the quarters over the garage."

"How many those are there?

"Right now, there's just Donovan and me. There were supposed to be two other guys with him but they didn't show."

"Guess what?" Riley replied. "They ain't coming. Now get in the trunk."

The guard folded himself inside the trunk and Riley pulled the lid down and locked it. Then he got behind the wheel and roared up the driveway between the towering Italian Cypresses. Reaching the front of the main house, he saw the multi-car garage off to the left. There were windows at the top. Riley guessed those were part of the quarters the guard mentioned. Alongside the garage was a staircase leading to an entrance on the second floor.

Reaching over and grabbing the shotgun, he exited the car, stood behind the open door, and pumped a round into the chamber. Then, as the rain continued to fall, he heard what sounded like a gunshot coming from the main house. Riley stood there for a moment, not sure whether to head for the house or the garage. Then, a moment later, he heard a second shot from the house. He slammed the car door shut and was walking around the Ford to head for the front door when he heard the door bang open on the second floor of the garage. Riley stopped behind the car and looked across the driveway to see a shoeless man in dress slacks and a white undershirt racing down the stairs. He had, what looked to Riley, like a revolver in his hand.

The man reached the bottom of the stairs and started running across the driveway toward the main house. Riley called out,

"Donovan?"

The man stopped and looked over at the Ford. He didn't see anyone.

The voice shouted again. "Donovan…Ian Donovan?"

"Yeah…where are you…what do you want…what were those shots?" Ian spat in rapid order.

Riley came round from the back of the car and stood between Ian and the house. He was holding the shotgun across his waist.

"That gun in your hand," Riley said, "is that the gun you used to shoot an unarmed woman in Texas?"

Ian stood still. He wasn't sure what to think. Who the hell was this cowboy? And what was he doing here? He tried to change the subject. "Did you hear those shots? Something's going on in the house. We need to get up there."

"She died, Donovan. She didn't deserve to. God knows she didn't deserve to. But she died…by your hand."

Ian then realized the man in front of him wasn't from LA. *He must have trailed me…all the way from that damn bank in Texas. Jesus! What do I say? What do I say?* "Look…it was an accident. Yeah, an accident. She started running…and I swung around…just swung around to see what the noise was…and my gun went off…it accidently went off. I swear. I swear that's how it happened."

"Drop the gun on the ground. By your feet. I'm taking you back."

"This is California. You don't have any jurisdiction here. Who the hell do you think you are?"

"I'm the husband of the woman you killed. And I'm carrying my jurisdiction in my hands. Now…for the last time…put the gun on the ground."

Shit! Shit, Ian thought. *Why do these things always happen to me? Why can't I ever catch a break*? "I tell you what…I'll put it down. That's what I'll do…I'll put it down so it won't go off if I drop it…you know…like it did before. Okay? I'm bending down.

Look, I'm bending down now to put it on the ground."

Donovan had squatted almost into a ball. He was reaching out and moving his hand down. Riley was watching, but his focus wasn't on the gun itself, it was on Ian's eyes. He knew they would telegraph what the killer was going to do. And they did. In milliseconds, Donovan's eyes widened, his mouth tightened, the muscles in his neck clinched and suddenly he was swinging his arm back up to take a shot. Riley swept the shotgun from his waist to his shoulder in one swift motion. He fired and blew Donovan halfway across the driveway. The hail of lead caught him in the head, thorax, knees, and feet. He lay supine where the force of the twelve-gauge blast had carried him.

Riley walked over slowly, looked down, and saw a shredded face with dead eyes staring up at the gray sky. The rain continued to come down, washing the red blood across the black asphalt.

Chapter 61

Inside The House

"That's the most sickening thing I think I've ever heard," Paul said. "Why did you see fit to tell me? Is this some sort of ridiculously delayed remorse on your part?"

"Certainly not," Zell said. "I told you, because as I said earlier, you are weak, and naïve, and even if you can't be blackmailed, I'm sure whoever wins this election can be. It may cost a little more money. But the eventual outcome will be more than worth it."

"And you seriously believe I'm not going to expose what you did in the war, and what you're trying to do with the candidates and politicians of this state?"

"Yes," Zell said. "I seriously believe that. Why? Because of your naïveté. You came here without telling anyone where you were going. Consequently, wherever you are found…there will be no connection to me."

"Wherever I'm found...what are you talking about?"

"Paul, the immutable fact is…you are no longer of any use to me. Therefore, I wanted you to understand how truly inferior you are to the Reich you think you defeated. I wanted that to be the last thing etched in your mind for all of eternity."

With that, Zell moved the folder on his desk that had been covering a Luger. He picked the pistol up, and without another word, fired point blank into Paul's heart.

The crack of the shot jolted Rémy from his stunned paralysis. He threw the drape aside, and stepped from behind it. Before Zell could turn and face him, Rémy had pressed his automatic against Zell's temple.

"Drop the gun," he said.

Zell let it fall from his hand onto the desk.

Still holding the automatic against the side of Zell's head, Rémy looked over and saw Paul slumped in the chair. Then he walked part way round so he could see Zell's face…and Zell could see his.

"It is you," Rémy said. "And it was you all along."

"To state the obvious," Zell said, "you have the advantage of me. I do not know you."

"You don't recognize me? Understandable. I'm much older than I was then."

"Please," Zell said, "have I not the right to know who has entered my house illegally and shot my friend, the Congressional candidate, Mr. Cassidy?"

"There is no end to your treachery, is there?"

"Enough of this. Tell me who you are, if you have the courage," Zell demanded.

Rémy looked into his eyes and said, "I am the one you just referred to as the little French bastard. I am the son of Colette Auteuil."

Suddenly, the shock of recognition came over Zell's face. He started to speak but Rémy spoke first. "And to your other question…the answer is no. You do not have a right. Evil such as yours has no right to exist."

Then he pulled the trigger.

Chapter 62

Pacific Shore

The public memorial service for Paul Cassidy was held at the First Lutheran Church on the corner of Via de La Paz and Albright Street in Pacific Palisades. The white stone building was packed with family, friends, campaign workers, print and broadcast reporters, gawkers who had seen his likeness on billboards and posters, and voters who had hoped he would be their next congressman. All were admitted entrance.

The private memorial service for Paul Cassidy was held on an isolated stretch of California coastline that bordered a public beach often frequented by Angelinos of every stripe—families of Japanese gardeners, Mexican field hands, black porters and elevator operators, white collar businessmen and blue collar laborers. But the only two at the service itself were Gwen and Riley.

The Los Angeles Police Department had requested that Riley not leave town until their initial investigation was concluded. He had been the one to telephone the police after finding Paul and the man known as Zellenski dead in the study of the Benedict Canyon home. Riley told the police that he killed Donovan in self-defense and then entered the house because he had previously heard gunshots. He said he found both men dead where they sat, and no one else in the room. He also pointed out to the investigators a large wet spot on the carpet just below one of the drapes. When contacted by the LAPD, Sheriff Harris Totter confirmed that Deputy Cross had been on the trail of a man wanted for bank robbery and murder in Texas. And when the ballistic tests were concluded it was apparent that neither man in the study had been shot by any of Riley's weapons. Forensic tests showed that the bullet found in Paul came from the Luger on Zellenski's desk. No one however, could determine who fired the seven-point-five millimeter slug that was found in the German's brain.

Waves gently caressed the shore as Gwen and Riley walked along the foamy edge of the incoming tide. He put his arm around her as she let the contents of the urn spill softly into the sand and surf. She couldn't hold back the tears and she didn't try. After a while, they walked to higher ground, sat down and stared out at the vast blue Pacific.

"This is the way he wanted it, Riley. This is where he wanted to be. He told me if anything ever happened to him, I should do this."

"Can't think of any place more beautiful."

"Sure is big, isn't it? Did you think you'd ever see any place like this when we were back in school?"

"Don't know that I gave it that much thought. Back then I seldom got beyond homework and the next basketball game. Not necessarily in that order."

"When I came to California, Riley, I had no idea what would happen. But I was game. I was ready for whatever life might offer. It didn't seem to matter then. Everything felt so new."

"Back in the war…you couldn't think much about your future. You didn't know if you were going to have one. So you just concentrated on what was coming next. And how you might deal with that."

"He was special, Riley. A special kind of person. You thought so too, didn't you?"

"One of the best."

"And when I think of what he might have become…not just Congressman, he might have—" Then she caught herself—realizing she wasn't the only one who had her world shattered recently.

"I'm sorry, Riley. Forgive me. Forgive me for acting like it's only me who has lost someone."

"Nothing to forgive."

"Does it get easier, Riley? Does it get easier as the days go by?"

"It hasn't yet."

"Do you think there's something wrong with us, Riley?

"What do you mean?"

"Do you think there's something we've done…some reason I've lost Paul, and you've lost Sharon? Do you think God punishes people, Riley? Do you even think there's a God at all?"

"I don't know. I hope so."

"You do? Why do you hope so?"

"I guess I just don't like the idea of believing in nothing. There doesn't seem any point to that at all."

"Think there was any point to Sharon and Paul being killed?"

"Bad things happen, Gwen. From the time we're all little kids, we learn that in one way or another. There's no figuring it. I mean…look at all Paul was up against in the war. All the times he could have been killed…should have been killed. He gets through all that…and then this happens."

"But why, Riley? Why did Zellenski kill Paul?"

"The police will eventually find out, Gwen. They always do. They'll find out why Paul was there but his car wasn't. They'll find out why Zellenski killed him. But as to why he was taken so young…why, like Sharon, he was pulled from those of us who are left behind…I'm not sure we'll ever know that."

"I guess no matter how old we get…or how lucky we are…or how smart we think we are…there are just some things people will never be able to truly understand. Maybe it would be worse if we did."

The sun began to slip below the horizon. Low hanging clouds that had hung around for days after the storm were tinted with a salmon glow that dropped a shadow beneath them, embossing their place in the sky.

"Wish you could stay longer," Gwen said. "Wish you didn't have to leave so soon."

"I have to get back to my son."

"You miss him, don't you?"

"More than anything."

With twilight encircling, they started walking back to where the Ford was parked near the main section of the beach. For some reason a crowd had gathered near the water's edge. Everyone was looking toward the sea. Some pointed. Others gestured back toward the highway.

"Do you mind if I stop for a second?" Riley asked Gwen.

"No. Go ahead. See what it is."

Riley left her standing alone and walked a few yards to where the crowd was milling. He asked one of the men, "What's going on?"

"This guy…I couldn't believe it…this guy…he just started peeling off his clothes, Hat, coat, shirt, pants, shoes, even his underwear, just peeled it all off and started walking."

"Started walking where?" Riley asked.

"Out there…right out there in the ocean. He just kept going. Kept going farther and farther out. He finally disappeared. I don't think he's coming back."

My God, Riley thought. *A suicide. That's the last thing Gwen needs right now.* He quickly asked the man, "Has anyone gone for the police?"

"Yes, I think so. Somebody went to find a phone booth."

Riley hurried back to Gwen. "Come on," he said. "Nothing to see here. Just some people who thought they might have seen something. But it was nothing."

"Look," Gwen said. "I found these while you were talking. They must have washed up on the beach." She held out her hand and showed Riley a pair of wire-rimmed spectacles. "Maybe they belong to someone in the crowd."

Riley took them from her saying, "You go on up to the car. I'll check to see if anyone's lost them."

Gwen headed toward the car parked by the highway. Riley went back and spoke to the man he had just talked to. "Here," he said, handing the glasses over. "Show these to the police when they arrive. They might belong with his things."

When he reached the car, Gwen was standing beside it holding a bulky envelope.

"What's that?

"Don't know. There's something heavy in here. It was wedged behind the windshield wiper."

"But I didn't tell anyone we were coming here."

"Well, maybe someone followed you or something. I don't know. But it's hard, and it feels weird, and look how the thing's addressed."

She handed Riley the envelope. He looked at the name on the front. Hand-printed were the words, Private First Class Riley Cross.

Riley unlocked the car and they got in. "Well, aren't you going to open it?"

"Do you mind?"

"No...go ahead. I'll just sit here and enjoy the evening stars coming up."

Riley opened the envelope and looked inside. He saw a Walther PPK semi-automatic pistol and a letter. He took the letter out, unfolded it and began to read. At the top of the paper, the first words were, *I'm sorry*. What followed was a story. A story of a small boy who was awakened one morning bound and gagged. The story explained that he was taken by a man with one arm to his mother's bedroom. There, he endured the most painful memory of his life. And he was told this horror was inflicted by Americans. The story went on to detail an unquenchable quest for revenge, an epiphany in the form of a long forgotten After Action Report, a hunt for murderers, the unforgivable killing of Private First Class Brendon O'Byrne, the stalking of Private First Class Riley Cross and First Lieutenant Paul C. Cassidy, an overheard conversation of attempted blackmail, the refusal of a good man to submit to evil, the murder of an honorable man, and the execution of a monster. The story neared completion with an admission of guilt for the murder of one innocent man, and an acknowledgment that another innocent individual died due to hesitation on the part of the storyteller. The ending announced his intent to atone for what he had done by taking his own life. In this way, the storyteller concluded, though he could never be forgiven by man for what he had done, perhaps he could be forgiven by God. The story finished as it began; with the words I'm sorry, and the signature, Rémy Auteuil.

When Riley finished reading, he looked out the car window toward the sea.

"Riley? Are you okay? What is it? What did it say?"

Slowly, he folded the letter and put it back in the envelope with the gun. Then he turned to her and said, "Let me take you home, Gwen. Let me take you home, and then I'll tell you everything."

Epilogue

Austin, Texas 1955

As usual, Riley was up before the sun. His routine hadn't changed much even though his life had. There was the walk down the hallway to check on Dwight, who was sleeping soundly and would continue to do so for the next couple of hours before he had to get up and get ready for school. There was the making of the coffee and the time spent on the back porch with his hands wrapped around the warm cup and his eyes on the red sun creeping over the rolling hills. There was the mental planning of the day to come and occasional flashbacks of the days that had preceded his move to the Texas capital. Memories don't announce their impending arrival, Riley accepted. They just flow in and out of your head with a will of their own. This morning, they were flowing back to the days just before he left Los Angeles.

Riley had taken the gun and the letter that had been left on his car to the LAPD. In addition to the confession, a ballistics test confirmed the bullet that killed Zellenski had been fired from the Walther. The officers in charge of the investigation told Riley they would contact the Chicago police. If there was an unsolved murder on their books of an individual named Brendon O'Byrne, it could now be wrapped up.

When he shared the contents of the letter, and the story of Colette Auteuil with Gwen, she said it made her sad that Paul hadn't felt he could tell her about it. Riley told her that most men who had been in the war found it easier to lock bad things away in their minds rather than sharing them. When she asked him if he had told Sharon about it, he simply said maybe he wasn't like most men. She silently agreed.

After returning to Pilot Hill, Riley took up his duties again. For months he tried to bury the pain of losing Sharon in daily routine and the rearing of Dwight. But his heart and his energy didn't seem to be in his job like it once was, and it showed.

Sheriff Harris Totter came to believe that Riley wasn't the same man he was before everything befell him. But he was sure that he could be again. And even though the last thing he wanted was to lose him, he thought that perhaps the best thing he could do for Riley was to get him away from the environment that was a daily reminder of all he had lost. So he contacted a friend he had in the Travis County Sheriff's Department. The first time a deputy position became available, Totter's endorsement landed Riley the job.

There was plenty for a deputy to do in a county that housed the State House and an ever-growing population. So it wasn't surprising that being knee-deep in petty thievery, property disputes, providing security for legislators, and helping his son with homework, Riley managed to slowly put the past behind him. Not completely of course, but far enough behind him that he didn't take it to bed every night and wake up with it every morning. He did occasionally wonder though, what his life might have been if he had asked Gwen to marry him before he left for the army. Then he'd always rationalize that it wouldn't have been fair to her…that she never would have had the chance at her own life and career…and that he never would have known the love of Sharon or the gift of Dwight. Eventually, he'd always reach the conclusion that try as we might, we never really control life. We just live it as best we can.

The train station off Lamar Boulevard was always Riley's late afternoon stop. It was his job to be there when the train arrived in case passengers or railroad officials required the assistance of the county Sheriff's department. Few seldom did. His attendance was almost always ceremonial. Riley would pull his car to the side of the station so it was in clear view of all those disembarking. In this way, he believed, a dual purpose was served. The meek saw a symbol of protection and the miscreants saw a deterrent to hassling the meek on train station property.

This afternoon's passengers seemed a mixture of both, Riley thought, as he watched them step down. Their path to the station required that they walk right past him. Repetition had enabled him to master the art of tipping his hat and saying hello with an economy of movement. The strong, silent lawman was what they really expected to see in Texas anyway, he assumed. So he was more than willing to oblige. An elderly couple were the last to disembark from the train and make their way past Riley. At least that's what he thought. But then he looked down the concrete walkway that ran parallel to the track, and he wondered for a second if he wasn't seeing one of those mirages you always hear about but never actually see. The sun was making him squint and hold his palm atop his eyes. But when he looked beneath it, he swore he could see a silhouette between him and that bright orange ball. A silhouette that took the shape of one of those fashion models right out of the pages of a glossy magazine. As the figure got closer it became a moving picture in a small, stylish hat with a feather, a tight suit that accented a trim waist, apple curves, sculptured calves, and thin ankles on high heels. Riley didn't have to wait for her face to come into focus. He knew it was Gwen. The lump in his throat gave her the opportunity to speak first.

"You the official greeting committee, officer?"

"Suppose I am. Of course, if I had known a big time Hollywood actress was coming, I might have scared up a few more folks."

"I like the crowd just this size."

"Is this one of those bizarre coincidences," Riley said, "or did you know I was in Austin?"

"Well, Riley Cross, that's the most conceited thing I think I've ever heard. You think I'd come all the way to Texas just to see you?"

"A fella can hope, can't he?"

"Well, if that was what you were hoping for, why didn't you write and invite me?"

"You never know how long it takes people to get over things. And you seemed to have everything you wanted right where you were. I mean the movies and all."

"That's the thing about movies, Riley. They seem real, but they're not. And frankly…they got a lot less real when I lost Paul. And somehow…found you again."

"How'd you know where I was?"

"I called your former Sheriff's department and got a friendly lady named Hazel. She told me all about your new job…your new city…your new life."

"Is that what we're living now? New lives. Can anyone do that? Completely?"

"Never completely. I don't think anyone would want to. But new enough to make the world a little warmer place to be…maybe."

"Gwen, I —"

"Riley, we've both had a lot of time to grieve, and a lot of time to think. I decided that I didn't want to waste any more time waiting for you to realize that. Look… we're not the kids we were. I'm not trying to get that back. I'm just taking a chance on making the rest of my life as good as it can possibly be. I didn't think I could do that without you. Now…if you don't feel the same way…you can just say so. I want you to say so if that's the way you feel. Or, don't feel. Oh…you know what I mean. I can get back onboard that train and return to LA this instant. I even have a round-trip ticket in my purse just in case you want to say thanks, but no thanks. See how practical I've become."

Riley looked into those gorgeous brown eyes, the eyes he had never truly gotten out of his head, and said, "When's the last time I kissed you?"

"Oh, let me see. I'd say it's something like twelve or thirteen years ago."

"Think we should try one again? Just to see how it feels."

"Well, I don't know. Are you on or off duty?"

"I couldn't care less."

Riley brought her close and kissed her. Kissed her like he'd been wanting to for a very long time. Then he said, "You really have a round-trip ticket in your purse?"

"No."

"Thought I'd be a pushover, huh?"

"No. Just hoped so."

"Well," he replied, as he walked around the car and opened the front passenger door. "Then come have a seat, and let's go for a ride. There's a young fellow I'd very much like you to meet."

About The Author

Joe Kilgore lives with his wife, an accomplished artist, and various animals in Austin, Texas. His short stories have been published in magazines, creative journals, anthologies, and online literary publications. His previous novels are:

The Blunder

The Golden Dancer

Sin And Sombreros

When not engaged in his own work, Joe reviews other writers' novels plus non-fiction books. You can learn more about him and his fiction at his website: http://joekilgore.com

TOP HAT
BOOKS

Historical fiction that lives.

We publish fiction that captures the contrasts, the achievements, the optimism and the radicalism of ordinary and extraordinary times across the world.

We're open to all time periods and we strive to go beyond the narrow, foggy slums of Victorian London. Where are the tales of the people of fifteenth century Australasia? The stories of eighth century India? The voices from Africa, Arabia, cities and forests, deserts and towns? Our books thrill, excite, delight and inspire.

The genres will be broad but clear. Whether we're publishing romance, thrillers, crime, or something else entirely, the unifying themes are timescale and enthusiasm. These books will be a celebration of the chaotic power of the human spirit in difficult times. The reader, when they finish, will snap the book closed with a satisfied smile.

If you have enjoyed this book, why not tell other readers by posting a review on your preferred booksite. Recent bestsellers from Top Hat Books are:

Grendel's Mother
The Saga of the Wyrd-Wife
Susan Signe Morrison
Grendel's Mother, a queen from the Old English epic, Beowulf, threatens the fragile political stability of windswept England.
Paperback: 978-1-78535-009-2
e-book: 978-1-78535-010-8

Queen of Sparta
A Novel of Ancient Greece
T.S. Chaudhry
History has relegated her to the role of bystander, what if Gorgo, Queen of Sparta, had played a central role in the Greek resistance to the Persian invasion?
Paperback: 978-1-78279-750-0
e-book: 978-1-78279-749-4

Mercenary
R.J. Connor
Richard Longsword is a Mercenary, but this time it's not for money, this time it's for revenge…
Paperback: 978-1-78279-236-9
e-book: 978-1-78279-198-0

Black Tom
Terror on the Hudson
Ron Semple
A tale of sabotage, subterfuge and political shenanigans in Jersey City in 1916; America is on the cusp of war and the fate of the

nation hinges on the decision of one young policeman.
Paperback: 978-1-78535-110-5
e-book: 978-1-78535-111-2

Destiny Between Two Worlds
A Novel about Okinawa
Jacques L Fuqua, Jr
A fateful October 1944 morning offered no inkling that the lives of thousands of Okinawans would be profoundly changed—forever.
Paperback: 978-1-78279-892-7
e-book: 978-1-78279-893-4

Cowards
Trent Portigal
A family's life falls into turmoil when the parents' timid political dissidence is discovered by their far more enterprising children.
Paperback: 978-1-78535-070-2
e-book: 978-1-78535-071-9

Godwine Kingmaker
Part One of The Last Great Saxon Earls
Mercedes Rochelle
The life of Earl Godwine is one of the enduring enigmas of English history. Who was this Godwine, first Earl of Wessex; unscrupulous schemer or protector of the English? The answer depends on who you ask...
Paperback: 978-1-78279-801-9
e-book: 978-1-78279-800-2

The Last Stork Summer
Mary Brigid Surber
Eva, a young Polish child, battles to survive the designation of "racially worthless" under Hitler's Germanization Program.

Paperback: 978-1-78279-934-4
e-book: 978-1-78279-935-1 $4.99 £2.99

Messiah Love
Music and Malice at a Time of Handel
Sheena Vernon
The tale of Harry Walsh's faltering steps on his journey to success and happiness, performing in the playhouses of Georgian London.
Paperback: 978-1-78279-768-5
e-book: 978-1-78279-761-6

A Terrible Unrest
Philip Duke
A young immigrant family must confront the horrors of the Colorado Coalfield War to live the American Dream.
Paperback: 978-1-78279-437-0
e-book: 978-1-78279-436-3